Other Titles by TW Brown

The DEAD Series:

DEAD: The Ugly Beginning
DEAD: Revelations
DEAD: Fortunes & Failures
DEAD: Winter
DEAD: Siege & Survival
DEAD: Confrontation
DEAD: Reborn (coming September 2013)

DEAD Special Edition

DEAD: Steve's Story
DEAD: Vignettes
DEAD: The Geeks
DEAD: Compendium 1

Zomblog

Zomblog
Zomblog II
Zomblog: The Final Entry
Zomblog: Snoe
Zomblog: Snoe's War
Zomblog: Snoe's Journey (coming October 2013)

Miscellaneous

Gruesomely Grimm Zombie Tales Vol. I
That Ghoul Ava
That Ghoul Ava & The Queen of the Zombies
Dakota (as Todd Brown)

Siege & Survival
(Book Five of the *DEAD* Series)

Written by: TW Brown

Cover Art and Design by Shawn Conn

Dead: Siege & Survival
©2012 May December Publications LLC

The split-tree logo is a registered trademark of May December Publications LLC.

ISBN—978-1-936730-73-5

To all the NaNoWriMos

A moment with the author…

I sometimes wonder if anybody really reads these. I mean, they have nothing to do with the actual story. This is just me taking a few moments and "talking" to you…the reader. Still, how else would we get to know each other?

So, if you have been staying with me through this series, you have started to notice a few shifts. For one, zombies are less frequent. Sure, they are still around waiting to take a chomp out of the unwary individual, but as the first winter sinks in teeth of a different sort, people are realizing that there are some drawbacks with getting far from the cities. Supplies are a real problem. One of the things I set out to do with the *DEAD* series is give some realism to a horrific fantasy realm.

I hope that you enjoy this newest book in the series. This is the fifth book in the series, but it is also the second book in this three-book arc. So yes, there will be a lot of unresolved issues. As I did in *Fortunes & Failures* (the third book of the series and the end of the first arc in the story), I will wrap up a lot of things in the next book. This is the set up…again, I refer to the original *Star Wars* trilogy. I was one of the kids who stood in line on a rainy day, May 21, 1980 for the premiere at the Westgate Theater (which was demolished years ago…sigh). I remember the ending well. I had to wait three years and one week for closure. So, while this is certainly no Star Wars, I understand that many of you are heavily invested in the characters and want answers. No worries. The next book will be out on May 30, 2013.

Thanks to all of you who keep coming back. And if any of you have something you would like to see in the next set of Special Editions where I compile Steve's story, The Geeks, and Vignettes into their own book and pump in around 15,000 words based on your requests, feel free to send me an email.

I love some of the stuff that sticks in your minds. I would venture to say that many of you know this world better than I do now. My biggest surprise in the first books had to be all the people who asked for Garrett's back story. I thought you would all be happy to see him gone and just want to move on. That was the most requested thing to show up in my box, second was what happened to the Geeks in Pittsburgh. I can't wait to see some of you fixate on this go round.

Many if you have been so kind in your emails. And some of you have become friends over the past couple of years. I would be lying if I said that I did not want to 'hit the big time' whatever that means. But I hope I never lose contact with you. So maybe that is why I write these introductions. Perhaps we have not spoken in a while.

I want to get to my 'thank you' portion, but first I want to say that if you did enjoy this book, tell a friend. I have some great memories of reading *The Stand* with my best buddy back in junior high. We had some great conversations that summer—we even cast the movie (can you believe we had John Ritter as Stu Redman?). In fact, as many of you know, that is the book that inspired me more than any other. And if you are one of those types who write reviews, you can bet I read each and every one. Good or bad. I try to comment on many of them to at least thank you for taking the time.

And now the thanks…I don't mean to slight anybody, and those of you who have been with me through thick and thin know exactly how I feel. I owe a thanks to Malina Roos and Susan Burdorf for their amazing help and outstanding proofreading. But this book is all about my daughter Ronni. This book is set to release on December 15, 2012. That is her 18th birthday. I want to thank her for being my daughter.

They say it's your birthday…
TW Brown
November 2012

Table of Contents

1

Geek and a Guest

Kevin leaned out the door as the Snow Cat rumbled to a halt. The dazzling brightness reflecting off the snow hurt his eyes. Every time he closed them, he saw spots. Still, he didn't need perfect vision to see that there was big trouble up ahead.

"I guess the ride is over, Kevin," Willa said as she shut down the motor. "Grab your bags, looks like we're hoofing it from here."

Kevin didn't say a word. There wasn't really anything to say. He looked at the herd that packed the breadth of the highway up ahead. Even from as far away as they were, he could hear them moaning and crying. There was one other noise under it all. It took him a moment to realize what he was hearing.

"The snow," Kevin whispered.

"What?" Willa asked as she shouldered her pack and buckled the weapon-laden webbed belt around her slender waist.

For some reason, Kevin found that simple action amazingly sexy. He had to shake off the inappropriate thoughts starting to bloom involving her wearing *only* that belt dripping with blades and a few more exotic hand-to-hand items.

"You can hear them walking though the snow," Kevin said with a nod towards the approaching mob.

Willa tilted her head slightly and peeled back her tight-fitting knit cap. With one finger, she tucked a strand of black hair behind her ear. Kevin couldn't help but stare.

"Hey," Willa said with a big smile, "you're right." She

1

tugged the hat back down. "Not much gets past you does it?"

There were a few seconds of silence between them as Kevin struggled to banish the thoughts in his head. The only sounds carrying on the cold winter breeze came from the approaching wall of undead. He shook his head clear and focused on the situation...and Aleah.

"The best choice for us would be to head north. The river should be that way. If we can come across a bridge at any point, I say we take the opportunity to make the move."

"You lead the way," Kevin nodded in agreement.

The rest of the day was spent in relative silence. It didn't seem that the herd saw them. If they did, they chose not to pursue. The zombies they did encounter were usually singles or small groups. Kevin continued to insist that they only engage the ones that took an active interest in them.

"You ain't worried about bringing a bunch of them with you on our heels?" Willa asked at one point.

"We have so many places we will be ducking in and out of that I just don't see the need for the waste of energy."

At one point, just after they had crossed an open field and began winding through a scattering of trees, Willa grabbed Kevin's shoulder and motioned for him to keep quiet. She swung a crossbow off her shoulder and loaded a bolt, bringing the weapon up and tracking something in the distance. He looked around for what she might be taking aim. All he saw was snow...and more snow.

With a thrum and a hiss, there was a puff of snow about twenty yards away. Willa clapped her hands and bounded off to retrieve her prize. Reaching down, she stood and waved a plump rabbit in the air. Five more times that day the ritual was repeated. Four of those times resulted in a dead rabbit.

As it began to grow dark and the first snowflakes of the evening began to fall, Kevin spotted the shadows indicating a scattering of residences. He veered off course, searching for the first intact home.

Luck was with them as the very first home they came to

looked to have all its windows and doors. As an added bonus, the picket fence surrounding the front yard was in excellent condition. At first, Kevin thought the residents might still remain. He discovered that he was only partially correct as he drew close enough to see the large front window. It was smeared with filth, a clear indication that a zombie (or two) was inside.

"Let's go around back," Kevin whispered when he came to a stop across the street from the two-story home.

"You see something?" Willa let her crossbow slip down her shoulder and into her hands.

"Nope." Kevin shielded his face with his hands to cut back the glare. "But I don't want our tracks to advertise where we went. It's bad enough that anybody who wanted to could follow us, but if we circle around to the back of the house and make tracks to each of the five houses in this little area it will help me relax."

"You are something else," Willa said appreciatively.

Kevin headed around the side of the house, his face turned away to hide the blush and the grin. All his life, he had been the awkward one…the geek…the nerd. Now, he had the most beautiful woman he'd ever seen waiting for him back where he currently called home while he was out in the middle of nowhere with another very pretty woman who lavished him with compliments and openly flirted with him. Not to mention the fact that he'd had to fend off the advances of a teenaged high school cheerleader that he'd saved from a horrific situation.

It took them about a half hour, but Willa did exactly as he asked, and they eventually had tracks all over the place; each house in the area had multiple sets of them leading to and from.

When it came time, Kevin pulled a small case from his own bag and made short work of the locked door. He drew his machete and nodded for Willa to open the door. Slowly and cautiously, so as to make as little noise as possible, she turned the knob and pushed it open. There was a tearing sound as the weather seal and the door, gummed together from the combination of not being used for months during the hot summer and now this freezing winter, separated. Then…the metallic rattle as the door chain reached its end and kept the door fast—open no more than a few inches.

A second later, the stench of rot and death hit them both square in the face. Kevin staggered back and shook his head, but Willa stumbled as if struck by something physical. The sounds of her retching were met by a low moan from the other side of the door.

Casting a glance back, he paused only long enough to be certain that the nausea was the worst of his travelling companion's problems before throwing his shoulder into the door. The tiny links of chain tore free, and Kevin found himself just inside a main entry hall. The hardwood floor was stained with what had to most likely be blood. Still, it was the lone finger with the ring still on it that drew his focus.

He only had an instant to consider the solitary digit when the torso of a small child pulled itself around the corner at the end of the hallway. Close behind was what Kevin first mistook for a middle-aged man. However, as he took a step forward and raised his weapon, he realized that it was, in fact, a woman with a crew cut.

With a quick swing, he buried the blade deep into the head of the zombie his mind had named Annie Lennox. Allowing Annie's weight to act in his favor, he stepped aside and yanked up to free his weapon. The creeping child was already at his boots by the time he recovered and was ready to swing again. It was probably the combination of Willa's violent heaving just outside the door, the echoes of bodies crashing to the floor, and the mewling of the creeper at his feet. In any case, Kevin never heard the zombie that had staggered down the stairs behind him and to his right.

A cold hand brushed Kevin's face, knocking his goggles cockeyed. Startled, Kevin threw his body down the hallway, landing on his shoulder and rolling up to his knees in what had to be one of the biggest kitchens he had ever seen. It also brought him face-to-face with a toddler-sized zombie.

Quickly shoving his goggles out of the way—he would not have the time needed to take off his gloves and make sure they didn't have anything on them that might get into his eyes and possibly infect him—Kevin shoved the toddler away with a strong forearm. It slid across the grimy floor and slammed into a very solid cabinet door. Pulling his Ka-Bar from its sheath, he spun and found the approaching zombie that had snuck up on him standing in the hallway with its head cocked to one side as if considering him and the scene at its feet.

There it is again, Kevin's mind screamed. Once more he was faced with a child-zombie that seemed to be thinking. Its expression was still slack and void of emotion, but its body language was sending a very different story. It kept its distance just over an arm's length away and tilted its head one way and then another in jerky fits.

The thumping of tiny feet made him glance back into the kitchen just in time to see the toddler take quick—for a zombie anyways—steps in his direction and reach for him with chubby, gray-green hands. With a backhand swing, Kevin brought the Ka-Bar around and plunged it into the left eye.

He turned back to the ten- or twelve-year-old girl in the hall. It hadn't moved and continued to study *him*. Had he been a second quicker, he would have been able to possibly wave Willa off as she came from behind and drove a spike-fisted hand into the back of the zombie's head.

"Crap," Kevin sighed, his shoulders slumping.

"Umm...you're welcome?" Willa planted a booted foot in the zombie's back and yanked her gloved hand free.

Kevin explained how he'd noticed peculiar behavior from some of the child-aged zombies. He watched her face closely for any signs that she might think he was crazy. So far, his theories hadn't been too warmly accepted by any of his group; that included his girlfriend Aleah who had been present for one such encounter. Willa's face remained impassive the entire time. After he finished by telling her that the zombie in the hallway she'd just put down was exhibiting similar signs, and that he would have liked to find a way to observe it for a bit before putting something through its skull, she shrugged and nodded.

"You are probably one of the smartest people I have ever met. If you say zombies are acting weird then who am I to say otherwise." Willa wiped off her gear with a dusty curtain.

Together, they searched the house for signs of any other nasty surprises. It was in an upstairs bedroom where they found a fresh horror. In a small bedroom, a little child looked to have wasted away to almost nothing.

"What the…" Willa's voice faded, and for the first time, Kevin saw a hint of real vulnerability in the woman.

Entering the room, Kevin was curious how this person could possibly have existed in the same house as the horrors downstairs. Not to mention that one of them had actually been up here and caught him by surprise.

Checking the desiccated corpse, he noticed a few things; first, the child was a girl, and second, the child was practically hairless. He noticed a pink diary sitting on the nightstand and picked it up.

After thumbing through a few pages, he set the book back down. "Cancer."

"Huh?"

"She had cancer."

"I don't get it."

"Neither do I." Kevin gave the room one more look.

"Yeah…" Willa let that word hang for a moment before continuing. "But I think we don't get it on different levels."

"I guess I am trying to figure out why the zombies didn't touch her." Kevin walked back out to the hallway and spent a few minutes wandering from room to room. He opened drawers and closets, but could not seem to find anything that satisfied him. He was several minutes in to his search when he realized that Willa was nowhere to be seen.

"Willa?"

"In here," a voice drifted from the dead girl's bedroom.

Kevin didn't want to go back in the room. He'd become accustomed to the walking dead. He'd seen plenty of death in the past several months. What he didn't like was the emaciated look of the girl in the bed; the fact that she had died a slow lingering death hurt him down to his soul.

"I'm going downstairs to make sure everything is as secure as we can make it for the night," he called over his shoulder.

"Her name was Linda." Willa stepped out of the room holding the diary. "Her family refused to go to the area FEMA shelter because they wouldn't take her in due to her condition. It started with her dad."

Kevin paused for a moment, and then continued on down the stairs. He didn't want to hear it. He didn't want to know any more about this girl's suffering. Suddenly, all he wanted to do was get back on the road and return home to his group. He wanted to bring Valarie her medication so that she would stop seeing people who weren't there. He wanted Aleah to hold him and tell him it would be okay...even though it would never really be okay.

As the shadows grew into an inky blackness the two sat in the bathroom where the rabbits roasted over an open flame in the tub. Willa let Kevin prepare the meal as she seemed unable to take her nose out of the diary. He only burned it a little.

They ate in silence and when he was finished, Kevin climbed inside his sleeping bag and drifted off to sleep. The dreams came in a torrent. Every face seemed to be screaming silently in pain.

Cary.

Mike.

Darrin.

His only friends in the world and the group he had left Virginia Beach with on a mission to survive the zombie apocalypse. Those faces gave way to Ruth and Angela Bergman. Shaw and his band of lunatics. The deranged teacher, Mr. Abernathy.

His sister.

Valarie.

His sister.

Valarie.

***

"Wake up," a sweet voice whispered in his ear.

"Aleah?" Kevin rolled over and pulled the blurry figure close, his mouth seeking hers.

"Open your eyes, Romeo," Willa snapped, shoving him back.

Kevin jolted awake. A wave of embarrassment made his face burn and his hands tingle. He tried to apologize, but not one word out of his mouth was understandable.

"Just relax," Willa chuckled. "You didn't do nothing wrong. But I need your ass awake right now."

"What is it?" Kevin wanted to climb out of his sleeping bag, but certain…physiological responses made that an embarrassing proposition at the present time.

"Lots of noise outside."

"Like zombie herd noise?"

"Like living people on the run and more living people chasing them."

Kevin wiped the sleep from his eyes and the slight trace of drool from his chin as he struggled to fully awaken. His body ached all over, and it took him a while to realize why. He hadn't just been out for a walk…he'd been slogging through almost knee-deep snow all day the previous day.

As he went through the ritual of packing up his gear, Willa kept pacing. As he picked up his pack, she almost seemed to be ready to run for the door. He hadn't ever seen her this rattled. Of course, he had to admit that he didn't know the woman all that well to begin with.

"Something bad was happening out there. I heard crying…definitely crying," Willa insisted.

"Okay," Kevin nodded, "but what is all this about?" He made a gesture with his hands that encompassed Willa.

"I don't know what all you've seen out in the world since

8

this happened…but there are some pretty bad people out there now that nobody is making folks behave."

"I've seen my share of bad."

"Yeah…but things have been happening to women that I don't think you can really appreciate. You asked why that outfit I was with just had women? It's because over half of us have been victimized in one way or another by men…often *groups* of men."

Kevin felt a slight twist in his gut. He'd saved one young lady from an unimaginable situation and killed her captor in a rather violent fashion. He still had nightmares about it. However, it was in this moment that a wave of guilt washed over him. His guilt had not been for what Heather, the young woman he rescued, had endured. Rather, it was for his taking of a human life.

"Well I won't let anything happen to you as long as I am still breathing," Kevin vowed. It was as much to himself as it was to the normally strong woman who now stood before him seeming more like a frightened child.

Willa appeared to consider Kevin for a moment with a different eye than he was accustomed. A sad look clouded her expression and she shook her head. "That's sweet, Kevin, but you're just one person. There is a whole world out there…and a lot of really bad people are out there in it."

"But you can't believe that," Kevin insisted.

"I can…and I do."

"Then what are we fighting to stay alive for?"

"It's in our nature…most of us anyways. Lots of folks took the easy way out a long time ago."

"So you're telling me that all that's left out there in the world are monsters…rapists…"

"Not *all*," Willa said with a sad smile. "There are a few men like you out there. However…most of the good guys died early on trying to save everybody around them. The cowards hid and waited for a world that they could poke their heads out into and finally crawl out from under their rocks."

"I refuse to believe that."

"You aren't a woman...a girl...or a child."

Kevin considered that statement and then held a hand out to Willa. She took it and they headed out the back door of the house and listened to the stillness that was only interrupted by the occasional sounds of branches bending under the weight of the snow.

"Well whoever came through seems to have taken no notice of our tracks or these houses," Kevin whispered. "Let's get moving."

Together, they trudged out into the snow. By midday, they had discovered a series of tracks that wove in and out of the trees. They also discovered that their bodies could not endure much more. Between the exposure to the cold and the strain placed on the body involved in walking through the knee deep powder, the pair were exhausted beyond the ability to continue. For Kevin, this would simply not do; Valarie was waiting. She needed him to keep moving.

"We need to find a residential area," Kevin announced as he handed his canteen to Willa.

"You want to make camp this early?"

"No. We need to find snowshoes, skis...anything. Otherwise we are not going to make it."

Kevin sought out the highest ground he could find and searched. The biggest problem was one that he had noticed during the journey to Newark from the golf course compound where his friends waited. Before the world had been plunged into darkness, most buildings gave off heat. That caused the snow to melt. Now...buildings were harder to see in this glaring white landscape. They were buried under snow just like everything else.

It took him a while, but eventually he found what he was looking for and led the way. The monotone colors of the landscape played tricks with distance and it ended up being much farther than it initially looked. To add to the frustration, it was well to the south of them, taking him away from his ultimate destination.

On the positive side of things, the zombie presence was nil.

There were no signs that anything—living or otherwise—had passed through the area. About an hour into the trek across the open countryside, the sun made an eventual appearance. That was a mixed blessing in that it actually felt warmer. The downside was the glare. Kevin's eyes began to blur and water. Early on, Willa stopped him and wrapped his scarf around his face and pulled his cap down low.

"You will get the worst sunburn of your life on any exposed skin," she answered his questioning look.

He didn't see how he could possibly be much more uncomfortable. His skin was already raw and chapped in so many places. Small sections were beginning to bleed and scab over. His hands and feet felt like blocks of ice grafted on to the end of his limbs. In short, he was miserable.

They finally reached the entrance to a housing development. A decorative brick façade announced it as: Picnic Palisades. *Did everything in this area have ties to that damned basket-shaped building?* he wondered acerbically.

The development looked to be set up in a razor-straight grid. All of the houses had postage stamp-sized front yards. The place had not fared well and Kevin was immediately reminded of the neighborhood that the Sarah Polley character lived in at the start of that *Dawn of the Dead* remake.

Several of the houses had suffered from a fire that had been allowed to burn out of control. The wind must've been blowing to the east that day, he figured as he surveyed the scene. Between the chaos that had obviously reigned in those first days and the subsequent looting, this once upper-scale residential area now more closely resembled an inner-city slum or a war zone.

From some of the homes up the street, Kevin spotted dark figures moving. This was going to be tricky.

"Should we split up to speed up the search?" Willa whispered.

"I don't think that is a good idea."

"It's not like we both haven't been fighting and surviving since day one. I realize the advantage of sticking together, but we aren't going to be so far apart that we couldn't rush to the other's aid. Plus, I think you should leave your bag of meds in the street or something…just in case."

Kevin had to admit that she made excellent points. Still, years of horror movies screamed in his brain that this was a terrible idea and it never ended well when people split up. However…

"This ain't the movies," Kevin grunted as he unslung his pack and set it up beside the nearby bank of mailboxes.

"Huh?"

"Nothing." Kevin selected his trusty machete and his Ka-Bar from his weapons. He wanted to be as light and mobile as possible.

"So how do you want to do this?" Willa set her gear beside Kevin's. She seemed to fidget over her weapon choice for a few seconds before settling on a garden variety machete and her crossbow.

"I say we leapfrog down one side of the street until we reach the end and then return. Don't enter your next house until I've come out of mine."

"Sounds good."

They walked up almost three blocks to clear the heavily burned section. Along the way, a few zombies crawled out from the charred ruins, but were easily dispatched. Finally, they reached the first houses that looked safe enough to enter. The first one only had minimal fire damage on one side of the structure. The pair patted each other on the shoulder and Kevin headed for the second house.

He tried the door and was happy to discover it unlocked. Entering the small foyer, he was greeted by a grand staircase on either side that allowed access to the second floor. He really didn't think the upstairs bedrooms would hold what he sought.

The house didn't smell, and other than a layer of dust, seemed in excellent condition. He was mildly surprised that looters hadn't sacked it, but he imagined that, like any other resource in the post-apocalyptic world, even looters had to be in short supply. With so few people living, they couldn't hit everything.

This actually gave him some hope. There were still places where they could seek supplies once he returned to the others. He knew from the exterior of the house that the garage would be to his right, and so he moved cautiously down the hall and turned right into a kitchen that was almost the size of his apartment. An oak door was on the other side of the enormous refrigerator.

He opened the door to a pitch black three car garage. The slight illumination came from the open doorway he now stood in. A quick sniff didn't raise any alarms, but he would not drop his guard.

For some reason, he really struggled with taking that first step into the darkness. Hugging one wall, he inched his way in and eventually reached the sturdy roll-up door. It took a considerable amount of fumbling around before he was able to find the mechanism and then figure it out enough so that he could manually open the garage.

The door inched upwards on squeaky rails and Kevin winced as he realized that any zombie for blocks...maybe even miles...had probably just heard his actions. Realizing he had nothing to gain in opening the door slowly, he heaved it up.

Sure enough, coming up the driveway were several undead. Quickly surveying the situation, he decided that his best move was to step in between the fancy sports car and the never-been-in-the-mud four-wheel-drive truck that would require a step stool to climb inside. This offered him a perfect view of the approaching threats as well as funneling the zombies to him in a very defendable space. It worked even better than expected. In a matter of a few moments, the snowy driveway was strewn with bodies, and as an added bonus, he had multiple pathways to walk in. He could trace each zombie back to its point of origin if he so desired.

A look around the garage proved to be a disappointment as far as transportation was concerned. He had returned back inside and been tickled to discover a set of hooks with key rings dangling from them, However, none of the cars rewarded him by turning over when he tried the ignition.

He went out to the sidewalk and waited for Willa. She'd had no better luck than he, so they moved on. House by house they searched. They encountered every possibility inside from mass suicide to an undead family waiting on them like they would a pizza delivery. Many of the homes were looted, some showed signs of having hosted squatters who eventually figured out the obvious—a residential neighborhood was no place to ride out the zombie uprising. The only real benefit thus far proved to be an occasional pantry with canned food on the shelves.

As the shadows grew long and the pair grew weary, Kevin began searching for a spot to stay the night. He found it in the back yard of one of the houses that had yielded nothing beyond a zombified family that consisted of father, mother, teenaged son, pre-teen daughter and a Golden Retriever. The irony came when he searched the garage. He hadn't really expected to find anything outdoorsy considering the obesity level of the entire family—dog included. Still, he couldn't stifle his chuckle after he opened the main garage door to shed some light. On the back window of a huge blue Suburban was a variation of the stick figure window decals. A zombie family paraded across the tinted glass under the words: "My zombie family ate your stick figure family!" In that family's above average-sized back yard was a large oak tree with a deluxe tree house.

He signaled Willa to join him in the garage when she exited the house she'd just finished searching. She was not nearly as amused by the window decal, but she was more than happy to climb up into the tree house for the night after they retrieved their packs,

Kevin tried to hide his excitement behind the discovery of a bookshelf in the tree house that would make any zombie nut jealous. There were several titles he was familiar with: *World War Z, Monster Island*, and every single *Walking Dead* comic book and compendium. However, there was also a plethora of titles he had never heard of by names he was unfamiliar with like Mark Tufo, Armand Rosamilia and John O'Brien.

"You've got to be kidding," Willa sighed as she flopped down on the cot shoved against one wall.

"Hey...it was a lot more popular than most folks realize," Kevin replied, warring against his inner desire to grab a book from the shelf.

"Yeah...well no need to read that crap anymore. Just go outside."

Kevin considered a few of the titles, but decided that Willa was right. He realized that he no more wanted to read any of those books any more than one of those soccer players in that plane crash probably wanted to read about the Donner Party.

They settled in and began opening up an assortment of cans. Despite being cold, his body was starved and the food sent tingles of contentment through him. Once they were both full, they opened up their sleeping bags, crawled inside, and drifted off to sleep.

***

Kevin woke first to the hair-raising sound of a baby cry. He rolled over to shake Willa and discovered that she was gone; her sleeping bag nothing more than an empty shell. Sitting bolt upright, he almost broke his legs trying to get out of his sleeping bag. The room was still dark—the inky blackness of a dead world combined with a thick cloud cover—making it impossible for him to even see his own hand in front of his face.

Feeling around, he tried to recall the layout of the small cubicle. The back of his hand struck the bookcase and he was unable to stifle a yelp of pain. That only encouraged the crying zombie somewhere down below.

A thought entered Kevin's mind, and he quickly forced it back into a dark corner. By the time he managed to discover the floor hatch that they had climbed through the night before, Kevin could not stop his hands from shaking. He tried to convince himself that it was the cold, but he knew better. He tugged the hatch up and actually managed to make out a handful of shadows moving around at the base of the tree.

"Willa?" he hissed in futility. He knew damn well that no answer would be forthcoming. Still, until the dawn broke and he could see for himself, he was not prepared to accept the reality of the woman's fate.

Over the next two hours, he had plenty of time to consider just what in the hell had happened. He could not ferret out any situation where she would simply leave in the middle of the night. The only fly in the ointment of his defense that there had to be a reasonable and rational explanation for her absence continued to be blown up by the growls and cries coming from the base of the tree.

Finally, a dull glow shown from the open square in the floor and the curtained windows, signaling that morning had indeed broken. Steeling himself for the sight he was certain waited for him down below, Kevin crawled to the square and peered down.

It was still too dark to make out anything beyond individual shapes. He flopped back and looked around the tree house. He had hoped that perhaps she might've left him a note…anything. He didn't like the idea of staying up in this place any longer and wanted to get moving. He turned his head and considered his former companion's pack. If nothing else, he would take the crossbow. Rummaging through, he was disappointed to discover that it was not there amongst the scant few belongings left behind.

A peculiar thump sounded down below. Followed by another…and then another. Kevin drew his Ka-Bar and moved to the hatch. He was unprepared for what greeted him. Three of the zombies—dawn had given way enough for him to actually begin to make out details—were pinned to the trunk of the huge oak. A hiss and a thump were accompanied by a dark flash as another of the zombies took a bolt to the head.

Kevin leaned down farther and looked in the direction of the house. Standing in the yard on a pair of long, slender skis, Willa was bringing her crossbow back up to her shoulder. A second later, the noises repeated and another zombie was finished. This one had the bolt pass all the way through its head, and it fell to the snow.

"What in blazes!" Kevin hissed. "You scared me to death. I thought...well...never mind what I thought, but what could you have possibly been thinking?"

"I had to use the bathroom," Willa talk-whispered back.

"But you could have told me."

"I did," Willa replied as she slung the crossbow over her shoulder and picked up a pair of ski poles that were lying at her feet.

"Huh?"

"I shook you and told you I needed to use the ladies' room." Willa came to a stop directly under the hatch. "You said, and I quote, 'Don't fall in!' end quote."

Kevin searched his memory and came up blank. He plastered his best scowl of disapproval back on his face and scolded, "You should know that there is no way I would have let you go out there in the dark all alone like that."

"I'm a big girl," Willa retorted.

"Not the point—"

"You're right," she snapped, cutting him off. "The point is that we are wasting time while you sit up there bitching. We need to get moving. I found these cross-country skis in the house I picked to use the ladies room, along with a set for you. I will warn you that yours are not going to fit well...they will be a bit small, but I think you can force your feet inside the ski boots. Beggars can't be choosers and all."

Kevin opened his mouth and then shut it with an audible click. With one final glare, he tossed down their gear and then climbed through the hatch.

As he shouldered his stuff, Willa placed a hand on his shoulder. "I'm sorry." Kevin shot a glare in response. "I honestly did not think that I would have to worry about any more zombies. I thought we had put most of the ones in the area down during the course of the day."

"But you went to a house that we hadn't cleared."

"Actually..." Willa paused.

"How did we miss something like this?"

"You missed it," Willa said cautiously.

"How did I miss it?"

"By not paying attention."

"I don't get it...what do you mean?"

"I went to the house to use the bathroom. The thing is, you can't see worth a damn. I stumbled around until I found the kitchen. I just went through every drawer. Rich or not...everybody has a junk drawer. That's where all those single batteries, loose nuts and bolts...and candles are usually found."

"Okay, but that doesn't explain the skis."

"I lit my candle with the nifty lighter I found in that same drawer and headed up the stairs figuring it would be the safest choice for a bathroom break. On the way up, I was just looking at some of the pictures hanging on the wall. Most of them showed the family up in the mountains someplace. They were skiing."

Kevin had moved into the open garage so he could sit down someplace dry to put on the boots that would fasten to the skis. They were tight, but not so bad that he couldn't manage. The big thing was that he could at least get his feet into them...mostly. His toes were going to look like he'd been practicing the old Asian tradition of foot binding when it was over, but he would make it home today.

"So where were they?"

"In the attic."

Kevin scowled, but said nothing.

"Hey," Willa adjusted her own pack just a bit, "you can't have *all* the answers or pull *every* rabbit out of your hat."

"Something that obvious could have cost us," Kevin finally mumbled.

"I'll settle for a 'Good job, Willa' and call us even."

"I'm sorry," Kevin let out the breath he'd been holding as if that would make his foot slide into the boot easier, "you did great. You made up for my carelessness."

"A bit of a backhanded thanks, but I guess it will have to do."

Five minutes later, the pair was gliding across the snow. Their progress was by no means smooth, but it was marginally better than just walking. As the sun broke through the gray canopy, the landscape became more familiar...with one exception...there were signs of a considerable amount of foot traffic, and it was all headed for the golf course.

2

Vignettes XXV

"Send the first vehicles," Aaheru called down from the balcony. "Ensure that the women have a truck in front and behind the bus."

"Yes, my Pharaoh," the two men called back up.

Aaheru watched the frantic scurrying as his children prepared. As the self-proclaimed New Pharaoh, he was not just considered the Father of all Egyptians, he was also their GOD. These people were here by his mercy and in his service. In a few minutes, he would be demonstrating his power.

"Your truck is ready, my brother," Ahi stepped up beside him.

"And everything is prepared down on the docks?"

"Our teams have the vessels cleared and the engines are running."

"And how are we situated for supplies?"

"That is where we still fall short." Ahi dropped his gaze. One of the tasks given to him specifically had to do with organizing the foraging parties. Of the three he'd sent out, only one had returned.

Aaheru listened to Ahi as he gave the bleak report. However, Aaheru knew something that his friend did not. Any good ruler not only expects insurrection, but has measures in place to deal with those occasions should they arise. Still, he let the silence hang in the air for a moment before putting his friend and advisor at ease. That was another trait of a good ruler; keep even your closest allies on their toes.

"Did you send Jaakan or Faakhir?" Aaheru retreated from

the balcony and into the hotel room he had claimed for their brief stay on the outskirt of Alexandria. A large carry bag was certainly not befitting his status, but it was all he had for now. Considering the fact that most of his subjects had been wearing the same clothing for days, weeks, or even months, his few changes were an extravagance.

"Both, my brother. I also sent Nabeh."

"I thought the boy fell victim to one of the returned," Aaheru said with a slightly raised eyebrow.

"He did. And we left him beside the road as you have instructed for any who are bitten. Yet, he caught up with us just yesterday. His wound heals."

Aaheru spun around. The look on his face was one that had Ahi taking a few steps back before he even realized it.

"Why was I not informed!" In two long strides, the much larger man was across the room and had Ahi by the open collar of his shirt.

"I did not think—"

"You place is not to think," Aaheru roared. "Your place is to do and to tell."

"I humbly apologize, my Pharaoh."

Aaheru took a deep breath and loosened his grip on the much more diminutive man. He brushed away the wrinkles and placed his arms firmly on Ahi's shoulders.

"The last broadcasts before the city went dark had reports of rumors that there were those who did not succumb to this plague. Since I can already assume that the two who did not return were Jaakan and Faakhir, I want you to bring me the boy. Bring Nabeh to me immediately and tell no one."

Ahi had no idea what Aaheru was talking about when it came to Nabeh. He had only heard that the boy was bitten. He had never seen the injury, but when it was reported to him, he had done what Aaheru had ordered long ago; he had given the order that the boy be left to die. He was given no provisions, but simply left beside the road with the warning that if he pursued the convoy, he would be shot. When he caught up with the group five days later, Ahi had to assume that the boy was not bitten. Nobody lasted five days after a bite. Also, the wounds do not heal; rather, they begin to fester and stink despite any treatment given. Nabeh's wound was now an ugly scab. In other words, it was healing. A bite from one of the returned never heals.

As for Jaakan and Faakhir, he had never told Aaheru who he sent. When he asked for volunteers, these were the men who stepped forward. Obviously Nabeh wanted to prove his worth and redeem himself after having been cast aside. As for the others, Ahi just assumed that they wanted to gain favor with him, and by proxy, the pharaoh.

Aaheru watched Ahi's face as his friend and advisor tried to process the information. It was time to reveal a small kernel of knowledge.

"The two who have not returned are loyal to Markata."

Ahi's eyes went wide. The implications were quite frightening. It was against his own advice that Aaheru had given Markata the honor of driving the bus that would hold all of the women. If Markata had men working for him, then the situation was even more serious than he first realized. His belief was simply that the snake of a man wanted *his* job. However, if things were as they seemed…he had even grander aspirations.

"I do not mean disrespect, my Pharaoh, but I warned you that I believed Markata to be treacherous."

"Yes, my *son*…" Aaheru let that hang in the air for a moment. Up until this moment, he had allowed this man certain familiarities; the time had come to fully embrace his role as the man who would return Egypt to her glory…and with it…the power of a true pharaoh. That meant it was time to make a subtle assertion of the role. He would hope the man proved to be as smart as he portrayed himself to be and catch the hint. It would actually pain Aaheru to order a disciplinary action against his friend. "You are right to distrust Markata. And I value your judgement, but I had to see for myself the depths that the *ibn il-Homar*, son of a donkey, was prepared to sink."

"So now you will remove him from the bus?"

"No."

Ahi was confused, but he had heard the tone Aaheru used when he addressed him as 'my son' and knew that much was changing in the dynamics of the relationship he had with this man who laid claim to the title of pharaoh.

"And the two men who have not returned?" Ahi decided that was probably the safest question.

"They are of no consequence. The possible supply problems are a concern, but no one man can survive out in this world alone any longer. They will perish in time." Aaheru glanced at his bag and headed for the door.

Ahi did not like this new relationship. Still, it would be to his benefit to maintain it as is for the time being. He still had his own agenda. It would simply need to have its approach altered slightly.

***

"You...lady," Juan barked causing the young woman to almost trip over her feet. "What's your name?"

"April Cable," she replied after choking on the words a few times.

"Okay, April, here is what I need you to do..."

Juan paused and looked back towards the hill. The brush was shaking violently, and even many of the more slender, young pines were bending and disappearing as the mob poured down the ravine. At this point, none of them would remember what they were chasing or why; they simply continued after the last visible food source.

He snapped his head back to the young man and woman who had made it with him this far. "I want you to climb up on one of those trailer rigs and look for any signs of the others. If Thad beat us here, he wouldn't have taken all the boats. That means they are somewhere close if they made it across. Also, if you see anything out in the water, track it with your eyes and look for a landmark if they beach."

"Okay." April licked her dry lips and tried to swallow back the fear that had threatened to overwhelm her the past several minutes. Without another word, she ran to the rear of the trailer and began climbing up.

Juan turned to the guy and his eyes froze on what looked like a nasty bite just above the left wrist. "And what's your name?"

"Al Kincaid," the young man replied. He followed Juan's gaze and his eyes froze on his wound. He looked back up with tears already brimming.

"Al, I want you to head down the beach here and see if you can spot anything that looks like it might possibly float. That bend in the river is as far as I want you to go. If you get there and see anything, you haul ass back and let April up there know about it."

"What about—"

"Don't worry about that right now," Juan cut him off. "You might be immune."

"But what if I'm not?"

"We can worry about that later."

"Later!" Al's voice cracked and was almost a shout.

"Listen…you want me to put this blade in your head right this minute? Or do you want to see about getting us the hell out of here and letting us deal with your problem when it is for sure that you are gonna be one of them deaders?"

Al seemed to consider his options for a second, so Juan drew his weighted machete blade. That seemed to prompt a response in a hurry.

"I'll go see if there is anything," Al said in a rush as he backed away from the well-used and heavily stained blade.

Juan took another look back to that steep hill they had bounded down in an attempt to escape the hundreds of undead that had followed them across that narrow bridge. The ploy hadn't worked, and now they were trapped between a seemingly never-ending wall of deaders and the Willamette River. This entire mission had been an utter failure, and if a miracle didn't happen, he might never see Mackenzie again.

Juan started heading in the opposite direction that he'd sent Al. They probably had ten minutes at the most before they would have to bug out and start running again. That would lead to another decision—which way would they run?

He hadn't gotten too far when the girl up on the trailer, April or Amber, Juan really had to work on remembering names, hollered. "I see the boats!"

Juan spun around and then tried to track the direction that she was pointing. It was towards him! Juan spun back around and caught a glimpse of something just before it slipped behind a severely listing tug boat and a partially submerged barge.

"Can you still see it?" Juan jogged back and began to climb up onto the top of the trailer.

"Yeah, but I don't think those are our people," she said as she stepped aside and made room for him next to her. She pointed, and Juan quickly located the four boats they had arrived in running parallel to the uneven shore.

"How old you think they are?" Juan asked.

"So I'm not crazy?" April sighed with audible relief. "Maybe early teens?"

"What the hell are they doing?"

"I may be wrong...but it looks like they are chasing a dog."

Juan shielded his eyes to try and get a better look. Sure enough, he saw the head of a dog jutting up from the dark water of the river. The kids looked like they were trying to cut it off from heading out to the middle of the Willamette and force it back towards the shore. That was where the next problem arose.

Juan looked back towards where he expected the zombies to appear, and sure enough, the first couple were stumbling from the bushes and tall grass. They would move towards the first sight or sound that caught their attention. Right now, the first handful were already turning towards the kids in the boats.

"You think those kids know what is coming?" April asked in a voice barely above a whisper.

"I doubt it," Juan replied. He took a look towards where Al

had gone in search of boats. The man was jogging back, and as soon as he saw that Juan was looking his way, he started waving his arms wildly. It was only a few seconds later when the first figures came around the distant bend in the river.

"Damn," Juan sighed and hung his head. There didn't seem like any way out of this particular situation.

"Oh no." April actually staggered back and ended up in Juan's arms; it was either that, or she would have fallen off the trailer.

"Wha—" Juan started to ask, but the words died in his throat. Thad and at least one of his group had arrived. Unfortunately, they were covered in blood...all of it obviously their own. Juan could only watch helplessly as Thad stumbled and fell. Three nearby zombies got to him before he could reach his feet. The familiar scream pierced the air.

The one thing that came from that scream was the fact that the kids out on the river all turned towards the source of the noise. One of them stood up in the boat and seemed to scan the area. Eventually they spotted Juan and April atop the trailer. Juan breathed an inner sigh of relief when all four boats gave up chasing the dog and began to speed towards them.

As he reached the ground, Al arrived. Juan managed to keep his cool, but April let the cat out of the bag with a gasp. "Your eyes," she breathed.

Al looked to Juan for confirmation and received a curt nod. He slumped to the ground and buried his head in his hands. Before Juan could say anything, the four motor boats came roaring into the little inlet where they had originally been tied off.

"Hey, you guys might want to hop in," a young boy called as the engines dropped to an idle.

"You make it a habit to offer rides to strangers?" Juan asked as he stepped habitually in between these new arrivals and April.

In unison, the dozen occupants of the four boats drew an assortment of weapons that would make an action hero blush.

"Huh," Juan snorted for lack of anything else to say.

"What?" April peeked her head around Juan's large frame.

"Oh."

***

"So what is the plan?" Chad stepped out into the hall with Scott. It had taken a few hours and a lot of crying, but finally, Ronni drifted off to sleep. He was only mildly surprised that several of the people who had been there when he first returned to his room from the mockery of a trial remained just outside of his door.

"This place is splitting into factions faster than we anticipated." Brett stepped out from between a pair of older men who reminded Chad of the men from the balcony on *The Muppet Show*. "Word is that we hold this hotel and the other group is in the lodge where the trial was held. If you can believe even half of what is flying around, folks are killing each other in the street."

"What in the hell triggered all of this madness?" Chad asked. *Surely*, he thought, *this can't all be over me killing the men who were trying to rape my daughter.*

"Somebody let it slip that we are almost out of the dry stores in the hotels," a man Chad had never seen before stepped out from the bunched up crowd. His light caramel skin tone was only enhanced by the well-kept goatee and pencil-thin mustache. "The fight at the trial was just the match that was needed to blow this powder keg straight to the moon."

"That doesn't make any sense," Chad said as he shook his head. "Why would everybody go all Hatfield and McCoy like this when we obviously need to come together and pool our talents and resources?"

"Because those guys you went after had managed to gain access to the store rooms. They were setting themselves up with a sweet little black market operation. They would have had all the food, which would have meant that they would have had all the power. When the folks went to their rooms during the investigation, some of the supplies were found. That guy you killed in you room was the ringleader."

"Still not following you…" Chad paused. "I'm sorry, but I don't seem to know your name, and you have an awful lot of information."

"Clark," the man said with a warm smile. "Michael Clark."

"Okay, Mike—"

"My dad was Mike…I go by Michael."

Chad felt himself bristle a bit. He chalked it up to the events of the past few days. "Okay…*Michael*…how come you know so much?"

"Because I was in on the deal."

All heads whipped around his direction at once. None of the expressions were all that friendly.

"You want to run that by me again?" Scott stepped up next to Chad, his hand on the handle of the blade strapped to his leg.

"Look, folks," Michael held up his hands, "it ain't like it sounds."

"Really?" Chad snapped. "Because right now it sounds pretty messed up."

"I didn't sign up for what these guys were pulling." Michael kept his voice calm despite the fact that the crowd had closed in around him. "They came to me and said that they were going to force a rationing plan…that food was being wasted, and that we wouldn't make it through the winter at the rate we were going. They wanted me for security."

"Security?" a few voices said in unison.

"I am a former Marine, and I was a cop when this whole thing went off. I am the only person to make it out of the Chico police department alive as far as I know. I wasn't about to get this far and die of starvation. I honestly didn't know that these guys were gonna flip."

"So when did you find out what they were up to, and why didn't you let anybody know?" Scott asked with a sneer.

"I was trying to figure out exactly who I could tell and get any support. With Sarge dead, there really isn't any authority figure here, and I wasn't ready to go heads up with these guys on my own. I was already starting to discover that they had all kinds of folks working for them in some capacity or another. That was also when I started eavesdropping on a few conversations and discovered that a whole bunch of these guys were on a prison transport bus that crashed. They were talking about a stockpile of weapons and all sorts of crap. Then…you went and killed most of the top guys in this little organization. You left a void in the power structure, and all the underlings made a grab. On the good side, they are just as set on taking each other down as they are you…the bad news…they don't care what it takes for them to reach their objective."

"Objective?" Chad sputtered. "Why can't we just work as a cohesive unit for a common cause…survival? Why does anybody have to be in charge?"

"I don't have any answers for you on that one, man." Michael gave a shrug, and then swept his gaze across the group. "But what I do know is that we need to prepare for one of two scenarios."

"And what might those be?" Chad asked.

"Battle…or siege."

***

Basingstoke, Hampshire, UK—Victoria Kirkpatrick, Vix to her mates, set the shovel down and stared out across the lightly snow-covered grounds. A few months ago, there had been thirty-seven of them hiding out in the Audleys Wood Hotel. Now there were seven, and she didn't think any of them would make it through the next few weeks.

She blamed Nigel Longstreet and that vile little rat-faced woman, Claudia Jones. Kneeling beside the mound of dirt she had been working at busily since just before dawn, Victoria fought back the tears that had been threatening to spill all night and into the morning.

"You stupid, wonderful man," she whispered.

Her husband was underneath all of the cold earth she knelt

beside now. And it was all Nigel's fault. He had been the one to insist that they venture in to town for supplies. She had argued, saying that the city was thick with the walking dead and their best bet was to search the outlying areas. They would not find a concentrated amount of food and such going house to house, but nobody had listened.

When volunteers were asked for, Ivor, her husband and the one thing she had known she could rely upon, had stepped forward. He and seven others set out with empty packs and three rolling carts that they pulled along using a shoulder harness. Ivor was the only one to return. He was empty handed…and covered in blood.

Nigel had flown into a fury about how "careless and foolish" Ivor had been in returning to their sanctuary. "Those monsters could be following you! You may have brought death to us all!"

Weak from blood loss and obviously in the final stages of the infection before he turned and became one of the undead, Ivor had enough energy and spirit left to land a punch with enough behind it to knock Nigel out cold.

The handful of survivors that remained all stood in silence for a moment, and then erupted in a very un-British display of emotion. The cheers and yells were a sign that Nigel's reign as the self-proclaimed leader of the group had come to an end.

Claudia had stepped forward and looked as if she were going to strike Ivor from behind, but Victoria had moved in between the two. The women locked eyes for just a second. Obviously Claudia saw something that made her step back.

"If you touch him…I will kill you." That was all Victoria said.

She had no idea that two more members of the group had stepped up behind her in support. Nobody could be sure if that had been what caused Claudia to backpedal and then flee the room, but the fact remained that she had, and Nigel had followed behind once he finally came to.

By that time, Ivor had succumbed to the infection and

closed his eyes as a living person for the last time. Victoria had been at his side in their room when a long exhale rattled his once sturdy frame.

"Stupid lummox," she said through the tears. Then, she drove a metal trowel through his forehead.

Despite the fact that it was still dark, she wrapped her husband and love of her life in some sheets and stitched the ends shut. After that, she dragged him down the hallway and out into the open grounds of the hotel.

A wave of nostalgia hit her as she stood under the glow of a full moon that was amplified by the light dusting of snow. This was the hotel he had taken her to the day he asked her to marry him. She knew something was up when they pulled into the main entrance of the luxurious hotel. Places like this were not usually to Ivor's liking. He was more at home in a small pub with a few blokes, a full pint, and some chips. Even their dates up to this point had been out of the ordinary. She still remembered their first date. Ironically, it was to see the local American flag football team, the Zombie Horde, in action. She had the time of her life that evening being with a man who had encouraged her to just be herself and "the world be damned."

Now, here she was, committing his remains to the ground. All because of the bastard Nigel. Nobody had listened to her. Of course, she blamed herself. She knew better. One of her passions before this whole nightmare began all those months ago was reading. Her favorite guilty pleasure was zombie fiction. Truthfully, her interest in the zombie was due to a misplaced assumption centered on that first date. The team name had been Zombie Horde. She mistakenly assumed Ivor was a fan of zombies; when in truth, he was addicted to American football in any form.

Still, she had read well over a hundred titles in that particular genre. One thing she felt qualified to give advice on was what to do and what *not* to do in this undead world. Sending a few of their people in to town was a monumentally bad idea.

When the first cases appeared in Basingstoke, she had been

the on duty nurse at Parklands Hospital. She had been at the central nurse's desk sipping at her tea and reading when the woman had stumbled through the doors. The front of her blouse was a crimson mess and she was clutching her neck with blood-slicked hands.

Before Victoria made it out from behind the desk, the woman had collapsed to the floor. Grabbing the phone, she had paged the emergency doctor and security. By the time she had pulled on rubber gloves and returned her attention to the downed woman, she was back on her feet. Her head moving with jerky fits as she seemed to scan the room. When those eyes turned Victoria's way, her body suffered a massive chill. They were covered in a milky film that was shot full of black tracers. When it opened its mouth and let loose with a low moan and began moving towards her with outstretched arms, she had no doubt what this was.

"Oh bloody hell," was all she managed to utter.

She ran back behind her counter and looked for anything that might be used to defend herself. Finding nothing, she made a decision. Victoria ran out the fire exit. She saw a few dark shadows in the car park as she searched frantically for her own vehicle. That ride home had been terrifying. When she burst through the door, she found Ivor asleep in his favorite chair, television droning.

He hadn't even questioned her when she woke him and told him what she witnessed. The next several weeks were a blur. She had refused to seek shelter in one of the locations mentioned on the telly, telling her husband that those places never fared well in her books. It proved true as each of those locations fell in the first few days.

With a few friends and neighbors, they had done okay for a while. Then they met up with Nigel's bunch and joined forces. At first, things had been okay, but soon, it became clear that Nigel was set on being the leader. Since he had the only gun—a fact that he never was quite clear on how it had ended up in his possession since it was a Glock 17 in a harness that had police markings, but it was clear that this man had absolutely no ties to law enforcement.

Eventually, the suggestion was made to check out the Audleys Wood Hotel. Practically empty, the place had been easily cleared out. It was fortified, and its secluded location was very helpful as they hastily erected a barricade around the central grounds. That was the first, last, and only suggestion of hers that had been heeded.

Looking up into the gray sky, the first few flakes of a new snow were drifting on the morning breeze. Victoria rose to her feet, wiping what she vowed to be her last tears from her eyes, she returned inside. Things were going to change…she owed Ivor that much.

***

"On your feet and outside!" Jody barked. On his flank, two of his fellow grunts had M4s leveled at the bleary eyed residents of the tiny home. The same scene was being played out this very moment in the four other homes in this cul-de-sac.

The men of the 3rd Battalion, 153rd Infantry, had been given their orders. The citizens of Bald Knob, Arkansas were to be brought to the high school. Any resistance was to be dealt with accordingly. Bald Knob was now considered the official property of the United States Army.

A little girl of six or seven clutched her mother's side as the family was ushered out into the cold rainy night. Jody felt his heart tighten at the sight of the absolute fear on the girl's face. Her fear was not due to the threat of being eaten by one of the walking dead. No…she was scared of the living monsters that had stormed into her home, jammed the stock of a rifle into her daddy's gut, yanked her mother out of bed, and shoved her into the hall.

"Y'all can't be doin' this," the girl's father coughed, still hunched over from the assault inflicted on him by one of Jody's men. "We're Americans…we gots our rights!"

"Right now," Jody leveled his gaze at the man and did his

best to look threatening, "the only rights you have are the ones we allow you."

"This is America—"

"Shut up!" one of the soldiers barked. He raised his weapon as if to slam it into the man's ample belly once more.

"Private!" Jody barked. "At ease."

The soldier gave the man a cold sneer, but he stepped back and lowered the stock of his weapon. The family stepped outside and quickly huddled together to try and fend off the cold. From one of the other houses there was a sudden outcry and a short burst of weapon's fire. Thankfully, this was the last street. If this had happened earlier in the evolution, it is likely that many, or at least some, of the residents of Bald Knob would have been alerted and gone on the defensive.

The 153rd was a skeleton of its former self. Even with the few locals who had volunteered, they only had forty-one men in the outfit. Compared to the thousand or so residents of Bald Knob, they were grossly outnumbered. The only thing they had on their side was the element of surprise and the lack of hesitation when it came to pulling the trigger when the target in the sights was a living, breathing human being instead of a walking stiff.

One by one, the call rang out. "Residence secure!" Every living soul was to be kept in the gymnasium of the local high school. Once they were secure inside, the next phase of the evolution was to commence. Every home would be tossed. Anything that could be considered a weapon would be confiscated.

"Slider wants to see you, Sarge," one of the men announced as he arrived on the double-time.

That was the other part of the problem for Jody. Chuck "Slider" Monterro was a bit of a legend to the men of the 153rd. He had been a covert op "hiding in plain sight" as the old saying goes. As far as anybody knew, he was just a soldier…a member of a stateside unit. Since training was an integral part of military life, it was always just assumed that he was attending any number of the available specialty schools. In reality, he had been performing "behind the lines" operations.

"Where is he?" Jody asked.

He had to do his best not to show any emotion. So far, everything he had done was strictly a manner of self-preservation. Slider had come to him and asked him to lead the men in this operation. He had no doubts that any sort of refusal would have resulted in his elimination. He would be replaced by the first man who would be willing to carry out orders. At least this way, he had a say in the operations.

"Ops tent," the soldier reported.

"Benny?" Jody removed his goggles, no longer needing their night vision capabilities.

"Hey, man," Benny Brazil slung his M4 over his shoulder and reached out to shake Jody's hand.

"Haven't seen you since the last patrol."

Jody's first opportunity to lead the men on an actual mission had not gone well. Benny had been on that run, but Jody realized with a slight feeling of concern that he'd not seen the man since their return. Having only spoken with Slider on a couple of occasions, he was now dosed with a healthy amount of paranoia. He had little doubt that there were individuals already being groomed to replace him should he stumble or fail.

"Got sent out on a RECON patrol."

Alarm bells began to ring.

"Funny...never heard of any outbound missions." Jody slung his own weapon and did his best to appear nonchalant.

"The captain got rumor of another small community holding out just to the south...turned out to be a bust."

More bells...and a bit more volume. Shouldn't he be made aware of such things if he were now the leading NCO of the Gunslingers of Arkansas?

"Too bad...it would be nice if we could bring in some folks who weren't set against us," Jody said. Benny just stared back silently.

Clang! Clang! Clang!

Jody headed across the wide open field and steered himself

towards the glow of the operations tent. As he walked, he tried to figure out just exactly what Slider would want from him. When he reached the tent, he fought the urge to ask for permission to enter. That was what subordinates were required to do. He was not a subordinate...at least not to Slider. *Supposedly*, they were co-commanders of the remnants of this unit.

Stepping in, a rush of warmth hit him in the face. A large barrel in the center of the tent had a nice fire going in it. Standing beside the barrel was Slider...and Captain Timothy Gould, the commanding officer of the 153rd.

"Sergeant Rafe," the captain stepped forward with an outstretched hand. "I understand congratulations are in order."

Jody remained silent for a moment and cast a quick glance at Slider. The man seemed to be more concerned with warming himself over the fire than what was happening in this tent.

"All the citizens have been accounted for, sir," Jody finally responded, returning his focus to the man standing before him.

"And the second phase of the operation?"

"In progress as we speak, sir."

"Excellent."

Jody considered his situation and decided that if he was going to be eliminated, then he had nothing to lose. That prompted his next question.

"I understand a mission was sent outside the wire recently."

"Just chasing a rumor, sergeant," the captain said with a shrug.

Jody's eyes darted over to Slider for any hint of reaction, but there was nothing. He studied the captain. He seriously doubted this young, green ROTC boy had the same ability to mask his feelings or motives that Slider possessed. He was met with a blank stare.

"Perhaps it was not the right decision to send out one of your men without informing you." The captain made a slight nod of the head. "It won't happen again. You should be aware of any operations involving *your* men."

Jody wasn't sure what to think. The captain sounded sincere. Yet there was still a great deal about all of this that he held reservations about.

"So what will be our next course of action?" Jody asked.

"That is what we called you here for," Slider spoke, causing Jody to jump just a bit. "We will be separating the women and children from the men. It is our belief that by keeping them separated, the men will perform as requested."

"Don't you mean as hostages?" Jody couldn't help himself. He had been raised by a Pentecostal preacher who had instilled in him the core value of truth and honesty. His father had wept the day Jody rebuffed an offer to continue the evangelical family tradition in lieu of a military commitment.

"I imagine it could be seen as such." Slider shrugged. His voice held absolutely no emotion and reminded Jody of what a snake would sound like if given a human voice. "But the fact is that we need leverage to hold our position. Logistics are not in our favor. We are grossly outnumbered and need to ensure our authority."

"So what will we be doing with the women and children?"

"The women will be kept safe and secure. They will be tasked with support services." The captain went over to the desk with a series of maps of Bald Knob and the surrounding areas. "The children will undergo an educational program and, based on age, some will begin military indoctrination."

Brainwashing, Jody thought. Why couldn't they call things as they were? The women would cook and clean and the children would be brainwashed.

"And what do you require of me next, sir?"

"We want you to see to the separation and housing of the women and children," Slider said.

Jody looked back and forth between the two men. He felt like he should be concerned. This was not the job you placed under the command of the leading NCO.

"Look, Sergeant Rafe, it is no secret that your...a bit more compassionate than Sergeant Monterro here," the captain explained. "The men are going to need some convincing to do what we require. That is his forte. The women will need to be made to feel safe. I believe that is yours. Don't read anything into this."

Jody looked back and forth between the two men. Neither one gave away even the slightest hint of emotion.

"Will I be doing this alone, or will I be given support?" Jody asked.

"How many men do you think you will require?" the captain returned question for question.

Jody considered what he wanted versus what he felt might be granted him. He knew that, despite what they were saying, this assignment was not one that he was being given due to his compassion. They wanted him out of the way.

"Give me one man...and I want to handpick him."

"Done," the captain agreed.

"Just remember one thing, Rafe." Slider moved away from the barrel and faced Jody with a blank, emotionless expression. "You are being given this job for a reason."

Jody did not need the hidden meaning of that statement to be explained.

***

Hanover, Ohio—Major Wanda Beers looked back at the column marching alongside the few vehicles that they were still able to maintain. *The fuel tanker would need to be topped off again very soon*, she thought, *if the gas was still even any good.*

She turned her attention back to the front. The blue piece of cloth fluttered from the street sign indicating that they were still on the right track. That idiot Paul James better not screw this up; she grimaced at the idea that her entire outfit was at the mercy of possibly one of the stupidest men she had ever met in her life.

He had been one of the first to sell out his group during their last stop. He had been under some delusional state of mind that the military could help his wife. The only help for that snarling, drooling, walking sack of guts was a bullet in the head.

Dead: Siege & Survival

Once the appropriate arrangements were made for all the supplies to be loaded up and all the willing recruits had been conscripted, the rest of the citizens were forced outside of the walls of their little barricaded outpost.

Wanda had taken great pleasure in throwing this particular group out into the wild. This was one of those gated communities full of people who bitch and moan about the military, protest their actions, and elect politicians who don't have a problem cutting defense spending so that little Johnny can go to school and be a juvenile delinquent. They all drove around in their Hybrid cars and chanted things like "No blood for oil!" What did they care? It wasn't like those rich pricks or any of their children would ever serve. None of them would ever hold a dying friend in their arms that had just had his lower half blown off by an insurgent's IED.

The day before they were set to leave, she had informed Paul James that his daughter would not be joining them on the journey. The girl was positively useless. She had failed in every task assigned and done nothing by cry and complain when they had placed her on kitchen duty. The only other choice was to put her with the whores who serviced the soldiers. He had absolutely refused.

Wanda had created the "Brothel Brigade" early on. As a student of history, she knew that it had been common in the ancient times for armies to have useable whores travel with them— usually in the rear, and they normally performed other menial tasks like laundry and such to earn their place. Apparently what was good enough for the father was too good for the daughter— Paul had been put in rotation with the men and women in the brothel tent after he had proven to be loyal but useless. Sadly, he wasn't much better as a whore.

Paul had come to her tent the night before they were prepared to roll out. He said that he knew of another outpost. He admitted that his group was just getting ready to approach them with an offer of joining forces. Ironically, they were concerned with the possibilities of raiders coming along and trying to take over their happy little homes.

He went on to say that this other group had even fewer people, but that they seemed exceptionally well organized and supplied. He didn't want to reveal the location unless he had assurances that his daughter would be allowed to remain with the group. He said that he would even take a second job to pick up her slack. She could have brought his useless daughter Mary in right then and held a knife to her throat to convince him to talk, but she was feeling generous that day.

"You will go, and your daughter will go with you," Wanda decided. "A group might be hesitant to take in a lone man. She will help soften them up. You will leave blue strips of cloth as markers and an indicator that you have made contact."

She could roll with the direct frontal assault, but she didn't want to waste precious manpower if it was not necessary. Having a man on the inside was the perfect Trojan horse scenario. He would gain this new group's trust, and then open the gates to allow their access.

Yesterday, one of her scouts returned and reported that blue banners had been spotted. She had slapped herself in the forehead with her palm when she looked on a map and determined the direction led straight to the Longaberger Golf Course. This little tidbit of information had put her on a higher state of alert. There was the possibility that this group might be better prepared and actually led by somebody who knew what they were doing.

When the next round of scouts returned to report that a military vehicle had been spotted, Major Wanda Beers actually considered cancelling the run. She decided to risk one scout who would attempt to get inside the wall and observe.

Four agonizing days passed, and her people were starting to run low on supplies—keeping a hundred and thirty-five people fed was no easy task these days—when the scout returned. Yes, they were very well fortified against the walking dead, but there were no signs of soldiers anywhere. In two days of observation, the only people seen coming and going besides Paul James and his useless daughter were a couple of young females and one male who was often seen using a set of crutches.

The sun was just coming up...somewhere. Here, it was a solid blanket of dark clouds that threatened snow. They stopped at the front entrance to the country club. There were several vehicles in place as a barricade. No sense adding to the chaos by allowing the possibility of zombies to come in during their assault.

Major Beers sent her men and women over the wall. Like any commander worth a damn, she climbed over with the first wave. All the concern turned out to be for nothing. Besides her Trojan horse, all they discovered were three young females between the ages of fifteen and twenty-five, one male with a severe leg injury that looked to have received expert attention, and a severely disturbed black girl with Down's syndrome.

3

Hunker Down

"...and we hope that some way, somehow, Jamie found peace in the end." The words tasted like ash on my tongue.

What I wanted to do was scream. I wanted to cry. Unfortunately, I don't have that luxury. Every face seems to be numbed with grief and looking to me for something. I just wish that I knew what the blazes that could be.

"We will miss Jamie Blossington, and we will never forget him. Rest in peace, friend."

I looked over to Billy in case he wanted to say anything. He was simply staring at the pyre with the same empty look that everybody else had plastered on their wind-chapped faces. A quick glance told me that nobody else was going to step forward. I truly believe that we have all had about as much as we could handle if we managed to live a dozen lifetimes.

I touched the torch to the base and stepped back as the flames began to devour everything. There would be little more than a pile of ash and bone in a few hours. Once the fire burned out, everything would be shoveled into a cart and taken to a burial site. A small monument was being fashioned by Melissa, Thalia, and Emily, and would be placed next to Teresa's in our little graveyard.

One by one, everybody walked away until it was just me and Billy and Dr. Zahn. And that was my newest problem. Of all the people I'd met since this nightmare began, Dr. Francis Zahn was probably one of the most hard-nosed, nothing-can-bother-me person I'd ever met or would ever meet for the rest of my

43

life. That woman had vanished in the past few days. She was replaced by a frail, feeble old lady, who looked like she might crumble in on herself at any minute.

The past several days had been her undoing. It started with Teresa's death. Teresa, the teenaged GI Jane of the group—and pregnant with Jamie's child—had come down with the zombie virus or whatever it was. The problem being, that she'd not been bitten or scratched by a zombie. The eventual answer to the mystery: sexually transmitted.

Jamie had been bitten several weeks earlier during a skirmish with a mob. The saving grace had been that he was one of the few who showed immunity to being turned. However, we had eventually discovered that, immune or not, once the virus is in your system, it remains there. A person who displays immunity will still turn if they die from other causes. Nobody made that connection until Teresa came down with the virus for no apparent reason. Dr. Zahn blamed herself for the girl's death…and now it seemed she chose to shoulder Jamie's suicide as well.

"Billy…" I went to stand beside the young man.

And then there was one, I thought. Billy had joined up with me shortly after this whole thing began during a crazy escape from a FEMA shelter that was overwhelmed from the inside. He was with three other high school friends who had all fallen one by one.

"He just gave up on me," Billy whispered.

"No," I corrected. "He just gave up."

"I don't understand."

"And we probably never will."

I stood in silence beside the young man. I just didn't have any more words. The only thing that I was sure of at this very moment was that it was freezing, and I wanted to go inside. I glanced over at Dr. Zahn who stood shivering on the other side of the pyre. It was like being at the edge of the river while two friends were drowning. Which one do I jump in and save. I patted Billy on the shoulder and headed over to the doctor.

"Come on, Doc," I said, and took her gently by the elbow.

She looked up at me with red, puffy eyes and tears stream-ing down her face. I truly thought I would never see this woman lose it like this over anything.

I took another look at Billy and hoped that he had the sense to eventually come in out of the weather. I'd made my selection so to speak and began guiding the doctor back to the huge, log cabin-style forestry building that we all called our home. In just the short time since we'd come out to send Jamie off to the heavens or wherever, the snow had already added a couple more inches.

The weather was not showing any signs of letting up, and the blanket of white that covered the ground was already past my knees. This area wasn't too bad because we walked around enough to keep it tamped down. However, I seriously doubted that we would be leaving this camp very often anymore for any-thing except water. We had snowshoes and skis, but the weather was becoming so harsh that even suited up as warmly as we could, it was simply not a good idea to flirt with Mother Nature.

When I reached the long porch that ran the length of the front of the building, Jon Saunders was there waiting with Sun-shine. Jon was and will probably always be a United States Marine, Sunshine is the kind of gal you imagine running around with flowers in her hair sticking daisies in the barrels of a sol-dier's rifle. Lately, the two had become a secret couple. The only thing secret about it was that we all knew it before they did.

"We need to talk," Jon said in lieu of a greeting.

"I don't think I can take anything else right now," I said with a sigh.

"I wish it could wait, but it really can't," Jon insisted.

"Fine." I glanced at Dr. Zahn beside me. She seemed to be showing little more life than the walking dead. She stared straight ahead, tears still running down her cheeks made rosy by the wind and cold. I did notice that her lips were moving. It was as if she were talking to herself, but I didn't hear so much as a peep.

"First, I am sorry as hell what you've been put through the

past several days," Jon apologized. "I am as big a part of the problem as anybody else. We all simply just got complacent...well...everybody but you. You need to know that you have all our support from here on out."

I really didn't care, but I let him continue because I could tell he was just building up to something.

"Also, I hate to be the one to add to what is already a huge burden on your shoulders, but Sunshine just finished a full inventory of the food pantry. We may not be as set up as we initially thought."

"We weren't really paying attention to a few of the things like flour, rice, and things of that nature," Sunshine took over as she stepped out of the shadows. "Plus, I was not making notes on how much it took for each meal until recently. We have all been eating very well, but we are eating like people who can go to the grocery store anytime we want."

"So how bad is it?" I asked. I didn't really want the answer, but since I'd been elected as the so-called leader of this group, I guess it fell on me to listen.

"We are good for at least the next six weeks."

I let that sink in and tried to figure out what the problem might be. Six weeks was plenty of time to remedy the situation. I guess they anticipated my response.

"You haven't ever lived out this way, have you?" Sunshine asked.

"Seattle born and raised," I replied with a shrug.

"This is just the start of winter, Steve," Sunshine said with a leading edge to her voice like she thought I might figure out whatever secret code she was apparently speaking.

I looked at her and then at Jon. "Look, I imagine you have a point, I'm just too burned out to pick up on it so spill it."

"This is just the start of things." Sunshine used her arms to gesture at the heavy snowfall coming down behind me. "Unlike what you might be used to in the city where this sort of weather clears up in a few days or a week, this will go on for weeks if not months."

"That is why the porch to this place is eight or so feet off the ground," Jon cut in. "And those tall posts along the road the lead to this place? Those are snow markers. This place could realistically see enough snow to reach the windows...or worse. Back in the day, they used plows to keep this place cleared. And that little Snowcat they have here is probably operational, but we don't have any fuel for it. This whole thing kicked off in the spring. They had probably just put her away for the season and hadn't gotten around to stocking up on fuel and such."

"So what's the bad news," I sighed. I guess I really had not planned on having to hunker down for three or four months. Once again I doubted my ability to lead this bunch of people effectively.

"I want to make one more run," Jon said. "I will take my boys with me and we will gas the cat up using the truck fuel. I already checked and that baby had a big forty gallon tank as well as a twenty gallon spare. We should be able to get to La Grande and Enterprise fueling as we go. This will be a food only supply run using the list that Sunshine has given me."

"You want to go out in this and then try and deal with zombies...possibly raiders...and then get back here alive?" I just didn't see the likelihood of anybody—not even a Marine and a pair of soldiers—making a run like this.

"I think we are the *only* ones who can do it," Jon stated matter-of-factly. "We have the training to deal with extremes and will have the best chance if it comes to a living enemy. That is why it has to be us three despite your previous decision that foraging runs were not to be gender exclusive. This has got to be more of a military operation."

Everything he said made perfect sense. My only problem with it was the fact that if, like they were both saying, the bad weather was just getting started, then I could be sending my three best fighters to their death.

"I don't like the idea any more than you do, Steve," Sunshine said with a hitch in her voice. "But if they don't do this, we might all die of starvation."

"How long before I should worry?" I asked.

"My best estimate puts us out for three weeks tops."

"So we hit the halfway point on our stores before we know if we will be surviving the season?"

"You can still hunt for game in the area, but if you have noticed, it has been scarce. It has either migrated, or it has been chased away by the herds of undead that have come through," Jon said.

"When do you intend to leave?"

"First thing in the morning, I already told Jake and Jesus to prep...I didn't want to go outside your wishes, but I had to assume you would see the necessity."

Jake Beebe and Jesus Sanchez were the two soldiers from the United States Army who showed up with Jon a couple months back. My relationship with them had been tenuous at best ever since they took Thalia and Emily—ages five and ten respectively—out into the woods and had them kill a walker. Yes, they had disabled it by taking its legs out, but I still had a problem with the whole thing. The worst part about that situation was that I was beginning to see where I was wrong. I was the one preaching vigilance and preparedness, but I was balking when it came to the girls.

"Just do your best to hurry back," I sighed.

We stood in silence for a moment. I noticed the uncomfortable looks on their faces any time they so much as glanced Dr. Zahn's way. She had been a rock for all of us. Nobody was comfortable with the shell of a woman she'd become almost overnight. With a nod, I led her inside and let the two "secret" lovebirds have a few moments of privacy.

Inside the giant visitor's center cabin we called home, the mood was as expected. Even the two new arrivals, Doug and Cheryl Coates were in a corner leaning into each other for emotional support and they'd only been with us for a day.

As I peeled off my coat and gloves, my eyes sought Melissa and I found her with Thalia and Emily each snuggled under an arm with faces buried in her side. She saw me and her eyes immediately flashed to Dr. Zahn and then back to mine.

Dr. Zahn pulled away from me and went to her little emergency room/trauma center/office and shut the door. I felt something warm on my hand and looked down to see Buster, the red and white Border Collie licking tentatively. That was odd in the sense that the dog seemed to ignore me almost entirely. He was Thalia and Emily's dog. Period.

I scratched the small dog behind the ear and was rewarded with a belly that was apparently a much more desirable location for the aforementioned scratching. Kneeling down, I gave the dog a good belly rub and remembered my beloved Basset Hound. Pluck had basically saved me that first night. For some reason, the emotions hit me like a firestorm and the next thing I knew, tears filled my eyes.

I don't know if I stopped scratching Buster's belly or if the dog was turned off by my pitiful crying, but at some point I found myself alone on my knees weeping like a baby. I looked up to find Thalia standing in front of me. She took my face in her tiny hands and stared into my eyes with a very serious expression of concern.

"It's okay, daddy." She placed her forehead against mine. "Jamie is in Heaven with Teresa and Emily's daddy and my mommy."

I was dumbstruck. This was just more proof that I was absolutely clueless when it came to the ability of children to process through absolutely debilitating emotional trauma and find happiness in a world that has fallen apart.

***

"Don't take stupid chances," I said as Jon climbed into the Snowcat with Jake and Jesus.

"And you need to take it easy on that leg," Jon whispered. He glanced over my shoulder at Melissa. I appreciated his discretion. "You are starting to show a very noticeable limp. It is all over your face when you get tired or start to push yourself beyond what you should."

"And if it looks bad, just come back and we will figure something out." I ignored his ministrations.

"You know as well as I do that there isn't anything to figure out. We need to do this. And next year we will have that full blown garden and we will hunt with a new purpose. We have to treat this like the pioneer days."

I watched as the Snowcat roared down the hill and eventually vanished in the trees. Once it was gone I turned to get a look up in the crow's nest. Fiona O'Hara was on watch.

"Fee," I called.

"Yep...I know...keep an eye peeled for anything that might have been attracted by the noise."

Everybody else had gone inside within the first few minutes; everybody except Melissa that is. Not even Thalia and Emily wanted to stay outside in this cold to play. It was bitter cold—and that was a phrase I really hadn't appreciated until recently.

"You want to talk?" Melissa came and put her arms around me and snuggled in close.

"About?"

"Everything."

"That doesn't narrow it down much."

"Dr. Zahn? The food situation? Jamie? There are a number of choices." Melissa ticked them off one by one like charges in a courtroom.

"I don't know what to say anymore," I conceded.

"Steve, you need to give yourself a little slack. Every single thing that happens is not your fault any more than they are your accomplishments when something works. We are a unit."

"But you all voted me your leader."

"And when the tough choices need to be made, we will rely on your ability to think clearly and rationally."

"But so much has gone wrong." I felt that strangled feeling in the back of my throat again. Man, I was sick of crying or feeling like I was on the verge of it. I didn't think men were supposed to get this way. They sure didn't in any book or movie I could recall. Maybe this was what a nervous breakdown feels like. Did men have those? I wasn't sure.

"And so much has gone right. You have two little girls that you have kept alive, we have this place—"

"And we may all starve and die here," I cut her off.

"We will figure it out," Melissa insisted.

I looked around at the smooth, white landscape. The curl of smoke rising from the chimney added to the idyllic look that this place gave off. That was the problem with an illusion; when it shattered, you were left holding nothing.

"Okay," Melissa's tone grew stern and serious and she spun me around to face her. "Have you confronted Dr. Zahn for her carelessness that resulted in Teresa's and Jamie's death?"

I stood there shocked. This woman and every single one of us probably owed our life to that poor lady. How could she even consider being so cruel? I tried to respond, but I was seriously pissed.

"You haven't, have you?" Melissa pressed, and I shook my head because I could not find the words to express not only my anger, but also my disappointment in this woman who I thought I'd come to know. "And you won't...because it is not. Her. Fault."

I stared. At first it was in confusion. But that soon gave way to something else.

"You set me up," I gasped.

"No, I helped you see something a bit more clearly. You are so buried in the problem that you often lose sight of the big picture. Also, you put unreasonable demands on yourself that you wouldn't dream of putting on others." Melissa slipped her gloved hands behind my neck and pulled me down.

When I withdrew from the kiss, she looked up at me with a look that I really had no idea could exist. I only hoped that what I felt in my heart for her was as clear on my face as her feelings for me were at this very moment. We walked back to the cabin holding hands. Suddenly it didn't feel so cold.

***

"At least five." DeAngelo Cribbs came in from the front porch after stomping his feet to knock away the snow. DeAngelo and his wife had arrived a couple months ago. I don't think I will ever get used to standing around shooting the breeze with one of the most sought after linebackers to enter pro football. The fact that he played for my beloved Seattle franchise made him a bigger star than Tom Hanks or Brad Pitt in my eyes. And did I mention that the man was freakin' huge?

"And they are coming up to us for sure?" I asked.

"Seem to be."

"Then let's get out there and meet them in the parking lot. That is the flattest ground. It will be the safest location," I announced.

"Three more!" Fiona called down through the trap door.

"Here's your big knife." Emily handed me my large sheathed blade.

"Thanks, sweetie." I took it and kissed her on the cheek. As I fastened it around my waist Thalia arrived with my gloves.

"Here, daddy." She held them up by the tips of the pinky fingers. "They're stinky," she huffed, and once I took them from her she made over-exaggerated waves of her hand in front of her nose accompanied by a scrunched face.

I gave them a sniff and she was right. I never knew that gloves could smell like dirty socks. I guess it makes sense. I know that my hands get sweaty.

Nickie Bailey was already waiting beside the door. She had a wicked looking curved blade in one hand and an unlit torch in the other. Her friend Christina Gavi was whispering something in her ear. The two hugged, and then Christina made her way back to the rocking chair next to the fireplace.

Christina and Nickie hadn't been with us long either. When they'd arrived, it was actually Nickie who had sought us out in hopes that we could help her wounded friend. It had been more miracle work by Dr. Zahn that had saved the woman. Maybe I needed to remind the good doctor of all of *her* successes. I could try to trick her like Melissa had done to me earlier, but she probably wouldn't fall for it.

DeAngelo, Nickie, and I headed out into the gloomy winter night to take care of the stragglers who were finally arriving to investigate the sound of the Snowcat firing up several hours ago. That really showed how single-minded they were; a noise they heard several hours ago drew them from wherever they had been, from whatever direction they had been heading. There was absolutely a way to use that in our favor…I just had to figure out what that might be.

Standing on the porch, I looked down across the expanse between our cabin and the tree line. I had to remind myself of my own lecture about the dangers of the zombie. The problem I faced was trying to be concerned by these pathetic creatures spread out and struggling to make it through the snow.

"I want to see if we can take these things down before we need that torch," I said.

"That means meeting them down below," Nickie pointed out. "I thought the idea was to meet them up here on the flat ground."

"We can't be sure they will all come up here." I pointed to a couple of the zombies that had stopped walking for whatever reason.

"So what's the plan?" DeAngelo asked.

"Let's move down to the Killing Tunnel with me and Nickie on the left, you take the right," I said.

"Are you sure that you want to split up?" Something was bothering Nickie. I didn't know her well enough to know what, but whatever it was, it had her shook. She kept looking away from me. That made my alarm bells start to jingle a little bit.

"We have zombies coming in from both sides," I pointed out. "If we don't use both berms, then we will lose sight of the ones on the opposite side. It is better for us to keep them in view."

Nickie nodded, but she still seemed off just a bit. I was suddenly glad that I chose her to pair up with me. I needed to keep my eyes on her.

We headed down, and it didn't take long for things to get tough. Once we cleared the huge flat rectangle that was the gravel parking lot in front of the cabin, we were in thigh-deep snow that slowed us down. Maybe I should have thought this through better. Would this be another huge error on my behalf? It's not like we don't have snowshoes inside.

Moving along the top of the berm was no easy feat. Even though it had a flattened top, it was covered with snow, and therefore, impossible to tell exactly where to walk.

Dusk seemed to be racing us to our places as the shadows grew, swallowing the surrounding landscape. It was already almost impossible to tell if anything else was coming out of the trees.

"Hey!" I barked as loud as I dared, causing the zombies to turn my way. Behind me, I heard Nickie hiss between her teeth.

"What?" I turned. Had I missed something? What on earth could go wrong?

"That's Mark," Nickie said with a sob threatening to overwhelm her ability to speak.

I turned back the way she was pointing. Scanning the zombies, I saw one that might have been fresher than the rest. He was wearing a tattered winter coat. One hand was still gloved...the other was missing.

"Who is Mark?"

"He was just the sweetest person you could ever meet," Nickie sobbed. She obviously decided that fighting those tears was a futile exercise. Her voice trembled and verged on not being understandable. "I thought it was him when we went outside. He wore that coat all the time...even in his sleep."

"That's what was bothering you," I mumbled.

I felt like a perfect heel for thinking that something might be up. That was an indication of just how suspicious I'd become of everybody and everything. This was just not me. I was not that guy. In fact, one of my problems early on was not being suspicious enough…not being assertive. It had almost cost me Thalia. Had I swung too far in the opposite direction?

"I wasn't sure it was him…or I didn't want it to be…" Her voice faded and she was looking past me now. "Oh, Mark," she whispered, "I'm so sorry."

"You want to go back inside?" I asked.

"No, he deserves better…he doesn't deserve to be one of *them* for eternity."

Before I could say anything else, she plunged down the side of the berm and began driving herself through the deep snow. It fell away from her like blue-white waves crashing from the prow of a ship. Weapon raised high, she was sobbing and saying something unintelligible. Despite not being able to decipher the words, the meaning was clear. Grief. Sorrow. Heart-wrenching sadness.

Halfway there, she stumbled, the snow building in front of her becoming too great of an obstacle. She vanished from view for just a moment, but came up in a geyser of white and barreled forward.

"What's going on?" DeAngelo called from the other berm. "Where's Nickie?"

"She knows one of them." That was all that needed to be said. It was getting dark fast, but I still saw him nod, I still saw the look of sympathy on his face.

I turned just as she shoved the first zombie she came to aside. It vanished under the snow, but I knew full well it would get back up. By the time I reached the bottom of the berm and took off in pursuit of Nickie as fast as I could—which wasn't very quick considering how my leg was starting to throb—she had bulldozed past two more walkers.

I was just reaching the first one as she closed in on her friend or travelling companion; I wasn't entirely sure of their relationship status. I jammed my Ka-Bar in the eye of the apparently confused zombie that was struggling with the idea that it could not grab the snow and use it to help regain its feet.

Pulling free, I looked and did some mental calculations. I would be able to get to one of the zombies that she had knocked aside. However, she hadn't given the other one enough of a push, and it had remained on its feet. It would reach Nickie before I could. To make matters worse, several others had now homed in on us and we no longer had the advantage of being above them in a position of superiority. Hadn't I just dismissed them as a threat a few minutes ago?

Nickie seemed to be hesitating. I had no idea what she was doing, but I was pretty certain that I would be adding her to the target list if she didn't do it soon.

I reached the second one that she had knocked over and swung my blade with a solid overhand that brought it down on the crown of its head. The blade stuck and my split-second decision was to leave it and keep moving.

To my relief, Nickie reared back with her sword and ended Mark for good. Unfortunately, that relief was short lived as she let loose with a cry of anguish and went charging into the midst of a half-dozen more that were just now coming out of the tree line to her left.

I was able to hear her now and quite frankly, I was more than a little surprised at the string of obscenities she was putting together. This from a woman I'd seen crack her shin with the head of the splitting maul and say, "Jiminy crickets!"

"…send you all straight to Hell where you belong you flesh-eating mother fuckers!"

That was the *least* profane thing that she said over the next minute or so as she waded through the snow from one zombie to the next and administered the lethal stroke. I decided that my best course of action was to take down the ones that had been making their way across the open field but were now coming back. Every single zombie in sight was headed towards Nickie as she did a fairly good impersonation of the Tasmanian Devil and whirled around to take the tops of skulls off and send the scalp and cranial matter flying away to land in the snow.

I was about ten or so yards away when something moved

under me and sent me falling sidewise in an awkward heap. It almost seemed like the world was moving in slow motion as I watched my just drawn machete fly end over end through the air in a near-perfect arc and then vanish in the snow about five feet away.

The weapon hitting the snow and vanishing was the last thing that I saw before I face-planted in the cold wetness myself. Something was clutching my left leg and trying its damnedest to bite through my shin guard. *Thank God I hadn't gotten so complacent so as not to fully suit up for this like I've seen others do*, I thought.

My relief was short lived as I felt something gouge into the flesh just below my knee. I cried out and kicked, but already I had the feeling that I was done for. Just like when Ian had been bitten not too long ago, my belief was that Jamie's immunity was a gift that we should not expect to see duplicated in any other members of our group.

With a groan I rolled over...or tried to at least. My situation had just gone from bad to worse. The snow had me entombed and mobility was a serious problem. Couple that with my leg not being a hundred percent, and the fact that me trying to turn over sent an explosion of agony up that leg and straight to my mouth where, despite the snow, I managed to let loose with quite a scream.

I flailed as best I could, but I was now certain that I was a goner. Not only that, but without me watching her back, Nickie stood little chance. There were too many for one person, and she had basically run to the middle of them and rang the dinner bell.

The hand or hands grasping my ankle continued to squeeze and tug and claw at my pants. I moved as best I could, but it all seemed like a lost cause. The pain in my left leg was agonizing, but the blood I felt running down my right was the reason for concern.

Suddenly I was being hoisted from the ground and then just as unceremoniously tossed aside. I only saw enough in that brief second above the snow to catch a glimpse of DeAngelo. This time I landed on my back and found myself staring up at the dark gray sky.

I heard a roar followed by a shrill shriek. When I sat up, DeAngelo was swinging his long sword in huge arcs and cutting down everything that stood. A head flew one way and an arm the other as he used absolutely no discrimination in his attack. He wasn't taking the zombies down so much as he was taking them apart.

The next thing that I noticed was that there was no sign of Nickie. I knew in my heart that she couldn't have been bitten and turned that quick so as to have been minced by DeAngelo's whirling dervish routine. Still, with the way things were going, I couldn't shake the fear that something very bad had happened to her.

I struggled to my feet as the creeper that I had unwittingly stumbled over was yanked up rather harshly and dispatched with a Bowie knife to the temple and then discarded like a ragdoll. DeAngelo spun and his eyes instantly went to my right leg. I looked down and could see the dark stain that was obviously not just dampness from the snow just below the knee.

"Steve..." he started, but couldn't say anything more.

"What the hell!" Nickie sputtered as she sat up, appearing as little more than just a head hovering over the surface of the snow.

"Exactly!" DeAngelo spun so that all I saw was his big broad shoulders. However, I could still see Nickie's face and her expression had changed from outraged to chastised in a heart-beat. "What in God's name possessed you to run down here like that and leave the berm? You gave up all of your safety and en-dangered everybody with that damn fool move."

"I...I..." Sounds stopped coming out, but Nickie's mouth kept moving like a landed fish.

"We need to finish these bastards and get over to my berm before the dozen or so on that side start making it up towards the cabin," DeAngelo said and turned to help me to my feet. "Can you go?" he whispered.

58

I nodded.

"Wait," Nickie called as she stood up. She waded towards us and came to a halt beside DeAngelo, her eyes glued to my right leg. "Oh, Steve," her eyes filled with fresh tears, "what have I done?"

"We can deal with this later," I said. ""Right now we've got company, and I don't have a weapon."

DeAngelo yanked a long machete from its sheath and handed it to me. Without another word we took down the seven remaining zombies that had come out on this side. As I was putting down the last one, he and Nickie were already headed up to the berm.

Once we got back and climbed up on the other mound—a feat that was not as easy for me as it sounds with my previously injured leg throbbing and my new injury burning—it was just a matter of attracting the zombies' attention.

I stepped forward just a bit and lifted my bleeding leg. "Come and get it!" I crowed. I tugged at my pants leg and fell over backwards down the back side of the berm and into the Killing Tunnel. I couldn't stop laughing.

Nickie and DeAngelo both gave me a nervous glance. I could see it in their eyes. They were certain that I was already in the grips of delirium brought on by the infection.

Geek Insurgent

Kevin scooted forward on his stomach just as Willa had instructed. She had wriggled under a thick hedge that had probably acted as a natural fence back when such things mattered.

They were on the west side of the country club and had been systematically working their way around the entire complex. What Kevin saw made his blood run cold...even colder than the weather.

"Two more," Willa whispered. "Both are armed with an assortment of blades. No sign of firepower here either."

"That makes at least twenty individuals," Kevin hissed. "What the hell happened?"

"If I had to guess, I would say a band of raiders found your little set up and decided to claim it for themselves. I would also say that they don't intend to give it up any time soon or without a fight."

Kevin shot a withering glare. "First, I was being rhetorical. Second, I need to figure out a way to get in there and save my friends."

"I don't want to be the bearer of bad news, but your chances are absolutely nil. These people have patrolling guards. We have seen at least twenty separate individuals since we arrived last night. There could be any number inside that we haven't seen yet. We have no idea what the response might be, but it is safe to assume that if they have not already killed your friends, an attack would likely prompt such a thing."

"What is wrong with you?" Kevin hissed.

"What do you mean?" Willa didn't even turn her head in Kevin's direction as she continued to scan the area.

"Is that your idea of a pep talk?" Kevin snapped.

"No." Willa finally turned his way and looked him in the eyes. "I am telling you the truth...these are facts."

"I lost people to goons like this before," Kevin said with as even a tone as he could muster. "I won't just abandon them. I waited too long the last time to act and somebody I cared about ended up dying a terrible death. I won't do something stupid, but I won't do nothing."

"You can't do anything, Kevin," Willa whispered. "I know that you are—"

"You *don't* know!" Kevin snapped. "I can't fail. That is not an option for me. People are counting on me, and I will not let them down. That girl in there needs the medication that I went through hell to get...that probably one of the last doctors in the freaking world died to get! If this is how I am going to die...then so be it. I don't give a damn anymore."

Willa looked back at the two men walking across the rolling hill, apparently down the middle of a tree-lined fairway. They were wearing snowshoes and had some upper end cold weather gear. From everything she could see, these were not just a bunch of thugs. These people were organized and had their act together. Any sort of open assault would end quick and with disastrous results.

"We are going to have to use some insurgency tactics," Willa finally said.

"Huh?"

"Over in Afghanistan, the locals knew better than to go heads up with us—"

"Wait," Kevin interrupted. "You were in the war?"

"Did you think I just borrowed these clothes?" Willa quipped.

"No...yeah..." Kevin was at a loss. Yes, he knew that she had been in the US Army, but he had never even once considered that she might have been in combat. "So you like...got into firefights and all that crap?"

"Yeah," Willa said with a chill in her tone. "I did all that *crap*."

Kevin shook his head in a mixture of disbelief and wonder. When he'd first met Willa and her band of female fighters, he was given the impression that some of them were actual soldiers, but that many were simply individuals who had joined the group for a "safety in numbers" sense of security. The last thing that had ever crossed his mind was that he was running side-by-side with an actual combat veteran.

"Hey," Kevin rolled on his side and faced her, "I'm sorry. I have this problem where I don't think. I say things that sound one way in my head and come out of my mouth in an entirely different fashion."

"If we're gonna do this, we do it *my* way." Willa dismissed Kevin's apology. She'd spent years having to prove herself to her male counterparts. She'd long since decided that she didn't have to prove a damn thing to anybody other than herself.

Kevin listened intently as Willa laid out the plan. A few times, he had to ask her to explain certain aspects or clarify exactly what she expected from him. The hardest part now was the waiting. One of the first things that she had insisted upon is more reconnaissance of the grounds. Also, she was insistent upon making at least one solo run over the country club wall by herself. When Kevin asked why he couldn't go, she asked him how many actual covert ops not involving a video game console he had made in his life. That had ended the discussion.

As nightfall came and more snow began to fall in large, fluffy flakes, Kevin sat in the house he and Willa had chosen as their base of operations. From the second floor window he could see a faint glow in the direction of the country club.

Less than two miles away from his friends...and Valarie. He would not fail them. He would not fail *her*. He had a chance to redeem himself for failing his sister. He would not be able to undo what had been done, but he could do something for somebody who needed him.

On the street below, a lone zombie stumbled into view. It struggled through the snow. When it reached the tracks made by him and Willa, it paused. Kevin leaned forward. He almost expected the thing to pick up their trail and come to the door. Instead, it continued on its course, struggling to stay on its feet as it moved down the dark street and was eventually swallowed in shadows.

***

Kevin moved down the side of the house. He and Willa had been preparing for Willa's first run when they heard a series of short, sharp whistles. There was no doubt in either of their minds that some of the individuals who had taken the country club were out in the area.

Willa had pulled Kevin up and told him very clearly, "This changes everything."

"So what do we do?" he asked.

"*We* do nothing," Willa said with a shake of her head. "You will stay put, and I will go out and assess the situation.

That had been a while ago, and he was getting antsy. He told himself that he was just taking a peek. The neighborhood was quiet now. There was no movement, and except for the occasional gust that whipped up some of the surface snow and made little snow devils, all was quiet.

He hadn't heard a sound since Willa had taken off, leaving him feeling rather useless. The problem was, he wasn't useless. He had survived this long because he spent his life—or most of it since his teen years—preparing for the most unlikely scenario imaginable.

Not even he had really thought something like this could or would ever happen. Seriously. Zombies? But he, Mike, Cary, and Darrin had been certain that *they* would endure just such an event. They would find a location far away from the main populations and erect a compound. They would set up a farm and add solar and wind power to their little grid. They would be kings among men and the women would all come and beg to be let in. They would all be beautiful and beholden to their saviors.

"What a load of crap," he hissed.

Speaking of which…so was staying in the shadows beside this house. He needed to be out there doing something. He wasn't entirely sure what; but he needed to be acting instead of waiting. He moved to the driveway and crouched by the bumper of the snow-covered car that would eventually rot in that very spot.

Nothing.

Nobody jumped out of the shadows and captured him. Nobody fired off a weapon or hollered out that he'd been spotted.

He crept alongside the vehicle towards the end of the driveway. From the rear bumper he scanned the cul-de-sac. Empty. To his left would be the highway and just across that, the country club. Something dark was sprawled in the snow just to his right. It was definitely a dead body. The question he was unable to answer was if it had been living or dead; was it one of the people who had taken his home, or was it Willa.

He tried to remember exactly what she'd been wearing when they split up and was embarrassed to realize that he hadn't been paying attention. After all, why would he? This was such a simple thing. How could he have been so careless? He was making stupid mistakes and forgetting obvious things and couldn't tell if it was the cold, the exhaustion, the hunger, or the combination of all the above.

He considered his possibilities and decided that he would observe from this position for a few minutes. To him, that was even more proof that Willa was overlooking his usefulness. He knew not to rush out into the open.

Almost on cue, three men appeared, coming around from behind the house across the street and two down to the right. It took him a few seconds to realize that he recognized one of the men.

Paul James and his daughter had just joined their little group shortly after they'd found Valarie. Right after that run, Kevin had returned to discover Erin's baby near death from a respiratory illness or some such malady. He'd turned around and gone right back out to search this very neighborhood for medication and stumbled upon the father and daughter. Initially, he had been cautious, but it just seemed like a dad doing his best to care for his little girl.

Oh my God! Kevin thought, and had to stifle a gasp. This was his fault! He had brought Paul and his daughter back to their home—back to the country club.

He watched the men stop in the middle of the vacant driveway to discuss something. From this far away, it was impossible to hear anything that was being said, but he didn't need to hear to know that they were arguing. Also, it was obviously two against one and Paul was on the short end.

Kevin tried to press himself as close the wheel of the car he was using for cover as possible. He heard the buzz of angry voices, but could still not decipher anything being said.

And he wasn't alone.

A pair of zombies came stumbling into view from the direction of the highway. They made slow and steady progress through the snow towards the men. At first, he thought they were not aware, but then Paul pointed and made huge gestures with his arms. The other two men looked, but they simply shrugged and resumed laying into the agitated man.

Kevin took the time to study the approaching undead. Both looked old. They were coated in a layer of frost and the man on the left had a long rip down one side that exposed the ribs underneath. That rip looked like the edges would shatter if struck. Kevin marveled at how the zombies remained mobile. Their food source had undeniably shrunk, yet they remained. A normal human body would have liquefied and rotted away to next to nothing by now. Then there was the cold. They did not generate any warmth. So why were they not frozen?

The three men turned to deal with the approaching threat. Kevin knew what was about to happen. Paul wasn't paying attention to the other two men. He never saw them as they dropped back. That is why he also did not see them bring their bats up and swing at the backs of his knees.

Even from this far away, Kevin heard the crack. When Paul screamed out, the zombies almost seemed to forget about the other two men. As one, the pair fell on the injured man and began to claw and bite.

Paul tried to crawl, but his legs were ruined. One zombie had found purchase on his back. At first there were the repeated cries of "No!" But it soon turned to pleading, begging, pleas for God…and finally that certain sound made by somebody who is literally being torn open and forced to watch themselves be fed upon.

Kevin had turned away long before that.

Once the screaming stopped, he chanced to take a look. He watched as the two men began to walk away. As they passed, each took a single swing at the zombies still hunched over and feeding. They were actually laughing as they picked up their packs that he had not noticed until now sitting beside a hedge that looked like a car had driven through it at some point.

They were just crossing the highway when the one on the left stopped suddenly. He turned to his friend and his hands came up like he was going to hug the other man. It took Kevin a few seconds to notice the shaft of a crossbow bolt jutting out of the man's chest. By that time, the second man was staggering back a few steps. He fell to his knees and face planted. Kevin had spotted the bolt sticking out of this one's head much quicker.

Looking around, he was not surprised to see Willa come out from behind a large conical-shaped pine tree that looked as if it would only take a few more snowflakes to send it toppling to the ground.

"I told you to stay put," Willa barked, thrusting her weapon against a mailbox post, drawing the string back, and securing it with the lever. She stomped over to the downed men and yanked the one bolt sticking out of the second man's head after planting her boot on the face; with little apparent effort, she yanked it free and dropped it into place. Turning, Willa fired from only a few feet away as what was left of Paul sat up. Kevin winced as the bolt struck the forehead and apparently had enough energy left to come out the other side. Still, he had gotten enough of a glimpse to see that the man's lower lip had been pulled down below the chin, a hairy piece of meat dangled, and Kevin could still see it swaying in his mind's eye.

"If you want to have any chance of saving your friends…you need to do *exactly* what I say." Willa stepped right up to Kevin and thrust her face at his until they were so close you couldn't slide a credit card between the space separating their noses.

"I just came out to see what was going on," Kevin insisted.

"No, you were coming out into the open where anybody who knows anything about watching for people could see you."

"Just because—"

"These people are military!" Willa snapped.

"What? Because they happened to be dressed in fatigues? I dressed as Spiderman one year for Halloween…that didn't make me him."

"No, because I know them." Willa shoved Kevin back. "And you better pray that your friends didn't give them any crap when they came in and took over. The commander of this outfit is Timothy McVeigh crazy. She was a reservist that was being investigated by the feds before everything went sideways. She is a militant extremist who believes that the New World Order was due and *she* was the person to make it happen."

"You have a lot of knowledge on a bunch of people we haven't even met yet," Kevin retorted, but his heart wasn't really into it.

He'd had his fill of the militant types. It had been one such man, Charlton Shaw, who had shot his friend and taken some of his travelling companions. He couldn't imagine having to—

"Wait…" Kevin ran his hand over his face as if he could wipe it clean of whatever had hampered his ability to hear. "Did you say '*she*'?"

"Yep," Willa confirmed. "She."

"So how do you know this…person?"

"She was the commander of one of the recalled units assigned to us. Early on, when things went so bad so fast, she snuck away with her unit. We kept following reports of an Army unit running around the area, hitting civilians. They would arrive and be seen as a signal of hope and relief. Folks would drop their defenses and welcome this unit in with open arms in most cases."

Willa paused. Her eyes took on a far away quality like she was staring at something in the distance. Kevin chose to remain quiet. Obviously she was fighting with some serious emotions. There had to be a lot more to the story, and Kevin could tell that she wanted to get it out…off her chest.

"We caught up with the unit just west of Columbus. We had been following the fires. They were burning out civilians who had managed to set up fortresses or barricaded camps and *confiscating* their supplies. At first we thought that they might be killing all the civilians, but in Columbus, we found our first survivor…a girl of about nineteen."

Kevin spotted a few more walkers heading their way. Apparently all the commotion had drawn some attention. Willa, in contrast, seemed not to notice. She'd gone to a very dark place in her memory. Nothing in the real world was registering. He thought he saw tears welling up.

"They put out an offer to the citizens once they'd been allowed inside," she continued after a deep breath. "Anybody who wanted to join them would receive the 'protection of the United States Army' according to this young girl. Those who refused were taken in their sleep the first night. I guess that they didn't want to waste any bullets, so they would simply throw the people out of their own compound and then fire a flare to attract zombies. The people who were thrown out could either try and defend themselves, or they could run.

"No time was wasted. All the supplies were rounded up the next morning. Everything that had any use, all the food, tools…whatever…all taken by this band of looters operating under the banner of the United States Army."

"Sounds bad," Kevin said after Willa had taken another pause for several seconds. "But why would people let them in? I have yet to see one movie or read a zombie book where the government was any help. Most of the time—"

"Not everybody in the world watched those movies, Kevin," Willa interrupted. "Despite the small percentage of crazy conspiracy theorists and anti-government types, most people rely on the powers that be when disaster strikes."

"Yeah…I guess," Kevin said with a shake of his head.

"Anyway," Willa continued, "I was on the trail of this renegade group for almost two months…always a step behind them. They were scouring Columbus and cleaning out everything and everybody. When we arrived at the airport, we finally thought we had them. We sent a person in to mediate with them…see if they would talk…they sent back her head."

"That seems kinda harsh," Kevin gasped.

"My sister-in-law."

Now it clicked for him. The rest of the story was irrelevant at this point. This would be as personal for Willa as it was for him. The fact that time had passed was not important. But if that was the case, why had she been so hesitant.

"So she killed your sister-in-law and sent her head back," Kevin said by way of prompting her to continue.

"No," Willa turned to Kevin with tears in her eyes and rolling down her cheeks, "the woman running that outfit *is* my sister-in-law."

Kevin was just about to take down the first of the dozen or so zombies that were now making slow progress towards him and Willa. His swing missed its mark and dug into the shoulder of the zombie. He shoved the creature away and drew his belt knife.

"You want to run that by me again?"

"Major Wanda Beers is my sister-in-law and she is a power hungry megalomaniac."

Kevin plunged his knife into the temple of the zombie. *What were the odds?* he wondered.

"So how many people?" he asked as he looked around to determine which of the zombies would be the next closest threat. "Is this an army...are we talking a couple hundred?"

He felt the dread grow in his gut. If that was in fact the case, he had absolutely no chance. The problem he faced was that he positively refused to leave Aleah, Heather, and Valarie. He felt only the slightest tinge of guilt over not really being all that concerned about Matt, Shari or Erin, but he couldn't really force himself to feel anything.

"Actually, I have no idea how many of them there are." Willa admitted. "Who knows how many individuals they have conscripted...or how many they have lost."

Kevin trudged through the snow towards an elderly woman missing both arms. He had become very adept at *not* seeing any of these things as people. They were just pests. He felt nothing more than he would if he swatted a mosquito or stepped on a bug.

"So what is your plan?" Kevin asked.

Willa seemed to think very seriously for a few moments. That gave Kevin enough time to take down the remaining zombies. He actually went all the way out to the highway for the last one and noticed that there were several dark shapes in contrast to the dazzling white snow that were heading their way.

"I think I know how we can do this," Willa said from directly behind him, causing Kevin to drop his knife in the snow as he was wiping it off on his latest kill.

***

Kevin sat beside the wall. On the other side, the country club and his friends waited. *No*, Kevin thought, *it isn't just a country club, it's my home.*

This situation wasn't anything like Shaw and The Basket. Sure, they had executed his friend in cold blood, but when they

71

kidnapped the Bergman women, he had only known them for a very short time. What he had with Ruth had been a crush…nothing more.

His mind turned to Aleah. He was not entirely sure how it had happened, but the most beautiful woman he'd ever seen was in love with him. One thing that he was sure of was that he knew that he hadn't ever felt this way about anybody before. He'd be damned if he was going to let some crazy militant take the tiny bit of pleasure that he'd managed to find in a miserable world and keep it from him.

"…much longer and I'm gonna kill that brat myself," a male voice grumbled.

"I doubt Major Beers is gonna let her stay much longer," a female voice replied. ""She don't come out of her bed…not even to use the bathroom. I guess it reeks in there, and she is starting to smell worse than the stiffs."

Kevin felt his stomach twist. He had no doubt who they were talking about.

"Brady suggested hauling her bed and all out to the parking lot," the male voice laughed. "She'd be a shitcicle by morning."

"That's nasty, Lee!" the female voice quipped in such a way to make it clear how she felt about the matter. Kevin would make sure they each choked on those words.

"C'mon, Cindy, you tell me you wouldn't feel just a little better with that crazy retard and her ghosts gone once and for all," Lee said.

Kevin had almost all he could take. Willa better hurry up or he was going to blow the whole thing. Thankfully, the next voice he heard was hers.

"Wow, I sure didn't expect to find anybody here…hope I'm not intruding," Willa said in a voice that did not match the woman he knew. This woman sounded like some mall bimbo who had wandered into the wrong department store by mistake.

There was a commotion and Kevin had to resist the urge to peek over the top of the wall until he heard the signal. What he did hear was the distinct sound of a sword being drawn from its scabbard. He looked down and double-checked Willa's cross-bow to ensure for the hundredth time that it was cocked and loaded.

"Put your hands behind your head and get on your knees," Cindy ordered. If Kevin were a betting man, he would guess that Lee was too busy checking out the merchandise, so to speak.

"Whoa!" Willa exclaimed. "I wasn't looking for any sort of trouble…I'll just go."

"You'll get on your knees or I will run this thing through you and toss you over the wall," Cindy insisted.

"I bet you can't guess why I'm here," Willa said.

Kevin took a deep breath; that was the signal. He stood just as the pair of sentries reached Willa, one on either side. He adjusted for the female since she was the one with the drawn weapon. The guy seemed content to take a more hands on approach it seemed. Kevin pulled the trigger. A second later, the female sentry staggered to the side, the feathered bolt sticking out of her back caught the sun and shimmered a bit when she fell facedown.

The man spun—just as Willa had told him would happen—and never saw the government-issued bayonet that plunged into the side of his neck. The blood came in the bright red arterial variety and caught Kevin a little by surprise. After killing zombies for so long, he had almost forgotten what happened when you shot or cut one of the living.

Kevin vaulted over the wall and slogged through the knee deep snow to where Willa was already striping the pair of anything useful. Kevin suddenly felt a bit queasy. He'd had all that anger fueling him when he took the shot. But now he was staring down into the face of a female who didn't look much older than Heather.

"Make yourself useful," Willa whispered.

Kevin knelt down beside the dead man and began rifling through his pockets and pouches. The weapons were an easy grab. He also found a set of handcuffs and a key ring.

Together, they headed back, staying in the footpath that had been carved out in the snow by numerous sentries. Kevin had a million questions, but he kept his mouth shut. Within just a couple minutes, he could see the large building that he had claimed as home. He cleaned it out and ensured that there were no zombies still inside. He had set everybody on tasks that would ensure their survival through the winter months.

One of the first things he'd done is figure out their food situation. He made sure that they secured enough food to make it for almost six months. Even with the addition of Valarie, they would be fine. Of course, the loss of Dr. Peter King had made it even more of a certainty. To think that some lunatic military faction had probably stripped the food storage made his blood boil.

Yet, no matter how much he tried, his mind could not clear itself of thoughts of Valarie. When he and Shari had found the girl alone, it had brought memories of his little sister Sara who also suffered from Down's syndrome. He would go to his grave with her death on his conscience.

Willa froze right in front of him and he almost collided with her. He held his breath and looked around for what she might've seen. It took him a moment, but at last he saw what had caused her to stop. The edge of the flat landing before you dropped down and entered the actual course itself was visible through the trees. There were at least a couple dozen people out there dressed in combat fatigues.

Very slowly, Willa lowered down into the snow. Kevin moved in beside her. He couldn't make out faces or anything, so he couldn't tell how many men and women made up the group. The realization that he might die…his friends might die…all came crashing down. What had he been thinking?

"I give them twenty minutes before the sentry is missed," Willa whispered.

"Why?"

"Because I watched them pass by twice before I approached them. And there are at least two other patrols that I spotted from where I had climbed over. That is at a minimum. I can't say for sure how many patrols are out here."

"Maybe you were right—" Kevin began.

"I don't want to hear it," Willa cut him off. "You went through hell and back to get medication for some little girl you just met. You can't and won't give up. We both know that you won't be able to walk away from this. Odds are absolutely against us...but then none of that matters."

Kevin considered her words. He knew she was telling the truth. There was absolutely no way that he would be able to live with himself if he walked away.

"So what do we do?" Kevin asked. "Now that we've seen what we are facing, is the plan still the same?"

"It's the only option."

Kevin felt a lump build in his throat. So many things could go wrong. What if he ended up being ultimately responsible for the deaths of all of his friends? He glanced over, but Willa was already scooting back. The pair slipped into the woods and made their way back over the wall.

***

Making sure to stay in the tracks that had been previously made—probably by Paul and his two companions—had proved to be difficult and nerve-wracking. Eventually, they made it to a wooded area and were able to forge their own trail. From that point, Willa actually deferred to Kevin. He knew the layout of the surrounding area better, and after specifying what she was looking for, he was able to think of the perfect spot.

They circled around to the north side of the golf course and climbed the fence where a thick copse of white pines offered them plenty of cover. It took them all day, and Kevin spent the entire time worrying if what he'd done—the killing of the two sentries—would result in repercussions for his friends.

It was almost dark by the time they reached their objective. Kevin was cold, tired, and hungry, but since Willa kept quiet, he remained silent. Once they cleared the wall and ducked into the trees, they scooped out a small pit to hide in while they ate what proved to be the last MREs in their packs.

"What was the last home cooked meal you ate?" Willa asked as she squeezed the last of the pot roast and gravy from the pouch and into her mouth.

"You'll be mad," Kevin opened his candy bar and popped it into his mouth, an audible moan escaping his lips.

"Why would I be mad?"

"Because it wasn't that long ago. One of the best finds we came across was an Italian restaurant. We were pretty well stocked when it came to pasta and that sort of thing."

"So you guys have been eating pretty regular meals?"

"Mostly."

"I guess it's just so much harder when there are twenty or thirty of you than when there are just a few."

"Simple mathematics," Kevin said after swallowing. He tried to savor every second of that flavor from the chocolate bar as it melted and trickled down his throat. "I walk into a house and discover a full pantry and I can eat for days…maybe weeks. A group of thirty might make it a day…if that."

"So are you saying we shouldn't band together?"

"No, because you also need security, and that is where the numbers come in, but you need a balance."

"And what determines that balance?"

Kevin had a feeling there was more to Willa's question than she was letting on. She wasn't making eye contact, which was very unusual for her.

"You know that when this is all over, I'd like you to stay…I don't want you to think that once you've helped me out that you need to go." Kevin leaned back against the side of their little snow pit.

"What about the others?" Willa finally spoke after a moment.

"They will be thrilled to have you," Kevin said with a dismissive wave.

"No," Willa sat up straight and looked Kevin in the eye, "I mean *my* others…the rest of my group."

Kevin scratched his chin thoughtfully. He hadn't ever considered it. When she'd shown up in Newark and offered to help, he just assumed she'd left her other group.

"How many?" Kevin finally asked.

"Never mind," Willa dismissed his question and turned away.

"Wait!" He was pretty sure he hadn't done anything wrong. He simply wanted to know what they were looking at in terms of logistics. He'd acquired farming tools and even scored the location of a serious farm where he would be returning in the spring to gather up even more stuff. If he did it right, he would never need to head west for the Dakotas. He could continue to develop and fortify this location. It would allow them access to several cities and towns without being smack dab in the middle of populated areas where the probability of large numbers of zombies would be likely.

"I'm asking because I plan things," Kevin explained. "I think it would be fantastic to have your group join mine. I bet we have fewer problems like what is happening now."

"Twenty-seven," Willa whispered. She looked up at Kevin through a lock of hair that had fallen across her eyes.

"That's not so bad," Kevin said with a shrug.

"And you wouldn't have a problem with all of us joining you?"

"Let's get through this first," Kevin said. "But no...I wouldn't have any problem and neither would my friends."

"We'll see," Willa said and closed her eyes. "Now get some rest, we will move out a few of hours after dark. It is gonna be a long couple of days."

5

Vignettes XXVI

Aaheru stepped out of the hotel and into the unseasonably cold afternoon. The breeze coming in off the sea was a mixture of salt, sand, and death. From this location, he could see down into the city of Alexandria. With the sky clear and the sun just starting its climb, he could see their route almost perfectly.

In the parking lot, a flurry of activity was taking place, but it was as if the world had been muted. Nobody spoke much above a whisper as they loaded equipment into the various cars, tucks, busses, and vans.

"I am ready to depart, my Pharaoh," a soft female voice said at his back.

"Ahmes, my child," Aaheru said as he turned to face the young, dark haired girl. Her body was extraordinarily developed for only just celebrating her fifteenth year. "Have all the preparations been made?"

"Yes, it has been done as you demanded."

"The sacrifice shall be rewarded." Aaheru placed his enormous hands on Ahmes' tiny shoulders.

"It is at the pleasure of our pharaoh that we serve in any way demanded."

Yes, Aaheru thought, *he had chosen well in all aspects*. His advisor was unflinchingly loyal. The woman he'd recently selected to replace his previous companion was turning out to be precisely what he needed. Being pharaoh was more than simply assuming the title; there was a certain air of authority and power that he must exude if he were to truly revive the entity and office of a true Egyptian pharaoh. This young woman tended to his needs in a manner befitting a god.

A god, Aaheru mused. The pharaohs of old were considered the representations of the gods on Earth. Their edicts were not placed before anyone for approval. They simply were law. The time had come for Aaheru to demonstrate his power.

He looked across the parking lot to the bus being loaded with all the women—the Mothers of Egypt as he had named the remaining women of child birthing age. Standing beside the door was Markata.

Since almost the first day he had arrived, Markata had used his conniving ways to avoid any sort of work. It came as no surprise that he had been a cabinet member under the Egyptian president. That entire administration had spent years weakening Egypt's standing in the world. They had abused the people and used the military like a father's correctional rod. Unfortunately for Markata, he thought things like paper money still had meaning.

When the first man had come to him and reported that Markata had offered him useless paper to be eyes and ears around camp, Aaheru had told the man to accept the offer. That man had found himself living in one of the nicer tents and having extra portions of food and water. *That*, Aaheru chuckled inwardly, *was the new currency*.

Food, water…and women.

All of those were under Aaheru's control despite what Markata believed. When the first rumblings of insurrection surfaced, Aaheru welcomed them with what was almost able to be called relief. So he waited for the perfect moment. It was important that his message be seen, heard, and felt by all.

"The women are all on the bus," Ahi said. He had come up beside Aaheru unnoticed. "Markata has all of our women…and he will make an attempt to break away from the caravan the first sign of trouble. We will not be able to avoid some rather tense moments during this journey. The opportunity *will* present itself, Pharaoh."

"Yes...it will," Aaheru said with a smile. "Now please see to it that everybody is loaded up and that we are ready to depart in the next five minutes."

Ahi nodded in affirmation. He knew better than to say anything more. It was clear that Aaheru remained unconcerned about Markata. Perhaps he did not value the women as he claimed...or perhaps he had some sort of an arrangement with the man and chose not to divulge the details to a simple underling.

Growing up as a homosexual male in Egypt, being paranoid had become an art as well as a way of life. The laws strictly prohibited such things and the current regime...*former regime*, Ahi reminded himself, maintained that they were punishable by death. It was all kept very quiet to avoid any sort of global intervention, but the secret police made many late night visits to individuals who were reported. None of the men Ahi knew that had been "taken in for questioning" were ever seen or heard from again. Perhaps this was just another case of being paranoid.

It took a little longer than desired, but eventually, the convoy rolled out of the parking lot. The first few blocks were almost like a normal early morning drive. They only had to weave around a few abandoned vehicles until they hit the highway that would lead directly to the waterfront. Having used it a few times already as supplies were ferried to the ships that awaited their arrival, the zombie traffic was a problem early on.

On the roof of every vehicle were men who Aaheru handpicked to dispatch the walking dead that might manage to gain a hand hold on any of the vehicles. On the lead vehicles, each of the men had a black case with several pipe bombs made with propane canisters. If the concentration became too great, it was hoped that they would be able to blow a hole big enough to drive through.

Aaheru was in an armored bank truck and just two vehicles behind Markata. He watched everything with intense interest. He was confident in his intelligence reports regarding the man, but had he missed anybody? For the first time, he felt like little more than a soldier in the Egyptian Army. He had been given orders, and he followed them without question. Now…he was giving them.

Just ahead, one of the men atop the rickety van lost his footing and fell over the side. A sea of undead arms that waved back and forth like stalks of wheat in the wind caught the man, he vanished from sight in seconds. There were so many of those walking abominations that Aaheru could not even hear the man's final screams.

The caravan had slowed to a crawl by now. As they passed an on-ramp, it looked like Markata had chosen the time and place to make his move. He veered to the right just as the front end of the convoy emerged from the first huge mob.

The bus made a wide U-turn and headed for the ramp. Aaheru was impressed. There was no way anybody could react in time and at the top of that ramp was a business complex that would be easy to hide in. Markata had indeed thought this out.

Well…almost, Aaheru thought as a huge smile spread across his normally serious countenance.

The bus accelerated right after a man's body tumbled out the door and rolled several times on the road before coming to an awkward halt up against the burned out husk of a compact car that looked more like a toy than a means of transportation.

Just as it reached the crest, there was a huge explosion. The bus literally broke in half and both pieces spun away in flames. An oily black cloud rose in a thin column that resembled an accusatory finger that pointed at the heavens.

The caravan began to increase speed as many of the walking dead that barred the way turned or veered off towards this most recent stimulus. Aaheru glanced back at Ahi, his smile still wide enough to cause his cheeks to cramp.

***

"We're just trying to be helpful," one of the older boys, no older than eighteen, spoke up. "But if you'd rather stay here…"

He looked past Juan, April, and Al at the seemingly never-ending wave of undead flowing down the hill and across the four sets of train tracks.

"No, we'd love a ride in *our* boats," Juan said as he jumped to the ground.

"Ain't no *our* or *my* anymore," one of the girls snapped.

"Cool it, Betty," the first young man said. He turned back to Juan who was helping April down. "You two can come, but we can't let your other friend on board."

Juan looked down at Al. His eyes told the story. The young man was infected, of that there was no doubt.

"We can't just leave him like that," April insisted.

"You don't have time to debate this." The boy reached out a hand as the other three boats began to pull away from the shore.

Juan looked back at Al. He could see the fear in his eyes. There was no way he could leave the man behind to be torn apart and eaten alive, but he wasn't about to stay. He made eye contact with the youngster in the boat and nodded. Juan grabbed April and shoved her forward into the boat. He hopped in behind her as the report from a high caliber rifle drowned out any protests.

The boat lurched and then spun around to take them out into the river. Juan sat up as April shoved him and scrambled out from underneath. She looked back to shore just in time to see Al disappear under a swarm of zombies.

"Would you rather he be alive for that?" Juan said in answer to her angry glare.

"So where did you folks come from?" the boy asked.

"You mean in *our* boat?" Juan shot a withering glance at the one called Betty. "How about we exchange names first."

"My name is Frank."

"Juan Hoya, and this is Amber."

"April," she whispered,

"April," Juan corrected.

"Well I could give you everybody else's names but it wouldn't much matter would it?" Frank laughed and flashed a smile at April who smiled back oblivious to Betty's glare.

"It's been a rough afternoon," Juan grumbled.

"So what were you guys doing down by the old lumber treatment facility?" Frank asked.

"Actually we were trying to make a run on the Freddie's," Juan explained.

"That many zombies came out of Freddie's?" Betty exclaimed.

"No," Juan turned to the girl, "they came from somewhere and followed us. We lost most of our group."

"So where did you guys come from?" Frank asked.

"Sauvie Island," April spoke up.

"And what was the deal with you guys chasing that dog?" Juan asked. "You guys planning on eating him?"

"First off," Betty snickered, "*he* is a she. And *Gidget* is immune to the bite. We just took the bandages off her leg and she took off and went straight to the water."

"So you guys are kinda young," April made the blatant observation.

"We were counselors at Outdoor School," Frank explained.

"Huh?" Juan scratched his head.

"It's a program with the area schools where they send sixth graders to camp where they learn about nature and ecology in the best classroom in the world," Betty said.

"The local high schools provide the counselors," Frank continued. "I went as a kid and couldn't wait to be a counselor. We were waiting for the busses when Mr. Zachery showed up in his car with the news...we thought it was a prank. There are no televisions and we are required to turn in our phones and stuff, so we really didn't know."

"We stayed up at the camp until we ran out of food," one of the other boys said. "There was plenty of stuff in the woods that we could forage, but Mr. Zachery insisted that we try and sneak down into the closest town; Troutdale. It went badly. We lost over half of our numbers and Mr. Zachery. To make matters worse, we had used a school bus when we came down and it ended up in a ditch."

"So you kids have been living where?" Juan asked, not hiding how impressed he was with this group of youngsters.

"An old warehouse just up the river a ways," Frank said.

"So what are you doing here besides chasing a dog?"

"Donna, one of the girls in our group, took off in search of her brother. She said that he kept coming to her in her dreams and so she knew that he was alive and where to find him," Frank answered.

"Did you find her?" April asked.

"No," Betty whispered. "Gidget lost her scent almost as soon as we made it out of the parking lot."

The boat turned up river towards Sauvie Island. A somber silence fell over everybody as each considered the terrible losses of the past several hours. Juan looked over at April who had sunk down on the bench seat and closed her eyes. Flecks of blood were dried on her face and he could see a single tear trickling down her left cheek. Her wavy red hair was matted in places. How would he explain to everybody that the two of them were it? They were the only survivors of the failed expedition.

"How many of you are on the island?" Frank scooted in next to Juan.

"I don't know," Juan said with a shrug. "Twenty...thirty."

The two sat in silence for a couple of minutes. Juan peeked over at the young man a few times and could tell what was on his mind. He looked tired and like he had all the weight of the world on his shoulders. If he had been leading these other kids since this whole thing began, then what he had accomplished was nothing short of a miracle.

They came up on the island just as the clouds drifted apart and the deep magenta color of the sky turned the water a bruised purple. The beach was empty, but Juan didn't expect a welcoming committee. When the boat ran aground, Juan jumped out and extended a hand to April who declined.

Great, he thought, *she thinks I'm a bad guy*. It couldn't be helped. He had done what needed to be done and her anger would not convince him otherwise. He watched her start off across the beach after climbing through the fence.

"So what gives with the fence?" Frank asked.

"Keeps the deaders away," Juan answered. "If there were a bunch, they could break through, but we shouldn't see more than a couple at a time. We come around a few times a day to be sure, plus we have observation towers."

Juan considered the faces staring back at him. For the first time, he really looked at the kids in the boat. They all looked exhausted. There was something in their eyes that gave away more than their outward attempts at bravado.

"You are welcome to stay here," Juan said.

He saw a different look from all of them at almost the same instance. Relief. Hope.

"What about the others?" Frank asked.

"We couldn't just bail on them," Betty added.

"The offer is open to all of you," Juan said. He saw them all look to Frank, Juan decided that was good to know. However, at this exact moment, he just wanted to go home. He was exhausted.

"Sort it out," Juan said as he shook Frank's hand. "I'm going home. I'll see ya or I won't...the choice is yours."

***

Chad looked out the window. The moon reflected off the snow giving everything a dazzling blue glow. Across the way he saw a shadow moving slowly along the roof.

"There." He pointed for Scott's benefit.

Scott nodded and drew back on the heavy compound bow. There was a hiss as the arrow sped away towards its target. A strangled cry told them that the target had been hit. The shadow disappeared for just a second, but rose up. Both men watched as it obviously struggled with a few steps before falling. After several seconds, it was obvious that whoever it was would not be getting back up.

A shrill whistle broke the silence and both men jumped. Obviously on cue, a pair of flaming bottles arced through the air and exploded against the front of their hotel in a gout of orange flame.

"Be ready," Chad hissed.

Scott had already nocked another arrow and was scanning the grounds. He pivoted with the bow, trying to sweep the full hundred and eighty degrees before him.

"Damn all these trees," Scott complained.

"Maybe we should—" Chad was cut off by a whoop of some sort followed by the clang of metal on metal.

"If this is what it was like in medieval times...it is a wonder we survived this long as a species," Scott grumbled.

"If we keep this up...we won't need to worry about it much longer," Chad said as he ducked just as an arrow bored into the wooden front of the building.

A yelp sounded from the dense group of trees to their right. Chad thought it sounded female. That made him immediately think of his daughter. Ronni was holed up in one of the enormous honeymoon suites on the top floor just under their feet. Never had he felt so far away from her while being so near.

Down below, three people emerged from the hotel. Two held detached doors that acted as shields from any sort of projectiles that might be launched as the other began scooping and tossing bucket of snow on the flames.

"They should start getting really desperate soon," Scott said as he held the fletching of the arrow against his cheek for a second before letting go. His shot was high and the figure he'd targeted scurried back into the impenetrable gloom of the shadows.

"I can't believe that *all* of the food was stored in this hotel." Chad breathed a sigh of relief once the fires had been extinguished. He'd been so involved in watching the operation down below that he had forgotten about the flaming arrow burning just over the side and hastily yanked it free and tossed it out into the snow.

"I don't think anybody planned for a civil war."

"Maybe not, but what if we got trapped inside by a huge mob...if you are in the wrong building you would be screwed."

"If it got to that, I think we would all be screwed anyways," Scott snorted. "Once those things get your scent or whatever...they don't let up."

The two men sat in silence for a few moments as they scanned the grounds. Night time was the only time when either side attacked the other. It was the only time when there might be even a glimmer of a chance for success.

Dark shadows could be seen scurrying from one place to another. Most of the movement came from the other faction. Chad's group had the food, so they were mostly content with protecting it. They had a few people out on patrol, but that was about it. Of course there were also the individuals that took it upon themselves to wage their own private war. Chad hadn't seen any logic or reason for such actions, but he was not about to tell anybody else what they could and couldn't or should and shouldn't do.

"How long you figure they've been without anything?" Chad finally asked.

"If you believe that guy Clark, then it has been at least three days."

"What has you and Brett so twisted about this guy?" Chad asked.

"He's military, but he says that he didn't realize what those bastards were doing until after the fact."

"If his job was strictly security like he says, then why would he know?"

"Plus the simple fact that he was involved in that whole thing to begin with," Scott insisted. "It wasn't right in any sense, and had things not shaken down the way they did...he would still be with them sitting on all the supplies and acting like he was lord of the manor."

"Lord of the manor?" Chad laughed.

"You know what I mean."

A huge explosion caused both men to start. Towards the center of the village, an enormous ball of flame rolled skyward. The entire eastern horizon was silhouette against the bright light of flame for a few seconds. That was all it took for Chad to see the hundreds of dark figures heading their way.

"Jesus," Scott breathed.

The door to the roof flew open and Brett was standing there with Michael at his side. Brett was far more out of breath between the two and stepped out of the way.

"We have big trouble." Michael's face was shining in the glow of the flames. Steam rolled off of him in wisps that were carried away in the wind.

"No kidding," Scott snapped.

"What is the problem?" Chad asked, shooting a scowl in Scott's direction.

"There is a freaking thousand of those things coming up Village Drive," Michael answered.

"What!" Chad exclaimed.

"I told you that all of the noise from the fighting here would bring them," Michael reminded.

"But what the blazes blew up?" Scott said.

"I had been in the process of rigging perimeter defenses before the big split."

"Were you thinking of letting anybody know?" Scott snapped.

"My fault," Brett wheezed as he finally made his way over to the other men. "He told me about it the other day, but then that girl threw herself off the roof of that other hotel and I forgot in the excitement."

"Still—" Scott wasn't done, but Chad cut him off.

"Any other set-ups we should know about?"

"I have two other similar set-ups, one to the west and one to the south."

"Fine," Chad said. "So what do we do now?"

"Do you want to end this fight and be rid of those other

people once and for all?" Michael asked.

"No."

"Yes."

Chad and Scott answered in unison.

***

"We still need to deal with the problem of food," Nigel insisted.

"Then why don't you go to the market," Victoria snapped. "You're the bloke with the gun...a point you never fail to mention. So why not be the big man and use it on a few of the zeds out there. And while you're at it...I fancy some crisps."

A few snickers made their way around the room. Nigel's face turned red and Claudia looked like she could chew nails and spit tacks. Victoria didn't care. She was finished with this charade.

"Maybe I'll send you." Nigel pushed himself up from his plush chair and brushed his coat aside just enough to flash his pistol.

"Maybe you'll try," Victoria said in a flat, emotionless voice. "You like to talk big, but when it came down to it, a man weak from the infection knocked your lights out. You didn't do a thing but fall and bleed."

"Oh really?" In a jerky movement that was made even more awkward when he got tangled in the hem of his coat, Nigel pulled the gun free from its holster and pointed it in Victoria's face.

"Is that it?" Victoria's lips twitched in a smile. "You think I fear that gun when I know what is out there?"

Pressing the barrel to her forehead, Nigel said in a loud voice that was supposed to sound intimidating but only sounded to Victoria like a naughty child who didn't want the doctor to give him his shots, "You'll do well to remember just who has the gun and who no longer has a husband to protect her."

Victoria did not so much as blink as she continued to look

up. Inside, her mind was racing and demanding that she not display any weakness. However, it took all her muscle control not to wet herself. She'd never realized how big the barrel of a gun could look up close.

She was beginning to have thoughts about how it might be if he pulled the trigger. Would it hurt, even for just that split second? Then she saw it; his hand trembled as he held the gun, and at his temple, a tiny bead of sweat bloomed and then trickled down the side of his face.

"You're nothing but a loud mouthed wanker," Victoria said with the same flat tone. Her eyes flashed to Claudia who was pacing like a caged tiger. *Now* she *would have no problem pulling that trigger*, Victoria thought.

"What makes you think I won't do it?"

"For starters," a voice said from behind Nigel causing him to turn his head, "you're too bloody careless."

Victoria was no hero. She had no false notions that she would be able to go out into the English countryside and become a one woman zombie-killing machine like in those silly *Resident Evil* movies. Still, she was no fool, either. She reached up and snatched the gun from the hand that had gone slack the moment the wielder's attention was diverted.

There was an audible crack, and Nigel scurried back like he'd just been scalded. He clutched his hand to his body and sucked in a huge breath through his clenched teeth.

"Why'd you do that?" he whimpered.

"Do what?" Victoria was confused and almost forgot that she was holding a pistol in her hands. She glanced over at Claudia and flashed a look that said she wasn't the only woman in the room who would not hesitate to pull the trigger.

"Broke my finger!" Nigel thrust his hand forward to display an index finger with an awkward bend between the first and second interphalangeal joints.

"Well I didn't mean to," Victoria huffed as she tried to figure out what to do with the weapon she now held in her possession.

"You want to throw them out, Vix?" Gary Munford asked with a nod at Nigel and Claudia. Gary was a school teacher, or at least he had been before all of this. "Not a soul here will think poorly of you if you do. Just say the word and it's out in the snow with the pair."

"No." Victoria shook her head and stuck the gun in the waist of her loose-fitting jeans. That had been another thing about this whole end-of-the-world situation that had actually been a plus. She'd finally shed the last four and a half kilos that she set out to lose every year before going on holiday.

"You sure?" Gary cast an uncertain glance at the sour-faced couple.

Victoria gave it serious consideration. In all the stories, letting the bad guy stick around always ended poorly. The only dilemma was that this was not one of her stories; this was the real thing and she couldn't just send two human beings out to certain death.

"I'm absolutely sure."

"Then at least let us take them down to the storage room in the cellar. We should lock them up for now and consider their fate once all the emotions are in control."

Good old Gary being just the perfect example of an Englishman. The dead had risen and were eating the living. Most of the city of Basingstoke was either overrun or a charred ruin from all the fires that resulted from the chaos of those first days. Instead of reacting and using his human emotions, he went the British way of "stiff upper lip and all that" as the world spiraled out of control.

"That is fine," Victoria agreed.

Once Nigel and Claudia were locked away in the cellar, the remaining eleven gathered around a table in the dining room. Somebody had managed to dig up a map of the town.

"We need to get out of this hotel and secure something a bit more open that will allow us to ensure that we live and not merely survive," Victoria announced. Every pair of eyes looked up at her expectantly. She had called this meeting and told them that she actually had a plan. It was mad, but she believed in her heart that she could do it if she had the support of the group. This would also allow them to add more numbers to their ranks if they did it correctly. "It starts here," she touched her pen down on the map where she intended to make her stand, "at the Thornycroft Roundabout."

***

"I'm tellin' ya, Danny," Jody Rafe said around a mouthful of cold powdered eggs and burnt toast, "Slider and the captain are plum crazy. They want to turn this place into a prison camp."

"Maybe they're just sending a message after our guys got roughed up pretty bad by those locals," Danny reasoned.

"I was in that office, Danny. I heard it all with my own ears."

"How are they gonna justify this to the others, there has already been some grumbling about that late night round up."

"I don't know but—"

"Attention, all personnel," the voice on the bull horn was unmistakably Slider. "Everybody is required to muster in the high school parking lot in twenty minutes. That is all."

"Jesus," Jody sighed, "what now?"

"You think maybe we should split?" Danny whispered. "I know it can be bad out there, but maybe staying here is not such a good thing."

"These people trusted us," Jody shook his head. "I realize they sorta turned on us toward the end, but maybe we gave them a reason. And we sure as heck didn't do anything to prove their fears wrong."

"Well I'm with you to the end." Danny took the last drink from his coffee and stood up placing a hand on Jody's shoulder. "And there are others who feel the same way."

Jody watched Danny O'Leary leave as he finished his own cup of coffee. He wondered how many residential houses had to be raided in order to provide the men with this luxury. Coffee was going the way of bullets. Sure, you could still find it, but it was getting rare.

Shouldering his rifle, Jody exited the empty mess tent. As he walked along the muddy road that led into town, he began to take a closer look at the faces of the men. They looked tired. Many stared at the ground as they walked, their heads hanging as if it were too much effort to keep their chins off their chests. These men were beaten up and simply operating out of pro-grammed discipline.

As he reached the high school, a queasy feeling began to build in his gut. His coffee suddenly felt like it had changed to concentrated acid, and he could feel an unpleasant burning in the back of his throat.

In the center of the parking lot was a hastily erected plat-form. It looked like little more than a few saw horses side-by-side with a sheet of three-quarter inch plywood on top. It was positioned directly below a sign that used to welcome students to Bald Knob High School—Go Bulldogs! Draped over the sign were two nooses and standing beside them was Captain Gould and Chuck "Slider" Monterro.

This could not be good, Jody thought.

As the men arrived, Jody was struck by just how few of them remained. He began to do a head count. Counting the lo-cals who had been conscripted, there were a total of fifty-three men and women gathered minus the captain and Slider.

It took Jody a moment to register the fact that the two hood-ed figures beside them were wearing uniforms. This could not be happening. He began to scan the faces of the men, but everybody was so haggard that even familiar faces were hard to recognize. He wondered only briefly if he looked as worn out and beaten as these other men and women.

As he continued to scan the faces trying to figure out who might be under those hoods, his heart began to race. He couldn't find Danny. He looked back to the hooded figures and tried to see if the body types might match his friend. It was impossible; they had just been eating breakfast and talking. Yet, he couldn't see Danny anywh—

"What the fuck is this?" a voice whispered in his ear making Jody jump almost out of his boots. And that would have been a feat considering the fact that it felt like his socks had melded into his skin and that the boots were grafted on by way of the filth.

Jody spun to find Danny standing at his shoulder. He resisted the urge to hug the man. However, the look of relief on his face told the story.

"You thought one of those guys might be me?" Danny gasped. "Well I've walked the rows and I can tell you who it is. It's Livius Nedin and Robb Olson."

"What?" Jody had to bite his tongue and lower his voice. Several heads had turned his way and two of those heads belonged to the captain and Slider.

"A couple of the guys said that three of the civilian conscripts came into their tent and cuffed them while reading from some piece of paper listing a series of UCMJ violations that they supposedly committed," Danny whispered.

"This just keeps getting worse," Jody moaned.

"Men of Charlie Company...a-ten-hut!" a large woman that Jody vaguely recognized as one of the local bartenders bellowed. She was decked out in an ill-fitting uniform that looked as if the buttons might pop off at any moment and burrow into somebody's eye. The spaces between each straining button bubbled out revealing her pale, cottage cheese-like flesh underneath. Her jowls quivered with each syllable and continued to sway just a bit for a few seconds after she spoke.

The soldiers came dutifully to attention. Heads came up and eyes stared straight ahead, but Jody didn't think they were seeing anything. The captain climbed up onto the sheet of plywood and Jody couldn't help but wish for it to break along with the man's neck. Slider and the woman—Jody thought she resembled those pig-faced guards in Jabba's palace in the *Star Wars* movie—manhandled each of the hooded men up onto the platform and then each took a place on either side.

"We have among us men who do not feel the need to follow

orders…men who would take for themselves…not just of supplies, but liberties with those we are sworn to protect," the captain announced, using the bullhorn so that everybody could hear him clearly.

Jody noticed both men squirm, but the nylon line used to bind them had secured their arms tightly to their sides and they could do little more than shudder.

"We have been given a solemn duty and I will not have our honor damaged by a few…"

He droned on, but Jody had tuned him out. This was wrong. He knew both of those men well. Neither would do what they were being charged with. He puzzled over the situation until a collective gasp snatched his attention back to the scene up front. Both men had been fitted with his noose and shoved off the platform. The drop wasn't severe enough to snap their necks, so they flopped at the ends of their lines for what seemed like an eternity.

It was too much. Jody's coffee had swirled with his stomach acid and created a toxic mixture. Doubling over, he vomited his breakfast all over his filthy boots.

He wasn't alone.

***

"Just what do you think you're doing?" The girl yanked her arm free of the two female soldiers who had brought her outside.

Major Wanda Beers continued to use her knife to clean under her nails. When there was no response, the girl did exactly what Wanda hoped for; she approached within arm's length.

"Hey…I'm talking to y—" she started.

Quick as a flash, Wanda's gloved backhand connected with the young female's cheek sending her sprawling in the snow.

"Shari!" an even younger girl exclaimed and rushed to the one laying on the ground with blood trickling from the corner of her mouth.

"Erin, no!" the oldest of the females hissed, but made no effort to move.

Wanda looked up and appraised the group. The one who had just spoken showed some usefulness. *Well,* Wanda chuckled inwardly, *at least to the point that she knew to stay still and keep her mouth shut.* There was another girl who stood beside her with a look of disdain etched on her face. Oddly enough, it seemed directed more at the two huddled together in the snow than for the soldiers standing around with an assortment of weapons on display—less than half actually had any remaining ammunition, but nobody needed to know that.

"What is it that you want?" This question came from the only male in the bunch, He obviously had a stronger attachment to the pair of females standing than the two on the ground, but it was clear that he would pose little physical threat. He could barely walk.

"Let's start with names." Wanda continued to work at her nails as she spoke. "My name is Major Wanda Beers, United States Army. I am the commanding officer of the expeditionary element of Ohio's 371st Sustainment Brigade. My mission is to seek and secure a location for citizens to use as a safe zone."

"You look more like a bunch of looting raiders to me," the young man said. Wanda nodded and that earned him the butt of a rifle in his gut.

"My name is Aleah Brock," the older female spoke. Wanda looked up and made eye contact. She also looked around at her men. Some of them were already eyeballing this one. She would have to have the word spread once everybody got settled in that unless this girl volunteered for the brothel, she was not to be harmed.

"Okay, Miss Brock, do you want to tell me where your doctor is?" Wanda asked. She heard a gasp from the one she had backhanded.

"What have you done to Peter?" the one identified as Shari screamed as she struggled to her feet.

"So you *do* have a doctor," Wanda said.

"We did," Aleah replied. "He went out on a supply run and

didn't return."

"You had a doctor and let him go outside these walls?" Wanda said with a disbelieving shake of her head.

"We didn't *let* him do anything," the girl next to Aleah spoke up.

"And what might your name be?" Wanda's eyes flicked to the girl. She neither blinked nor flinched, which scored her points in Wanda's book.

"Heather Godwin...from Heath."

"Okay, Heather Godwin from Heath." Wanda pushed away from the truck and slid the knife in its sheath. "So how do a group of girls and one gimpy boy manage to secure a place like this? Who is the brains behind it? Because I have seen some of the work that is done and somebody knows their stuff. So...which of you is it?"

"None of us," Heather answered. "One of the people who used to live here did it. He left on the same run."

"Okay..." Wanda had been through this before. Whoever it was had probably hidden during the commotion when they had burst through the doors and began dragging the residents of this place out into the snow. "Nobody so much as utters a word. Any of you who do will be shot. Nod if you understand." Everybody nodded. "By a show of fingers, and on the count of three, how many weeks ago did he leave? If it was longer than three months ago, just hold up all ten fingers." She saw the expressions on their faces and already knew what the results would be. "One...two...three."

As she figured, none of them matched. She walked over to Heather and leaned in very close. "I will give you to my soldiers as a plaything if you lie to me again. Are we clear?"

"Yes."

"I need to be sure." She looked over her shoulder to the female soldier standing beside and nodded. Without hesitation, the soldier put the barrel of her handgun against the young man's temple. "So...how long ago did he leave?"

"Eleven days," Heather whispered.

"And where did he and the doctor run off to?"

"Newark. They are trying to find medicine for Valarie."

"The retarded girl?" Wanda glanced over to the bundled up black girl who was standing just outside the doorway staring into space.

"She has Down's syndrome!" a voice snapped from behind her. Wanda turned and was more than a little surprised to see the girl she had backhanded come to her feet. Her entire demeanor had changed.

"Excuse me?" Wanda asked.

"She has Down's syndrome. Calling her retarded is...ignorant!"

Perhaps she had misjudged this one, Wanda thought. "Well whatever the case, she serves no purpose and will only be a drain on supplies. How you could allow your doctor and the architect of this little sanctuary to risk everything for a girl who will contribute nothing to the group in any productive way is beyond me."

"What does that mean?" Shari stood up and brushed the snow from her hands.

"It means that we will not be keeping her," Wanda said.

"You can't—" Shari began, but Wanda cut her off.

"I can do whatever I like, little missy."

"If it's food, I'll give her some of mine...if it's something else, just tell me what I can do, but you can't just throw her out or shoot her or whatever you plan on doing."

Wanda glanced around at the group and sort of expected the same looks of outrage from the others. Instead, she was greeted by gaping mouths and looks of obvious astonishment. Now she really wanted to meet the person who had held this all together.

6

Staring into the Void

The plastic shin guard had split and caught the skin just below my kneecap in between the pieces. Somehow they had acted like scissors and cut deep into the flesh. I hadn't been bitten! I guess I now knew what hysterics felt like, because I couldn't stop laughing. The tears filled my eyes, and I really thought that I was going to pass out.

"Watch him, Nickie," DeAngelo growled. "I've never seen anybody get delirious like this after being bit. I'll take out these on this side. Yell if he loses consciousness."

Nickie nodded in the affirmative, but I was still unable to say anything. God help me, I tried. I finally got enough control of my body that I was able to wave her over. She was really cautious.

"Go. Help. DeAngelo," I managed each word between fits of maniacal giggling. Then I showed her my knee.

Now it was Nickie's turn to act like a loony. She fell on top of me and hugged me. Her knee also caught me in the solar plexus and knocked the wind out of me. Oh well, at least I'd stopped laughing. It's hard to laugh with no air. Anyways, she jumped off of me and took off after DeAngelo.

I was lying in the snow trying to get my wind when I heard the slow and steady crunch…drag…crunch…drag. I wiped my eyes and found myself looking up at a zombie child. She couldn't be any older than six or seven. The poor thing had been torn open something terrible. Her entire torso was bullet ridden and she had a wound to the neck that looked like a knife had been plunged in and gone all the way through.

I tried to reach for a weapon only to find that I couldn't really move. Having the wind knocked out of me had left me defenseless as a baby. I managed a croak when I tried to call for help.

Just that fast and all my hysterical joy was gone and replaced by fear and dread. I waited for the child to throw itself on me and start biting. I very briefly wondered how long it would take me to regain my breath, and would I be able to scream once I did.

I was overwhelmed with horror. That is why it took me a few seconds to realize that this child-zombie was just standing there staring at me. All it did was cock its head to one side and then the other like that certain way a dog has when you just know they are trying to figure something out.

I could feel my fingers twitch and I thought that I was going to start sobbing when that first teensy bit of oxygen made its way into my lungs. The entire time, the child-zombie simply continued to…study? That is the best way to describe it. I actually felt like it was trying to figure me out.

Once I was able to flex my hands, it was just a few seconds before I could move my entire arm. I kept my eyes glued on the little girl as I sat up very slowly. The only weapon I still had handy was an oversized pocket knife. I tried to move my hand for it, and that is when the situation changed in a hurry. Just that quick, it was just like any other zombie. It stumbled for me with arms outstretched. I heard it make a squeaky mewling sound as it tripped and stumbled in the snow. The only thing that saved me was that the snow was almost at its waist, her being so small and all.

Something whizzed past and the child toppled over backwards. She wasn't even heavy enough to sink completely in the snow. The handle of a pretty fancy looking knife jutted up from her face. I looked up to see Nickie standing at the top of the berm with two more matching knives.

"My brother told me I should join the circus," Nickie said. I stared back blankly because I really had no idea what she was talking about. She waved the other knives at me. "Throwing knives? Like when that guy has a girl hold a balloon or tied to a big spinning wheel?"

"Oh," I said. Actually, that was kind of what I said. It came out as more of a croak. I was still a bit tender from having the wind knocked out of me.

"DeAngelo is right behind me, he went after two other zombies that tried to get away."

"Excuse me?" I was positive that I did not hear her correctly.

"Well not really try and get away," Nickie said with a frown. "It was like they just decided not to come after us."

"Were they younger?"

"Who?" Nickie looked at me like I was still hysterical.

"The zombies!" I snapped a bit harsher than I intended. I got to my feet and started the rest of the way up the berm.

"I guess…" Nickie was backing up as I climbed like she thought that I was coming for her.

I had this stupid image in my head. I could see DeAngelo chasing down the two escapees, and just as he reached the woods, a bunch of the little bastards would jump out and attack him. My fear seemed even crazier when I reached the top and DeAngelo was already walking back across the snow.

"Nickie told me about your knee," he said as he reached the berm. "Gotta say I'm relieved. Not just about you not being a zombie…but I didn't want to be the one to break the news to the little woman."

"So what was the deal with the two you chased?" I asked as casually as possible. I had no idea what exactly I thought I'd witnessed with that little girl zombie. The problem was that things just refused to sit right in my mind.

"Kinda strange," DeAngelo said as we started back towards the cabin. "These two little ones hung back through the entire ordeal. I didn't think anything of it. It was just weird that every single time that I looked their way, they hadn't moved. I swear to God that it felt like they were studying me."

He paused for a second. I couldn't tell if he was trying to make sense of things in his own mind or what, but eventually he continued.

"When I started towards them, they both just turned and walked away. It wasn't really like they were trying to escape, just that they had seen all they cared to see and were ready to leave."

"So it seemed like they were studying you?" I asked.

"I guess," DeAngelo shrugged. "To tell you the truth, I was a little busy dealing with the ones I had on the ground coming after me."

"You two mind letting me in on what y'all are goin' on about?" Nickie demanded.

"That zombie that you nailed with the throwing knife?" I shot a quick glance at DeAngelo. "Did you know that she threw blades like William Tell?"

"William Tell shot an apple," Nickie huffed.

"Okay…she throws a knife like William Tell would if he wasn't shooting a bow and arrow. I mean the girl is freakishly good," I corrected.

"No idea," DeAngelo shrugged.

"Anyways, that child-zombie was standing there for several minutes," I explained. "She just stood there watching me and didn't react at all until I went for a weapon."

"Wait? What?" DeAngelo and Nickie said in unison.

"How long had it been there?" Nickie asked.

"Not sure," I admitted. "I closed my eyes and when I opened them a few moments later, she was there. I heard her coming, but I couldn't do anything about it."

"Why not?" Nickie asked.

Crap on toast, I absolutely did not want to melt her confidence this close after her last mini-meltdown. She'd been the saddest looking person I had ever seen; if I told her that she had inadvertently knocked the wind out of me and I'd been in danger of being eaten, she might shut down.

"I was just having trouble is all," I explained, and quickly went on with my recounting of what had happened minus the whole part about having the wind knocked out of me.

"That's weird," DeAngelo said as we reached the stairs to the cabin.

"I can't even begin to guess what the heck that is all about," I said.

Just before we opened the door, Nickie grabbed our arms. "If what you are both saying is accurate, then maybe we keep our eyes open and snag one for Dr. Zahn. I bet she could run some tests and maybe tell us what the dickens is going on. That might pull her out of her funk."

She had a good point.

***

The next few days were blessedly dull. The snow let up and it actually seemed to warm up a bit. Not enough to melt the snow in any visible amount, but enough so that everybody made a trip outside; even Dr. Zahn went out onto the porch for a while and sat on a stump that doubled as a stool and a even a card table on occasion.

That entire time, not a single zombie was sighted. The look-outs reported a few distant pinpoints of light that were likely camp fires, though I could not imagine being outside in this sort of weather for more than an hour or two, and that was with the knowledge that I could duck inside and get warmed by the raging fire in the massive hearth. Face it...as far as zombie apocalypse survival went...I was spoiled.

"Steve?" a voice whispered from right behind me as I was standing out on the porch watching Thalia, Emily, Rabia and Levent make a snow family.

"How's things, Doc?" I said without taking my eyes off the children. They had decided to create a snowman to represent each of us and were building DeAngelo's at the moment. They'd enlisted Fiona and Billy to help with the base. This snowman would easily be three or four times the size of all the others. That said a lot about how they saw this gentle giant of a man.

"Tell me everything you remember about that encounter."

I didn't need to ask which one. I'd already given her a narration at least a dozen times by now. What could she possibly gain from another re-telling of the story? Still, if it got her going and in any way contributed to getting her out of her funk, then I was obviously going to do what needed to be done.

I related all the details by rote as I had every time before. Periodically, she would ask a question or two. Sometimes she would ask the same questions with a few different words—once a doctor always a doctor, I guess.

When the interrogation was over, she went inside with her pencil tapping furiously on her notebook. I went back to watching the kids, the dog, and a pair of assistants building our snowclones. That is why I was outside when the distant growl of an engine broke the relative quiet. Actually, Buster heard it first and cocked her head to the side in the same way I'd seen that child-zombie do just a few days earlier.

When the Snowcat came through the natural canopy that framed the entrance road, I could tell that something was up. Jesus and Jake were both sitting on top of the cab waving their arms. It was a wave of greeting as opposed to the "grab the guns and be ready" wave. To their credit, I noticed that all the kids were frozen in their spots and watching the arrival of the cat.

I waited as patiently as possible for them to come up to the parking lot area. I actually had to chuckle when Thalia plowed through the snow to the driveway's entrance and acted as a traffic cop, indicating where they could park. Meanwhile, I noticed that they had a huge load of supplies in the trailer…as well as five new faces.

"How's the leg, Steve?" That was the first thing out of Jon's mouth as he climbed out of the cabin and went around to the trailer and began untying the straps. Not, anything about the supplies or the people, I took that as a message.

"It is as good as can be expected." I raised my eyebrows in

the universal symbol for 'What's up?' as I made my way to the cat, but he seemed satisfied with the answer and moved on.

"Where is the doctor?" Jake asked as he slid down from his perch and landed in the snow.

"Inside," I replied. By now, the rest of the gang was making their way out onto the porch. I knew I would only have a few seconds before they made their way down and could hear normal voice tones. "So what's the deal with these folks?" I kept my voice as low as I could.

"We found a small group." Jake looked past me like he wanted to be sure that nobody else heard. "These were the ones we felt comfortable traveling with, but we left a dozen back at their camp."

"Comfortable?" I asked. I didn't like where this was headed. A look came across Jake's face that I couldn't read. Then Jesus came down beside Jake. I wasn't close with the man, but I'd never seen him like this. He was pale, and if I didn't know better, I would have sworn he was infected.

"Jon made us promise to keep our mouths shut, he said he wanted to talk to you," Jesus said.

Jesus went to the cab of the cat and opened the door. The stench that poured out of that rectangular opening was almost enough to make me sick. The first person to be helped out had a face that looked like one of those people from the old concentration camp pictures. I seriously could not initially tell if the individual was male or female.

I don't know how long I stared, but the person did not seem to notice. Even with the layers of clothing—all of which looked recently acquired—I could tell that this person was nothing but skin and bones. One by one, the others were helped out. They just huddled close and waited until each of them was out, then they followed Jake like ducklings would a mother.

By now, everybody had come at least part way, but at some point the children had run up to the house. I could see them, Thalia and Emily clinging to Melissa while Rabia and Levent each had a grip on DeAngelo. Even Buster had retreated and was in a crouch at the base of the stairs.

As Jake approached, everybody either backed up or moved to give them a wide berth. In a way, it was kind of embarrassing. Obviously these people were in dire straits, and here we were acting like they were the walking dead.

"We need to head back out right away."

At some point, Jon had come up beside me. Jesus was still standing beside the Snowcat with a haunted and blank expression. I had to know what was going on. And going back out? I better have some answers first, because I was prepared to use my so-called position to veto any further activity until I had the whole story.

"What is going on?" I asked as I turned to face the man. Then I took a step back. Even Jon looked awful. Whatever it was, it had a man that showed no fear shaken to the core.

"Go up to the house and see," Jon said. "I will give you the details, but you have to see first hand and hear their story. Then, if you can tell me not to go back out there…well…I guess we'll see."

Each of us grabbed a box of supplies and headed up to the cabin. As I approached, I noticed everybody had stopped short of entering. My entire group was out on the porch, crowded around the doorway or the windows.

"Make a hole!" I barked, causing them all to jump.

"Steve?" Melissa had a look that went way past concerned etched on her face.

"I have no idea," I said with a shrug as I shouldered my way past everybody and entered the cabin.

The group of five had stopped right where Jake did and simply stood motionless while he peeled off their outer garments carefully like he was afraid he might injure one of them.

I had to do a double-take. The first one that I'd seen turned out to be a male. I could not put an age on him, but he was young enough to not have gone through puberty because his face was devoid of even a trace of fuzz. However, it was the left arm that I could not tear my eyes from. Rather, it was what remained of that left arm. It had been severed at just below the elbow and looked like it had been cauterized by shoving it in a campfire with the skin all black almost to the shoulder.

That was just the beginning. One by one each of them were stripped of their jacket and moved close to the fire. Each had the exact same injury. Everybody, that is, with the exception of what turned out to be a woman. Again, the malnutrition had made determining the age next to impossible.

Of all the members of the group, she was the only one without the missing lower left arm. However, there was something in her face that seemed far worse. It was just the expression, but she actually looked more damaged emotionally than the others.

"What is it?" Dr. Zahn grumbled as she came out of her office with Sunshine dragging her by the wrist. "I've got—"

Whatever else she was about to say died in her throat as she saw—and most likely smelled—the new arrivals. I was about to say something when I saw a flicker of the old doctor in the eyes of a woman who I had thought to be lost for good.

"Get these people into the back room. I want everything we can use put to the task of getting me as much hot water as possible. I want rags and I want the cleanest clothing we have as well as a minimum of three blankets for each." Doctor Zahn was back.

The room was silent for a few seconds until she stepped into the middle of it and clapped her hands together once. "Now, people!" With that, it was like roaches in a room when the light came on; everybody took off in different directions. Some bumping into each other.

I caught Jon's gaze and we both headed back out to the cat to get it unloaded. As we walked down the stairs, Jesus caught up.

"I can't stay in there with those people right now," he said.

"You can help us unload," Jon offered. "But then we are going back."

If it were at all possible, Jesus turned even paler. "I just don't think—"

"Your job isn't to think, soldier," Jon barked, sounding very much like a Marine sergeant. "You will do as you're told. Do you understand me?"

"Yes, sir."

"So are you gonna give me the details?" I asked.

"I will, but believe me when I tell you that words can't actually relate what we found." Jon's voice seemed to grow quieter with each word.

"When we got just outside of La Grande, we started to find signs of people. Every so often we would come across a few zombies that had been taken down. The fact that we were seeing them meant that they were recent kills; otherwise they would have been buried.

"Then we saw what looked like a small trailer park with a corrugated metal fence built around it with lots of extra reinforcement and no visible gate." We reached the Snowcat and Jon paused as he climbed up into the attached cart.

Once he started tossing things down, he continued. "We tried to hail anybody inside and thought it might be abandoned or that maybe everybody inside had turned. Then we heard a cough."

"Otherwise we would have moved on and never found them and they would have stayed there to..." Jesus started to talk, but his voice trailed off at the end.

"We climbed over, and my first thought was that they had turned and that sound hadn't been a cough, but rather just some random noise from a walker. However, there was a small fire burning in a metal barrel and that had to mean that they were alive." Jon stopped again and I looked up at him and saw what I thought might actually be tears in his eyes. I kept my mouth shut and waited.

"They were eating themselves, man," Jesus finally spit out, unable to keep it in any longer.

I looked from Jon to Jesus, unsure of what I heard. They couldn't be meaning what I thought they were, could they? Jon gave a slow nod. I looked back to the cabin as if that would help me understand. I had that image in my head of each of those people missing their left arm to the elbow. All but the one. It must've shown on my face because Jon sat down on a large burlap bag of rice or beans or something of the sort and folded his hands on one knee like he was settling in to tell a story. Only, I had the distinct feeling that I would not like the ending, and that nobody lived happily ever after.

"The woman was pregnant," Jon began, but already he was having trouble speaking. He kept swallowing like there was a huge lump in his throat that wouldn't clear. "According to one of their group, she miscarried at the seventh month...probably due to lack of nutrition."

Suddenly I wanted to hug Melissa. I was becoming increasingly aware of just how good we had things...even during our worst times.

"They ate it," Jesus whispered. "They were so hungry that instead of burning the child...they ate it."

When had I sat down? I wondered as I found myself seated in the cold snow.

"We brought the ones we felt comfortable moving without the doc taking a look. And we left the strongest behind to try and protect them, but I don't know if they can fend off a stiff breeze at this point," Jon explained.

"So that is what you meant when you said you had to head back out?" I was at a loss.

I had several thoughts flood my brain, and I'm not proud of many of them. What would this mean for all of *our* supplies? The entire reason that we sent Jon and the men out in the first place was because we would not last the winter. The first five were already here, but how many more were there. And as messed up as they were, what possible diseases might they be carrying? How would this affect the kids?

I was the leader of this group. It had been voted on and been unanimous for the most part. Supposedly my word was the final say. They had chosen me because I thought through things with what they considered more clarity, but I called it a bunch of guessing and making it up on the fly. If I made the call to leave things as they were—there was no way I could toss out the people they had already brought—would everybody agree? I had a feeling that Jon might oppose me on that decision. However, that was the least of my concerns. I doubted with all seriousness my own ability to simply ignore the problem. It would mean that we would need to endanger ourselves further and go out for more increasingly-hard-to-find supplies. But it would also mean that I would be able to look myself in the mirror.

An image flashed in my mind that made me shiver. I pictured Thalia, Emily, and Melissa looking like those new arrivals. If I was wrong and we were unable to meet our supply needs, that might very well be the fate that I consigned them to.

"I will get a few helping hands to unload the supplies you brought," I finally said. "Then you and I and the doc will roll out."

"Are you sure that you are in any condition—"

"I'm going," I said with as much authority as I could muster. "But we do this on one condition, if the doc says that one or any of those people will not survive...we leave them. You do what needs to be done to lessen their suffering, but I will only do this under that condition."

"Understood," Jon agreed.

I glanced at Jesus and am fairly certain that I saw relief on his face when he realized that he would not be going.

Each of us grabbed what we could carry and headed back to the cabin. When we arrived, everybody was still standing around in stunned silence. I could only speak for myself, but I had a feeling that everybody was seeing a glimpse at a possible future. As for the survivors, they had all been hustled to the back.

"Everybody listen up," I called out. A few people jumped. "We have supplies outside that need to be unloaded yesterday. Jon, Dr. Zahn, and I will be heading out to the camp where the rest of these people are staying. While we're gone, I want Billy, Melissa and Fiona to inventory the supplies and make a reasonable rationing list that will give us an idea how long the food will last. Calculate it for an additional..." I glanced at Jon who flashed both hands once and another hand, "...fifteen people being added to our ranks."

"Excuse me?" Cheryl Coates spoke up.

"Yes?" I was not sure where this would go, but I was seriously hoping that this would not turn into a debate on the idea of bringing these survivors into our camp...especially by our newest additions.

"I don't know about anybody else, but I feel rather useless just standing around. Is there anything that needs to be done to set up for these incoming people?"

"And is somebody going to explain what happened to their arms?" Nickie added.

I took a deep breath. After a glance at Jon and Jesus, I figured that they had relived this situation enough for now. I related the story as it had been told to me. I forced myself to relate even the worst details. Everybody needed to be aware of what we were doing and why.

When I was finished, I scanned the room. Everybody seemed to have drifted off into his or her own private little world. The children were huddled together and whispering to one another. I had no idea what that conversation might sound like, but it was clear that they understood at least some of what was going on.

"I will need a couple of you to volunteer to help Sunshine. Since I have to bring Dr. Zahn with me, she will need a few helping hands." I considered my statement just long enough to wish I'd used different words.

"So will you be going solely to pick up the other survivors, or will this also be a supply run?" Doug Coates, Cheryl's husband, asked.

"This is simply a rescue mission," Jon answered. "There would not be enough room for anything else, and even if there were...it is paramount that we get these people transported here as quickly as possible. The ones here represent the healthiest with the exception of the two we deemed to be the most able to take care of the others."

I don't think I had made it clear that the rest who had been left behind were even worse off than the ones with us. I saw a lot of winces in the crowd.

"So what is the deal with the left arm?" Christina asked a very reasonable question that I hadn't really considered up until that point.

"It was considered the least useful since all of them were apparently right-handed," Jon explained. "From what they told us, each week, somebody's name was drawn at random. That person endured the amputation and then the cauterization by the blade of a machete that was left in the fire for however long they saw fit."

"So what would they do after they ran out of left arms?" All heads in the room turned. Levent stood there behind Rabia with his hands on her shoulders and a questioning look on his face. "Would they make more babies?"

"Oh my God," Nickie gasped with her hands to her mouth.

"I don't know," I said. "But we are going to help them."

I headed for the door and was pleased that everybody fell in on my heels. It took less than an hour to get all of the food unloaded. It looked like so much, but I already knew that it was not nearly going to be enough. For one, it was less than we had currently in our stores. That did not bode well, but I could only deal with one crisis at a time.

With everything unloaded, I went back to get Dr. Zahn. She was bustling around her five new patients with an energy that I had not seen in a while. I almost hated to pull her away from it.

"Time to roll, Doc," I said. She looked up for just a second and then returned to whatever it was that she was doing with her current patient. I cleared my throat and she continued to tie off something that she had wrapped around the stump of this patient's left arm.

"Hey, Doc, I said—" I started, but her head popped up and she cut me off with a tone of voice that I did not realize I missed so much.

"I heard you, Steven, but unless you want to return and find all four of these men dead, I suggest you wait the ten minutes more it will take for me to finish cleaning and redressing these injuries.

"No problem," I said, raising my hands in surrender and backing out of the room. I stopped to kiss all my girls and assure them that I would be careful; then I returned to the Snowcat and climbed in with Jon.

"Don't expect to see too much zombie action until we get down the hill," Jon said. "I don't think they can make it up here without a lot of difficulty. Which reminds me…how much activity did you guys get when we left?"

I related all that happened, including the bit about the child-zombie. He nodded thoughtfully a few times and didn't say anything for a few minutes.

"Are you totally sure that you should be out?"

"I am probably slowing down the healing process, and I may be doing a bit of damage, but the days of being able to convalesce for any reasonable amount of time are long gone."

Jon didn't have anything to say to that. I think he knew damn good and well that he would be acting the same way…if not worse. Dr. Zahn did not take ten minutes, it was more like twenty. She gave us both a look that dared either one to say anything.

Once we were out of the campgrounds and had made it up to where I guess the road should be, Jon filled us in on some other aspects of this run. For one, we would not reach their location until tomorrow afternoon at the earliest. Also, we would need to stop and refuel. He already knew of a tanker that would do nicely.

Also, they had seen signs of human activity in the vicinity that we would have to camp at tonight; but the only other option was to forge an entirely different trail and hope that there were no nastier surprises. Having not been out in a while, I had a hard time recognizing anything and absolutely deferred to his judgment.

"Besides," Jon said with a shrug, "we don't know what the nature of these people are, and may just be worrying about nothing."

He had a good point. It was just that we'd had some bad luck with the living lately. I did not want to put any of us at greater risk than need be…especially Dr. Zahn.

The rest of the day was driven in relative silence with only the steady growl of the engine as our travel soundtrack. When we did finally stop, I noticed that the huge fuel tanker was obviously being used by any who passed. There were all sorts of cryptic messages painted or etched all down the side of the vehicle.

Jon and I climbed out. I was surprised to see an elaborate and obviously handmade setup for siphoning the gas out of the tanker. Not only had somebody gone through a great deal of trouble, but they had left it behind for others. I was amazed and ashamed, because I hadn't realized how pessimistic I'd become about my fellow man.

The entire time we filled up our tanks, I kept hearing the animal kingdom type show's British narrator. *The tiger waits in the high grass beside the watering hole as he watches for the perfect victim to act as the evening meal.*

Less than thirty minutes later, we were back on the road without incident. By the time we reached the rickety looking apartment complex that would serve as the evening's camp, I was exhausted from being so vigilant the entire time. When I climbed out, my butt still buzzed from the vibrations felt while sitting in the hard plastic seat of the Snowcat and trundling over the uneven and snow-covered terrain.

The place was only ten units. One two-story building housed six of the apartments and a long, one-story building on each side housed a pair. We went upstairs and into the one in the middle. I was only a little surprised to discover that a small cache of supplies was in place. After getting a fire going in the bathtub—a small hole was cut in the ceiling to allow the smoke to vent, obviously Jon has staged a few runs from here—we drew straws for watch rotation. I have the second shift. Time for a nap.

7

Geek Attack

Kevin pulled himself forward just a few inches on his belly. The snow was making him numb and a bunch of it had just gone down the opening at the neck of his coat and was sending cold trickles down his chest.

From where he had positioned himself, he could see all of the entries to the country club's main building. Two figures stood at each set of doors. Of course it was impossible to tell the gender from where he was at, but he had to keep telling himself what Willa had drilled into his head all of last night.

"They are not men or women…they are soldiers and they will kill you and your friends without hesitation."

Of all the days, the sun had chosen today to shine. The crystal clear skies were only allowing the temperatures to plummet further. Any time he stayed put for longer than twenty minutes, he had to break free from the crystallizing snow. The surface was almost a sheet of ice as the sun warmed it enough to melt slightly and then the near zero temperatures re-froze it. Thank goodness for the military grade arctic gear that Willa had for the two of them.

As the sun began to set, the world was turning a reddish-purple. Within an hour, the front of the building would be completely shrouded in shadow. Kevin kept checking over his shoulder. Behind him, a tree-lined fairway unfurled a couple hundred yards before hooking left. He was in the perfect position to see all the way down the slope, and could even see part of the grounds of the dogleg as well as the tattered flag marking the

119

hole's oval green. It was from there that he expected the foot patrol to appear.

Twice he thought he saw *her*. Twice, a figure paused at one of the expansive windows. Of course he could no more see the details of that face as he could the sentries at the doors, but he knew it was her.

Aleah.

He knew that the primary motivator for him was to not fail Valarie. Yet, when he was being honest, it was Aleah's face that he saw every time that he closed his eyes. It was her voice in his head telling him that she believed in him.

His head snapped and he realized that he had drifted off. He scanned the area and looked back over his shoulder. Still nothing, but he couldn't be sure that they hadn't passed by while he had been asleep.

It was the cold. It was sapping him of his energy. Already, even though he knew he needed to be alert, he could feel the lure of sleep tugging at him. He scooped a handful of snow and rubbed it on his face. He hoped that darkness would come soon.

Less than fifteen minutes later he saw a team of ten leave the country club. That was not part of the plan. They had waited this extra day because Willa insisted that they let them discover and react to the missing sentries that they had killed.

Of course there was no way that they would find the bodies. Kevin had made sure of that by lugging them to the wall and tossing them over and emptying his pack. He and Willa scooped up all the bloody snow and carried it out like the garbage. Using a branch to brush the snow and obscure their tracks, they had made their escape and hauled the bodies away.

Of course he realized that there was no way to completely erase their tracks, but it looked like there had been a lot of foot traffic by the soldiers as they obviously had been searching the area. He hoped they were simply scavenging for food; he wanted to have the complete element of surprise. If they were searching for him, that might prove to be a problem.

The ten soldiers were all equipped with an impressive array

of weapons and split up into two groups of five. One group headed up the driveway. They looked to be heading out of the golf course's entry drive. The other five were headed almost directly towards him!

He held his breath, afraid that the fog created by it might give him away. Fortunately, they veered to the left. They would be heading down the fairway at his back. He could hear them talking, but was unable to make out anything being said.

Not long after the darkness laid claim to the land, he saw a single flash on the far left of the main building. That would be Willa. She had some of those glow sticks and had determined that the signal to move would be her setting one of them off. Of course she would cover it and bury it immediately after activation; they didn't want to risk the chance of it falling out of a pouch or pocket at an inopportune time and giving them away. That was just another one of the beauties of a dead world. With such complete darkness, something so small as a glow stick grabbed immediate attention.

Kevin pushed himself up from the snow. His entire body felt as if it were in the throbbing stage after a bee sting. He had to grab ahold of a nearby branch to keep from sinking back to his knees. After stomping his feet a few times to get his circulation jump-started, Kevin ducked down low and moved along the tree line. He needed to stay in the shadows because the moon had the entire landscape lit up in a soft blue light.

Now that the sun was gone, he could see into the shadows of the country club enough to know that there were still sentries out. He wasn't sure if whoever was in charge in there had made the decree after two of their own came up missing, but it was 'lights out' inside the huge building.

Eventually he came to the tree-lined path that would lead up to the country club's small bar, not surprisingly named 'The Nineteenth Hole'. As expected, there were two sentries here as well. Here is where the plan's success hinged. Kevin was able to get within ten yards of the doorway and remain unseen.

He squatted down and pulled the six bottles from his knapsack. It took him a while to unwrap them. Willa had insisted that they bundle them with cut up blankets to prevent breakage or noise. His hands didn't want to do exactly as he directed because, despite even the best gloves, his hands had gotten cold and were slightly numb. Next he pulled out the collapsible wind screen. After he dug a small pit in the snow and lined up the bottles, he wedged the screen into place.

The idea was to keep his location a secret for as long as possible. Of course, if the sentries were paying serious attention, then this entire elaborate set up was all for naught. Willa said that it was typical for the folks on the night watch to be lulled into a bit of a stupor by the lack of activity.

Kevin thumbed the wheel of the lighter. The rasp of flint and steel sounded like an explosion in his ears. He looked up and instantly remembered Willa's other word of caution.

"Don't look into the flame when you light it," she warned. "You are gonna lose your night vision any way, but every extra second that you can be aware of your surroundings is to your benefit."

He also remembered his response. "I know!"

At least he didn't hear anybody yelling or sounding any sort of alarm. Once Kevin lit the first two Molotov's he snatched them up. He cocked his arm and launched the first one. It sailed high and slammed into the wall just a few feet away from the entry.

In the flash of near blinding light, Kevin saw both of the sentries duck and dive away from the flames. Human instinct is a wonderful thing. No matter how well trained most people believe themselves to be, the instinct of self-preservation kicks in on its own before training and discipline has a chance.

Kevin didn't wait to admire his work for more than a second before he hurled his second fire bomb. There was a crash of glass and an orange glow began to illuminate what had once been a huge dining and reception room. As he knelt down to grab the next two, he heard a muffled cry. When he looked up, a third shadow had joined the sentries—that would be Willa.

Selecting another large window to the right, Kevin hurled one and then another of his Molotovs, and then quickly scooped up the last two. This would be the trickiest part, and also the part where he might unknowingly injure his friends. He targeted the second-floor balcony windows of the spire-topped circular portion. The first one crashed into the railing and Kevin adjusted his second throw accordingly.

The flaming missile smashed through the window and an additional crash was heard seconds later. Just as he'd tossed that last one—the entire operation had taken less than twenty seconds up to this point, but felt like an eternity—the guards from the front of the building came running around the corner. That was his cue; Kevin turned and ran back into the woods that bordered the long fairway.

He had gotten a decent distance when he heard the yelps. That would be the trip line he had strung between several of the trees catching at least one of his pursuers. A few seconds later, he heard a yelp of pain. That would be Willa nailing one of his pursuers in the back with her crossbow. She had made it clear that she would try and take a couple of shots if the sentries went after him and didn't bother to look back her way.

They still had no idea how many people they were dealing with, and any chance to pare down the numbers had to be taken. Kevin ducked just before he reached the edge of the tree line. This was the most dangerous part for him. He would have to run all the way across the open ground of the dog leg. He hoped that he'd built enough of a lead.

As he reached the halfway point, he heard a strangled cry as another of his pursuers apparently 'discovered' the line he had rigged at about throat level. He dove into the waist-high, snow-covered shrubs when the first arrows flew past. The solid 'thok' of one of the projectiles burying itself into the trunk of a nearby tree made Kevin scramble to his hands and knees and keep moving.

He knew that there was no way he would be able to give his pursuers the slip. His only hope was that Willa had everything handled on her end. A few moments of running in the snow was worse than an hour of just plain running, and his lungs were on fire. He came out into the open once more and took stock of his position. As he passed a ball washer, he cut left and saw the long, gentle downhill slope just ahead.

His mind went back to one of his favorite James Bond movies, *For Your Eyes Only*. There was a really great chase on skis where Roger Moore's hair barely moves. What he was about to do would not be nearly as cool, but he was willing to put it up on the fun-meter with the water slide scene from *The Goonies*.

He spied his target and veered just slightly. Grabbing the Snow Disc, he took two more steps and flung himself forward, landing belly first on the round, metallic disc and taking off down the hill. He kept his feet up just enough so as not to drag in the snow and slow him down. A glance over his shoulder allowed him to see three dark forms reach the crest of the hill. He was almost in the clear. Kevin looked forward just in time to notice that we was starting to veer towards the small frozen pond to his left. Leaning slightly, he corrected his course.

As the slope leveled out, he coasted to a stop. He did not see the trio of pursuers any longer. That could be good or bad. However, there was a pronounced glow back towards the country club. The fire had caught, and if he could make his judgment based solely on the brightness, he would guess that it was well past out of control. He just hoped that all of *his* people made it out. In the back of his mind, he still struggled with taking such a drastic measure, but Willa said that it was either this, or else leave them to their fate. When Kevin had asked about going back to her people for help, her explanation had been simple.

"Every single day you give them allows the possibility of something happening to Valarie. Didn't you say that you heard she might be in danger? Besides, the more pieces you add to our puzzle, the more complicated you make it. Haven't you ever seen the movie *Red Dawn*? A couple of motivated rebels can accomplish a lot."

"Didn't they all die in the end?" Kevin had asked.

"Lea Thompson and that other boy live," Willa shrugged.

Kevin couldn't argue with logic like that. He kept pushing on until he reached the wall. He tossed his knapsack over and hauled himself up. He lost his footing when he landed and submerged under the snow. He surfaced and found himself face-to-face with a zombie. It was close enough for him to smell the rot coming from its putrid innards and he gagged.

C'mon," Kevin sighed. "You guys are hardly around for days...and you just *happen* to be here?" He drew his knife and drove it into the eye.

Getting to his feet, it was a bit more of the tougher going until he reached the highway. At least there he had the numerous tracks made from those who had taken his home. He glanced again over his shoulder and was surprised to see flames shooting skyward. He heard a popcorn sound and it took a moment before he realized that it was probably ammunition cooking off. The fact that there wasn't much noise meant that they either got the majority of it out of the building, or they simply didn't have all that much to begin with. He hoped it was the latter.

"Kevin!" a voice whispered from the darkness ahead.

He veered towards that voice and found Willa leaning against the side of a house. He was only slightly relieved to see her as out of breath as he was at the moment.

"We need to get moving," she said between gasps for air.

"And how will we know if my friends are okay?" Kevin asked as he followed Willa into the garage to put on the skis.

"We won't," Willa said. "At least not right away."

"So what do we do next?"

"We wait." Willa fastened her bindings and made her way out to the driveway. "But right now, we need to get out of here."

They had selected a distant farmhouse that sat far enough back from everything but high enough up on a slight ridge to allow them to keep an eye out. They couldn't actually see the highway from the house, but it was a simple matter of crossing the yard and weaving through some trees. They would keep watch in shifts.

***

Two days had passed. Kevin had taken the first watch after promising that he wouldn't 'run off on some fool mission' if he saw something. The fire had burned most of the night. By dawn, it was a wisp of gray smoke curling skyward. The winds had died down to nothing, so the column had risen high and then seemed to flatten like it had been squashed flat with a giant hammer.

Now, as he stood leaning against the sturdy trunk of one of many in a grove of some generic looking deciduous trees. He was beginning to doubt Willa really had a plan. Every single time that he approached her, she simply said that it was not the time. He'd begun to wonder about the peculiar convenience of meeting her when he did. And then there was the deal about her unit of women.

He struggled with the seed of doubt in his mind that had given way to a weed infested garden. He'd read the books…seen the movies. This was starting to pan out like some elaborate scheme. The only problem was that he couldn't rationalize why anybody would go to the trouble for him and his friends.

With sunset an hour away, he decided that it was time to start taking things into his own hands. Willa would come out to relieve him soon. When she did, he would give her a dose of her own medicine. An hour into her watch, he would make his move. He would slip out and make his way back to the country club.

A hand on his shoulder made him jump.

"You want to get us killed?" Willa whispered.

"Huh?"

She grabbed his shoulders and turned him about forty-five degrees to the left. At the entrance to the housing development that they had escaped through, a group of the soldiers were gathering around one of the now-useless streetlight poles. They had placed a ladder beside it and one of their group was climbing.

Kevin watched as the person tossed a rope over the extended arm that had the light mounted at its end. The group at the bottom stood in a cluster waiting for the climber to come down. Kevin didn't realize that he had started moving forward until Willa grabbed him and yanked him back.

"Stay put," she hissed.

"What are they doing?" Kevin felt his throat tighten. He knew what he was seeing, but he was trying his hardest to make himself believe that he was wrong.

"Shut up!" Willa hissed. "They are trying to draw you...us...out into the open."

Even from this distance he recognized the coat. A sick feeling filled his stomach. He'd met some despicable people since this whole thing had begun. He'd met people who had done things that he did not imagine possible. However, this...this was simply more than he could stand.

He yanked away from Willa and his eyes widened when his fears were confirmed. He recognized that coat. Valarie never went anywhere without it on. He couldn't see her face from this distance. Actually, he couldn't see much of anything because the so-called soldiers were all gathered around. One of them draped the noose over the hooded figure and then three of them hauled on the rope, hoisting the helpless figure in the air. It swayed back and forth and Kevin could tell that the arms and legs had been bound.

The group yelled and cheered and made all kinds of noise. The legs were barely three feet off the ground. They were hoping for zombies. Kevin could have told them they were wasting their time. Valarie was immune to the bite, but since she'd already been bitten—numerous times at that—she would turn soon after death.

A surge of emotion filled him and Kevin decided that he no longer cared if he lived or died. Shoving Willa back, Kevin drew his sword. His mind did not bother him with the futility of going after several men with bows while carrying nothing more than a knife.

"Kevin, no!" Willa pleaded.

"Go to hell," he snarled. He took two more steps and never actually felt the blow to the back of his head. All he knew was that somebody had turned up the brightness on his vision in a hurry; and just as quickly…everything went dark.

***

Kevin felt sick. He wanted to open his eyes, but he had already tried it once and the room had flipped on its side causing him to blow chunks. He felt somebody wipe at him with a warm, wet cloth and decided to just stay still for the time being.

While he waited for the woogy feeling to pass, he flexed his hands and was surprised to discover that they were not bound. The next problem was trying to figure out why he would have expected them to be. He began to search his memory, but it was a bit hazy.

He could see images start to form in his mind's eye, but then they would vanish like the sun behind a cloud. One picture kept trying to force its way in…a face. He knew that face. He knew the name. Sara? Valarie? Why couldn't he decide on which was correct? It wasn't like they were similar.

As he sat with his back against a wall, Kevin continued to focus. He kept seeing scenes from some of his favorite movies pop in with a clarity that almost disturbed him. And he started realizing that he hadn't seen any of these scenes in any movie.

"Oh, God," he moaned. It was real! And just like that, the past few months came pouring back. In the middle of the memory pile-up was his sister…and Valarie.

Kevin's eyes opened and the room swam. He felt the cold sweat break out on his face as he struggled to keep from heaving again. The face a few feet from him took a few seconds to match up with a name floating around in the soup of his memory.

"What did you do, Willa?" Kevin said through clenched teeth.

"I couldn't let you go," Willa said in a choked whisper.

"You wouldn't have made it anyway. It was too far away and done before you—"

"You don't...have that right!" The first words came out at almost a yell. He squeezed his eyes shut tight as if that would also help force the bile rising in his throat back down to his stomach where it belonged.

"Look beside you," Willa said with a nod of her head.

Kevin looked and actually tried to push himself away from what sat next to him on the floor. The first thing he recognized was the coat. It was definitely Valarie's. However, that was it. Other than that, it was only a bunch of clothing. He looked at Willa with a question etched on his face.

"Snow," she said. "They stuffed a bunch of her clothes with snow, put her jacket on it, and then strung it up."

"So she isn't..." Kevin's throat burned and tears spilled from his eyes.

"Dead?" Willa asked. "I have no idea, but I can't imagine they would have gone through all of this trouble if she was."

"So then what the hell was all that about?"

"It was about what you almost gave them," Willa said matter-of-factly. "They were trying to draw you out for some reason."

"Why?"

"I have no idea," Willa said with a shrug.

Kevin leaned back against the wall and closed his eyes again. He tried to make sense of what could possibly be the motivation behind such an act.

"Go change," Willa said.

Kevin went to stand and the room tilted. He slid back down against the wall. "I'll wait."

He eventually reached the point where he could keep his eyes open without feeling sick. By the time he was able to stand, the room had become noticeably darker. At some point, Willa had gone back outside to keep watch. As he sat there, things came back. At first it was just in bits and pieces, but eventually he was able to recall everything...or at least he thought so.

Making his way into one of the bedrooms, he saw a bunch of their stuff laid out like it had been gone through. He couldn't worry about that now, he needed to focus. First he peeled out of his sick-fouled clothes and wiped himself off as best he could. He didn't put too much effort into it because he really didn't care.

Once he was dressed, he grabbed a few things and stuffed them into his knapsack. A quick peek out of the room confirmed that it was still empty. *Good,* he thought, *I don't need much of a head start, but every bit helps.* He walked on tip toe until he realized how silly it was with her outside and him in.

He opened the back door and had an immediate appreciation for how warm the fire in the bathtub was keeping the house. It was cold enough to hurt his teeth when he breathed. Kevin had never really been one to wear scarves before, but they had become a valued part of his wardrobe lately.

He made his way across the back yard as carefully as possible. The surface of the snow was a hard crust that broke instead of just being smooshed underfoot. A few times, he'd had to actually tap hard with the heel of his foot to break through. By the time he reached the trees, he was starting to question his wisdom. His head still throbbed a bit, and he probably should have eaten something before taking off.

He kept his mind occupied with the importance of taking one more step...then one more step...and so on. A good bit of time passed when he found himself at the edge of the trees and looking down a pretty steep slope. The moon lit up a frozen stream below and was so bright that even the crystalized moisture from his breath sparkled like tiny diamonds. He couldn't feel his nose, and his eyelashes felt like they stuck just a bit when he blinked.

When he reached the bottom of the hill, he had to look around a bit and get his bearings. It took him just a few seconds to figure out where he was, and he quickly set off for the golf course. As he moved along the highway, he crossed over and stayed in the shadows. On the off chance that Willa had not come inside from her watch to discover his absence, he did not want to reveal himself to her.

As soon as he saw the stone wall, he climbed up and over. He had to weave through some trees, but eventually he found himself on a long, narrow fairway. Using what he remembered about the place, he made his way to where the club house should be.

He moved cautiously, knowing that he would be no match for any real soldier…especially in his current condition. The one thing that kept him moving was the idea of what he had resigned the Bergman women to by waiting to act. He had wanted to formulate the perfect plan. He now realized that there was no such thing. All he could do is move, act, and improvise.

When he finally saw the camp, he felt his heart sink just a bit. There were at least three dozen tents along with a huge central tent. He guessed that to either be the headquarters or the mess tent. Whatever the case, it was too much. Anything he did would be futile and end in failure and probably death. Worse still, if he hadn't condemned them to death already by torching that building, it was very possible that he would do so now.

Willa had made several statements to that effect. He had chosen to ignore her. He hadn't wanted to hear just how hopeless it was. *Just once*, his mind screamed, *why can't it be like in the movies?* In the movies, the "good guy" eventually triumphed over bad. He knew that because it was always the part he and his friends complained about when the movie was over. There was always some convenient miracle that signaled the doom of the bad guys. Couple that with how the good guys never missed and the bad guys couldn't hit a stationary target ten feet away with an M-16 and you had the typical Hollywood scenario.

He'd already lost his friends. He'd lost the Bergmans only to get two of the four back…and then lose them again. He'd had a chance at redemption with Valarie. His run to get her medication had been full of miracles. At least that had been the case until Dr. Peter King got bit.

And then there was Aleah. Of course Hollywood casting

would have utilized one of those "nerd chic" types. A change in his eyeglasses and a new hairstyle would transform him like a geeky Cinderfella. That would make somebody as gorgeous as Aleah the princess who kissed the toad and helped him transform into a prince.

"Fuck," Kevin hissed.

He didn't know how long he stood there, but the longer he did, the more he felt his resolve start to fade. It was now or never. Kevin unslung his knapsack and dug through it. The medication was there just as it had been the other four or five times he had checked. He slung it over his shoulder and stepped out of the trees. Lacing his fingers behind his head, Kevin began the walk across the open ground of where the putting green would be if you could see it and towards the shadowy form that he was pretty certain had to be a sentry.

Vignettes XXVII

Ahi stared in disbelief. He looked back and forth between the obviously pleased Aaheru and the bus that was now little more than twisted metal, smoke, and flames. All of the women, the Mothers of Egypt as the seemingly mad pharaoh called them, were on that bus. Physically, it was of no consequence to Ahi. He preferred the company of men and had a secret lover among the boys who had been recruited from the City of the Dead.

"Did you think I was that big of a fool, my brother?" Aaheru laughed loud as if he'd just heard the most humorous joke.

"B-b-but the women—" Ahi stammered.

"Are in the armored car directly behind me," Aaheru said, clucking his tongue. "I would not be fooled by somebody as greedy or power hungry as Markata."

"But I saw the women board—"

"Did you see their faces?" Aaheru asked with a raised eyebrow and a smirk. "You saw several *figures* board the bus wearing the traditional burqa. Allah will forgive the transgression, but those were young men that I hand-picked for their willingness to make the ultimate sacrifice when needed. They were needed today."

Ahi thought it over. On one hand, he could see the need to send a clear message to any future potential rebels…but to sacrifice twenty-three men to kill one? It didn't make any sense to him.

"They served you well, my Pharaoh. I hope they find glory and honor before God."

Aaheru returned his attention forward. The waterfront district was just through an arch. They had arrived with minimal casualties. He glanced in the mirror at Ahi. The man was far too grim after such a victory. Of all people, he would have thought that the man would delight in seeing the demise of the only person who sought to unseat him as the pharaoh's advisor. Perhaps he had gauged this man incorrectly.

The caravan came top a stop. Aaheru looked and was annoyed to discover that they were still a few hundred yards away from the actual docks. One of the men from a vehicle out front came sprinting back. The fearful looks that he continued to cast over his shoulder gave Aaheru a clue as to the most likely problem.

"Two climbed in the first car," the man panted. "The windshield finally gave way after hitting several of the cursed things. There are over a hundred between us and the ships."

This was not good. Aaheru would be sure to deal with the men tasked to keep the ships secure and waiting for his arrival. This was no way for the new era to begin.

Opening the door with enough force to send the man outside it sprawling, Aaheru stepped out of the vehicle. He did not look back, but rather strode forward with purpose. He should not need to look or give an order; his people should instantly react and move to ensure the safety of their pharaoh.

"Perhaps you should return to your vehicle, my Pharaoh," Ahi said as he stepped up and matched stride with the larger man.

One of the undead stepped out from between two idling vehicles of the caravan. Aaheru drew his curved scimitar and swung with a ferocious backhand. The blade dug deep but did not completely pass through the top third of the skull. With a slight turn, Aaheru brought up a booted foot and kicked the now truly dead creature away. Several more of the abominations were headed their direction.

Looking in all directions, Aaheru felt a brief flutter of the closest thing to fear he'd experienced in years. They were so close, and in such great numbers, that it took him a few seconds to realize somebody behind him was screaming.

The armored truck directly behind his vehicle was already surrounded. The man he had assigned to ride on top had apparently tried to stop one and lost his footing. He was on the ground with at least twenty of those things fighting for a piece; that was all Aaheru needed to see.

"Sons of Egypt!" he bellowed. "Gather on me and let us send these restless dead to their eternal slumber!"

From every nearby vehicle, the men who had not already come out with their leader poured forth. It was almost a contest as to who could respond quickest. Nobody wanted to be the last man to answer the call for fear of displeasing his pharaoh.

"You," Aaheru pointed to a small cluster of middle-aged men, "cover our rear. Kill anything that moves."

As one, they turned and rushed to meet the oncoming threat. He sent the remaining men forward with instructions to clear the path ahead. Once they were engaged, he turned to Ahi—who he had restrained from joining in on the attack.

"Gather the women and follow me," Aaheru whispered.

Ahi glanced over his shoulder at the men who had charged the mob at their heels. Already, several of the beasts were coming out from between the vehicles, effectively cutting them off from the group.

Once the women had been herded off the truck, they began the jog to the waiting vessel. On the brow of the closest, a few men stood idle. Aaheru moved to the front as his small entourage reached safety. Without a word, he grabbed the closest man by the shirt and, in one fluid motion, heaved him back at the dozen or so undead that had continued to pursue.

As the screams began, he stepped up to the man responsible for the detail. "Pray that you never fail me again," he hissed.

"How have I failed—" A backhand across his face cut off the question.

"You waited safely on board and did not think to clear the pier for our arrival? Are you a child who needs to be told every single detail? I had to sacrifice several of your brothers to reach this ship because you did not think to secure our way. Now begin untying us and get us out to sea."

Less than fifteen minutes later, they were navigating the harbor. The hulls of several partially sunken ships jutted up in a nautical representation of a graveyard. After a head count was taken, Aaheru went on a tirade, scolding the security teams and the men who had secured the ships. Once he retired to his quarters, he smiled. They had lost less than half of their numbers. Over three hundred souls remained. Things had actually gone better than he'd hoped.

***

"...and that was it...Thad and his group didn't make it," Juan said as he stood in the wash basin and continued to soap his body up and down.

"I don't think we should risk any more runs to the mainland until spring." Mackenzie set the bucket of warm water down and then hopped up onto the counter.

"Weather ain't gonna matter." Juan picked up the bucket and began to ladle the warm water over his body. He looked down in the tub and was disgusted by the putrid brown color. He wondered how many people's blood was mixing together at his feet. "I think we should stay away from any sort of city. The best bet is to make a run out to the sticks."

"You mean travel *farther* away?" Mackenzie was almost yelling.

"We got it pretty good," Juan admitted. "But finding those kids..." His voice trailed away and Juan felt something strange tighten in his chest.

"They are settling in," Mackenzie said with a smile. "April is getting them assigned places to live. Most of them want to stay in the same house, which is fine. We still have about fifteen or twenty that are empty, so we are really doing well in that respect."

At the mention of April's name, Juan tensed up. There was a long silence before he finally spoke. "She tell you what happened?"

Mackenzie hopped off the counter and came over to the wash basin. She opened the curtain and saw that same haunted look on his face that he'd had after JoJo. "She told me."

"And?" that single word held a ton of weight, and all of it was sitting squarely on Juan's shoulders.

"You did what needed doing."

"But—" he tried to protest, but she placed a finger on his lips. "April is fine. She realizes what had to be done as well. In fact, she feels awful for giving you such a hard time over it."

Juan finished washing up and slipped into some clean, dry clothes. He had just sat down with Mackenzie when the knock came at the door. It was dark. It was never a good sign when somebody knocked on the door after dark. He flashed an apologetic look to Mackenzie, who simply smiled and nodded for him to go answer it.

"This better be—" the words died on his lips. Frank was standing in the door with a dog in his arms. It looked dead. There was a slow expansion and contraction that indicated breathing. "Is that the dog you were chasing?"

"Gidget," Frank said through the tears in his eyes. "I don't know how, but the stupid dog followed us."

"Besides the long swim, what the heck happened to her?"

"Well, remember how we told you she got attacked by one of those…things. Well…as crazy as it seems, I think she got hit again."

"Bring her in." Mackenzie had stepped up beside Juan and already had rubber gloves on. She pulled the blanket away and hissed between her teeth at the bite mark. A good chunk had been taken from the left front shoulder.

"There's more," Frank whispered. "A few of the guys took one of the boats and left about twenty minutes ago."

"This isn't my problem," Juan said. "I won't make anybody stay here against their will."

"They went looking for Donna."

"Still not my—"

"Juan Hoya!" Mackenzie snapped with enough venom and volume to cause the dog to raise its head.

"What?" Juan spun around with an expression that was part confused, part annoyed. "Didn't you just say something a little bit ago about no more supply runs to the mainland? You want me to go chase after ghosts now?"

"They're children," Mackenzie insisted.

"They were doing okay until they met us. They just lost *one* person. And now they want to go over and search for someone who is chasing somebody who comes to her in her dreams? We've lost how many in the past few weeks? It is the way things are now."

"No," Mackenzie whispered. "It is the way things will become if we do nothing."

"So what do you expect me to do?" Juan asked.

"I want you to help—" The dog made a whimpering sound and Mackenzie turned just as its eyes closed and it gave a single convulsive shiver.

"Mackenzie," Juan said as calmly as he could. "Step away from the dog."

She looked at Juan in confusion for a moment before the realization settled in. The problem she had was that she just hadn't seen what Juan had out on his supply runs. Her mind didn't immediately register the fact that dogs turned just like people. And even if somebody showed immunity, when they succumbed to death, the virus was able to complete its task.

Everything seemed to shift into slow motion at that moment. Juan saw past Mackenzie to the dog lying on the table. He saw its eyes open and shift to the nearest target available. He was vaguely aware of Frank saying something.

On instinct, his hand went to his belt...but who wears a weapon at the dinner table? There was nothing. All of his gear was either in the bedroom or hanging up on the wall on the other side of the room. As the dog's head rose and its mouth opened wide, all he could think was, *Why didn't I keep something by the door?*

***

Smoke curled skyward. From his position on top of the Yosemite Hotel, he could see perfectly all the carnage of the last few days. Michael Clark had been true to his word. The fight was indeed over. The bodies strewn about the snow, surrounded in halos of blood, were testament to the finality.

A solitary figure emerged from a clump of trees. Chad had to shade his eyes to be sure before he called out.

"Hey, Mike!" Chad called.

The man looked up. Even from this distance the scowl was visibly apparent. "It's Michael," the man hollered in response.

"Sorry." Chad was anything but, despite the fact that the man had been the key figure in ending the little war between the factions, he was not happy about the method. Also, he was not totally convinced that it had needed to be so final. There had been absolutely no attempt to negotiate a peace settlement.

"So...Michael...Brett says that you guys found the handful that tried to run."

"Yep."

"I also notice you aren't escorting any prisoners."

"None to be escorted."

"They all fall off of cliffs?"

That was a bit of a dig. After the initial explosion, a few of the residents had run for it; hightailing it to the woods. Michael had gone after them with a few hand-picked individuals. When he'd returned without any prisoners as Chad thought he would, he and Scott had asked what happened to the people.

"They fell off a cliff," was Michael's response.

"Hey, Chad?" Michael called up.

"Yeah?"

"Kiss my ass."

"I take it he didn't come back with any prisoners?" Scott

139

said over Chad's shoulder.

"Nope," Chad replied. "And the funny thing is, I didn't know he went out again. I thought you and Brett were making this trip."

"I was all set to leave and he came by and told me that there was something more pressing that he didn't think anybody would want him taking part in." Scott turned his back on the ledge and leaned against the waist-high brick wall.

"Sounds ominous." Chad leaned his rifle against the wall and gave Scott his full attention. The newest decision was that the precious ammo and the guns would stay in camp. Any patrols would take bow and arrow or one of the dozen or so crossbows. Firearms were just too precious to risk in the field.

"Actually..." Scott paused and Chad suddenly had a feeling that he did not want to hear what was about to be said. "It's about the food."

"Jesus," Chad sighed. "When isn't it? The last few meals have been crap and everybody is griping. They should be thankful they picked this team after what was discovered."

The rigged explosions that were set off in their enemies' stronghold had caused a pretty good fire. But it had burned out and left part of the building intact. Late yesterday afternoon, Chad and a few others went in to look around. Partially because they wanted to see if there might be anything worth salvaging. But also because Chad wanted to make sure that any survivors found would be taken in and offered a chance to step across the line. Of course there would be a probationary period and all, but it was a better alternative than just murdering them.

They had not found a single living survivor. What they had found was a horrific scene of butchery. With food obviously in short supply, at least some of the people had decided that cannibalism was an acceptable alternative to starvation. That one room smelled like a slaughter house with a repulsive mix of blood and shit and meat.

"I did an inventory and sat down with a few people who knew what they were talking about and our situation of food is…grim is the nicest way I can put it," Scott explained.

"Okay," Chad nodded, "what are we looking at?"

"A month tops if we ration carefully."

"So we have plenty of time to stock up. I don't see the problem," Chad said with a shrug. "We will send out foraging teams right now."

"And go where?" Scott asked.

"There should be plenty to hunt, and we can hit some of the small towns and communities."

"The zombies have scared away a lot of the wildlife, and besides, most of the herds are not this far up. They are hugging the line down where they can still graze."

"So we send out hunting parties."

"You aren't getting it," Scott huffed. "We came up here in a bus, so the few hours that trip took may not seem like such a big deal. However, none of our vehicles will get us out of here. A couple of guys have checked on the snowmobiles and the plowing rigs, but that cold snap we had a few weeks ago that hung in the sub-zero range for that stretch…it sapped batteries, caused cables to break and basically turned every motorized vehicle in this place into its own little monument."

"But we have bad weather gear…skis…all sorts of stuff."

"And nobody wants to take a trip that will last at least a few weeks with very little chance of success just to return with enough food for one or two people to eat for another day or so. We can't get out and come back with enough for the group. There are over fifty people here…feeding that many takes a lot more food than any of us realized."

Chad let it all sink in. He hadn't considered any of this a few months ago when they had left Modesto in search of someplace safe…or, as it turned out, at least sa*fer* from the walking dead. His only thought had been that staying in populated areas would keep them in constant danger.

When they'd first arrived, everybody had been so excited to discover kitchen pantries full of food. There had simply been so much, and when looked at with one or two pairs of eyes…it looked as if it could last forever. They had been so wasteful. Everybody was cooking for themselves those first days until Colonel Morris had stepped in and made some rules. As expected, folks had bitched…but a majority saw the logic. After a while, it was the norm.

Colonel Morris's death had lasting repercussions. The whole place had fallen into disarray in his absence. This latest news would cause a panic.

If it was just him, alone and free of responsibility, the choice would be easy. However, he had Ronni to think of and watch over. He would need to do something…the question was simple.

What?

He had no answer.

***

"Excuse me, miss?" the young girl climbed up on the wall next to Victoria.

"Who you calling 'miss'? My mum has long since passed," Victoria snorted.

"Sorry, Victoria," the girl mumbled an apology.

"And that's another thing…nobody calls me that. Just 'Vix' is fine."

"Right, then…Vix."

"And you're Glenda Baker's daughter, yeah?" Vix knew it was something like Jenna or some such thing.

"Gemma."

"Right." Vix considered her next words carefully and with as much sensitivity as she could muster. "So…your mum and dad didn't make it?"

She saw the pain on the young girl's face. She really didn't have a handle on being sensitive. It was one of the great things about her Ivor. He didn't get all caught up in the flowers and whatnot. He showed her how much he loved and cared for her in a million other ways that had much more meaning. For the past several years, it had been as much about them being best mates as being husband and wife. They joked and teased and made fun.

"...and I just hadn't ever seen so much blood."

Vix looked up with a grim face that she thought might pass for sympathetic. The poor girl had been pouring her heart out while she daydreamed. To make matters worse, a few zeds had spotted them atop the wall and were making their way over.

"We need to get moving," Vix said as she pushed off and landed in the snow on the other side of the wall. She took a few steps, but didn't hear anything behind her. After being certain that she still had enough open space between her and the trio of undead making slow progress through the shin-deep slush, she turned back to Gemma. "You coming or not?"

"I just..." the girl's voice faded.

Vix tried not to be angry. After all, she couldn't be much more than fifteen years old. Still, the girl had volunteered for this mission, it was a bit too late to fall back.

"I will do this alone if I have to," Vix said with as much calmness as she could muster. "But getting through that big, open parking lot is going to be a pain."

She heard the crunch-squish of the nearest zed and turned to discover that it had gotten closer than she realized. It lurched forward and its hands swiped at her, missing by inches. Too bad for the zombie that it lost its balance and fell face down in the wet snow.

Drawing the heavy fireplace poker that she favored, she drove it through the back of the downed zombie's skull. Planting her foot on its back, she tugged the weapon loose and cocked back for the next one. The swing was a bit low and caught the creature in the side of the neck. The awkwardness of the strike caused her wrists to turn just enough, and she yelped in pain. The poker tumbled from her grip.

Shaking her arms to try and work away the pain, Vix backed up and drew the decorative sword she had taken off the wall of the hotel. One thing about English history, it was chock full of plenty of tales about knights and swords...the bloody things were practically everywhere it seemed. As she was about to take a swing at the still approaching zed with the nasty dent in its neck, a figure flashed by.

Gemma drove the large kitchen knife into the eye of the zombie and the two went to the ground in a heap sending a wave of wet snow out in a big oval. Vix only glanced down as she stepped past to meet the final zombie of the bunch. In an anti-climactic thrust, the sword went all the way through the head and out the other side. The creature fell, taking the weapon with it. Vix's wrist hurt terribly and she was forced to let go.

Flexing her fingers, she retrieved all of her things and helped Gemma to her feet. The girl had a nervous smile on her face that was way too big. All of her teeth showed and she looked almost like she was about to cry again.

"That was a right good thing you did there," Vix complimented. "Though you should give a word of warning when you are gong to barrel past somebody who is about to swing a sword."

"I can't believe I killed it!" Gemma gasped like she had been holding her breath the entire time. "That is the first one I ever did in on my own."

"Wait…you haven't killed so much as one of those things?"

"No…I always ran. I kept waiting for them to chase me or something. I was worried that their slow walk was a trick, and as soon as I came after one…it would run after me and tackle me to the ground."

"Where would you get an idea like that?"

"The pictures. That movie *28 Days Later*—"

"Those weren't really zombies," Vix interrupted as she started across the road. "Those people were infected by monkeys and went raving mad."

"And then there was that show…*Dead Set*…I wonder if Davina finally got it for real?"

Great, Vix sighed inwardly, *I am facing the end of the world with a* Now *magazine junkie.* She reached the middle of the road and looked around. She had to peel her hood back and remove her glasses because the steady, cold rain was making it almost impossible to see. Up one way, she saw a nasty traffic snarl blocking most of the road; down the other were fewer cars...and several dark figures that were moving in their direction.

"What do we do?" Gemma asked as she came up beside Vix.

"We follow Hackwood until we get to War Memorial Park. It is a long bit, but we can hide in the college once we make it," Vix explained.

"But I thought we were going to Wickes?"

"Maybe we are, but in case you haven't noticed, none of the busses or taxis are about. We will be on foot the entire way. This rain is worse than the snow. I don't know about you, but I am already soaked to the skin."

Without another word, Vix crossed the M3 and quickly found herself in the parking lot of a huge fitness center. In one window, a woman stood with her face pressed to the glass, a gruesome rip across her throat giving away the cause of her demise. Her form-fitting exercise clothing still showed off a physique that Vix imagined hadn't seen too many candies or bags of crisps.

Lot of good that was doing her now, Vix thought.

***

"You think old Pitts had the right idea?" Danny stood at the door. Inside the gymnasium were all the women and young children.

"What do you mean?" Jody asked.

"Well...he grabbed his girl and headed for the hills. You think he had a line on what the captain was up to?"

"No...I think he ran because of the immunity thing and not wanting her cut up like sushi so that a bunch of halfwit military and government doctors could try and guess at what made her the way she was. He ran to protect his private piece of ass."

"Not much of a romantic?" Danny scoffed.

"Romance has nothing to do with it," Jody explained. "I am not entirely sure that the captain realized what he had with Slider until recently. The locals acting out gave him an excuse to act. Slider gave him the right weapon."

"So what are we gonna do?"

"Right now we are gonna go inside and get these women on our team," Jody said with a shrug.

"What good will that do us?"

"Don't be so sure," Jody cautioned. "You endanger a mother's child and you better be ready to reap the whirlwind."

Danny followed Jody inside. The first thing that they noticed was the smell. These people hadn't been allowed to wash, and their bathroom facilities consisted of a row of mob buckets behind a few roll-away classroom partitions.

"Holy Je—"

"Stow it!" Jody hissed.

He looked around the room at the faces that were all staring back at him and saw a lot of variations of fear in those faces. However, in a few...he saw something else. Jody Rafe saw anger. Not just the run of the mill public display of outrage and injustice that soldiers had endured over the years when called in to control the sometimes unruly citizens of the United States. Nope, this was the seething hatred that was commonly seen on television when footage of anti-American protests were taking place in countries like Iran, Iraq, and Afghanistan.

"Can I have your attention, ladies?" Jody handed his weapons over to Danny and nodded that he stay put. He walked into the center of the room where these women could easily mob him if they chose to do such a thing. "I realize that you are all probably angry, scared, and confused. I am here to—"

"Where have you taken all of our people?" a woman snapped, cutting Jody off.

He gave her a second look. This room had a wide variety of ladies and young girls. Any of the women deemed fit for service had been plucked from the mob and sent to what was being called "indoctrination" by the captain and Slider. Jody knew better. There seemed to be nothing wrong with this lady. She appeared to be in her mid- to late twenties. She was fairly tall, easily able to look him in the eye without craning her neck which put her a scant few inches under six feet. Most noticeable were her dazzling blue eyes and long blonde hair. She had that girl-next-door pretty in full effect complete with a splash of freckles across the bridge of her nose.

"I'm sorry, I don't know any of your names." Jody turned all his attention to this woman figuring that if she was bold enough to speak out, then she might just be what he needed.

"Selina," she said through clenched teeth. "Now…can we dismiss with the crap, and how about you tell me where my dad and brother are…as well as everybody else?"

"They are safe," Jody started. He had come in with an idea of how he was going to address the crowd but hadn't anticipated a confrontation this quick. "But I won't lie to you…they are not going to be treated fairly and all of you are the leverage that will be used to ensure that they do exactly as they are told."

Gasps and murmurs of dismay circulated throughout the room. All of the emotional outbursts triggered the younger children. In seconds, the room was awash in tears.

"I'm not asking you to trust me." Jody took a step closer to Selina so that only she could hear him. "However, I think I can help. It is gonna be risky, but I don't trust your chances otherwise. I will help, but I need you to keep quiet for now and convince everybody to do as I ask."

"And how do I know this isn't just part of the game?" Selina shot back in a voice just above a whisper.

"Why would I do this? Can you even remotely think of one reason for me to pretend?"

"So what are you planning?"

"Actually…it is still a work in progress," Jody admitted. "But I have a question for you if you don't mind."

"I have alopecia," Selina said and pulled off her wig.

"Is it terminal?"

"Hair loss? Not likely, but if you tell the goon squad that

went through and started picking off every able-bodied person in town that you have terminal cancer…"

Jody was confused. He had no idea what the hell alopecia might be. It sounded terrible, but her comment made it clear that he was missing something.

"Umm…"

"I have a condition that makes my hair fall out. When your soldiers came door to door, I pulled off my wig and told them that I have cancer."

Jody looked at Selina in disbelief. She was a fast thinker and obviously held no love loss for the current regime. She might very well be exactly what he was looking for.

"Can I ask you a question?" Danny leaned forward and whispered.

"Go ahead."

"Does that condition affect you everywhere?" He wiggled his eyebrows and flashed a smile as his eyes travelled down the length of her body.

The slap made a loud echo in the room, causing every head to turn in their direction. All the crying had stopped.

***

Major Wanda Beers stepped out of her tent. The cold was already seeping into her body and that pissed her off to no end. She'd had a sweet deal going when they had happened across the country club. Now, here she was, back to camping out in the elements. Sure, her tent had a woodstove, but that did little more than take the edge off of cold days like today.

She went about the daily business of organizing her camp. She was a little disappointed in her soldiers. A few had gotten themselves killed by being careless. That had done nothing to heighten their vigilance which was how this man Kevin and who knows how many others were able to wage a successful campaign of terrorism against the 371st.

Lately, there had been a few deserters to compound the

problems. This morning's muster had revealed the largest deser-
tion to date. She was starting to reconsider a few of her edicts.
There were two points that seemed to rub the soldiers the wrong
way—the first being the fact that she had forbidden anybody
from 'taking liberties' with one of the original residents of this
compound. Not being too fond of the current trend in music (she
preferred *real* music like the Stones or Pink Floyd), she'd had no
idea who Shari or her bratty little sister had been in the world
before all hell broke loose.

She'd been unimpressed when it was revealed that some
tabloid cover girl was in their midst. However, apparently some
of the men had offered her all sorts of 'perks' in exchange for a
bit of intimacy. The girl had refused...as was her right under
Wanda's rule.

That had been the big surprise. When they'd initially taken
over this location and the current residents had been presented,
Shari and her sister were deemed practically useless. However,
when a possibility had been raised that would involve getting rid
of the retarded girl—*Down's syndrome!* She heard Shari's voice
growl in her mind even now—it was like a switch had been
flipped. Now, Shari was usually one of the first people awake in
the camp. She worked from before sun up and went well after
sunset.

Wanda had forbidden any of the soldiers from forcing their
will on any female. She had been called a lot of things since the
dead began to walk. Most of them were deserved. She didn't really care. However, one thing she would not condone was rape.
That was still an offense punishable by death. When a few of the
troops decided to test that rule and had trapped not only Shari,
but the one named Aleah as well, and had their way forcibly
with the young ladies...Wanda had shown her resolve.

The hangings had been conducted immediately following
the tribunal where two of the men had quickly offered up the
other three members of this little gang of miscreants during tes-
timony in exchange for leniency. The three were declared guilty
and executed. The other two were given leniency. She had them

tossed over the wall with nothing but the clothes on their back.

Yet, there was still the problem of Kevin and his band of terrorists. They seemed to strike at will. Her guards were turning up dead almost every day. Obviously this guy had some serious training. He was managing to slip in, put an arrow through two walking sentries and escape with little trace…in three feet of snow!

She knew that the killings were a single person because of the few clues they had managed to glean. But it was the torching of the huge golf club's main building that made her realize that she was dealing with a well-organized group. The thing was, up to that point, she had been willing to offer the man amnesty. He obviously had a good head on his shoulders. He was a definite step above the normal ground-pounders under her command. However, now she just wanted his head. He was too dangerous to keep alive.

She had eavesdropped on a few of the conversations with the members of his group that she had, for all intents and purposes, captured and conscripted. They spoke of this Kevin Dreon person like he was some sort of perfect combination of genius, saint, and messiah. A person like that would eventually be a threat to her authority.

Walking through the camp, she could feel the tension. It was bad enough that she was trying to ensure the survival of all of these ungrateful bastards…but now the insubordination was something she was going to have to deal with directly. Her attempt to lure this Kevin in to her grasp by staging the execution of the young lady with *Down's syndrome* had failed to produce; further proof that this individual was savvy and a force to be dealt with as soon as possible.

"Excuse me, Major Beers?" a female voice interrupted her mental ranting.

"What is it?" she snapped as she turned to face the person bold enough to address her before her morning cup of coffee. It was that damned pop star.

"I was told that my rations are being cut?"

"You don't eat all your food," Wanda said with an indifferent shrug. "In case you haven't noticed...food is in short supply. Especially after that latest stunt by your beloved little friend, Kevin. Most of the stores that *you* put away were destroyed in that fire in case you don't remember. You are now relying on *our* stores for your meals and there isn't enough to waste."

"But I am only taking what everybody else is allowed...no more and no less."

"And you aren't eating it all."

"Because you completely cut Valarie off from the food line! We had a deal. You said that I could give her mine."

"Aren't you supposed to be on the wood cutting detail?"

"We had a deal!"

"There is a line in one of the *Star Wars* movies...not those horrendous so-called prequels, but the originals. I think it was Darth Vader who said, 'Pray I don't alter it further.' So get your skinny little ass back to work before I throw both of you over the wall," Wanda growled.

"He's gonna beat you, ya know," Shari whispered just loud enough to be heard. Whether on purpose or not, it still earned her a backhanded slap that sent her to the ground.

Wanda stood over the supposed pop star—she'd heard her singing to that damn retarded girl and hadn't been impressed— with clenched fists. She was on the verge of making an example of this one once and for all. The girl was sprawled on the frozen ground with a trickle of blood coming from the corner of her mouth. She was staring up with a defiant glare sparking with tears.

Several thoughts crossed her mind as the two looked deep into each other's eyes. She could give this one to the men. The rationale was simple: she was a way to reclaim the loyalty of her troops. Also, many of her men and women had expressed discomfort at the crazed ramblings of the retarded girl. She supposedly saw ghosts, she talked to thin air, and she had a serious problem with her sanitary habits. Tossing that one over the wall would ease a lot of minds.

"Kevin," Shari whispered.

Wanda waited. Obviously the girl had another smartass comment to make about how this man would ride down from the clouds in a flaming chariot and save the world...or at least her and her friends. *What the...?* She thought as she realized that the girl was no longer looking at her. Glancing over her shoulder, Wanda couldn't believe what she was seeing.

Coming through the camp was a man with his hands laced behind his head. Obviously, according to Shari's reaction, this was the elusive Kevin. She'd expected...more.

9

Surviving Ain't Livin'

Dr. Zahn sat beside me in the cat as we waited for Jon to come back out of the woods from his bathroom break. I could tell for a while that she'd had something on her mind. I figured the best way to find out was to just ask.

"What?" I let that one word hang in the air. I knew the doctor well enough to know that she was not one for small talk.

"I killed that poor little girl," Dr. Zahn whispered. "And before you start running at the mouth about all the things I've done, or how I shouldn't have simply known or whatever else you all have been yammering on about...I specialized in infectious diseases for almost a decade. I had a position with the CDC in the Eighties and saw it all. Aids. Ebola. Things that would scare you into taking full body dips in anti-bacterial liquid."

"Okay," I said after she sat quiet for a second, "but this isn't like anything you've ever seen."

"Still, there are simple rules that you *always* follow."

"So...like you told me not so long ago...don't make the same mistake twice."

"It's not that—" she started, but Jon running for us through the snow ended that conversation in a hurry.

He kept looking over his shoulder as he ran. I'd never seen him so visibly shook. Whatever it was, it was bad. And then I saw them. Wolves.

We'd dealt with them before and they were just disturbing. It wasn't that they were super fast or anything. It all boiled down to the eyes and the creepy groan they managed to produce that

153

was like nothing I'd ever heard before and after that one time, hoped to never hear again.

I climbed into the driver's seat and turned the key. Popping into gear, I got us rolling as Jon came up alongside. The doctor opened the door and held out a hand. She recoiled so fast that she almost ended up in my seat.

"Dammit!" the doctor cursed. I glanced over as Jon climbed in…with a huge rip in his hand.

"Just drive," the ever-stalwart Marine snapped (I will never say former because Jon still serves as a Marine despite the lack of any formal government to answer to any longer).

I kept my focus forward because I couldn't look him in the eyes. I didn't want to ask. I didn't need to.

As we continued down the general direction of the road— basically I drove between the canopies of frosted pine trees that bordered the path—Jon worked at cleaning and bandaging his hand with the basic first aid gear that he had obviously had the foresight to put behind the seat. I did mentally slap my forehead when he pulled the metal box out because something so obvious had once again slipped my mind.

I drove for an hour before the doctor nudged me. Jon was leaning against the door with his eyes closed. I pulled the big knife from my belt and handed it over. Doctor Zahn accepted it like it might turn into a snake and bite her.

"Don't be so hasty," Jon said. He opened his eyes and shot a sideways glance at the two of us.

I wanted to be relieved. So far there was no sign of the black squiggles. That didn't necessarily mean that we were out of the woods yet, so to speak. It was encouraging, but there was still the possibility that he could be infected. Maybe a bite from a wolf or dog took longer to cause a person to change. We really didn't have any idea.

"How are you feeling, Jon?" Dr. Zahn asked.

"I feel like rancid oil is running through my veins and my stomach is doing flips, but other than that…"

"I need you to do me a favor."

"Sure thing, Doc."

"I need you to stay awake."

"Okay."

"And I need you to keep your eyes open so I can watch you. Since that is the most definite way we have of knowing your condition, I will monitor you that way."

It took over two hours to leave the wolves behind to the point of not being able to see them. That only meant we had put distance between us. If wolf zombies were anything like their human counterparts—and we have no reason to think otherwise—once they get on a trail, they are relentless until something distracts them.

As it started to get darker, I kept glancing at Jon for directions. He simply sat silently staring straight ahead.

"I am assuming that you will tell me if and when I need to turn," I finally said.

"Of course," was Jon's only reply.

We drove for about ten more minutes when Jon pointed to a narrow opening in the trees on the right hand side of the road. I turned and began a slow climb.

"There are a handful of trailer homes coming up," Jon said. "We never stayed in any, so just pull into the first one. We can secure it and stay the night. We will have to finish this in the morning. It isn't far, but I don't want to make this last little leg in the dark. Up ahead is where we saw most of the zombie activity."

The first trailer we came to was set back from the road through a single row of scraggly looking pine trees. I pulled into the first opening I found and parked beside the partially collapsed fence that looked like it had been hit by something moving fast the way it was all twisted and mangled.

"Let me take point going in," Jon said.

I didn't see any reason to argue. After all, he was already bitten. If he was infected, another bite would not make it any worse. If he was immune…well, pretty much the same logic.

We climbed the cinder block stairs and stood on the three-quarter inch plywood square that acted as a porch. I was trying my best not to judge…but this was almost too stereotypical. Jon tried the knob at the top of the stairs. It opened and released a rolling wave of stench that made me think of what shoving my face in a dirty cat box might smell like.

I lit a torch and handed it to Jon so that he could get a better look. It seems that the windows were covered in aluminum foil. Jon only took one step in before backing out in a hurry. I had my machete in my hand and quickly stepped in front of Dr. Zahn.

"Don't bother," Jon said as he turned his back to the open door. "This was a meth lab. There is nothing moving inside."

We moved on to the next trailer. This one was a double-wide with no fence. As far as trailers went, this one looked okay. In fact, whoever lived here had put a lot of work into making it look like an actual house. The contrasts were so jarring that I almost missed the hand reaching out from the snow between the screened in porch and the big bush just beside it.

I brought my machete up, but never had the chance to swing as Dr. Zahn drove a wicked looking Buck knife into the snow-crusted face that rose from the powder in a slow motion eruption. I gave her a sideways glance. She simply shrugged and accepted my invitation for her to enter ahead of me.

A walk through revealed that the place was empty inside of anything that might want to bite our faces off. The rest of the night was dull. I did my best to relish the fact that the only problem we faced was staying warm enough. The temperatures plunged as it got dark and I would guess that it went well below zero.

The three of us barricaded the two doors and chose to rely on noise to wake us in the unlikely event that zombies showed up. We huddled under every single blanket and comforter while making a bit of a Dr. Zahn sandwich to maximize warmth from our bodies. It was still freezing. As I drifted off to sleep, I was reminded of a story by Jack London about a guy in the frozen wastes who dies of hypothermia.

Sweet dreams.

***

I woke to Jon shaking me. Dr. Zahn was already on her feet and I could see thick clouds of steam coming from their mouths and nostrils. The cold was so harsh that it made my face sting as soon as I came out from under the covers.

"Take this," Jon said, handing me a strip of a blanket that he had cut into wide strips. "Put this over your mouth and nose. It will make breathing easier."

I shrugged and did as I was told, but I also felt a bit of relief when I saw that he had clear eyes. Jon certainly knew more about survival that somebody like me. My idea of roughing it up until this whole zombie thing had consisted of fixing the non-microwavable macaroni and cheese.

"The one thing we have on our side is that there is no measurable wind." Jon headed for the door. When he opened it, a dazzling white light illuminated him like he was some sort of warrior angel come to lead us to salvation. "We should be at the camp within an hour or two."

We headed out in the Snowcat after a rather unsettling moment where it looked like the vehicle was not going to start. Did I mention that it was freezing cold?

Walking on the snow, you could actually stand on the surface of it and not plunge through it if you stepped carefully. When you did break through, it was accompanied by a loud crack that echoed in the deathly silent (no pun intended) forest. It took me a few seconds to realize how quiet it was before I brought it to Jon's attention.

"None of the snow is melting or falling off the branches for one. I will say this…if it warms up any, it could get interesting."

"How so?"

"If it keeps thawing and refreezing, not only will everything be a sheet of solid ice, but the snow will start to cascade down the branches and eventually the lower ones will become overburdened. This place will be a symphony of breaking wood."

We made the trip in silence. I was fascinated by one field in particular that we passed by. It was like a zombie farm. I counted a dozen of the things standing in waist-deep snow. They were stuck, but strangely not frozen solid. I know this because their arms were very animated as we passed by. They reached, and I bet if it were not for the growl of the engine on the cat, I would have heard them making their assorted zombie noises.

We turned down a long road with a deep ditch on either side. In the distance, I could see an obviously hastily erected fence. It was a mix of corrugated steel, chain-link, wooden slats, and aluminum siding all topped with coils of razor wire. What I didn't see was any signs of life. As loud as the Snowcat is, the inhabitants of that compound would have heard us coming several minutes before we even came into sight of their location.

When we pulled in and shut down, I looked to Jon for an indication of what to do. He seemed to be scanning the area with an abnormally—even for him—intense gaze.

"Did we come here to look at a fence?" Dr. Zahn finally broke the silence.

Jon said nothing, but he opened his door and climbed out while simultaneously allowing a painfully cold wave of air to fill the cab and ensure that neither the doctor nor I would simply sit in its relative warmth while he tromped around in the ice-crusted snow. I did a quick self-inspection of my gear. I didn't know what I was feeling exactly, but it wasn't anything good.

"Hello inside!" Jon called. Not exactly subtle, but I was nit-picking. Considering the fact that we'd driven here in the Snowcat and probably activated or re-directed every stationary zombie for miles, his little yell was probably not making things worse.

I hopped from the cab. That was my first mistake. I guess I really haven't been out much. That is my best excuse when it comes to what is a complete ignoring of common sense. I promptly sunk up to my thighs in the snow. Looking around, I realized that the Snowcat had plowed its way to where we were currently parked. I also noticed that we had driven in the tracks made the last time Jon had come this way. At the nose of the cat was a mound of snow that rose about three or four feet above my head.

"Took us three days to make it this far last time," Jon said with a smirk as I looked around for anything that could extricate me from my current situation. "Then we had to shovel our way to their wall. They'd made a path, but it was mostly filled in when we arrived. Wasn't sure if we were gonna find anybody alive."

"So what led you here?" Dr. Zahn asked. "This is obviously off the beaten path."

"Jesus saw a flare. The only problem we had with that was that once we got here, nobody admitted to firing one. We talked to everybody that was able to speak...but nobody owned up to it."

"And that doesn't seem a little weird to you?" I asked as I flopped down on my belly and tried to wiggle my way across the snow.

"Of course it does." Jon reached the edge of the unpacked snow and offered his hand to help pull me across. "But I stopped trying to figure out everything that *seems* weird to me a few months ago."

"Boy howdy," Dr. Zahn chimed in.

Boy howdy? What the hell was that about?

"And did they completely ignore your attempts to make contact with them when you arrived that first time?" I tumbled off the snow bank and came to a less than graceful and some-what painful stop against the rear treads of the Snowcat.

"Actually...no." I could hear the concern in Jon's voice, but there was something else that I couldn't quite identify.

"Maybe they're all dead," Dr. Zahn offered.

She wasn't being callous. Actually, the best way I could put it was that she was finally being 'Dr. Zahn' again instead of the strange person who had been walking around in a funky haze since Teresa and Jamie's death.

"So we are going to have to climb over," Jon said with a

sigh. "The best place is just around the corner. See that tree?" He pointed.

"I don't think I've climbed a tree since before you were born," Dr. Zahn grumped.

For some reason, that tickled my funny bone. It was something that I suddenly realized had been completely absent from my life these past several months—those spontaneous moments when you find something to be the most hilarious thing in the world. It is made worse by those around you who do not get in the slightest what you find so damned funny. Then, the harder you try to stifle the laugh, the worse it gets. Pretty soon your eyes are tearing up and you are laughing like a lunatic with no idea if you will ever be able to stop.

"Are you quite finished?" Dr. Zahn said as I wiped away the last of the tears in my eyes with my sleeves.

"I think so," I managed. I was so out of breath that I really have no idea if she understood the words as much as just picked up on the sentiment.

We made our way to the corner…and that was where we encountered our first 'surprise.'

"Holy Jesus," Dr. Zahn gasped.

I felt my stomach shift just a bit and my knees give way until I somehow ended up on my butt in the snow beside the almost still defined trail. It took my brain a few moments to truly untangle the image and let me know what it was that I was looking at.

My best guess is that she could not have been any older than Thalia—five or six years old. She was leaning against the fence. More accurately, she was frozen *to* the fence. Somebody had taken the time place her exactly as we found her.

From just below her neck, there was nothing. Not a speck of flesh could be found on her frame—and that is *all* that was left…her frame. They had left the head untouched. So that one cold, dead eye still stared out at the world. She wasn't alone. Beside her were seven others, all of varying ages. Each one had been stripped of every speck from the neck down, but for some reason, they'd left the heads.

Dr. Zahn pushed past me and knelt beside the first figure. She pulled something from her pocket and began to poke and inspect in a way that was far too clinical for me. I wanted to scream.

"They were boiled," Dr. Zahn said, not looking away as she continued to inspect the collection.

That was the name my mind could handle referring to this group of individuals. They would now be etched forever more as 'The Collection.'

"How do you know?" Glad to see Jon was still capable of forming words. I was just staring like an idiot.

"The bones are cracked and brittle." Dr. Zahn duck walked to the next one. "And if you look close enough, you can still see filaments of tissue. But for the most part, these people have been stripped clean of all the juicy bits."

Now I wanted to be sick.

"So why not the heads?"

"Who knows," Dr. Zahn said with an absentmindedness that let me know she was now fully engrossed in her inspection or autopsy, or whatever the hell you would call it.

"I never even stopped to ask," Jon whispered.

"Ask?" I tore my vision away from the doctor and tried to focus on Jon.

"There were these big metal garbage cans—"

A flood of images filled my mind so quickly that I couldn't shuffle them off to a nice dark place where they would only be able to torment me in my sleep. I fell on my side and threw up.

When I was finished, I looked up to see the doctor had moved down the line. Jon was at her heels and they were talking in low tones. I was too shook up to care. And now I understood the haunted look in Jesus' face. Now I realized why he did not want to ever see this place again. If this was what waited for us outside the compound…what in God's name was on the inside. What could be so horrifying that men like Jake and Jesus would make excuses in order not to have to return?

"We better get inside," Jon said with obvious hesitation.

"So why would they freeze them to the fence?" Dr. Zahn made her way back to us, doing her best to stay on the narrow trail of packed snow. "This is very deliberate. They sat each of these bodies here and then, by the looks of it, poured water on them to freeze them in place."

"Nothing about the fact that they left the entire head intact?" I gasped. "You fixate on them being frozen in place...not the fact that we have a half a dozen skeletons with heads staring out at us?"

"I agree that is peculiar," Dr. Zahn spoke in a level tone. "However, that can be attributed to a number of possible reasons."

"Such as?" I challenged.

"They wanted to remember the sacrifice these people made or simply the fact that there is little to be gained from eating a person's face. Or perhaps they were aware of the possibility of kuru."

"What the hell is kuru?" I wasn't sure I wanted the answer.

"Basically it is like mad cow...but in humans. It comes from eating the brain or spinal material of a human being."

Dr. Zahn said that with such matter-of-factness that I was stunned into shutting my mouth and simply going along. I followed like a scolded child as Jon climbed up onto a low hanging branch. I watched his face, but he remained as grim as always when he was doing anything that didn't revolve around Sunshine.

That got me to thinking. It was obvious that the two were a couple, so why was he so set on trying to act otherwise? That was something I would have to find out later. And now that he'd been bitten, what could that do to a new relationship. So many questions about what many would consider meaningless drivel.

I glanced at the doctor who was eyeing the tree like it was swarming with cobras...or zombies. She caught me looking at her and scowled.

"You go on up," she said with a curt nod. "I will require the two of you to pull me up as I will absolutely not be climbing that thing."

"You ain't that heavy, Doc," Jon called down.

"I would prefer two sets of hands if you don't mind," she retorted with an icy glare that held its own against the temperature that was providing us with this frozen landscape.

I grabbed the lowest branch and slung my leg up. Just as I did, a dry mewling sound came from the nearby pines. They shook a bit just before an elderly woman and young child of about four or five stumbled out into the open. The elderly lady took a tumble but wasn't quite heavy enough to break the icy crust that made up the top layer of the snow. The child stopped, glancing down at the struggling figure beside it that now fought for purchase and managed to punch one frail arm through the snow. That only made the situation worse for the pathetic creature as its left arm vanished up to the shoulder.

"I got this," Jon called out as he swung his crossbow up into his hands. His shot was true and literally vanished into the crown of the woman's skull. Not even the feather quarrel remained in sight.

The child looked up. I couldn't say for certain, but it looked as if it might actually be angry. It wasn't so much that the face changed. It remained slack just as all the other zombies that I'd ever seen. It was something around the eyes; almost as if they narrowed or squinted. I had to be imagining things and chalked it up to how few child zombies I'd actually encountered.

And then something strange happened. That is a statement I can make in a world where the dead walk and eat the living, so...

The child took a step back. It watched us intently, cocking its head from side to side a few times as if trying to consider exactly what we might be. In between those jerky head movements, it would glance at the downed woman. For some reason, I had a gut feeling that the woman must be this little boy's grandmother. For the first time ever, a zombie was retreating. It slipped back into the trees and, for a few seconds, we could hear it moving away through the woods.

"Okay..." I was at a loss.

"Have you seen anything like this in your travels out and about?" Dr. Zahn asked, looking up at Jon with a raised eyebrow.

"We don't run into many of the little ones," Jon admitted. "But I have to be perfectly honest when I say that we don't usually wait for them to get close enough for us to do any in depth studies."

"This wouldn't require too much depth," I muttered. "The damn thing walked away."

"And was giving us the zombie version of the stink eye," Jon added. At any other time, that comment might have elicited a few chuckles, but not after what we'd just witnessed.

"I really wish I had a research facility," Dr. Zahn grumbled.

"As much as I'd like to have an open forum about what we all saw, we need to get over the fence and inside this place."

Maybe it was me, but I was having a real problem with the fact that we'd been talking in conversational tones—which, these days when you are out in the open where the danger of zombies is so great, is almost like yelling—and nobody had come to investigate. That did not bode well for the inhabitants of this compound.

Jon and I pulled the doctor up. Next, Jon inched out along the branch and then swung over and dropped to the ground with a crunch as he plunged through the virgin snow. I went next and had barely hit the ground when the mixture of smells hit me in the gut.

"Look out!" Jon hissed as he shoved me out of the way. Doctor Zahn landed rather unceremoniously beside me. She was in the seated position and so only her head and the tops of her shoulders were visible above the snow.

"My goodness." The doctor squeezed her eyes shut tight and I heard her swallow.

"It's gotten worse." That was all Jon said as he headed towards the cluster of buildings that the barrier had encompassed.

I helped Dr. Zahn to her feet and followed. Every single step seemed to be a test of my resolve. I had no idea what could be waiting, but after what I'd already seen, plus the swirling array of various smells that seemed to lurk in the wind, I had absolutely no doubt that this was going to be unpleasant.

A sound that could have been a moan or a cry came from up ahead. Jon began to wade through the snow as quickly as he could. For some strange reason that I could not begin to explain, seeing him move in what was little more than slow-motion made me think of the opening credits of *Baywatch*. The wave of snow that was rolling off of him as he plunged forward and the fact that he was moving so slow had triggered this odd memory comparison, and now I was helpless to clear it from my head. It was as if my brain was already doing everything possible to minimize what I was about to experience.

I rounded the corner and collided with the back of Jon. Further proof of just how strong he was in comparison to basically everybody, he didn't even register the impact. I, on the other hand, landed on my ass.

"Hey there," Jon said in as soft a voice as I'd ever heard from him. He was already crouching down. That was the only way I was able to see the little girl standing in the much-too-dark doorway.

I had to actually think for a moment to realize that she was the spitting image of the girl frozen to the fence outside this place. The resemblance was made even more frightening when my brain allowed me to process just how terrible *this* child looked. Her face was so drawn that it would be easy to think that this child was dead. The only thing that gave hint that she was among the living were the eyes. Besides the fact that they lacked the white film and black tracers…zombies don't cry.

"Get out of the way, Steven," Dr. Zahn hissed as she pushed past not only me, but Jon as well.

"Can you speak, child?" The doctor had already halved the distance between us and the child in the doorway before I could get to my feet. Her voice had changed into something that was completely foreign sounding to me having been around Dr.

Francis Zahn for as long as I had. Sweet. Warm. Grandmotherly.

The child cast a look over her shoulder before taking two steps forward. As of yet, I hadn't heard a sound from inside that building. In fact, other than that one cry, I hadn't heard any sounds at all from inside this compound.

"Mommy…m-m-mommy can't walk," the little girl rasped. Had I not been staring directly at her, I would have thought that voice came from some chain-smoking truck driver of a woman. It certainly did not fit this wisp of a child standing before me.

"Is there anybody in there besides your mommy?" Jon asked.

Dr. Zahn's head whipped around like an angry snake. "You keep your eyes open for trouble and your mouth shut, Marine. From here on, this is *my* mission and *I* will ask the questions that need asking."

It was probably instinctive, but Jon snapped to attention and gave a slight nod of his head in acknowledgement. Just that quick, I watched the relationship between these two people transform. Suddenly, she was a military officer and he was an enlisted man.

"How many people are still inside, child?" Dr. Zahn asked. Just that quick, she was everybody's sweet old grandmother.

The child seemed to consider the question for a few seconds before holding up seven fingers. She looked over her shoulder again, and then extended one more finger, then another.

"Nine?" Dr. Zahn asked.

The little girl nodded.

"And do any of them have something wrong with their eyes?" By now, Dr. Zahn was only a few steps away from the child. I could tell by the way her head was moving that she was trying to crane her neck enough to get a better look inside.

The little girl nodded. Once more she looked over her shoulder. When she looked back, her expression had changed. I could see what looked to me like pain.

"Mommy promised me that she would not be like daddy…she lied."

166

Jon and I stepped up behind the doctor. The closeness to that doorway did almost nothing to improve our ability to see. It was still so dark that we could not even make out shapes.

And then the upper torso of a woman pulled herself into view. There was no mistaking that this woman was the child's mother. The blonde hair was the easiest thing to lock onto, but even their faces were so similar that it left no doubt.

"Mommy...Mister Patton says that you are supposed to stay tied up," the little girl said. Her voice had a scolding tone to it that reminded me of how Thalia spoke to Buster when she had a potty accident indoors.

The creeper raised its head and regarded the child standing a few feet away. After what I'd seen with that child-zombie outside the gate, I almost expected it to ignore the little girl and come after us. It didn't.

One hand reached out and snagged an ankle. With a tug, the child fell on to her back. Both Jon and I leapt forward with blades drawn. I actually got the inside track and had my heavy machete raised when the child screamed.

"Don't hurt my mommy!"

That threw me off and I hesitated. Jon didn't. His blade crashed down, splitting the skull open. The legless creeper flopped to the ground, its open mouth dangerously close to the leg of the girl. I came in with the finishing stroke. Dr. Zahn shoved me aside and scooped the girl into her arms. Unfortunately for the doc, the little girl wasn't having any of it.

"Let go of me!" she slapped Dr. Zahn and began to thrash about, her tiny balled fists raining blows on her captor.

"Hey—" Jon barked, but I cut him off.

"We got trouble!" I backed away from where I had taken position in the doorway.

In the shadows, I could make out five figures coming towards me. I looked over my shoulder at Dr. Zahn who had her hands full trying to get the child under control. For somebody so visibly malnourished, she had a lot of fight in her.

Jon and I took up a position on either side of the doorway

and waited. The first figure to step through was so heavily bundled that it was impossible to tell if it was a male or a female. I was closest and stepped into my swing.

The howl of pain that followed was answered by a shriek from the little girl. I almost broke my wrists trying to pull up on my second swing aimed at the shrouded head of the next figure that staggered through the door.

"Please," a voice whispered from the darkness, "we aren't infected. The infected ones are tied up inside."

"They killed my mommy, Mister Patton!" the girl bawled. "The bad man chopped her."

"But she..." I glanced down at the remains of the child's mother.

"She was infected," the man managed to say through a lung-rending cough.

I looked down at the blood pooling around the head of the person I had just cleaved. The child's mother might have been a zombie, but zombies didn't really bleed. Not like this.

I heard something change in the struggle behind me between the doctor and the little girl. Dr. Zahn had her arm around the girl's neck from behind. It reminded me of a sleeper hold that you might see on pro wrestling. However, unlike the dramatized version for entertainment purposes, this didn't take more than a few seconds. The child slumped and Dr. Zahn laid her down in a clear patch of snow.

"Each of you needs to step into the light," Dr. Zahn ordered. "And you two, as soon as these people are all out, go in and finish off whatever is inside."

As each individual stepped out, the only thing that came to mind was stories that my grandfather used to tell. He had been in the US Army during World War Two and served in the 6th Armored Division. He was one of the men present at the liberation of the Nazi Buchenwald prison camp. The descriptions of some of the things he saw just did not seem possible. I'd always felt that perhaps he had exaggerated. When those five people stepped out into the light...I suddenly believed that perhaps he had cleaned it up for me.

I didn't need to see what was or was not under the layers of clothing. What I could see of their faces told me more than I wanted to know. It was like seeing flesh-toned human skulls staring back at me. The mouths were a mass of scabs and sores at each end and it looked visibly painful when the man, obviously Mr. Patton, spoke. It was almost as if you could see the skin of his lips rip and tear with each word.

"There are three inside," Mr. Patton managed. "One...Kelli Scott...she was immune...but passed in the night. She's one of *them* now."

I followed Jon inside. At that point, I thought I'd seen all the horror there was to see. Hanging from the rafters was a body. Or, more accurately, what was left. With a burlap sack or something over the head, you could not see the face, but this woman had been almost entirely stripped of every ounce of flesh. One arm remained untouched from the elbow on down. I guess they didn't have to worry much about spoilage due to the cold, so they simply left it hanging and cut away pieces as needed. A large metal barrel was off to the side. I imagine that would be what they would boil the rest off at the end when nothing more could be carved away.

Next to that barrel was another. It sat on embers and steam rose from it, swirling around the covered head that bobbed on the surface. That must have been the last person to serve the masses. The smell coming from the bubbling barrel was very upsetting. It was strangely reminiscent of beef stew. The fact that my mouth began to water brought on a merciful sensation of nausea.

I didn't wait for Jon to say anything. I planted my foot against the barrel and pushed it over. The contents spilled out in a chunky rush that was made all the more disturbing due to the poor light given by the barely glowing embers of the fire that I'd kicked it off of.

He went over to a far corner and I soon heard the telltale sounds of heads being cleaved. It was over in seconds, but it would haunt me for however long I had left on this world. Once we were finished, I could not get out of that place quick enough.

Dr. Zahn had the five survivors sitting in a row as she went down the line giving them whatever sort of checkup that she deemed necessary. I kept finding my eyes draw to the little figure curled up in the fetal position at the feet of Mr. Patton. I tried to imagine what had led these people to this fate. I tried to understand what god could allow this child to endure what she had while Thalia lived in relative luxury by comparison. My brain sped through all the horrible events that my little Thalia had survived and kept returning to the fact that no matter how bad it had gotten for us...it had been infinitely worse for these people...for that child.

Suddenly, all I wanted to do was get home.

10

A Geek Reunion

Kevin knelt in the snow and looked up at the woman. Her close-cropped coif did nothing to lessen her beauty. The glints of silver sparkled like tiny filaments of precious metal against the fine black hairs. Her eyes were a dark brown, so dark they almost appeared black. Right now, those eyes were staring down at him with a curious mix of contempt and curiosity.

"All the stories…and this is the infamous Kevin Dreon?" she mumbled. "I half-expected Arnold, Bruce, or Sly to appear…and instead, I get a reject from *Revenge of the Nerds*."

"And you must be the infamous Major Wanda Beers." Kevin saw a flash of surprise in her eyes. "Oh yes…I know all about you. How you have gone against your sworn oath to protect and defend. How you are now nothing more than an armed mob, looting and enslaving. I also—"

The boot to the gut caused Kevin to exhale in a great 'woof' of air. He doubled over, his face resting on the cold, hard snow.

"Kevin!" a familiar voice cried.

He turned his head to the right to see Shari looking at him with tears in her eyes. A trickle of blood was a bright red and smeared across her chin.

"Hey there," Kevin managed. "Sorry I took so long."

"We can save all these happy reunion moments for another time," Wanda barked. "Get this one to my tent, and as for the girl, I've had about enough of her and the retard. If she wants to care for that useless burden, cuff 'em together. We roll out of here in two days. We'll see how much she sticks to her guns when we get out on the road."

Hands grabbed him under the arms and yanked Kevin to his feet. The first shove in the middle of his back sent him face down into the snow once again. He was escorted across the camp to the largest tent and shoved inside.

"Leave us," the major said with a wave. "Spread the word to the camp that we will be rolling out at sunrise the day after to-morrow."

The two escorts nodded and ducked out of the tent, leaving him standing just inside the entrance. Kevin looked around and noticed, to his surprise, that there was little in the way of luxury here. He half expected to find a collection of trinkets and such. At the least, he figured that the major would have more than a government-issue cot to sleep on.

"So, you have heard about me." The major leaned back in her chair and swung her feet up onto the desk. "That is interest-ing. That must mean Willa is still out there."

"I don't—" Kevin started, but the major was out of her chair like a cat and standing over him with clenched fists. He didn't quite understand how he had ended up on his back, but the dull ache on the side of his face told him all he needed to know.

"Do not play me for a fool," Major Beers spat. "I know very well that she has been out there hounding me with her useless band of castoff bitches."

"So what do you hope to gain by all this?" Kevin asked as he scooted back far enough to allow himself to sit up.

"Gain?" the major laughed and returned to her desk. "This is not about gain…it is about survival."

"At the cost of all those you come across?"

"You aren't stupid, we already know that much. But are you so naïve to think that survival can come without a price?"

"I don't know…we were doing pretty good until you showed up and raided us," Kevin said with a shrug.

"Is that right?" the major laughed. Pulling a bottle from her desk she twisted the cap and took a drink before offering it to Kevin who shook his head in refusal. "Just take a drink, Kevin.

We have some things to discuss, and maybe it will be helpful if you relax."

Kevin stood up and accepted the bottle of vodka. He took a sip and tried unsuccessfully not to choke. He handed the bottle back and took a seat after the major gave a nod.

"So…you say you were doing okay until we came along?"

Kevin nodded.

"But when we arrived, you had four women, a retard, and a gimpy teenaged boy holding down your stronghold."

"Actually, there was another man and his daughter—" Kevin began, only to be cut off again.

"Paul James and his useless daughter Mary? Mine. I sent them in search of you. Although I did not know who you were at the time. I had been made aware of your presence and determined that you might be a possible asset."

"So I didn't just leave *five* women," Kevin stressed the word 'five' to include Valarie. He struggled to push his concern for her down for the time being. As things stood, he was currently not bound, cuffed, or imprisoned. In his current state, he still had the opportunity to help his group.

"Let's not play with semantics." Major Beers waved a dismissive hand. "The fact is, you had one of the most precious commodities in your care if what I've been told is correct. Since you are alone, I will assume that you have either foolishly squandered that resource, or this doctor is still at large."

"Peter is dead," Kevin said flatly.

"Please tell me he did not perish in your foolish mission to acquire medication for the retard."

"She suffers from Down's syndrome," Kevin bristled. "And I would expect you to be more sensitive to the words you use."

"And why is that?" Major Beers raised an eyebrow, the look on her face was that of an obvious challenge.

"I don't know…but I'm guessing that if I started referring to you as a nigger, you might get just a touch upset."

"It's a word," Major Beers said with a shrug. "And you might use chink, slope, or slant if you want to include my mother's side of the family."

"And none of that bothers you?" Kevin asked, genuinely curious.

"It did before the dead started getting up and wiping everybody out. Now…well, I guess I have bigger concerns."

"Such as?"

"You know," the major rose from her seat and walked around to sit on the corner of the desk almost on top of Kevin, "for somebody who is supposed to be so smart, you are kind of an idiot."

Kevin sat silently. He'd said enough to get her going. He didn't want to give away anything. He was aching to ask about Aleah and Heather. Hell, he was even curious about Erin and Matt, but if he showed any sort of emotion, he was almost certain that this Major Wanda Beers would zero in on it and use it against him.

"All I care about now is staying alive. To do that, I've had to make choices. You can't possibly understand—" This time it was Kevin's turn to cut *her* off.

"You are pillaging folks who have struggled to carve out their own way and pressed people into service. You don't care about anybody or anything except wielding power over others. As for what I understand…I have fought from day one to survive. Along the way, I have met a few people that joined up and came along. At some point, I was made their leader, but not because I threatened or hurt others."

"Is that right?" The major leaned forward into Kevin's face. Her breath was tinged with a mix of the vodka and the funk of no recent applications of any sort of oral hygiene. Kevin wrinkled his nose, not caring if she was offended or angered. Apparently she either didn't notice, or chose to ignore him. She continued in a dangerous whisper. "Nobody has survived this long without having to do something bad. So why don't you stop sitting there like you don't have any blood on your hands."

Kevin remained silent.

"C'mon, Kevin," the major urged. "You are one of those zombie geeks. You saw the movies and played the video games.

How many people did you meet and supposedly put out of their misery? And how long after did it take you to discover that some folks are immune?"

Kevin felt all the blood leave his face. The major smiled, reading his expression perfectly. She scooted off the desk and returned to her chair. "So who was it? Friend? Relative? Who did you kill and then discover that you might have committed murder?"

"Actually..." Kevin let the word hang for a few seconds while he warred with what to say and how much to reveal. "It was somebody that I didn't kill."

"Go on?" the major urged after Kevin remained silent for a while.

Kevin related bits and pieces of what happened to Cary at the truck stop. It had barely been just over half a year since that day...but it seemed like an eternity.

"So where is he now?"

"Same place a lot of folks are," Kevin answered with a shrug. "And the law of averages says that we will all end up that way."

"So why fight it?" Major Beers asked, seemingly interested in Kevin's answer.

"That is a question I don't have an answer for," Kevin replied.

"So then why are you so dead set against me and what I do if all I am trying to do is ensure that I don't end up succumbing to this law of averages?"

"Because you are using innocent people to pave your way."

"There are no more innocent people," the major snapped.

"What about Valarie?" Kevin shot back. He hadn't wanted to allow any of his personal feelings to be used against those he cared for, but what he'd seen so far in regards to how Valarie was being treated left him feeling like he really had nothing to lose here on this one.

"Why don't you tell me why the re—" The major stopped and gave a slight nod of deference. "Why is that young lady so important to you?"

"Let's not pretend that you care about me, or that I'm gonna just open up my heart to you if you talk nice."

"So what would you rather I do? Torture? Maybe haul your friends out one at a time and have you watch while terrible pain is inflicted on each one?" Major Beers got up and walked to the tent flap. "Bring me the retard and the pop star," she called. Turning back to Kevin she gave a little shrug. "Sorry, they wouldn't know who I was talking about otherwise."

Kevin sat quietly and waited. He had no idea what to expect when he saw Valarie. Shari had already seen him, so that part was no surprise, but Valarie was a wild card draw. He didn't have to wait for long.

"...but Kevin just came to me last night and told me that he was sorry he missed my birthday, and he couldn't make it for dinner." Valarie walked into the tent speaking very matter-of-factly to Shari who was handcuffed to her.

"Valarie?" Kevin glanced at the major as he made a motion to stand. She nodded, but opened her coat to reveal a wicked blade strapped to her belt.

The girl turned. Her eyes grew wide and the biggest smile that any person could possibly display spread across her face. Right away, Kevin noticed (with just a hint of shame) bits of food stuck between the gaps of her teeth. However, he didn't have too much time to linger on that observation as she plunged forward, yanking Shari along as if the girl did not exist.

"Kevin!" Valarie shrieked. "You aren't a ghost anymore!"

Kevin caught her in his arms and felt a wave of queasiness turn his gut just a bit. Later, he would think that she actually smelled worse than some of the zombies he'd encountered. But at the moment, he forced his rising gorge down and threw his arms around the girl.

"No, Valarie, I'm not a ghost," Kevin said as he hugged the now-babbling woman close. He looked over her head at Shari. Tears flowed freely down her cheeks as she watched the reunion. Kevin only had a few seconds to reflect on the peculiar look in her eyes before Major Beers spoke.

176

"Okay, take them out before I get sick." Major Beers motioned for the two soldiers standing off to the side.

They stepped in and began to pull Valarie away. The young woman immediately threw herself to the ground and began to wail.

"Don't put me back in with the ghosts!"

"Hey." In an instant, Shari was kneeling in front of Valarie, holding her face up so that they were eye-to-eye. "I will be with you. We have these bracelets on so that nothing can take me from you."

Kevin watched in fascination. He couldn't help but think, *Who are you, and what have you done with Shari?* Even more amazing, Valarie calmed down in an instant.

"You are staying with me in my box?" Valarie said as she scrubbed at the tears making tacks down her grimy face.

"I will be right beside you always, Valarie," Shari soothed, caressing Valarie's hands as she spoke.

"This is all very touching," Major Beers scoffed, "but my nose can't take any more of this...*girl.*"

"Maybe if you could hold on just a minute," Kevin spoke up. "In my bag." He nodded to the pack leaning against the major's desk.

"These are the medications that you went after at the cost of the only doctor I've heard about surviving this nightmare?" The major returned to her desk and heaved the pack up, setting it before her.

"What?" Shari's head popped up. "Peter?" That one word hung in the air for a second. "Kevin, where is Peter?"

"This isn't how I wanted to tell you—" Kevin began.

"Just tell me, Kevin."

"He sacrificed himself to save me," Kevin admitted. Of course there was so much more to the story, but he was fairly certain that Shari would care little for the details. "He was bitten and as soon as he knew that he wasn't immune, he did what he had to in order to ensure that I made it out safely. He did say that he wanted me to tell you that he loved you and that he was sorry for everything."

So much had happened that Kevin wasn't sure exactly what words passed between him and the doctor at the end. Still, it couldn't hurt to say a few nice things if it brought even a shred of comfort.

"Did you put him down?" Shari asked in a voice barely above a whisper.

Once again, Kevin felt that the truth was not exactly the best way to go here. "Yes." He didn't dare say more for fear that he would have to remember details. That was the thing about a lie—the more details you gave, the more you had to remember.

"So what are all these bottles?" Major Beers spoke, dumping the contents of the pack on her desk. "OxyContin? Demerol? Percocet? Kevin, I don't think these have anything to do with that girl seeing things that aren't real."

"No, but I didn't see the sense in leaving those behind since I was right there. I also loaded up on antibiotics if you're interested."

"So which ones do you need for...*her*?" The major nodded to Valarie who had huddled in close to Shari, stroking her hair.

"I need the clozapine."

The major sifted through the bottles on her desk until she came up with one. She shook it and then tossed it to Kevin. "You get this one for now. If things go well, I might just let you have the rest of her meds."

"And the rest?"

The major laughed. That laugh was cut off by a loud commotion outside the tent. There was a wet slapping sound accompanied by a yelp.

"Kevin!" a familiar voice yelled. The tent flap opened and Aleah stumbled in clutching a bloody spike that looked like a tent peg.

Kevin caught the woman in his arms and barely had a chance to react as lips pressed to his. He felt Aleah clutch at him so fiercely that it bordered on painful. His breath was squeezed from his lungs and he almost tumbled when legs wrapped around his waist.

The reunion was short-lived as something hard struck him in the small of his back, sending the couple sprawling to the ground. A breath-stealing pain radiated from his kidneys, but Kevin instinctively covered Aleah's body with his own. Another blow came, this one to the back of his head.

There was a brilliant flash...and then...nothing.

***

"Kevin?" a voice whispered. He felt a hand brush his cheek.

"Aleah?" Kevin managed. For some reason, his mouth felt strange. However, he only had a second to reflect on that before the pain at the base of his skull blossomed. He tried to turn his head, but was not quick enough and began choking on the vomit that came in a rush.

Mercifully, somebody scooped him up from behind his shoulders and sat him upright. Kevin kept his eyes squeezed shut for several seconds as he fought the urge to be sick. It didn't help that somebody—most likely Aleah—was fawning and pawing all over him as if afraid that he might vanish if physical contact were broken.

"You took a nasty shot," a familiar male voice whispered. "Probably would have killed you if that major hadn't stepped in and ordered them to stop."

"Matt?" Kevin asked, still afraid to open his eyes for fear that the world would suddenly tip over and begin spinning around like it had a moment ago.

"I'm here, buddy," the male voice assured.

"And everybody else?"

"I'm here," Aleah whispered, patting his hand.

"Me too," a tiny voice whispered. That had to be Erin.

"Right here," Heather said from behind Kevin—the owner of the hands that had sat him up a moment ago.

"Shari?" Kevin asked.

"She and Valarie were dragged out," Matt answered. "Probably taken to lock up again. That is where she keeps Valarie most days. And for some reason, Shari was chained to her."

179

"I feel like I was hit by a truck." Kevin winced as he touched the damp lump on the back of his head.

"That would be Bryce," Matt said with an angry tone.

"Who is Bryce?" Kevin asked.

"Major Beers' second-in-command. He has a thing for Aleah, but the major won't allow any of the women to be touched against their will."

"That's at least something," Kevin tried to laugh, but it became more of a choking cough as the pain hit. Each cough made it increasingly worse, and in no time he was fighting back the tears of pain that wanted to come.

"That's the *only* saving grace of this lunatic," Heather spat.

"I'm just glad you are all still alive," Kevin said with a sigh. He felt something spread through his body, and it took him a few moments to realize that it was relief.

"Almost weren't," Matt said.

Kevin slowly opened his eyes. It took a second for the triple vision to drop to double, and then, finally he saw the faces of his friends staring back at him.

"A fire burned the club house to the ground," Erin sniffed. "Now we live in these stinky, cold tents."

"And considering the weather," Aleah spoke up, "they aren't too worried about us running away. They take our coats and shoes each time they bring us back here to our tent."

Kevin looked around and realized that they were all, in fact, shoeless.

"They come and check every couple of hours to see if you are dead or conscious…not sure which," Matt said with a half-hearted chuckle.

"So, about this Bryce person," Kevin probed.

"Imagine a hockey goon crossed with one of those fellas from *Deliverance*," Matt said. "He's a big guy and sometimes I think he is really smart…then he does stuff like what he did to you."

"And this has what exactly to do with the major not letting her soldiers rape at will?" Kevin asked.

"He has a thing for Aleah," Erin sing-songed like she was on a grade school playground.

"Knock it off, Erin," Heather snapped. "Or have you forgotten about how Aleah is the reason that you survived that fire."

"I was only kidding—" the girl started to defend herself.

"Enough!" Kevin snapped and immediately regretted it as light bloomed behind his eyes and the dull pain in his head became sharp. "Can you really be acting like this after everything?"

"What?" Heather asked, looking confused. "We aren't doing anything different."

"My point exactly," Kevin said in a voice barely above a whisper. "We are being held captive by a renegade military faction. Valarie and Shari are locked up...and you guys are acting like this is just a regular day."

"They said they wouldn't kill us if we agreed to join them," Erin said. "We get meals, and it's not like Shaw and The Basket. Major Beers won't let nobody rape us. We just have to work during the day, and do stuff like we were doing before you disappeared for so long."

"We thought you were dead," Aleah added.

"The choices were pretty limited," Matt chimed in. "It isn't like we have hurt anybody or had to do anything skeezy."

"That's because you guys have stayed here behind the wall," Kevin said. "Meanwhile, she had that James guy killed and staged a mock hanging of Valarie to lure me out. These people are no better than Shaw and his men. In fact...I'd say they might be worse. They are showing up like the US Army and when folks open their gates, they take what they want and toss any who they don't deem useful over the fence or wall or whatever."

"Then why haven't they tossed..." Matt began, but shut his mouth with an audible click. Kevin couldn't tell if the name he was about to mention was Erin's or Valarie's, and at the moment he didn't care.

"You all need to listen up," Kevin hissed. "The only way that we will survive is if we stick together. If we lose one, we become weaker."

"Then why do you seem so set against joining these people?" Matt asked.

Kevin looked at the young man closely. He hadn't really gotten to know him over the few weeks that he'd been part of the group. Most of the time, Matt was off with Heather. He didn't want to become suspicious of him this easily, but he had been too pre-conditioned by all the books and movies. There was always one guy who turned out to be something other than what he tried to pass himself off as to the others. He would keep his eyes on Matt and do his best to not let his Hollywood-induced paranoia taint his perception. Still...all movie stereotypes had some basis in truth. Right?

"Because I've been out there and seen what they have done...I have been traveling with somebody who knows the major personally."

"And where is that person now?" Matt challenged—at least that's how Kevin took it.

"I have no idea," Kevin said with a shrug. "We got separated a few days ago." At least he was giving up some truth. He tried to stuff them down, but the feelings of suspicion regarding Matt began to rise and spread its wings in the back of his mind.

"Who was this person?" Aleah asked. "And how did you get split up?"

"Her name was Willa, and we got split up shortly after the staged hanging of Valarie." Now Kevin was watching Aleah. If anybody deserved his suspicion, it was her. A solitary woman who looked like her just happened to stay alive on her own all this time. She "stumbled" across them in the middle of nowhere. And the real eyebrow raiser was her interest in *him*. Geek chic was one thing...but he was a lot of the former...and almost none of the latter.

"You have been out there with a woman?" Erin piped up.

"It wasn't like that," Kevin defended. He was now the focus of three sets of eyes. The trio all looked at him with something different in their expression: Matt—interest; Aleah—concern or curiosity (he couldn't decide which); Erin—glee? He was growing confused. In fact, the more he thought about it, the more he almost wished he was still out there fighting the cold and zombies with Willa.

"What was it like?" Aleah crossed her arms under what Kevin considered to be the most perfect breasts in the world. A tiny voice in the back of his mind told him he might want to lock onto the memory, because he was probably never going to see them in person again.

"She is part of an army detachment that has been chasing Major Beers and her band of crazies all across the state of Ohio. She is also her sister-in-law."

"So she wouldn't have any sort of ax to grind," Matt said with a chuckle.

"What's your problem?" Kevin snapped.

Everything about Matt changed in an instant. His smirk became a look of concern, and whatever he was about to say died on his lips.

Heather stepped beside him and took his hand. "Kevin?" she asked with obvious concern. "I don't think Matt was saying anything. I think it was simply the fact that with everything that has happened, and especially after discovering Paul James was working as a spy, we can't trust anybody."

"So much has happened since you left," Aleah said as she stepped in front of Kevin and effectively blocked his view of Matt. "And we had to start trying to figure out what to do with you gone."

"But I wasn't gone that long," Kevin protested.

"These days, a week is an eternity," Heather said. "None of our runs have taken longer than three days, and when you were gone almost two weeks, we had to start considering the fact that you wouldn't return."

Kevin listened. Had it really been that long? He tried to count the days, but they all sort of ran together. He knew that the initial trip out to Newark with Peter had been fast, but then things got jumbled.

"When these people rolled in, Matt was almost killed trying

to stop them," Heather continued. "And when the major rounded us all up, she promised that none of us would be harmed if we agreed to take part in the work. In fact, Matt was supposed to start working with the soldiers and start going out on scouting missions eventually. None of us were forced to work with the whores, and the major even protected Aleah and Shari early on when a few of the soldiers started getting a bit grabby."

"What about Valarie?" Kevin said in an even whisper that did very little to hide his anger.

"That's the other thing," Matt spoke up despite the warning looks he received from both Aleah and Heather. "I know you have some sort of soft spot for her, but she has been a danger to herself and all of us. She screams at things that aren't there, she is filthy...you saw her."

"Yet Shari of all people has taken it upon herself to care for the girl?" Kevin shot back.

"She almost killed us all when she caught the country club on fire—" Matt continued.

"What?" Kevin exploded. "Why would you say that?"

"Everybody knows it," Matt replied, not backing down from Kevin despite Heather's hands on his chest. "That lunatic kept screaming about fire being the only way, and then...whoosh! Middle of the night, we all have to jump through windows or whatever to escape as the building burns to the ground."

Kevin placed his hands gently on Aleah's that were—like Heather's—squarely set in the middle of his chest in a gentle effort to keep Kevin and Matt apart and pushed them aside. He leaned in close to Matt's face and smiled.

"Who told you that Valarie started that fire?"

"Nobody directly," Matt said with a scowl. "But everybody was talking about it. In fact, that major you have such a thing against, it was her that kept Valarie from being thrown over the wall. There were even a few fights and three soldiers ended up being sent to isolation for a few days because they got so mad when the major wouldn't just deal with the problem."

"I set that fire," Kevin said with almost no emotion in his

voice. "It was part of mine and Willa's plan to flush the soldiers out."

"You set a building on fire knowing that we were in it?" Erin stepped into the middle. Whether it was the fact that she had gotten tired of being ignored, or really had something to say was unclear.

"The plan was to force the major out into the open," Kevin said.

"And then what?" Matt laughed. "What were the *two* of you going to do against a military unit?"

Kevin opened his mouth, but nothing came out. He had turned everything over to Willa at that point. Sure, they had argued, but she was so set and certain that this plan would flush out the major. He hadn't thought to ask what they would do next. He had simply accepted that she had a plan. He was so determined not to fail Valarie that he had agreed. Had his judgment been too clouded? Had she taken advantage of that fact?

"We hadn't gotten to all the details yet," Kevin admitted sheepishly.

"But you had enough of a plan to set the building that we were in on fire?" Aleah asked.

"Look, I wasn't totally on board with everything that she planned, but I was getting desperate. It wasn't easy for me to be out here not knowing what was going on," Kevin protested. "I couldn't keep my mind straight. All I could imagine was the kind of stuff Shaw and his men did. I couldn't let that happen to you." He looked Aleah in the eyes. "I could not allow myself to just walk away...or to do nothing."

"You could have killed us all," Matt insisted.

"I could have left you in the middle of the road," Kevin snapped. "But since neither of those things happened, maybe you should shut your mouth and start deciding what side you want to be on."

"Kevin," Heather put her hand on Kevin's, "nobody is blaming you for anything...and nobody is changing sides, or whatever you think is happening. I think we are all just trying to figure out what is *going* to happen. To be honest, we all thought

185

that you might be dead. This is really the first time we have all been allowed to be together. They've kept us apart since they took over."

"I understand that you had to make some tough choices out there," Aleah added. "And none of us think that you would do anything to intentionally hurt any of us. It's just that you were working with somebody that *we* don't know. And now, just like you have your concerns about the major and her band, we are trying to wrap our minds around this Willa person and wondering if there is a lesser of two evils."

Matt and Erin were nodding as she spoke. Something on Matt's face changed and he stepped around Heather to address Kevin. "Man, I'm not going to ever forget what you did that day you guys found me. I didn't mean to come across like a jerk. It's just that things have been tense. I feel like I let everybody down when we got overrun. You've always been the man with the plan, and I have no doubt that you will figure something out here. I shouldn't have gotten in your face like I did."

The two men shook hands. But Erin was not ready to let things be. "I still don't understand how you could just set our only form of shelter on fire. I—"

"Enough!" Heather snapped.

"So it is okay with everybody that we were all starting to agree with the soldiers about them putting Valarie over the wall when we thought that she burned the place down, but since it was Kevin—"

"I said enough!" Heather spun on the younger girl. "And not *all* of us were okay with putting Valarie over the wall."

"Then why is it that my sister is the only person who has stepped in to take care of her?"

"I imagine it was because she was sick and tired of taking care of you," Heather replied. "You don't lift a finger to help anybody but yourself...you didn't before the soldiers took over, and you have done everything possible to avoid working since they came."

Erin's face turned red and she sputtered over words that

seemed to all arrive at the same time on her lips.

"Don't think we haven't heard," Matt added as he stepped up beside Heather.

"I don't know what you're talking about!" Erin blurted.

"You don't think the soldiers talk?" Matt raised an eyebrow.

"They...I..." Erin stumbled and stammered as she backed away.

"What am I missing?" Kevin asked with genuine confusion.

"Erin has been...performing favors...for some of the men in exchange for them doing her work," Heather said, her eyes never leaving the younger girl's.

"You mean—" Kevin glanced at Erin.

"Most of the soldiers don't actually know her real name...they just call her Bee-Jay," Heather said with a smirk. "It seems that she provides her...*services*...to anybody willing to take care of her kitchen shift."

"Does Shari know?" Kevin asked the young girl who was now glaring daggers at Heather.

"She spends all her time with that retarded girl!" Erin snapped. "She hasn't hardly spoken to me for..." Her voice faded and her words trailed off.

"Since you let your baby die?" Heather prompted.

In a surprising flash, Erin's fist lashed out, catching Heather on the nose with an audible crunch. There was a snarl of anger and then the younger girl tackled the older one, sending them both to the floor in a heap.

Kevin and Matt waded in to pull the two apart—Matt ending up with Erin and Kevin with Heather. The tent flap opened and a soldier stuck his head inside. He only seemed to take a casual glance before ducking back out.

"You two need to knock it off," Kevin hissed. Heather went to pull away and he jerked her back hard. "I mean it. If we are going to survive, we will all need each other before this is done and over."

"It won't ever be over!" Erin spat. "Those dead things aren't ever going to go away. Nothing is ever going to be like it was!"

"No," Kevin agreed, "it's not. And I won't lie to you and

say otherwise. However, we are still very much alive, and I intend to do everything in my power to keep us that way. What I won't do is victimize others in the process. I can't accept this major and her people as anything more than raiders and bad guys. They rolled in and *took* our place. And I'm not asking you to trust Willa and her group either. However, if it weren't for her...I might very well be dead. She actually left her group to come find me, and then helped me get back here."

"She sounds pretty amazing," Aleah whispered.

"And she also knows that I have an unwavering crush on a beautiful woman." Kevin wasn't sure, but he thought he detected something weird coming from Aleah. Having never really had a serous girlfriend—much less one that would display anything remotely resembling jealousy—he was on some uncharted ground.

"So what is it that you would have us do?" Matt asked, still keeping a grip on Erin; tightening it any time she struggled to get free.

11

Vignettes XXVIII

Aaheru gazed out at the sea. The surface was as smooth as glass; a delicate veil of mist swirled across the water in spots. The sun was still below the horizon, but its orange glow already gave the sky a lovely tinge of blood red that could easily be seen as an omen for what lay ahead.

"Pharaoh?" a soft voice spoke from behind him.

"Yes, Ahmes?"

"I have news."

Aaheru turned to face the girl. Her dark caramel skin was made even more radiant by the light of the breaking dawn. She stared at the ground, waiting for his acknowledgement. Her beauty made him pleased with his decision to do away with those cursed burqas. Women were truly a gift from God to be enjoyed by all the senses.

"Then do not have me wait, Child of the Moon."

"Your seed is strong and I am with child." Ahmes glanced up, her dark eyes betraying her. The pride was etched clearly on her face.

"Are you certain?"

"I have not had any tests by a doctor…but a woman knows her body."

Woman, Aaheru tried to conceal his smile at her use of that word. By most standards, Ahmes was still a girl. When he'd first laid eyes on her, he'd imagined her to at least be sixteen. The night in his bed that she revealed herself to be a mere thirteen, he'd almost sent her away…almost.

Who could fault him? The girl was a true Egyptian beauty.

189

Besides, the ideals of the Old World had considered her of a suitable age after her first bleeding. Those ideals were being revived as he assumed the title of pharaoh. If they were to give rise to a New Egypt, then they would have to bring children into the world in abundance.

"Are you pleased, my Pharaoh?" Ahmes whispered, a tinge of uncertainty clouding her eyes and forcing the glow of pride to hide like a sun behind scudding clouds.

"I am, my beautiful child," Aaheru said, scooping her up in his arms. When he brought her up to his lips for an embrace, he only briefly considered the difference in their size as he felt her feet brush his knees.

Eventually he set her on the deck and they stood in silence as the sun lit up the sky. Despite its radiance, there was still a chill in the air and Ahmes shivered slightly against Aaheru.

"So, where are we going?" Ahmes finally broke the perfect stillness, her voice barely audible above the deep—more felt than heard—resonance of the ship's engines.

"Off the shores of Greece there are hundreds if not thousands of islands. My vision is that we will claim one and make it our home. Over time, we will grow in strength and claim them one by one as ours. Eventually, we will be ready to claim the mainland."

"So do you aspire to be Pharaoh or Caesar?" the girl said with a tinge of laughter.

"You surprise me yet again, Ahmes," Aaheru said, turning the girl to face him.

"My name has more meaning than the one you chose," she said with that pride returning to blaze in her eyes. "It was also the name of a famous scribe."

"Still," Aaheru countered, "it is uncommon for a daughter to be so well educated except in the most wealthy of families where the thinking has a more...Western leaning than is the norm."

"My father was the Ambassador to Great Britain," Ahmes said with a sigh. "We were only supposed to be visiting for a dignitary's wedding. We were in the airport when they came in great numbers and overwhelmed the security force. I watched my entire family fall under a wave of those repulsive creatures. I managed to climb up on top of a statue. I sat on its cold marble shoulders for two days trying to be silent as those things stumbled over each other. Every time I thought I would be able to crawl down and run, somebody would appear and stir things up again.

"Sometimes one of them would spot me and begin to paw at the statue and make noise. This would bring others. Then, somebody in hiding would try to run and draw them away. Finally, I decided that I had no choice…hungry, thirsty, and covered in my own filth, I made a run for it."

Aaheru had a new appraisal of this girl. She was not so different from him. She would fight to survive at all costs. Her will to live matched his own.

"You are indeed the choice of the gods to be my queen and the first Mother of New Egypt." Aaheru felt a stirring deep down below his belly.

Scooping the tiny figure into his arms he carried her to the stateroom that he had claimed as his own. The soft moans of passion wafted from beyond the closed door a few moments later.

Ahi stood in the corridor for a moment. He'd come to speak with Aaheru about a disturbing discovery. The engineer had come to him moments ago to report that an attempt had been made to sabotage the engines. The perpetrator had escaped before being identified or apprehended.

The sounds of passion were rising in intensity and volume. Ahi shrugged. He'd been outside Aaheru's tent before during such instances. He could wait another minute or two.

***

Mackenzie felt the air swirl across the back of her hand as the mouth closed with a snap, missing her by a hair's breadth. She staggered back a step as the dog rolled over and landed awkwardly on the floor at her feet. Something struck her in the side knocking her over. Her head bounced hard off the floor causing a bright flash and then the sensation of the room tipping and spinning like the old Tilt-a-Whirl at the county fairs she had loved so much as a child.

There was a commotion and an odd gurgle, followed by a dull thud and sickly crunch. Mackenzie struggled to remain conscious and found herself looking up into a face that took her a moment to recognize.

"Juan?" Her hands went to his cheeks and she could feel the moisture of tears coating them.

"Are you okay?" Juan's voice was frantic.

"I'm fine," she moaned, "and if you would get your huge body off mine, I might even be able to catch my breath."

Juan rolled away and got to his knees. He glanced over his shoulder just as Frank was yanking his machete from the skull of the dog. The two shared a look and Frank quickly glanced around. His eyes came to rest on an old blanket thrown over the back of the couch in the living room. As he went about the task of wrapping the remains of the dog and dragging it outside, Juan helped Mackenzie to her feet. Twice he tried to lift her up, and twice his hands were slapped away.

"I hit my head, Juan," she said softly, wincing with each word. "I didn't break my legs."

"Maybe you should lie down for a while," he suggested.

"Actually, you get to stay up and be my alarm clock all night."

Mackenzie patted Juan's arm as she made her way to the bathroom where she used a make-up mirror and the one on the medicine cabinet to get a look at her head. She fumbled around in the cabinet until she found a bottle of hydrogen peroxide.

"Pour some of this on my bath towel and dab at the wound. It is going to bubble up, so don't worry."

"I know what hydrogen peroxide does," Juan grumbled as he did as she asked.

A few minutes later, they returned into the living room to

find Frank on his knees with a bucket, rubber gloves, and scrub brush, cleaning up the mess from the dog. Juan cleared the table, suddenly no longer hungry. He didn't think it had anything to do with the dog turning to a deader; he'd seen them before and it was only slightly less unpleasant than seeing a child, but not enough to put him off his dinner. No, he knew damn well what it was. He glanced at Mackenzie who was making small talk with Frank as he continued to clean.

He'd almost lost her.

Not wanting to wait another second, he pulled one of his field belts from the pegs in the hallway and strapped it on his waist.

"So you're heading out to go find those children?" Mackenzie asked.

"Not tonight," Juan replied with a shake of his head.

"But—" she began to protest.

"Going out at night in this weather is asking for trouble. We will end up with more people dead and nothing good to show for it," Juan cut off Mackenzie's protest. Frank opened his mouth and Juan held up a hand. "And I can't tell you what to do, but if we are going to have a chance at finding your friends and making it back alive, then we do it my way."

"So what does that mean?" Frank asked as he carried the bucket to the front door, stepped outside and tossed it. Almost on cue, a flash of lightning lit up the darkness to reveal a pouring rain.

"That means I will get a couple of others to come, and we will let you direct us as to where we search…but I have my conditions."

"I'm listening." Frank set the bucket down and closed the door on the storm outside.

"We go out there for three days. If we don't find anything in that time…I come home and bring my people with me. You aren't under my orders in *that* decision *only*. You want to stay out there and keep looking, then you go right ahead. But I am not going to risk a bunch of my people for some kid who wants to be an idiot." Juan paused for a moment before adding, "And I am bringing *all* my boats back with me."

"That's fair," Frank agreed.

"Juan," Mackenzie whispered.

"Yeah," he turned with a look of concern on his face. There had been something in her voice that he didn't like.

What he saw when he turned around brought a lump to his throat. His mind tried so hard to process what he was seeing, but nothing made any sense.

Mackenzie was standing in the arch between the kitchen and the dining room. She was paler than anything Juan could ever remember seeing in his life. She was holding out her hands, both were slick with fresh blood. Her jeans had a visibly growing dark stain at her crotch. She took a step forward and collapsed. Juan was just able to catch her before her head hit the floor.

"Go get somebody!" Juan screamed.

He was only vaguely aware of Frank's response. He didn't hear the door open and slam as the man left. He was focused with his entire being on the woman he held clutched to his chest.

***

"Why can't we just send out hunting parties?" a voice asked from the back of the room.

Chad had called a meeting of everybody in Yosemite Village in the large, open dining room of the hotel that was going to serve as their home for the foreseeable future. With the threat of rebellion and in-fighting seemingly over, now they had to focus on the task at hand of surviving the winter.

"The temperature has been hovering around zero for the past few days." Michael stepped up beside Chad after a nod. "We just do not have the gear to withstand being out overnight in that sort of weather."

"But I thought we had foul weather gear…and some of the shops had some pretty nice sub-zero rated clothing," another voice shouted back to be heard over the grumbles of the crowd.

"Clothing we have," Michael agreed. "What we are lacking is tents, sleeping gear, that sort of thing."

"So why can't we just hunt in this area?" another voice argued.

"Because all the fighting, fires, and zombies have probably run off every single animal for miles around," Michael answered with just a slight edge to his voice.

"We are going to have to cut back," Chad said. His statement was immediately met with a chorus of angry complaints. He let them go for a few seconds before raising his hands to try and settle the crowd.

"We are already practically starving," a woman cried. "My children can't keep going hungry!"

Another angry chorus rose. Michael stepped forward again. He clasped his hands behind his back and waited for everybody to notice him and quiet down.

"If I have three volunteers, I will take a small group down into the valley. Be aware that, if you come, you do what I say, when I say it. It is not a democracy. We will make a supply run and try to return within a month. We will be on skis going down, so if you can't ski, don't bother raising your hand. I don't have time to teach you. Once we come down out of the snow, we will be on foot. There will probably be someplace down there where we can find a snowplow or something that we can use to make the return trip. We will bring as much food as we can back with us."

A lot of heads dropped, eyes searching the floor rather than make contact with anybody and reveal the fear. Chad glanced at Scott who nodded. Brett nodded as well, but Chad gave him a slight shake of the head. Brett scowled, but stayed put when Chad and Scott raised their hands.

"No!" Ronni's voice broke the silence. "If you are going, then I am too!"

"No, you're not," Chad said with a shake of his head. "We'll talk about this later back in the room."

"No," Ronni pushed her way through, "we won't. We'll talk

195

about this right now."

"Ronni—" Chad started.

"No," Ronni snapped. "You have done more than your share. I don't know who you think you need to prove anything to here. These people all are all happy to sit back and do nothing because they know that you and Scott and Brett will handle things. And lately, with Mr. Clark happy to run around and kill zombies or rebels, or whatever he does when he takes off into the woods, every single person here just sits on their asses and waits for the next meal…waits for somebody else to go out and kill the zombies—"

Several voices rose in angry protest. Ronni stepped up on the small stage beside her dad, Michael, and Scott. Hands on her hips, she glared out at the faces. "Fine…prove me wrong! Which one of you wants to go with Mr. Clark down the mountain and back into town to search for supplies?"

It was as if somebody had hit a mute button as the room full of people became instantly silent. She planted her fists on her hips and swept the room with her eyes.

"Just like when we came up and found that bus," she scoffed. "Everybody stayed on the bus while my dad and a few others went out and dealt with the problem. Nobody wanted to risk it. And when those guys where stealing stuff and then tried to rape me…you all just stood there while my dad handled it. You let a bunch of people grab him and put him on trial like he did something wrong for protecting me. And when the fighting started…most of you hid in your rooms."

"Ronni—" Chad put his hand on his daughter's arm, but she jerked away.

"No! I am sick of it. I am sick of you being the one to kill the people who get bit…you going out when a bunch of those things find us. I lost my mom, and I know lots of people lost family…friends…but I have you back and I won't lose you again. Not when all these other people are here and should be helping."

"It's not that easy, Ronni," Scott spoke up. "Somebody has

to do this or we will all starve to death."

"Then let's just go. We can leave these people here to die and go down the mountain." Ronni spun to face Scott.

"This is the safest place to stay away from those things," Scott replied. "Sure...sometimes a few wander in, but down there...they are everywhere. We would never be able to rest. And then there are people like the ones who tried to hurt you. Zombies would only be a part of the problem."

"The girl does have a point," Michael spoke up. "If four of us go out there and risk our asses, then everybody else here is going to need to start stepping up. Before we leave, we will have a quick nomination and vote for a...mayor or whatever you want to call it. That person is going to assign every able body in this place with tasks that Chad and I will come up with and write down. Those tasks *will* be done."

"Or else what?" somebody shouted.

"Or else you will be tossed out of this place," Michael replied flatly.

"There are more of us than there are of you," another voice retorted.

"Then maybe the girl is right." Michael stepped beside Ronni. "Maybe a few of us need to pack up and head down for good to leave you people to starve."

"Maybe we won't let you leave," another voice, this one female, yelled.

A low hum of conversation began to swirl. Chad glanced at Michael who shook his head very slightly. He moved his hand to his hip and opened his coat just enough to reveal the butt of a pistol-gripped shotgun. Chad raised his eyebrows in surprise. Three days ago, all the firearms had been rounded up after it was announced that everything needed to be inventoried and matched up with the limited and almost exhausted supply of ammunition.

He considered Michael Clark for a moment. He knew very little about the man. What he knew for certain wasn't something that instilled too much confidence. The man had been a part of the gang stealing food...the gang that eventually tried to rape his daughter. Still, somehow, this man had convinced everybody to turn in their weapons for "inventory" just before announcing that there was not going to be enough food to survive the winter.

He might not trust the man, but it would sure be better to have the man on his side than be against him. He gave a slight nod to the man—whatever he had in mind had to be a better alternative than starving to death.

"You'll do what we say because if you don't, then we will toss your ass out in the snow," Michael said with absolutely no emotion in his voice.

"Oh yeah?" a man shouted back. "You and what army?"

"I'm so glad you asked." Michael drew his shotgun and jacked a round into the chamber.

As if on cue—and Chad would believe for the rest of his life that it was, in fact a pre-arranged cue—ten men stepped out of the doorways on all sides of the room and brought rifles to their shoulders.

***

"So what was he like…that man of yours?" Gemma asked as she shook the last bit from the can of beans they'd had warming on the fire.

The two of them had been in this lecture hall for two days while it rained ice cubes. At least that is what it felt like if you went out in it. It was so cold, and the wind blowing so hard, that if you were out in it for even a moment, your entire face went numb.

"Daft," Vix shrugged, "like any bloke." Her eyes clouded over as a million memories flooded her mind. *Why*, she thought, *do you suddenly remember every good thing a person has done* after *they're gone.*

"He seemed like a nice fella," Gemma scooped the last spoonful in her mouth and washed it down with a sip of water from her canteen. "Wasn't he always going out every single time we were needing supplies?"

"That was his way. Never one to sit when things needed doing."

"Handy 'round the house then?"

"Couldn't change a light bulb without breakin' something," Vix snorted.

The two shared a laugh and then lapsed into several minutes of uncomfortable silence. Growing restless, Vix got up and went to the door. She listened for a moment before opening it and stepping out into the hall. At the end of the corridor was a door leading outside. A soft glow shone through the window.

The sun! she thought.

Still, it wouldn't do to get all excited without making sure. Besides, they'd been in that gloomy lecture hall with nothing but a small fire that barely chased away enough of the gloom to see the person sitting across from you.

Drawing her blade, Vix stayed close to the left wall. She didn't know why, but she just felt more comfortable with something at her back as she moved along.

Reaching the door, she had to squint and shade her eyes to actually have a look. The sun was peeking through several breaks in the clouds. It was also obvious that she wasn't the only person...or thing...enjoying the break. Several shadowy figures could be seen moving about. Of course they could have just as well been moving about before, but when she and Gemma had been running for cover, they hadn't really taken much time to look around.

She cracked the door to let in a little draft of the cold, clean air. A hand grabbed her shoulder and Vix spun, bringing the sword across to hopefully decapitate whatever it was that had her in its grip.

"Easy, it's just me!" a voice squeaked.

Vix looked down to where Gemma was sprawled on her butt after diving away from nearly having her head chopped off. She felt anger boiling inside her. *That was twice*, she thought.

"Are you trying to get yourself killed?" Vix snapped.

"I didn't want to yell up the hall and bring a bunch of them things after us," Gemma said with a sniff.

"You still need to let me know if you are coming up behind me. It's a wonder I didn't slice you open."

"Actually..." Gemma let the word die as she held up one hand where a razor-thin slice across the palm wept tears of blood.

"Damn you, child," Vix hissed.

"I'm not a child!" Gemma stood up, actually stamping one foot as she folded her arms across her chest.

"Really?" Vix raised an eyebrow after a glance down at the offending foot. She huffed and turned back to look outside.

"So, are we going to the hardware store now?" Gemma asked as she moved up beside Vix and looked outside.

"Nope?"

"But the weather—"

"I didn't say we weren't leaving," Vix cut the girl off. "I just said we weren't going to the hardware store."

Vix opened the door and took a deep breath. The air was cold, but it smelled wonderful and seemed to fill every bit of her lungs. A few zombies were close enough to take notice and began shambling her way. She didn't wait and went to meet them. With a few quick flashes, the ground was littered with five corpses that would walk no more.

Looking skyward to get her bearings, Vix turned east. She stared off in the distance at nothing for a few minutes while her mind considered all the possibilities.

"But I thought we were going to fortify our location and—" Gemma spoke in a voice just above a whisper. She couldn't keep her eyes from darting every direction. It seemed that wherever she looked, she saw more of those things. And it seemed that some of them saw her, too!

"I am not going to be nursemaid or mother for a bunch of ignorant buggers who probably won't survive to see the coming of spring." Vix started across the open field, her footsteps making squishy sounds in the saturated ground.

"So where are you going?" Gemma asked scurrying to catch

up and match strides with the woman.

"London."

***

"So all of our people are going to be sent out on patrols?" Selina handed Jody a steaming mug.

"Yep," Jody nodded and sipped at the hot water. In his mind he imagined it to be a latte from his favorite barista, this little Vietnamese lady who'd run the stand just outside the base in Little Rock.

"But are they ready for that sort of thing?"

"Not at all," Jody said after a noisy sip that was more steam than liquid. "But that is the point. Casualties won't matter to the captain as long as they aren't his men. He and Slider have this whole thing figured out as far as logistics and what they consider optimal loss."

"What the hell is optimal loss?"

"It is a number of people that they *hope* to lose in the next few weeks so that our supply issue improves." Jody leaned back in the chair and closed his eyes. He was absolutely exhausted.

"You look like warmed over garbage…and don't smell much better," Selina said with more concern that disgust.

"They had me in last night for progress reports," Jody said with a sigh. "I am supposed to select ten percent of the 'nonviable' female population."

"What for?"

"They didn't say, but I got the feeling that it helps with their optimal loss numbers."

"But didn't you say that we were leverage to keep the others in line?"

"Yep, but as the casualties tally up, certain individuals no longer need to be pacified with your safety."

"So what is going to happen?"

"I think the chosen few that I gave them last night will be sent to a greenhouse complex about ten miles south of here.

They will be given instruction and limited supplies and left to fend for themselves."

"So what if they take off?" Selina opened up the two MREs that Jody had brought. She had insisted on serving everything up on actual plates. Jody couldn't recall the last time he'd used anything besides foil packs and tin trays.

"Then the losses make up part of their optimal target. And if they stay and accomplish the task, then there will be a chance at a better food supply...next year."

"That captain is a real bastard." Selina set the plate in Jody's lap and took a spot on the couch across from him.

"That's one way of putting it," Jody said before shoveling a mouthful of what was supposed to be roast beef in his mouth.

The long wail of the hand-cranked siren broke the silence that had settled as the two ate. Seconds later, the front door burst open. Danny stumbled in and then bent over with his hands on his knees as he tried to catch his breath.

"Herd!" was the only thing he managed to get out.

Jody jumped to his feet, his plate of half-eaten dinner falling to the floor with a splat. He moved past Danny and stepped out onto the porch. Selina's house was on the west end of town on a small rise. He had risked a lot sneaking her out of the gym, but he had grown very attached to the tall, strong woman. Together, they had convinced those remaining in the gym that it would be in their best interest to remain quiet about the arrangement if they wanted any chance at survival. He'd had less trouble convincing the captain to approve his requisition to confiscate a local residence in order to have someplace to base his own assigned operation from. Actually, the captain seemed enthusiastic at the prospect that Jody was beginning to fall in line with the program.

From the porch, he could see down the long, grassy slope and past the fields beyond for hundreds of yards. Sure enough, a long line of undead stretched out north and south. He guessed the herd to be at least a half mile wide. As for how long...that was anybody's guess as is vanished from sight, blocked by a dense woods and a higher bluff. In effect, the undead hoard was wandering down into a valley.

A quick look revealed something to Jody that he wasn't sure everybody else down in the central base—as well as Bald Knob proper—might be aware of. The valley ran in a bit of a crescent around the region. It would be no small stretch for the herd to eventually surround the entire area if there was sufficient numbers. And from what he was seeing, it looked very likely that there would be more than enough.

"Danny, where's your pack?" Jody asked over his shoulder.

"Back in my tent," Danny gasped, almost able to get a full breath finally.

"And what weapons are you carrying?"

"Just my spike and my three-foot brush clearer."

The 'spike' that Danny referred to was a weapon of his own creation. He'd bored a series of three holes in an aluminum bat, and then welded stainless steel tent pegs into place. Jody thought it was an awkward weapon, but Danny loved it when he could pipe up in his baseball announcer's voice. *"And now, stepping into the box for the Red Sox, Danny O'Leary!"* Then he would make what he thought was a good impression of a stadium crowd going wild, but to Jody, sounded more like bad static on a cheap AM radio.

"Selina, do you have a bug-out bag here?" Jody brought his field glasses up and scanned the area.

"Umm..."

"Get it," Jody barked. He didn't have time for her to decide if she could trust him or if this was part of some elaborate trick.

"What's the deal, Sarge?" Danny asked. "How bad is it?"

"Look." Danny handed his glasses to the man and continued to observe the scene with his naked eye.

"None of our perimeter fences can withstand that," Danny breathed.

"Anybody who doesn't run for it will be swept under," Jody said.

"I don't think the tower sentry can see as well as we can,"

Danny said as he handed the glasses back.

"Which means that the captain will issue a standard defensive order."

"Everybody in camp will retreat to the municipal building," Danny added.

"And the citizens will be left out in the open," Jody continued. "Only, there is no way that they can make any sort of real stand in that building. In fact, I don't think the first floor barricades will last an hour. They will be compromised with no hope for escape."

"We need to warn them." Danny took a few steps forward, but Jody stayed put. He was halfway down the cement walkway before he turned back to Jody with a questioning look on his face.

"I'm not going," Jody said with a shake of his head.

"You want to split up and head to the school?" Danny asked.

"I'm not going there either," Jody said.

"Am I missing something?" Danny glanced over his shoulder like he half-expected the massive mob of undead to be at the end of the driveway.

"You might make it in...but I doubt you will make it out." Jody came down off the porch and approached his friend. "And as for the school, most of them are so weak, they won't make it more than an hour before they need to stop."

"So tell me what you're saying," Danny challenged. "Are you prepared to just leave all of the guys behind...and the men women and children of Bald Knob that we are sworn to protect and defend."

"It's over, Danny," Jody said with a hitch in his voice. "I don't like it...but it is over. There is no more Gunslingers, no more United States Army...hell, man, there's no more United States. There hasn't been for a long time. All there is now is what is in your boots. You have to take care of you...and leave the rest for God."

"But you were going to stand up to the captain...you were

gonna stand up to Slider—"

"Who were we kidding?" Jody snapped. "Slider is a trained killer...the captain hitched his wagon to the only man he thought would keep him alive. They knew the score, they just went about it in a way that you and I wouldn't. They didn't care what they did to survive. If you don't think Slider knows every move we could possibly make beforehand, then you took too many fast-balls to the head."

"But—" Danny sputtered, but he couldn't find an argument that didn't have a million holes in it.

"I'm going north...Canada maybe," Jody said. "Maybe if we go far enough north, we'll either run out of people, or it will just be so damn cold that those things will be frozen solid."

"You bringing Selina?" Jody whispered.

"If she wants to come," Jody replied with a shrug.

"If I come...can I make a request?"

"Sure."

"If, for some strange reason, we end up near New York—"

"I said *away* from people," Jody snorted.

"Yeah...but you never know...I just want your word that if we are in New York, you'll let me piss on home plate in Yankee Stadium."

"Deal."

***

Charles "Slider" Monterro heard something wailing in the distance. He looked up at the sky and smiled. Pulling his knife out of the temple of the zombie, he let the body fall to the ground.

That one had been sneaky. It was another of those damn kids. For some reason, many—not all, but enough to be noticea-ble—of the zombies of children between the ages of what he had to guess to be five and ten were displaying some peculiar tendencies. He hadn't really noticed until he'd overheard a few of the soldiers talking about it around camp. He'd never let one live long enough to observe its behavior.

The past several days, he'd kept his eyes peeled any time he was out in the field. Up until today, he hadn't seen any kids. He imagined the reason that they were so scarce had to be because there was not enough to come back more often than not when one of the little ones went down.

"People McNuggets," Slider scoffed.

He glanced down at the one he'd just killed. A boy, maybe eight or nine years old. His left arm was gone and he looked to be wearing what remained of a set of coveralls.

Probably some farmer's kid, Slider thought as he wiped off his blade.

He continued through the woods, following the tracks of the deer he'd been after since before sunrise. Almost fifteen minutes ago—although it seemed like much longer after having to take down that zombie farm boy—he'd put an arrow in the damn thing. It had jumped just as he let go, which caused him to miss the heart and catch the poor animal in the flank.

Being out like this brought back memories of a mission in the foothills of the Arma Mountains in Afghanistan. He'd been tasked to finish a take down that another sniper had missed. Actually, he hadn't missed entirely, he'd winged his target. Unfortunately, the Air Force had not been aware that an operative was in the area and a drone had taken out the operative. Slider had moved fast and caught the target in a cave. The man was huddled by a small fire obviously no longer caring about remaining hidden. It was very seldom that a sniper had to look his target in the eyes. Slider had been a little disturbed by how much he'd enjoyed that kill.

After about an hour, he came to a clearing and his quarry. He felt a twinge of sadness at the obvious suffering the animal was experiencing. Small puffs of steam came in rapid bursts from its nostrils.

It took a staggering step away as he emerged through the trees. Slider already had an arrow nocked. He quickly drew back to his cheek and took very careful aim. He wanted to put the deer out of its misery as quickly as possible. He let go, the twang of the bow and the hiss of the arrow were almost loud in the peace of the forest…and a dead world.

Drawing his knife, he crossed to the downed animal. He was pretty sure that his shot had ended the deer, but it never hurt to be careful. More than one hunter had been surprised at the ferocity in which a deer will struggle for its life when mortally wounded.

After all, Slider thought, *they are wild animals*.

He knelt beside the downed animal and yanked the arrow from the eye socket. After inspecting the projectile and deciding that the cracked shaft meant that it was not reusable, he cast it aside and went to work field-dressing the carcass. This would keep him well fed for a few weeks.

He very seldom actually ate a meal in the mess tent. In fact, the only reason he made an appearance in there at all was to hear what the men were talking about. It was strictly low-level intel gathering tactics, but he was always amazed at how individuals felt that their conversations were confined to the space they sat in.

Once he was done and all the meat was loaded into his pack, he began the trek home—or at least the place he currently called home. He had to really think back to the last place he had stayed at for longer than a few months. The funny thing was, this place had been his home longer than anyplace else in the past fifteen years.

Slider was weaving through some young pines when he smelled something on the wind. Setting his pack down, he quickly adjusted his attitude. He'd been actually feeling pretty good about the day, and for him, feeling truly good about anything was a rarity.

Hunkering down, he duck-walked to the edge of the woods and looked down. What he saw was unsettling. He imagined that some people might think he was some sort of fearless warrior, unmoved by all that had transpired. Quite the opposite.

He'd been visiting an old buddy at the veteran's hospital

when this nightmare had unfolded. He still remembered fighting his way out of there from the eleventh floor. It had apparently started down in the ER with a few victims brought in with assorted bites. He still had nightmares of what he'd witnessed in the pediatrics and maternity floors. Back then, he had shifted into his "Protector" mode. He had left "Slider" behind, and mistakenly believed that that part of him was buried for good.

Within seventy-two hours, he had come to a decision. His only chance at survival was to take care of himself. He couldn't worry about anybody else. It was simply a sad reality. That night, he walked away from the small group he had been travelling with.

Now, as he looked down into the very slight valley with Bald Knob at its head. The sea of undead would wipe out everything in its path. He was very aware of the contingency plan put in place by the captain. He'd thought at the time that it was short-sighted and foolish. However, that was why he had his own contingency plan.

As he took a seat and watched the herd—he guessed it to number well over a hundred thousand—close in, he heard the first strains of the warning siren down in Bald Knob. From his vantage point, he could actually see the amorphous blob of walking corpses refine its direction and hone in on its target.

He wished that he'd brought his bug-out kit. There was so much gear that he knew he would miss. However, that was the beauty of the new world. Everything he wanted was still out there someplace. He just needed to find it.

He stayed for a while out of curiosity. He wanted to see what would happen. He wished that he had his field glasses. Hell, even a scope from a rifle would be nice. However, he didn't need either to see and hear the mayhem down in Bald Knob. The leading edge of the zombie mob slammed into the town full force. Slider almost chuckled at the logic that had gone behind the barbed wire fencing that surrounded the area.

He heard the screams along with the pathetically few echoes of gunfire. They had been dangerously low on ammunition for quite some time. However, it was what he saw to the east of his location that interested him the most. Three lone figures, each carrying what looked like fairly large and full backpacks, heading away. Of course it was too far away to make a positive identification, but he was willing to bet it was Sergeant Rafe.

12

Emily

As we turned down the almost invisible trail road that would dump us in the campground's opening in the dense woods, my mind was trying to shake off the numbness. With the exception of Mr. Dean Patton and the little girl—who still glared at me like I'd strangled a puppy in front of her—the rest of the survivors had died the first night.

Misty Dell, the little girl, had kicked and screamed when we'd put the dead bodies outside. Something in her mind was simply not processing that dead meant dead. *And why should it?* I thought. She'd seen so many supposedly dead people get up that I am sure it was more than a little confusing.

Of course this had brought on a whole new set of internal conflicts for me to resolve. I'd gotten into some heated arguments with Jesus and Jake—and pretty much everybody else for that matter—when it came to Thalia and Emily being exposed to the zombies and the day-to-day situations we faced. I could not imagine the lengths that people had gone to in order to keep little Misty shielded from the horrors of this dead world.

I'd asked Jon why they hadn't brought this little girl with them on the first trip. I wasn't too surprised when he revealed that they hadn't been aware of her existence. The group must've had her hidden for some reason or another. Well, we were almost home and I could get to the bottom of that later. When we made the final turn for home, I filed that one away with the million other unanswered questions.

As we drove between the berms, I could see a group out on

the porch waiting for our arrival. Honestly, I just wanted to wrap my arms around Melissa and the girls and not let go for a week.

"They've seen some action," Jon commented as we came to a stop just before the bridge.

"Huh?" I snapped out of my reverie and looked around.

"Lots of tracks in the snow over to the left all down that side of the hill." Jon pointed.

Well it couldn't have been any worse than what we dealt with, I thought as I pulled on my hat and gloves. Dr. Zahn was bundling up Misty, mostly since the girl wouldn't have anything to do with either Jon or me.

"When we get up to the house, you will meet Thalia and Emily," Dr. Zahn was saying as she zipped the girl's coat up.

We climbed out and I glanced at the huge makeshift sled that we'd loaded with food that we collected on the way back. As an added bonus, Jon had also dropped a pair of elk that first day after we left behind that nightmare of an outpost. I still could not get over how awful that group had had things when you compared them to us. Of course, if this Mr. Patton was any indication, they didn't have squat for leadership. He was curled up in the fetal position most of the time and whimpering. Even now, as we were getting out of the Snowcat, he was hunched up so tight that he more fell than climbed out.

I hadn't taken two steps up the winding trail that would lead to the house when Sunshine came barreling around the corner. At first, I envied Jon. After all, with Melissa being visibly pregnant now, she wasn't doing anything beyond a brisk walk. That's why I was more than a little surprised when Sunshine bee-lined for me. Of course that would give Jon some time to prepare an explanation about his hand.

"Oh, Steven, thank God you're here," she gasped.

I looked closer and realized that her gasp could be equal parts fatigue from running down to us and choking back tears. My heart skipped a beat as I tried to think as to whether or not I'd actually seen Melissa in that group on the porch awaiting our arrival.

"Just tell me that she is okay," I blurted. "I can handle it if she lost the baby as long as she is okay."

Sunshine looked at me for a second as if perhaps she'd gotten the wrong person. She closed her eyes and took a deep breath like she was about to deliver the knock out punch to my heart. I tried to brace myself for it, but I knew that it was useless. This was going to hurt.

"It's Emily."

Those words hung in the cold air for a second as if the sub-freezing temperatures had fixed them to the little cloud of condensation that had spewed from her mouth when she spoke.

I guess it took a few seconds for me to react, because all of a sudden, Dr. Zahn was at my side. She had me by the arm for some reason.

"What about Emily?" Dr. Zahn said in a voice barley above a whisper.

"She and the other kids were playing in the snow," Sunshine started slow, but her words quickly picked up momentum and seemed to be jumbling together in my head. "...place that they always ride the sled. Jake was there and DeAngelo was close by chopping wood. When she screamed, I think we all thought it was just girlish squealing. I think it was Fiona who saw the blood. She was on watch in the tower, so I guess she could actually see right down into the snow—"

"Are you trying to tell me that a zombie made it all the way across the field and to the hill?" Dr. Zahn snapped, cutting Sunshine off so abruptly that her teeth clicked when her mouth shut.

"No," Sunshine shook her head. "It was under the snow. A creeper."

Everything fell into place in a bizarre slow motion. When what had been said finally dawned on me, I took off up the hill. By the time I reached the flat parking lot at the top, my lungs were on fire and my head was swimming.

DeAngelo, his wife Melinda, Nickie Bailey, and Doug Coates were all standing on the porch. DeAngelo said something to the others and came down the stairs to meet me. It was at this point that the world seemed to shift into that dream-like quality where my feet were bogged down in quicksand and I moved in slow motion.

"Steve," DeAngelo said. His deep voice rattled around in my head, and I had this feeling that he was going to try and stop me from going inside.

"I want to see her." I kept forcing my feet to take step after grueling step.

I remembered back to when I'd thought that Thalia had been bitten. Maybe this would be like that time. Maybe Emily would be fine.

"She is pretty heavily sedated." DeAngelo made that sound important. For some reason, my brain wasn't making any of those connections right now.

"I want to see her," I repeated. By now we'd reached each other in the snow-covered parking lot.

"I'll take you, but I want you to know that we've done everything we can to keep her comfortable.

"When did it happen?" I asked. I wasn't sure if Sunshine had told me. In fact, now that I was thinking about it, I couldn't recall one single word that she'd said.

"Late yesterday afternoon."

I ran through everything in my mind. If we hadn't stopped at that small town on the way back...if Jon hadn't gone off for a few hours to bag those elk...if Dr. Zahn hadn't insisted on stopping to camp so early...if I hadn't insisted on making this run...

"It wouldn't have mattered if you'd been here or not," DeAngelo said as if he'd read my thoughts.

"How could this..." My voice trailed off. I didn't even know what to ask.

When we reached the porch, I saw the same look in every set of eyes that looked back at me: sorrow. There would be no miracle this time. I was going to lose one of my girls. I had failed Randall Smith.

The sounds of somebody running to catch up with me made my head snap around sharply enough to send a twinge of pain between my shoulders. Dr. Zahn was coming across the parking lot at a speed I don't think I'd ever seen her display.

"DeAngelo, go help Jon," she ordered, using that tone that left no room for discussion. "We have supplies and a couple of survivors, including a young girl that may present some problems. They are almost completely incapacitated."

With that, the doctor and I headed inside.

Melissa was there to greet me. I only had the briefest flash of concern when I didn't see Thalia. Everybody that hadn't been on the porch—except for Thalia and the stupid dog...and of course, Emily—was standing around in the huge entry room. As my gaze swept the room, all eyes told the same story.

"Where is she?" I asked. Actually, it took me three tries to get that out of my throat and past my lips.

"In the back room," Jake said.

My eyes met his and he looked away. I would worry about that later.

Surprisingly, Dr. Zahn let me lead the way. I reached the door and took a deep breath. My vision blurred for a second and I wiped away the tears. That wouldn't be what she needed right at the moment. I turned the knob and opened the door.

Immediately, the smell hit me. I hadn't smelled it in such strength since Teresa. What I saw when I entered the room brought an instant lump to my throat.

Thalia's head turned so slow that I felt like time had suddenly skidded almost to a halt. I only half-noticed Buster's head lift from the floor as well.

"Emily's sick, Daddy," Thalia whispered. "She got bit and her eyes are like the monsters."

For the briefest of seconds, I was amazed at how much she comprehended about the situation. It was a polar opposite of little Misty.

"Em, are you awake," I said in a voice barely above a whisper. I could scarcely hear myself say the words, so I have no idea how she heard me, especially in her condition.

"Can't sleep," Emily rasped.

I rushed to the bed and took her hands. This time I didn't even have to think about hiding the odd revulsion that comes from taking a person's hands who is in the throes of the latter stages of infection. I didn't feel the cold clamminess. All I felt were Emily's tiny, slender fingers.

"Didn't want to sleep until you got home," Emily continued after clamping down on her teeth to keep them from chattering. "I was ascared that I would become like my daddy before you got home."

"Well I'm here now, sweetie." I brushed a sweaty clump of her fine, dark hair from her forehead. The heat radiating from her face made my hand tingle.

"I'm sorry, Daddy Steve," Emily whispered.

I brushed the tears that started flowing from her eyes and cupped her face in my hands. "You don't have anything to be sorry about, Em."

"But who is gonna be Thalia's big sister now? Who is gonna help show her how to take care of the baby when Melissa has it?"

"Let's not worry about that," I whispered, kissing her on the forehead.

I felt a vice-like grip clamp down on my shoulder. Glancing up, I saw Dr. Zahn staring down at me with concern. She made a slight but curt shake of her head. I raised my eyebrows in concern and question.

"We have no way of being certain about the vectors of contamination. She is sweating profusely," the doctor hissed.

"So?" I didn't understand at first.

"Bodily fluids," the doctor reminded.

Teresa had died, not from having been bit, but from having sex with somebody who had. He'd shown immunity, but apparently that didn't matter. Of course, looking back, it had seemed so obvious. We already knew that even if a person was immune, if they were bitten and eventually died, they turned.

"Thalia?" I heard Melissa whisper behind me. "Why don't you come get some rest now that your daddy is home." It was a statement more than a question. "He can sit with Emily for a while and then you can come right back after you wake up."

"Is Daddy gonna have to kill Emily?"

That question smashed into my heart with all the force of a bullet. I glanced down at Emily to see her reaction, but her eyes were closed. For a brief moment, I felt like the monster that Misty saw when she looked at me. I knew right then that it would have to be me that took care of Emily at the end. Who else was there?

I didn't hear Melissa's response as the door shut, but it didn't matter. I took a few deep breaths and tried to clear my head. In that moment, I was hit with another revelation of just how secluded Misty had been kept by those she travelled with, and I was angry. The problem being, I didn't know exactly who to be angry at.

On one hand, we had Thalia who was more than aware of what was going on in the world around her. At age five, I think she was more aware of her situation than the one adult we'd rescued, Mr. Patton—

"The other survivors!" I blurted. In all the craziness of our arrival, I had completely forgotten about the people Jon, Jake, and Jesus had brought back with them.

"Umm..." Dr. Zahn seemed at a loss, which was very uncommon. "Come to think of it, I didn't see a single one of them when we came in. It was all the same familiar faces."

"You want to check on that?" I asked. "I will sit with Emily. Besides, I want a few moments with just her."

The doctor headed for the door, but paused and turned to face me with a very grim expression. "I mean what I said to you earlier, Steve. We don't have enough information to rule out any transmission vectors. I know that you don't want to do anything that would leave Melissa and Thalia to go on without you. In fact, I know that you want to hold and touch her, but I have to insist that you put on gloves."

"Jesus," I growled. "Have a little bit of a heart, would ya?"

"I do, Steve," the doctor whispered. "And my heart has to

be with the living. You have a child on the way, a wife, and a little girl. I need you to keep your head."

I wanted to say something…anything. But she was painfully correct. The only thing that I could do was nod…and put on a pair of Latex gloves from the nearby box. I waited for her to leave before I turned back to Emily who appeared to be sleeping.

"I won't ever leave your side, Emily," I whispered.

"Not even to go to the bathroom?" she mumbled.

I looked down in shocked surprise to see the tiniest of smiles on her lips. I took her hand. "Well, I guess for that," I answered. That little quip made my heart feel like at least one or two turns had been taken off of the vice that currently threatened to squeeze it flat.

"Okay, because I wouldn't want you in here if you are using the toilet."

"I thought you were asleep," I said, changing the subject.

"I keep my eyes closed because everybody stares at them when they are open," Emily said matter-of-factly. "I hate how sad they all look."

"So, how are you feeling?" I guess I had to ask the stupid questions.

"Like my body is floating…but my brain feels funny."

"Funny how?"

"It won't think about anything." I saw her brow furrow slightly. I knew that she was trying to express something, but couldn't find the right words.

"So how about the bite? Does it hurt?"

"Sometimes, but if I start to even breathe funny, Sunshine gives me another dose of that gross tasting medicine."

"Yeah…" I remembered back to my own recent bout with being incapacitated. "It was pretty grody stuff."

"Grody?" Emily asked.

"That is a word we used to say about something bad."

"Like when you say groovy or rad?" Emily asked with seriousness.

I had always been impressed with how bright she was. *Is,*

dammit! I scolded myself. *She isn't dead yet!*

"Yeah, like that," I agreed.

"I like that word. It sounds like the medicine tastes," Emily decided.

"So why don't you go ahead and open your eyes, sweetie," I urged. "I won't stare."

"Promise?" I heard a very tentative lilt in her tone.

"I promise."

She opened her eyes and I did everything in my power not to react outwardly. Still, inside I could feel that vice tighten again, and this time, I was almost certain that it would not stop until my heart was completely crushed.

"Don't cry," Emily whispered.

I hadn't even realized that the tears had begun to flow until she said something. I guess maybe I thought that my eyes were simply trying to live up to the promise that my stupid mouth had made. I leaned down, but her hands planted themselves in the middle of my chest with a surprising firmness.

"Dr. Zahn said you can't," she said, shaking her head.

"But—" I start to protest, but Emily cut me off.

"You have to take care of Thalia and Melissa...and the new baby." Her voice caught a little on that last bit and a tear trickled down her cheek. With one Latex-sheathed finger, I wiped the tear away.

"I will take care of them, Emily, but you..." I was at a loss. What do I say to a child that is completely aware that she is dying within the next day or so?

"I don't want to die," Emily whispered.

The words "I know" sprung to my lips, but I bit them down. What could I possibly say to this child that would bring her any comfort? I looked down into her eyes, trying not to focus on those dark squiggles that signaled her demise, and I had absolutely nothing to say.

"Will you stay with me at the end?" Emily asked. I knew what she meant, and I also knew that I had to be the one.

"I will," I agreed with a nod.

"Then you should go out there and see everybody," Emily said, taking my hand. "Besides, I need Sunshine to come give me more medicine."

"Are you starting to hurt?"

She nodded and I got up, but her grip on my hand tightened. "I'm glad you were my daddy and I got to be Thalia's sister...even for just a little while."

I left the room, but before I could even get the door open, my eyes were so full of tears that I could hardly see through the blur. Somebody grabbed my arm and I looked down to see Billy.

"How is she?" he asked.

"Not good." The words sounded weak, but how else could I describe her.

"I got that dress that Ian snagged for her birthday for when..." Billy's words trailed off. He finally just nodded his head and walked away.

If this is what it was going to be like, I would go absolutely crazy. I realized that everybody was grieving, we all felt this loss. Perhaps it was less for the newest members of our group, but the bottom line was that all of us felt this one in some way. Maybe it was because she was a child...who knew? But the bottom line was that this would hit even harder than the loss of Teresa and Jamie for the group as a whole.

To me, it was going to come down to dealing with the feeling that I had failed. Her father had entrusted his little girl to me because he believed that I would protect and watch over her. There was no way to see it other than a personal failure.

Why did I feel the need to leave the camp? Why did I have to go out there and leave behind those that I was supposed to protect? Well, from now on, things would be different.

I had been chosen to lead these people for whatever reason. If I was going to do that, then I needed to be here to take care of the daily grind. It wasn't about being a hero, or "doing my part" when it came to the care of the people here. I could accomplish all of that from this location. A true leader had to know when and how to delegate authority. At some point, I guess I had come to some conclusion that my hands needed to get dirty.

"Steve?" Melissa snapped me out of it and back to the present.

I hugged her close, realizing that I had come home and not done something that I'd been wanting and needing for the last few days. I felt Thalia's tiny arms wrap around my leg, so I bent down and scooped her up. The three of us stood huddled for a few seconds. My eyes scanned the room until I found Sunshine. She was with Jon and seemed to be examining Mr. Patton.

"Sunshine," I called across the room. "Emily says that she needs her medicine." I almost felt sorry for Mr. Patton with the way Sunshine just dropped what she was doing and jogged across the room and disappeared behind the door to attend Emily.

"I don't like that new girl," Thalia whispered.

"Thalia!" Melissa scolded. "That's not nice."

"She acts funny," Thalia insisted, holding her ground.

"She has been through a lot, sweetie," I said, squeezing her close for reassurance—whether hers or mine I wasn't sure.

"Jake filled me in a little." Melissa looked up at me with an unspoken question in her eyes.

"Well it was worse than that." I failed to suppress the shudder as the image of the things I saw in that camp came in a rush: skeletal bodies with intact heads; a barrel of what was, in essence, human stew; the partially stripped bodies hanging from beams; and that child zombie...

"...wouldn't even speak about it," Melissa was saying.

"What?"

"I said that whatever it was, it must have been bad because Jake will only give very brief details and Jesus won't speak about it at all."

"Thalia," I leaned down and set her on the floor, "will you be an angel and go get me a bowl of whatever that is that smells so good?"

In truth, I knew that it was some sort of stew and it was actually the last thing that I wanted to eat. However, I could tell that Melissa really wanted to know what I had seen. Thalia gave me one more squeeze and skipped to the table to find me a clean bowl.

I explained—omitting considerable detail—what we had found. I also let her know that I was not Misty's favorite person and why.

"That might become a problem, Steve," Melissa warned.

"How so?"

"Thalia won't let somebody talk bad about you."

"Well—" I began to speak, but Melissa was adamant.

"You don't understand. When that whole drama unfolded between you and Jake and Jesus, she let Jesus have what for. I guess he made some comment or other in her presence and she tore him up and made him apologize."

I was more than a little surprised. When I was being honest with myself—not a common occurrence lately—I was jealous of Thalia's and Jesus's ability to communicate in Thalia's native tongue. Throw in the fact that he is a real-life soldier, and my inferiority complex gets quite a workout.

"Steve?" Dr. Zahn seemed to appear at my elbow as if by magic.

"Did you find them?"

"Sunshine set them up in a corner in the back so they could all be together. It looks like they are all going to make it."

I know that was supposed to be good news, but I was having trouble feeling good about anything with the whole situation involving Emily. I gave her a nod.

The rest of the evening was a blur. We brought in everything that we'd managed to scavenge, along with the two elk, and let Fiona, Cheryl, and Nickie sort through it.

It was while everything was being brought in that I received a rather pleasant surprise. It seems that, in our absence, Billy and Jake had built five wooden tubs out of what looked like a huge tree. Each one was set up on a pedestal so that they could be drained completely after each use. To add to the surprise, a huge fifty gallon drum was constantly kept full of water and atop a bed of glowing coals just out back.

"You've got to be kidding," I gasped when I was led into the, until now, mostly useless public bathroom.

Already, Jon and Dr. Zahn were soaking in their own personal baths. Melissa drew the sheet so I could undress in privacy, but I wouldn't have cared in the slightest if there had been a curtain or not. Modesty flies out the door when you are presented with a hot bath for the first time in forever. I sank into the water and let out a huge sigh. It was wonderful.

"Sunshine said that we needed to be more conscious of our hygiene or we would be compounding our health risks," Melissa explained as she soaped up a sponge and began scrubbing at my back. "Billy and Jake went to work. It seems that Billy was a teacher's aid in shop class. He found the right tree, cut it down, segmented it, and then hollowed it out with fire. He said it won't be permanent, the wood will start to deteriorate, but it should get us through till summer."

"Where did he find the plastic tarps?" Each "tub" was lined with heavy duty plastic sheets.

"In the tool shed, folded up and stuffed in a corner."

I didn't care if these things only lasted a few weeks, to soak in a hot bath was absolutely amazing…until I got out and saw all the crud floating on the surface. It was like a disgusting oil slick or something.

"Yeah," Melissa said with a nod as she handed me a towel, "none of us realized how much grime had accumulated on our bodies until that first bath. Taking those one-bucket-showers is apparently about as effective as using a single Handi Wipe to mop your kitchen floor."

After dressing, I went in to check on Emily again. Thalia was on the floor beside the bed in her sleeping bag with Buster snuggled at her feet. The dog only opened its eyes long enough to see who had intruded, and then closed them after what sure seemed like an exasperated huff. Emily's chest was rising and falling in the slow steady rhythm of sleep. Jesus was in a chair against the far wall keeping watch. I noticed a set of straps around Emily's wrists and ankles.

"We have always kept an adult on watch," Jesus whispered. "Thalia hasn't left her side for longer than a few minutes at a time, so we started keeping her in restraints this morning."

"I didn't notice any when I came in earlier," I said.

"Sunshine had them taken off when you arrived. She didn't want you to walk in and see her all trussed up…figured that it was going to be rough enough on you just seeing her in this condition. Melinda slipped in as soon as you left and put them back on."

"I can watch her now." I appreciated the sentiment, but I wasn't too sure I liked the idea that somebody thought I couldn't handle the situation.

"You look like you are about to fall over," Jesus countered. "Get some rest. I promise I will come get you if there is any change. And I will make sure that Billy knows to do the same when he relieves me."

He was right, I felt like somebody had tied weights to my eyelids. Even standing, I struggled with each blink. My eyes really wanted to shut. Melissa took my hand and somehow I ended up in our sleeping bag.

13

Geeksicles

Kevin peeked between the slits in the tent flap. The person standing guard—it was impossible to tell if it was male or female—was leaning forward and rubbing his or her hands together over the fire burning in the barrel. A few flakes were drifting lazily. That wasn't a good sign. Fresh snow would be an automatic tracking device. He turned back to the expectant faces that, with the exception of Erin, all showed signs of being ready for action.

"It is dark enough," he barely mouthed the words.

Matt nodded and took his place at the entrance of the tent. "I owe you one," he mouthed back.

"Screw you!" Kevin yelled. He let his punch fly, catching Matt on the shoulder. Aleah timed slapping her hand on her thigh almost perfectly.

Matt fell backwards and through the flap. There was an exclamation. Kevin thought it sounded female. He shoved that piece of information someplace in the back of his mind where, hopefully, he wouldn't find it again. He bobbed his head once...twice...a third time and charged out of the tent, tackling Matt. The pair rolled twice, coming to a stop with Kevin on top.

"Clear," Matt whispered. His job, after being hit by Kevin and "knocked" through the tent flap, was to take a quick look around and see if there were any other guards in the immediate vicinity.

Kevin waited until he felt the hand on his shoulder and quickly grabbed the wrist, jerking the person forward and over.

225

She—he saw her face clearly in the glow from the fire in the barrel—landed with a graceless thud on her back. He brought one hand over her mouth and the other came down hard on her throat. He would never forget the feeling of the windpipe crushing under the blow. It took a little longer than he would have liked for the thrashing to cease.

Getting to his feet, he turned to find everybody staring with open mouths and wide eyes. He tried not to feel like an animal. Briefly he wished that Shaw hadn't been so damn altruistic at the end. If he'd survived, then it would not likely be his hands getting so damn dirty.

"Okay, lead the way," Kevin whispered to Matt.

The plan he'd come up with was not elegant. He was familiar enough with the grounds and had observed the camp enough to have a basic idea of the layout. Plus, he'd been very vigilant about identifying possible paths to take when the time came to make a hasty exit—he'd never doubted that it would come to such a thing. The others had helped him refine things as he drew a basic sketch of the camp on the dirty floor. He doubted that Lee Marvin or the other guys from *The Dirty Dozen* would be envious of his map...or his plan for that matter.

The idea he'd come up with was simple: Run away. After being assured that they knew exactly where Shari and Valarie were being kept, Kevin laid it all out. There were very few questions with the exception of the one that Erin blurted out while she was leaning in over his shoulder.

"What makes you think they will just let us get away?"

"Unless they have completely changed their patrol plan and have in-camp sentries, I don't think they are worried about us getting away," Kevin said in a voice just under a whisper to avoid the possibility of being overheard. "It is below freezing out there. They probably don't expect us to try and make a break for it...and if we did, they wouldn't expect us to survive. They took our coats and our boots. We would have to run through the snow and risk exposure...frostbite..."

"So why are we doing this?" Erin had pressed.

"Because it's not that far away to that housing development," Kevin replied. "And a few minutes of misery beats a lifetime of being somebody's prisoner. They could decide to kill us in the morning."

Kevin didn't think it would come to that. He had a feeling that the major truly wanted them to join her band of raiders. Kevin had more than just the logical, moral reason for not considering that offer. The "Bad Guy" never triumphed in the books or movies. Sure, he had told them all time and again that this was not the movies, but it was a nagging feeling in his gut that wouldn't go away. He'd never bought into karma or any of that other mumbo jumbo, but something told him that staying with Major Beers would cost him more than he could afford.

"So where do we go after we rummage houses for shoes and coats?" Erin pressed.

Kevin had bitten his tongue. For one, all the points that she was making were valid ones. He was actually surprised and just a little impressed with Erin and her line of questioning.

"The farm house," Kevin had answered.

The funny thing was, until that exact moment, he hadn't really known where they would be going. Her question demanded an answer, and thankfully, he had one. Several weeks ago, they had stopped at a remote farm house. It was there that they had met Aleah. During their stay, he, Aleah, and Heather had made a supply run. When they had eventually set out for the country club, Kevin had insisted that they leave a cache behind. Partially in case they came back that way—which seemed unlikely at the time—and partially to provide for a possible passer-by in need.

That's karma, you idiot, the voice in Kevin's head practically screamed.

Now that they were out, everybody huddled together, waiting for Kevin to lead the way. He took one last look at the face of the young woman he'd just killed. He didn't think he would ever be able to forget her...or what he'd done.

"Hurry up, Erin," Aleah urged.

It had been quickly decided that Erin would take the shoes

and coat from their sentry. This would hopefully keep her grip-ing down to a minimum. The girl was surprisingly quick about it. Of course, Kevin chalked that up simply to the fact that it was so painfully cold. Finally, she was finished and he and Heather dragged the body into their tent.

"Okay, Matt, lead the way," Kevin whispered.

The first several steps were made worse by the fact that the old snow had frozen and thawed and re-frozen so many times that is felt like walking on cold shards of glass. Kevin was a lit-tle surprised by how quiet the camp was. He had sort of expected them to encounter at least somebody. However, as they flitted amongst the shadows on the way to where Shari and Valarie were supposedly being held, there was absolutely no movement. Sure, they could hear the occasional muffled conversation com-ing from within the tents scattered about the rather unmilitary-like encampment.

They were passing one tent when a low moan sounded caus-ing everybody to freeze. Kevin had taken the small crossbow from the soldier and Aleah had taken the machete she'd had strapped to her thigh. However, it was only Kevin who brought his weapon up, fully expecting a zombie to come stumbling out.

"Easy," Aleah whispered. The others had to put hands to mouths in order to muffle their snickers—even Erin. "That is the brothel."

Kevin was thankful for the dark as he felt his face heat up in what was probably a serious enough blush to cast at least a little glow in the darkness. The warmth on his face served as a re-minder that his feet were very cold. He prodded Matt, and they wove through the dozen or so vehicles scattered about the park-ing lot.

Finally, they came to a stop at the small tool shed that sat just off from where the main club house had once been. There was no sentry, but a chain with a huge padlock was wrapped around the handles of the double-doors. Kevin was confused.

"I don't get it," Kevin whispered. "If they took their shoes and coat like they did ours, why bother with the security?"

"The soldiers insisted on it. They figured if Valarie could burn down the country club, they didn't want her wandering around," Matt explained.

"But Valarie didn't—" Kevin began.

"But the major has everybody thinking that she did," Heather reminded.

"It would have been nice to know this ahead of time," Kevin snapped.

"In all the excitement, I just didn't think about it," Matt admitted sheepishly. In the darkness he was able to make out heads nodding in agreement.

Kevin scowled and approached the padlocked door. By now, his feet felt as if they were on fire. He noticed everybody else—with the exception of Erin—dancing back and forth and rubbing their exposed arms. *Now what?* He thought. It wasn't like he had his lock pick set with him. Hell, he didn't even have a bobby pin or a piece of wire.

"We will have to come back for them," Kevin sighed.

"What?" Erin pushed forward, her voice just on the edge of too loud.

"We don't have a choice," Kevin hissed. "There is no way we can get past that chain, and all of us need to get something on our feet or we are going to end up losing toes."

"Kevin?" a voice whispered on the other side of the door. "Is that really you?"

"It's all of us, Shari," Kevin whispered.

"He says we are gonna have to leave you behind," Erin blurted, causing everybody else to look around nervously as if they expected a sentry to pop up out of the snow and shoot them all.

"The door is chained and padlocked," Kevin explained. "I don't have any way to get you out of there, but I promise we won't abandon you. I'll come back...tonight if possible...but we won't just bail on you."

"You need to just run, Kevin," Shari whispered. "You can't come back. You and I both know that would be foolish."

"I won't leave you," Kevin insisted.

"And Valarie," Shari added. "I know, Kevin. But we also both know that you will be lucky to sneak out of here alive. Coming back is asking for trouble."

"But I can't—" Kevin protested.

"I will take care of Valarie," Shari said. "The major sent over some of her medications. I read all the labels and I will make sure that she is okay."

"I can't just leave you with these people." Kevin swallowed a huge lump in his throat. He knew what she was saying to be true. Even worse, he didn't have time to stand here and debate the issue. They needed to run. "I won't abandon you…I will find a way to come back for you both."

"I'm not leaving," Erin insisted.

"Shut up and do what Kevin says," Shari's voice hissed from the other side of the door. "You need to grow the hell up, little sister. Nobody has time for your crap anymore." Erin let out a gasp in the darkness. "If you want to have any chance to survive, you need to stop thinking that this is all going to be over some day and start doing what it takes to be a part of the group."

"But—" Erin whimpered.

"No!" Shari snapped. "Get your asses moving!"

Kevin took a tentative step away from the shed, and then another. Pretty soon, he was plowing through the snow, heading down a gentle slope that ended at a wall of leafless trees. He thought he heard an occasional sob behind him, but he was in too much discomfort to pay that much attention…or care.

They spotted the six foot high brick wall on the other side of a clearing as they emerged from the thin strip of woods that once divided two fairways. By now, his feet felt like a pair of ice blocks attached just below the ankles. He and the other barefoot runners were starting to stumble, having lost all feeling in their feet. This, in turn, was leading to frozen, numb hands as they kept having to catch themselves as they fell.

When they reached the fence, they encountered a new set of problems. Everybody was so cold, that their bodies were sapped of strength to the point that getting over the wall posed an even bigger obstacle.

"I am going to get on my hands and knees," Kevin said through chattering teeth. "Matt, you get up on that wall and help the girls over. Erin, then Heather, then Aleah."

"No," Erin insisted.

"We don't have time for this," Heather managed, biting her tongue twice with teeth that were clicking so hard, Kevin wondered how they weren't shattering.

"I am the only one in a coat and shoes, I go last," Erin said, pushing Matt forward. "That way, I can help pull Kevin up."

It took far more effort than any of them could have managed without working together. In fact, by the time it was Kevin's turn, it was Erin almost single-handedly pulling him over the wall.

"I just want to sit down and rest for a few minutes," Heather sighed from where she had collapsed in a nearby snowdrift.

"No," Kevin urged, even though he felt exactly the same. "It is just a little ways now and we can warm up."

He led them across the freeway where the crustiness and jaggedness of the icy snow was at its worst. Kevin took up the lead, but kept looking over his shoulder to see that the others were following.

Finally, they reached the small housing development. Several of the homes had big spray-painted markings indicating that they had been scavenged, but Kevin didn't care. He'd been the one doing most of the supply runs and knew very well that they had left behind most of the clothing and linen. It simply hadn't been necessary to take it all.

Just the act of stepping inside and being off the actual snow was an immediate relief for them all. He'd been in this house a couple of times and knew that the bedrooms were upstairs.

"Follow me," he said, fighting the invisible pins and needles that began to pierce every inch of his exposed skin. With each step, it seemed that the gauge of those needles was getting bigger. By the time he reached the top step, it felt like his body was

231

being tattooed with a nail gun. He wasn't alone in his misery as whimpers and soft crying followed him.

In the first bedroom, he motioned to the twin bed against the wall with posters of Justin Bieber over it. *Obviously a young girl's room*, Kevin thought. At least he hoped so.

"I can't feel anything below my shins," Matt groaned. "But everything else is on fire.

"Frostbite," Kevin said as he opened the top left drawer of the dresser. It was crammed full with tee shirts. A distressed murmur rose from everybody, but Kevin began throwing clothing over his shoulder. "Help each other wrap up your feet, but *don't* rub," he instructed.

"Won't it get the circulation going faster?" Aleah asked through a whimper.

"You more than likely have ice crystals formed up in your feet. To rub them would be like taking tiny razors to all the veins and capillaries. Just wrap them tight and with several layers." As everybody got to work—Erin helping Aleah, Matt and Heather paired up— he sat down to start on his own feet.

"We can't stay long," Kevin said through his clenched teeth as he bit down against the pain. "I figure we have an hour tops before we are found out. I don't know if killing our guard will earn us a more serious search, but we have to get moving."

"Will you answer a question? "Erin asked as she tied off the tee shirt she had been wrapping Aleah's right foot in.

"I have no idea when we will be able to go back for your sister," Kevin answered, knowing very well what the girl would ask. "But I swear to you that I will not just abandon her and Valarie."

"That was *a* question," Erin said. "But it wasn't the question that I had in mind."

Kevin tied off his first foot, grabbed another shirt and looked up. "Okay, go ahead."

"Why does this lady want you so bad?" Erin asked.

Kevin cocked his head to the side for a moment. Finally, he looked up. "I have no idea," he admitted.

"It has seemed like she was a bit obsessed," Matt chimed in after struggling to stifle a yelp when Heather pulled his untreated foot into her lap.

"Sorry, thought you couldn't feel anything below the shins," Heather apologized.

"It's okay, just had this sensation like all the skin on that foot was peeled off with a rusty razor."

"That's a good sign," Kevin said. "I think that means you only have really bad second degree frostbite."

"And that is a good thing?" Matt grumbled.

"As opposed to third or fourth when you probably lose your appendage?" Kevin looked up. "Yeah, I'd say that is good."

"So," Aleah looked up as Erin finished tying off her other foot, "how long before we need to go back out there?" This question was greeted by several groans and complaints, but she cut them all off. "We obviously can't stay here. But I honestly don't know how far I can walk…shoes or no shoes."

Kevin looked around at the faces staring back at him in the shadows. The one thing about a snow-covered terrain was the fact that it really reflected the ambient light. He couldn't see them clearly, but he could see well enough.

Fear.

Uncertainty.

Doubt.

Whether it was directed at him or not didn't matter. These were his people, and thus, his responsibility. He needed to regain their confidence.

"I am not saying this is going to be easy. I also can't promise that, if you come with me, things will be good or easy or whatever it is you think I can do. I don't have any answers," Kevin said with a firmness that he wasn't too sure didn't sound like the "old" Kevin. Still, it wouldn't do to have these people following him around with some crazy idea that he knew what he was doing. If he was being honest with himself, he had lost the grip of what to do the moment he met Heather and found out she was immune. Nobody in the books or movies was immune.

That was simply proof of his axiom that "this ain't the movies."

All he could do was try his best…think things through…and try to never make the same mistake twice. Beyond that, it was all up for grabs.

"How long can we take for a break?" Matt asked. He stretched his wrapped up feet out in front of himself.

"I think we can safely wait an hour," Kevin said. "I don't like the idea of waiting that long, but if we absolutely have to, I think we can hold up for one hour."

"Do you really think they could find us that fast?" Heather asked, copying Matt by stretching out her legs as well.

"There aren't many places we could make it to," Kevin explained. "This is the closest development and has to be the first place they will look."

"Does this belong to you?" a voice from the doorway made everybody jump.

Kevin's head swung around, his hand going instinctively for the small crossbow. The figure standing in the doorway holding Erin by the scruff of the neck took a step forward. The shadows did not reveal the face, but he knew the voice.

"Willa!" Kevin had to work to climb to his feet and overcome the pain.

"Let me go," Erin snarled, struggling against the hand that had a tight grip on her.

"She's with us," Kevin confirmed.

Willa gave Erin a none-too-gentle shove forward and followed her into the room. Everybody else was struggling to their feet as well, but unlike Kevin who was relaxed, the other three were visibly on edge.

"I caught her sniffing around outside," Willa said with a tiny laugh. "She was trying to climb through a window."

"But—" Kevin started, only to have Willa cut him off.

"She was completely oblivious to the walker that was coming up to take a chomp out of her leg." Willa patted the large blade on her hip. "I thought she might at least notice when I cleaved it in the forehead…but no. She was still wiggling and squirming in a window frame, not a clue in the world."

"I heard a noise and was trying to get through and away from whatever was coming...but my coat got caught on a stupid piece of metal that was sticking up." Erin tugged at her jacket and stomped away from the woman.

"Umm..." Aleah moved next to Kevin and took his arm. "Maybe you could introduce us to your friend, Kevin."

"Everybody, this is Willa, that soldier that I told you about," Kevin had to swallow a few times before he could speak. For some reason, his mouth was extremely dry. "Willa, this is Aleah, Heather, and Matt. You already met Erin." He indicated to each one in turn.

"What in the world are you doing out here...and do I even dare to ask where your shoes went?" Willa stepped into the room and dropped a big burlap bag on the floor.

"We made a run for it," Kevin said with a shrug. "As for the shoes, Major Beers took them to discourage our departure."

"If she wanted to keep you from running, she would have cuffed you or locked you up," Willa said.

"She has my sister and Valarie locked up," Erin blurted.

"Ahh." Willa nodded her head. She glanced at Kevin. "So the girl you got the medicine for is locked up, but you, she just takes your shoes? That doesn't seem right."

"She had a guard on us," Erin offered.

"*A* guard...she had *A* guard on you?" Willa said with disbelief.

"We killed her," Heather said sadly.

"Crap," Willa hissed. She turned and bolted from the room.

"What's her problem?" Matt asked.

"You need to get your group out here," Willa hissed.

Kevin took a step and felt like he was on one of those stupid retreats where they had you walk across hot coals. Steeling himself, he continued out of the room and to the doorway where Willa stood. What he saw made his heart sink.

"What's that?" Erin asked. Of everybody, she was the only one in the group who had no trouble walking.

"We have to go!" Willa insisted.

"We won't make it ten minutes," Kevin sighed.

"Excuse me," Erin pressed. "I asked a question."

"You got played, Kevin," Willa said with a shake of her head.

"You think she would do all of this for you?" Kevin asked. He couldn't keep the doubt from creeping in to his voice.

"If she knew we were together, then she knew that I would still be in the area," Willa said.

"Can somebody please tell me what is going on?" Erin insisted.

It had taken that long for everybody else to reach the trio standing in the doorway staring out into the night. The low rumble was something you could hear as well as feel now.

"I didn't see anything like that when I reached the camp," Kevin said with a shake of his head.

"They didn't use those when they took us," Aleah gasped.

"They must think my entire group is with me." Willa turned to face Kevin and his group.

"Hello!" Erin stomped her foot. She was tired of being ignored. She was sick of being treated like she wasn't a part of things. "What are those?"

"Bradley Fighting Vehicles," Willa whispered.

"So what in the hell would make it so important for her to come after you like this?" Kevin asked.

"You guys stay here." Willa began stripping off her weapons' belt.

"What do you think you're doing?" Kevin asked.

"I'm going out there and surrendering. I'm telling her that I haven't seen you and I am giving myself up."

"What?" Kevin, Aleah, Heather, and Matt blurted almost in unison.

"She doesn't care about you guys," Willa explained. "She wants me. If I give up, she will probably roll out of here tonight."

"Wait," Kevin insisted. "Something about this is just not

adding up. For one, she wouldn't have even known that you and I were working together when she took my camp. So what am I missing?"

"Major Beers has been looking for me and my group almost since this whole thing went off," Willa started. She sighed heavily and closed her eyes. "I haven't been entirely honest with you, Kevin."

14

Vignettes XXIX

Ahi struggled to his feet. The bloom of heat radiated from his left cheek and the taste of blood was coppery in the back of his throat. He wiped at his face with his hand and was not surprised when it came away bloody. His feet betrayed him and he stumbled to the left a few steps before regaining his balance.

Aaheru still stood in his doorway. The towel that had adorned his waist when he answered had fallen to the floor, but the man paid it no mind. He rubbed absently at his left hand, the back of which had just caught Ahi squarely in the face.

"You thought it best to wait?" Aaheru snarled. "Then perhaps you know more about this little attempt than you are saying."

"I serve only you, Pharaoh." Ahi decided to end the war with balance. It would hopefully soothe the anger of the man towering naked over him at the moment. And while Ahi was not adverse to the idea of Aaheru doing anything to him while naked, Ahi would certainly wish for much better circumstances.

"Why would you think it to be okay for you to stand outside my door for several minutes?" Aaheru roared. "You have information regarding somebody who wants to try to kill us all and you decide to eavesdrop on my intimate affairs with one of my wives?"

Ahi glanced up—not at Aaheru, no, his eyes chanced a peek at Ahmes who sat naked on Aaheru's bed with a sheet pulled up to her chin. Just as he suspected, the young girl was not pleased with the idea that there would be other women sharing Aaheru's

239

bed. Pharaoh or no…a woman did not usually like sharing the affections of a man that she considered to be hers.

"I only just arrived, my Pharaoh." Ahi tried his best to sound contrite. What he would not say is that he did in fact show up just as the little tryst began. "I hadn't been there for more than an instant. It was clear that you were nearing completion. I did not want to incur your wrath by interrupting such a moment."

Aaheru felt a bit of his anger subside. Ahi made a good point. And a few moments would not make a difference. After all, it was a case of *attempted* sabotage. The engineer had discovered and thwarted the actual attempt. The culprit was still at large, but that was a problem that he could devise an answer for once he had a moment to think clearly.

Naturally he would not admit anything concerning his thoughts to Ahi. As pharaoh, it was his duty to instill a respectful fear in his subjects. This was actually a good thing to have happened. It reminded Ahi of his place; it also demonstrated his power in front of Ahmes. This would certainly be spoken of to the other women, which, in turn, would ensure that every one of his subjects would know the details before the sun set the next day. Even better, the way women tended to exaggerate, his power and strength would be amplified. *Yes*, Aaheru thought, *this would serve his needs*.

"Meet me on the bridge in ten minutes," Aaheru said to Ahi with a dismissive wave before returning to his stateroom and closing the door.

He dressed and ensured to equip himself with an assortment of blades. As he dressed, he kept noticing that Ahmes simply sat in the bed with her arms folded across her chest like a petulant child. Her expression was a perplexing scowl. Perhaps she was hoping for another powerful mounting by her beloved. Well, that would have to wait. There were people trying to kill not only the people that would serve as the stock for the start of a new Egypt, but they were trying to kill HIM!

When he walked onto the bridge, he was struck by a peculiar and unpleasant smell. He sniffed a few times, but could not place it right away.

"We are getting a strong breeze from the north, my Pharaoh," one of the men announced.

Aaheru tried not to let his annoyance at himself show. He had no idea what the man was trying to say.

"Likely we are getting a smell of one of the coastal cities from Turkey," another of the men added. "Perhaps Antalya...it would certainly have enough of a population to account for what we are smelling."

Aaheru was struck by how foul the stench was. He'd been surrounded by thousands of the walking dead and had the entire city of Cairo sending up its stink. Why would this be so much worse?

"Funny how you can learn to get used to something and just block it out," Ahi offered.

Aaheru glanced at his advisor and gave a nod. Once again, the man proved to almost be able to read his very thoughts. Yes, he had indeed chosen his advisor well. Surely he would understand that there would be the occasion that he would fall subject to his pharaoh's discipline. Even the best of children have their wayward moments.

"So am I to understand that we have had an attempt at sabotage?" Aaheru asked, bringing things to order.

"Yes," Ahi spoke.

"And who was it that discovered this attempt?" Aaheru posed the question.

"That would be me, my Pharaoh." A heavy-set man with greasy black hair yanked the stained cap from his head, rolling it nervously in his hands as he bowed and stepped forward.

"And what is your name?" Aaheru faced the man.

"Otmar Ali, my Pharaoh," the man replied in a voice that was surprisingly soft for a man so large.

"You are to be commended, Otmar Ali," Aaheru spoke, trying to sound gracious but still maintain the authoritativeness he decided that a pharaoh must always display. "I wish for you to dine with me this evening as a reward for your diligence."

"So what shall we do to try and find this person?" Ahi asked.

Aaheru cast an angry glance at his advisor. Did Ahi not see that he was trying to be a magnanimous ruler? Perhaps that cuff to the face was warranted after all.

"I want all hands brought to the dining hall. I will leave it to you, Ahi, to choose who will assist you in this task, but I want everybody assigned to another individual. Everybody will be confined to their quarters until we arrive at our destination with the exception of meals. I want you to also determine who will eat when. Everybody will be escorted to and from their quarters by your security team."

Aaheru answered a few questions, but quickly grew tired of the details. He had given his edict. To refuse or disobey would result in being tossed over the side. Beyond that, he didn't care. All of this had stirred his desires. He would go pay a visit to the women's quarters. *After all*, he thought, *it was time to start selecting his wives*. Once he had done so, he could begin to award the remaining women to those who excelled at doing his bidding.

***

April Cable and another woman emerged from the bedroom. Juan wished for the thousandth time that he was even remotely good at remembering names. That thought was quickly banished when he saw the red-rimmed eyes on both women.

"Is she…" He couldn't bring himself to say the words.

"She will be fine," April stepped up to Juan and took his hands. "But she lost the baby."

"The what?" Juan felt his knees give just a little.

"You didn't know she was pregnant?" April gasped. "Oh my God, Juan. I am so sorry."

He was sure that he could grieve later, but at the moment, all he truly cared about was that Mackenzie was okay. The woman with April was talking, and something she said brought Juan back to the situation at hand.

"...if not, we might suffer some needless casualties." The woman wiped her hands with a wet towel and stared at Juan expectantly.

He really did not like how everybody had turned him into some sort of leader. Didn't they know who he was? How about *what* you were, a voice in his head said with an accusatory tone. A street thug, a druggie, a thief...and so many other things—too many to mention—had filled a few pages worth of his "rap sheet" before the world had pressed a gigantic reset button.

"If not what?" Juan made himself ask.

"We need to find out some things like known allergies, medical conditions, and blood types," the woman repeated. Juan expected her to be angry at having to repeat herself, but she had simply glanced at April with some sort of sad look and nodded. "It's not like we can just rush to the hospital if something goes wrong. If we are going to set up here, then we need to get people like April and anybody else with her skills to start teaching others."

Juan glanced at April with a raised eyebrow. "What kind of people are you?"

"I was an EMT," April said. Something in her tone told Juan that perhaps this bit of information had been relayed to him before.

"I understand that you are going across the river," the woman resumed control of the conversation. "Perhaps while you are there, you can see if you can find some blood type testing kits."

"And what do they look like?" Juan asked.

"They usually come in a box that says 'Blood type testing kit' I would imagine," the woman made a slight laugh as if she had said something witty.

Juan scowled. "Maybe you should come with me, I might not remember...what did you say your name was?"

"I'm Jeannie Simons," the woman said with less laughter in her voice. "And maybe I could write it down for you if you need something to help you remember."

Juan was not always the most observant guy, but he knew fear when he saw and heard it. This woman wanted nothing to do with going on a run. Well, he could worry about that later. He wanted to see Mackenzie.

"So can I see her?" Juan started towards the door, not really caring what the answer might be if it was anything that would delay his seeing her for himself.

He opened the door and stepped into the room. It had a funny smell that he didn't place right away. Then his eyes found the bucket covered with a bloody towel in the corner.

He faltered just a bit as he stepped up beside the bed and took Mackenzie's hands in his. Her hair was spread out on the pillow, and even though she was unusually pale, she was still the most beautiful thing he had ever seen.

"How are you feeling?" The moment that he asked the question, he wished that he could suck the words back into his mouth.

"Tired," was her whispered response. She opened her eyes and he could tell that she had been crying.

"You want me to stay here beside you for a while?" Juan looked around for a chair to pull up beside the bed and was more than a little flustered to discover that there was no such thing in their bedroom.

"I want you to go with Frank and try to find that girl," Mackenzie replied. "But I do have a favor that I want to ask you first."

"Name it," Juan said with a severity that caught him by surprise. He had always figured that it was easy to say you would do anything for somebody, but at that very moment, he understood that, for the first time in his life, he was with somebody that he could say those words and literally mean it.

"I want you to take the baby and bury her beside my mom." A single tear welled up in Mackenzie's left eye, bloomed, and then spilled down her cheek.

"It was a girl?" Juan whispered. He felt his chest tighten.

Mackenzie's hands squeezed his.

"Do you...do..." her voice faltered as a few more tears joined the first.

"We could name her Maggie...sorta like your mom, but not quite," Juan offered.

"That would be nice," Mackenzie sighed and closed her eyes.

Juan struggled with the question that would not go away. "How long have you known?" he finally asked.

"Just a few days. I found out while you were out on that last run."

"Why didn't you tell me?"

"I wanted to make it a perfect moment." Mackenzie started to cry.

"Maybe I should stay—" Juan started.

"No!" Mackenzie insisted. "That girl is out there alone. You need to go help her if you can."

Juan nodded his head. He glanced over at the bucket covered by a bloody towel. He would bury little Maggie. First, he would find something more suitable to place her in besides that bucket. Then...he would go find the missing girl and the idiot boys who took off to find her.

***

Chad felt like his legs were going to burst into flames. It was as if he could feel each fiber of each muscle, and they were all burning like a firecracker fuse. He kept reminding himself of what it was they were hoping to obtain and why.

Michael seemed to be doing just fine up ahead. At the moment, if for no other reason than the way he continued to lead the four of them along like it was nothing more than a walk in the park; he hated Michael Clark.

They had left before dawn this morning. He'd had just as soon left the day it was decided. Ronni hadn't spoken to him once in the three days that Michael got everything ready. It would be him, Michael, Scott, and a lady named Trina. Chad had made the mistake of asking if it were short for Katrina like the hurricane. Apparently she had a few years to get tired of answering with a polite "no" to that question. Oh sure, the answer was still basically the same, there just happened to be a few expletives before and after the actual answer.

Chad didn't much like Trina either, and it had nothing to do with her less-than-positive reaction to his 'Katrina' question. She was gliding along beside Michael—laughing and talking! He could barely get enough oxygen in his lungs to breathe, much less carry on a conversation. It seems that Trina had been an employee at the Yosemite Village luxury hotel as a hiking guide in the spring and summer; and as a ski-trail guide in the winter and fall.

When Michael signaled for the first break, Scott came to a stop beside where Chad was sitting down on a fallen tree that he had brushed clear of snow. He gave a tired sigh and took a seat on a space after snapping off a few remaining branches.

"How you holding up?" Scott said. It was accompanied by a groan as he reached over his shoulders to pull his pack off.

"About the same as you by the sounds of it," Chad said with a sarcastic chuckle.

A nerve-jangling titter came from where Trina sat beside Michael sharing a canteen. Chad glanced over and did his best not to extend a particular finger in response to her way-too-enthusiastic wave.

"I should have let Brett make this trip," Scott said after a long pull from his own canteen. "Old age, a bum knee from my high school football days, and the fact that I really hate snow all add up to me wondering what the hell I was thinking."

"So, have you been noticing all the zombies trapped in the snow like it is quicksand?" Chad asked after they had both popped open one of the precious cans of chili that had been spared for them to take on the trip and scooped out a few spoonfuls.

"Makes you wonder how they keep showing up at our

camp," Scott said with a nod.

"They never need to rest," Chad said with a shrug. "Eventually, the right combination of jerking around probably frees them up. As for the herds, I think they are almost like a snow plow."

Scott considered the information and finally nodded. "Well, according to the Michael De Sade and Suzi Chapstick, we should reach the snow line before dark."

"That's good, because I don't think I could deal with another day on skis," Chad said. "When I used to go cross country skiing, it was for a few hours tops...we've been going for at least ten hours with minimal breaks, and honestly, these little breaks for some cold, canned chili ain't putting all that much energy back in the tank, if you know what I'm saying."

Yes, Scott nodded, he did know what Chad was saying. He had been fighting cramps for the past couple of hours. Not for the first time, he envied Brett for being left behind. Of course, Chad had asked the man to keep an eye on his daughter. And while Ronni could be a handful, keeping tabs on her seemed infinitely preferable to this trip.

As if on cue, Trina and Mike stood and gave the signal to get moving. Chad and Scott shared a miserable look and pushed themselves up to their feet. A few minutes later, the foursome were back on the trail, gliding along at a brisk pace. Occasionally, they would cruise past a zombie buried to its waist, chest, or even to its neck.

A few hours into the next leg, it was Chad who signaled for a stop. Michael and Trina both looked at him like he'd just let one go in church.

"Is anybody else noticing the fact that we are seeing more and more zombies as we go along?" he asked. This received blank stares form the 'dynamic duo' as he'd begun to refer to them in his mind. Thankfully, Scott came to his aid.

"I'd guess that we have passed a couple hundred in the past hour...more than we saw the whole rest of the day combined."

"Maybe there were just as many, but maybe they were all completely buried under the snow," Trina said with a shrug, clearly not grasping the seriousness of her own statement.

"You better pray that isn't the case," Scott shot back.

"In any case," Chad piped in, "we need to be vigilant from here forward. I say we pair up. One person keep eyes up, the other scanning the ground ahead."

"I will pair with Scott," Michael said. He shot a look at Chad that, if he didn't know better, he would swear conveyed the message, 'she's your problem now.'

It took a few minutes to get moving, but eventually the foursome were gliding along the snow. Some time that afternoon, they came to the top of a small rise. From this point on, it would be a long and winding run downhill. Chad had learned how to smile and nod a lot as Trina droned on about a particular tree or a rock formation. He began to realize that Michael and she had not been engaging in some sort of friendly banter; no, Trina was still in guide mode.

Oddly enough, it was Trina that shot out ahead of the group and then came to a skidding halt across what was probably the road underneath all the snow. She flipped up her goggles and the three men saw the fear in her eyes.

Trina pointed down and to their left. Chad, Scott, and Michael looked down the embankment to the switchback. Packed shoulder to shoulder and stretching down and all the way around the next curve was a herd of undead.

"There has to be hundreds...thousands of them," Scott breathed.

"What do we do now?" Chad asked, glancing at Michael. "I'm not too familiar with the area, but I'd wager that they are using the same road that we drove up when we came here. As far as I know, that is the only way up or down the mountain."

"We don't have a choice," Michael said in a voice barley above a whisper. "We have to go down. If not...everybody is going to starve to death."

"They might not be there when we get back," Scott spat. "There is no way in hell that we could fight off that group."

"What makes you so sure they will end up in Yosemite Village?" Trina asked.

"Where else would they end up?" Chad retorted. "Like I said, I don't know the area, but I don't recall any turnoffs or forks on the trip up here."

Trina's face scrunched in deep thought. She didn't need to speak to relate her deductions; it was all over her face. The steep incline leading down to the next relatively flat area would shame any ski resort's "Double Black Diamond" run. Looking down, Chad could almost swear that the face of the mountainside curved inward at one point.

"But we can't go back...not empty handed," she insisted as the men began to turn their skis back the way they'd come.

"And how would you suggest we get around that!" Scott snapped, his arm flailing wildly in the general direction of the oncoming mob. From below, the volume rose on the moans of the undead as they locked in on a new stimulus.

"You three go back," Michael said. "I will try to find a spot and wait them out. Once they have passed, I will head down the mountain and find supplies."

"You think that is a good idea?" Chad asked.

"Nope," Michael shook his head. "But I also don't envy what lies in store for you guys either. You have to go back and tell everybody that a wave of zombies is coming...and then wait for them to arrive and *hope* you can fend them off."

"Well we can't stand around any more and talk about it," Scott said, pointing to the first of the zombies rounding the distant corner about a half mile down the way.

As Chad, Scott, and Trina began the grueling trip back up the hill and towards Yosemite Village with the sounds of the dead growing louder, Chad began to wonder if there was any point in fighting to survive. The only thing he could come up with was enough to make him push on well into the night; he even urged the other two on well after dark.

He had to get back to Ronni.

***

Vix climbed up onto the car and spun around quickly but carefully. It wouldn't do her any good to fall at the moment. The blue-gray face was at the perfect level and distance. As it opened its mouth to let loose with that horrible baby cry sound, she kicked it right in the teeth with her steel-toed boot. The head snapped back and the creature stumbled. Unslinging the spike-tipped pole from her shoulder, she brought it around and drove the point directly into the thing's eye socket just as it brought its head back to try and snap at her.

A few lanes over, Gemma was on top of a blue van. A group of five of those cursed things had her circled, but she was making steady work of them. They'd thought that the road had been clear when they set across it. And it had been for the most part. Then Gemma had spotted that Dasani truck and squealed with delight.

This was the equivalent to discovering an oasis in the middle of the desert. The sliding door was open wide, revealing stacked cases of the bottled water. While it was obvious that others had taken the time to help themselves, there was still more than enough.

Vix had climbed inside and was handing a case down to Gemma when she saw the first head come bobbing along behind another nearby vehicle. And it wasn't like the cars were bumper-to-bumper here. Vix had seen more than one zombie movie where the freeways were stuffed with miles long traffic snarls. She hadn't entirely understood that image. Sure, there might be a few tie-ups where people had tried to flee and ended up smashing into each other, but she didn't think that many people would be out on the roads after the first few days.

It was while Vix was busy pulling out a case and handing it to Gemma that they both heard the most chilling sound imaginable in the post-apocalyptic world: a baby's cry. Gemma dropped the case she'd been handed and almost broke her leg scrambling back from the truck.

As Vix hustled out, she saw five of the cursed things coming up out of the drainage ditch that ran alongside the M3. She wasn't too worried; five of them were manageable even if she'd been alone. Then that sound came again…from the other side if the M3. At least three dozen more were coming up. She would have a talk later with Gemma about being a bit quieter when they were travelling.

Snapping back to the here-and-now, Vix scanned the area to make sure that there were no other immediate threats. She did see a few shadows bobbing in the distance back the way they'd come, but nothing they couldn't out run once they cleared up things here.

Vix moved around the boot of one of those expensive sports cars that her husband always said that men bought when they "lacked the necessary equipment to satisfy their women." She peeked inside and was able to glimpse a hand clutching a bottle of pills.

"Took the easy way," she muttered as she moved in behind the last few zombies that were trying their best to get at Gemma up on top of that van.

She paused, unable to keep from wincing. Two of the undead were children. So far, she had managed to avoid killing any little ones. She'd gotten used to killing zombies. It was the first few that she'd struggled with simply because they were familiar faces. However—and she credited this to all those books and movies that she loved so much—she knew very well that a person could not hesitate when dealing with the undead or you would join their ranks.

As a gift one year, her husband had managed to contact one of the cover artists who did the work for one of her favorite series of zombie books. For Valentine's Day, he presented her with a framed picture of her as a zombie. He'd been a very lucky man that evening. That was as close as she cared to ever come to being a zombie.

She moved quietly. If she could keep from being noticed, then perhaps she could take down at least one of the child-zombies without having to see its face. Taking a few steps forward and raising her blade, Vix paused. There was something about these two zombies that didn't seem right.

She watched them for a few seconds before she realized that they were hanging back from the others. They had moved just outside of Gemma's range and seemed to be more intent on observing than getting in there and trying their hand at the futile exercise of reaching for Gemma. It was as if they knew that they could not reach her, and what's more, if they tried, they would meet the same fate as their cohorts.

But that's silly, Vix thought. *Zombies don't reason or think or do anything else except try to eat people.* At least that had been her view until now. Vix glanced up at Gemma, who seemed to be unconcerned with her situation at the moment. That was fine, that meant that there was no reason to rush in and attack at the moment. She could afford to watch for a few seconds longer.

One of the children, a girl judging by the silky blouse that was almost ready to fall off the frame due to a combination of being snagged and dragged and who knows what else, kept shifting from one foot to the other. It reminded Vix of how children act when they had to pee. The other was almost a statue. It simply stood there making no move forward or back.

"Oi!" Gemma called, snapping Vix out of her observation. "You gonna stand there, or are you going to help me with these two. They don't seem to want to join their friends."

Vix shook her head to clear it and started forward. They must have heard her footsteps or something, because they both turned to face her. Vix froze in mid-stride; one foot still in the air as if she were afraid of what might happen should it touch the ground.

She could see their faces now. Her heart wanted to break. The little boy had a jagged bite taken out of what had once been a pair of plump cheeks. The little girl had fared worse. Her belly had been ripped open. And now she knew why the shirt was still on. It had fused to the wound with filth and dried gore.

The little boy's head tilted to one side and its eyes locked on hers. She would swear for the rest of her life that it glanced down at the weapon in her hand and then back up to her eyes. The pair took a step back.

Vix had no idea what to think now. She had never known a zombie to back away, and yet, here were two doing exactly that. They took another step…right into range of Gemma's spear. Her first thrust drove into the back of the little boy's head. The girl turned just in time to catch the next jab in her right eye.

"Good work," Gemma sighed, sliding off the van and landing on the ground between the two children. "Nice plan to get their attention and scare them back to me."

"I didn't," Vix whispered. For some reason, she couldn't take her eyes of the two downed bodies.

"What?" Gemma only asked with partial interest. She was already walking back to the water truck to reclaim their prize.

"I didn't try to scare them back towards you," Vix explained. "In fact, I am wondering how you didn't notice the way those two were acting."

"Acting?" Gemma had that confused expression that Vix was becoming accustomed to whenever the two of them were talking about zombies.

"Never mind," Vix said with a scowl. Maybe she had been imagining it. After all…everybody knows that zombies don't think. "A couple more miles and we will be at the M25 interchange. We should be able to find a place to rest for the night."

***

"Down here, quick!" Danny hissed, waving Jody and Selina over from where they were crouched behind a Dumpster next to the alley.

The sign coming into town read Newport, Arkansas. The population was, according to the sign, 7,342. Judging by what they'd seen so far, none of the town's citizens had survived…and none had left. Zombies were everywhere.

The two scurried across to join Danny in the dark stairwell.

A half dozen steps led down to a metal door with a small window. The door was currently propped open by a chunk of concrete.

"I used to get in a little trouble when I was growing up," Danny said in response to Jody's arched eyebrow. "The one that put the nail in the coffin was when I broke into my high school. I had this stupid idea that I could get into the school, hack the computer, and then tweak my grades."

"Got caught?" Selina chuckled.

"As I was breaking into the main office. I guess the school had some sort of silent alarm as well as motion detectors. The cops said that the person on the radio basically told them my entire route."

"Talk later, let's get inside," Jody urged.

The trio slipped into the long, dark hallway. Doors lined both sides, just offset from each other. The gloom outside didn't do much to light the way. Plus, the cold had seeped inside to the point where icicles hung in places from the ceiling.

"So tell me what good we are doing by coming in here?" Selina managed through teeth that were already chattering.

"We can find a spot to build a fire that hopefully won't attract attention," Jody whispered. "Now please be quiet for a moment...I thought I heard something."

Selina bit back the response that initially came to her lips. However, she had learned her lesson after last night. They'd had the luxury of stumbling across, of all things, a car that had several bags of groceries in the back seat. It had run off the highway and was nose down in a deep ditch barely visible from the road.

"Probably swerved to avoid hitting a zombie," Danny had quipped.

A lot of the food had spoiled, but there were a couple of bags of canned food that were in perfect condition. That night, they had beef stew cooked over a fire that Jody made in a hole that was almost waist deep.

During the meal, Danny was spinning tales and cracking jokes—which was the same thing he did most of the day as they hiked along in the slush. It helped her keep her mind off of how miserable she was and how very cold her entire body felt…especially her hands, feet, and face.

After one of his more humorous jokes involving two blondes, a step ladder, and a platypus, Selina had laughed so hard that stew actually came out of her nose. Of course that only made her laugh harder.

Jody kept insisting that she quiet down. She had given him some flippant retort about being out in the middle of nowhere and that he should just chill out. Five minutes later, four walkers stumbled into their camp.

"Sorry," Selina whispered, nodding for Jody to lead the way. She thought she caught Danny mimicking her out of the corner of her eye.

They reached the second door and Jody held up his hand to signal a halt. Danny moved up beside him and the two made a few hand gestures. Without any indication that she saw, they burst through the door and disappeared into the room. A rasping moan sounded for a split second, followed by the familiar crunching splat of a head being crushed or busted open with Danny's or Jody's hand ax.

The two emerged and they all continued up the corridor. Jody checked each room very carefully. When they reached the end, they discovered a stairwell leading up. Jody signaled that they retreat back up the way they'd come. He led them into an empty classroom and shut the door.

"If we rig a trip wire at the stairs, we should be able to camp here tonight. This room is perfect. It is big enough that the smoke won't overwhelm us." His voice was still above a whisper.

"Won't it all go out the window if we just open it a crack?" Selina asked.

"Sure, but some of it will still build up in the room," Jody answered. "We don't want to end up suffocating or being overcome by smoke inhalation."

"I'll rig the line," Danny offered as he slipped out the door.

Jody began gathering books and creating a pile. He had a good sized stack, and was about to light it when Selina grabbed his hand. She reached down and plucked a ragged paperback from the pile.

"*Wuthering Heights*," she said with a wistful sigh. "I loved this book when I was in Honors English my junior year in high school."

"I was a fan of *Tom Jones*," Jody said as he started the blaze.

"The singer?" Selina asked with a giggle.

"No…it is an old English comedy," Jody said with the first thing close to a laugh that she'd heard from him since they left Bald Knob. "In fact, if you read it, you will see the genesis of probably three-fourths of the sitcoms ever written."

"Huh." Selina sat down and flipped through the pages of the book.

"I'm gonna go out for wood as soon as Danny gets back," Jody said peeking out the door. "I saw a stack of pallets over by that knocked over school bus. Those should be well seasoned and burn nice."

"Do you need any help?" Selina asked.

"You could come hold the door," Jody said with a nod. "If I am on the run from anything, I don't want to worry about setting things down and opening the door."

She hopped back up to her feet and followed. Jody gave Danny a brief explanation in a loud whisper before heading back down the corridor. Just before they reached the door, Jody froze and raised his hand to signal a stop. Selina didn't need to be told; she could smell it.

Pulling his blade, Jody put his hand on the knob. Selina drew hers and took a few steps back. She had learned from a few of their incursions into abandoned homes that it was always best to give each other room. When you are swinging a blade at something that is trying to eat you, there isn't a lot of time to make sure you have enough space between you and your fellow travellers.

Cracking the door just a bit, Jody peeked out. The stairwell was empty. He pulled the door open and crept out. Step by step, he climbed until he could see over the lip and out into the parking lot. A few feet away, a handful of zombies were crouched on the ground. From this close, he could hear the smacking of mouths and the wet rip of pieces being torn away. What puzzled him was the fact that he hadn't heard anything.

A rock bounced near his head causing Danny to flinch and duck down. His heart felt like it was going to come through his chest. He glanced back at Selina with a scowl.

"What?" she mouthed silently.

"The rock?" he mouthed back. She shrugged.

Danny crept back up and looked again. His eyes scanned the lot more carefully, looking for anything that might be out of place. *There!* Up on top of a school bus a small figure sat hunched over but waving one hand.

Creeping back down to Selina, he whispered in her ear, "There is somebody up on a school bus across the parking lot. It looks like a kid. I'm gonna take out the few in the parking lot and then haul ass back with what I think is just one person. Have the door open."

He didn't wait for confirmation. He'd already wasted enough time. The zombies would be finished with the poor individual that they were snacking on very soon...if they weren't already. He reached the top of the steps and was only momentarily upset to find out that he would now be facing six zombies instead of five. The group was already wandering off and the person on the ground—a young boy in his early teens by the looks—was trying unsuccessfully to stand. It seemed that there was too much damage to the left leg for it to bear any weight.

Jody came in low under the first zombie and brought his blade up under its chin. He shoved it back and it hadn't even hit the ground when he swung with a backhand, catching the next closest threat in the forehead. He knew well enough not to bother with that weapon any more for the moment and drew his Ka-Bar. A stab into the eye took the next closest.

A hand clutched at his sleeve and he quickly shoved off and brought the weapon around and drove it into the temple. The fifth one was a few steps away and Jody moved in with a strike to the forehead. He let his arm relax as the zombie slumped to the ground. This time, he put one foot on a shoulder and yanked the knife free.

He turned around just in time to see the figure from the bus crouching over its undead former companion. A hand ax came out from the thick coat the person was wearing and smashed into the face of the most recent addition to the zombie population.

"C'mon," Jody hissed, "we need to get out from the open."

The person ignored him, pulling the ax loose, but continuing to squat down over the body. Jody moved closer, but stayed beyond what he guessed to be a few feet past arm's reach.

"Hey, you in the coat?"

Still no acknowledgement, but the person did stand up. It was a girl. She turned to face Jody, tears running down her face.

"I know you're upset, but we need to duck out of sight for a bit. Down those stairs." He pointed and took a few steps. The girl did not budge. She glanced at the stairs, and then returned her gaze to Jody. There was something in her eyes.

"You don't trust me?" Jody sighed. "Look, I get it. There has been some crazy shit going on, but you threw the rock at me to get *my* attention." She seemed to consider his statement. "My name is Jody—"

"And my name is Selina."

Jody jumped and spun around with his arm half-cocked. He only took a fraction of a second to appreciate that she had wisely stayed out of range before the anger at being surprised resumed control.

"What have I—" he started.

"She's mute," Selina cut him off and moved past Jody to the girl. Jody turned to see the newcomer nodding vigorously.

"How could you tell?" Jody was perplexed.

"She put her hand over her mouth and shook her head," Selina said over her shoulder.

It took a few moments for them to get inside and for her to get out a dog-eared notebook full of scribbles, but eventually Jody, Selina, and Danny were introduced to Katherine Yares.

***

Slider kept to the shadows. He had been having no trouble following the trio as they travelled north. It wasn't like they seemed to be trying to hide. Then, shortly after they reached the outskirts of a town called Newport, he lost them.

It had been almost two weeks since they'd left Bald Knob to its fate. Once or twice, he had considered making his presence known to the trio. He didn't think that he would be welcome just yet. Besides, he was somewhat curious to see how that kid Jody handled himself.

Now that he was no longer working under the command of the captain—an idiot with an over-inflated view of his abilities in Slider's personal opinion—he was no longer bound to carry out the last orders he'd been given: Kill Sergeant Rafe.

Despite his ability to become detached in the field, Charles "Slider" Monterro was no monster. He did not take joy in killing. It was simply his job. Nothing more. Nothing less. He'd been aware that Rafe and his buddy with the thick New Englander accent were devising something involving the women. He was a little surprised when the young man departed Bald Knob with just one.

So, Slider had followed. Always keeping his distance. He'd been almost certain on more than one occasion that they would fall prey to the walking dead. Once, he'd even moved close enough, prepared to come in at the last second and save the day. In Slider's mind, that was the only way he would be ingratiated to the group.

He was just about to give up. After almost two hours, he was willing to move on. It would have been nice to fall in with a group; he held no illusions about the likelihood of survival if a person were to remain on their own. It was not a matter of *if*, but *when*. He was preparing to climb over a fence that enclosed a golf course when he saw two small figures dart across the road about a half of a mile ahead.

Sticking close to the fence, he started to move after them. He had a difficult time figuring out how two youngsters could be out by themselves with conditions being what they were. A moment later, three men emerged from some sort of shack that he was almost directly across from. One of them was limping and they were whispering angrily back and forth to one another.

"...told you to tie that one up before fucking her," one of the men hissed.

Slider didn't hear the rest of the conversation. He didn't care what else was said. He now had a purpose. He tried not to laugh at his inner-monolog...the one that had insisted that he didn't kill out of pleasure. He was about to enjoy what he did.

Taking the crossbow from his back, he quickly dropped a bolt into place and brought it to his shoulder. He gauged the distance and figured that he would have two shots before these goons were on him. He chose one without a limp, aimed, and fired.

The first shot caught the man in the center of the chest. No need for a head shot here...center mass would be just fine. He dropped the crossbow, jammed his toe into the metal hoop, caught the drawstring with his two handles and pulled to cock the weapon. He looked up as the surviving goons were charging his way. His training was serving him well as he blocked out everything except the task, preventing the rush of adrenaline from causing him to make foolish mistakes.

He brought the weapon to his shoulder, sighted, and fired. The second man dropped, the look of surprise almost comical on his face as he ended up on his knees staring down at the feathered shaft jutting from the middle of his chest.

Slider had no time to admire his work. He drew his knife just as the man with the limp skidded to a stop about ten feet away. He threw his hands up in the air in surrender.

"I d-d-don't want no p-p-problems, f-fella," he stammered.

"Those kids," Slider growled.

"What? Them muties? You want 'em...hell, have 'em both," the man couldn't get the words out quick enough. "If that was all this was about...well we could have worked somethin' out, man. No need for violence. In fact, we got other stuff to trade as well...food...even a knife bigger than that 'un." The man pointed to the Ka-Bar in Slider's hand.

"Run," Slider whispered.

"Huh?" The man appeared to be confused by the word.

"I said run," Slider repeated. He slid the knife back into its sheath.

Apparently the man mistook the intention. "You want me to hurry and go get what we got for trade?"

Charles "Slider" Monterro walked up to the stranger. He brought up his right hand and the man reached out to accept what he assumed was a proffered handshake. Like a snake, Slider grabbed the extended hand, used it to whip the man around, and grabbed under the chin with his left hand while cupping the back of the man's head with his right. In a single action, he jerked hard. The satisfying crack sent a shiver down Slider's spine.

Yes indeed, he thought as he began up the road after the two small figures he'd seen run away, *sometimes it was actually enjoyable killing another man.*

15

Tough Choices

Dr. Zahn's voice would make an excellent alarm clock. It has that certain quality to it that makes you want to smash the button and shut it off...for good. I'm not proud of the fact that this was my first thought as I opened my eyes.

"...can't simply expect him to do everything when it comes to the dirty work." The doctor was ripping somebody a new one by the sounds of it.

"I'm not saying that," a voice responded defensively. It took me a second to place it: Nickie Bailey. Of all the residents, she was the only one with that peculiar Southern accent. I say peculiar because this is the Pacific Northwest. While some folks may adopt a lazy form of speech, hers was definitely a real, honest-to-goodness Southern drawl. I keep meaning to ask her about it, but I'll be damned if things don't keep cropping up.

"I think it is best if Sunshine makes her concoction and then we administer it when the child is on the verge. Ease her into it if we can."

That made me sit up. They were discussing Emily. I already had my mind made up. I would be the one to take care of her in the end.

"And that is fine," Nickie countered. "However, Jesus has said that he would step in and take care of her after. Steve has enough to deal with...why should he have to be the one to put that little girl down for good?"

"Because she is my responsibility," I said, causing both of them to jump.

263

"Steve, I am sorry if we woke you," Nickie sputtered. "We were actually outside when this conversation began. I guess we just lost track of where we were and how much volume we were using."

"Don't worry about it," I said with a wave of my hand. "But as for Emily...I will be the one to deal with her in the end."

"Steve—" Dr. Zahn started, but I didn't want to hear it.

"That's not open for discussion."

"Oh good...you're up." Melissa pushed into the open room past the two women who were still giving each other the evil eye. "The newcomers are starting to come around and we have a problem."

"Never a shortage," I huffed. "Now if you all don't mind, I would like to change into some clean clothes before I go out there."

For some strange reason, all three of them looked at each other, and then at me like I'd sprouted an extra appendage somewhere in the middle of my forehead. *Fine*, I thought. I dropped my pants and hooked my thumbs in the band of my underwear. When I looked back up, Nickie was gone. *Well, so much for that.*

"Doc...do you mind?"

"Oh, sorry," she said with a slight shake of her head. Obviously she had gone on to other things in her mind and could care less if I were about to drop trow.

"I guess now is as good of a time as any to ask," Melissa began with just a trace of hesitation in her voice.

"Sure," I shrugged, "why not."

I pulled on a clean set of boxer-briefs and sighed as they almost slipped back off. Who needed fancy pills or expensive gym memberships? I hadn't been exactly fat before all of this, but on those rare occasions when I would work out with a few buddies and we got around to doing sit ups or whatever the latest thing one of them had read about in some fitness magazine, the rally cry would go up. "Time to do abs!"

"You mean *ab*," I always corrected them. I had a very well-defined one pack. It sorta looked like the hood of a VW Bug.

Now, I could actually see three of the mythological—to me at least—six-pack. Why is it that I could see the top two and the second one down on the left side? Weird.

Anyways, I would need a smaller size next time we sought out those sorts of supplies. I pulled on some pants and fastened my belt, realizing for the first time that I was now three notches past the original ones.

"...ever you did has not only got that child all stirred up, but also that other guy, Potter or Palmer or whatever his name is," Melissa was saying.

Oops, I guess I was distracted. Still, I think I was catching the gist of what she was saying.

"I was the one who put down her mother and a few others," I explained. "I guess they have been shielding the kids from what is going on. She thinks I was actually killing people."

"That's terrible," Melissa sighed.

"I know," I agreed. "I mean, how long did they think they could keep that up?"

"No," Melissa scolded, "I mean how could you kill the zombies, especially her mother, right in front of her, Steve?"

What?

"That had to be very traumatic. No wonder the little girl is terrified of you."

"It wasn't like I was the only one," I snapped. Why in the heck did I have to defend myself? She should know damn good and well what it is like out there. We never shielded Thalia or Emily. In fact, she was one of the big proponents for getting the girls exposed to *more* of what went on. "Jon was in the barn taking them out, too."

"I bet he was inside and out of sight of that poor little girl."

Honestly, the way everything was starting to blur together, I couldn't really remember. What I did remember, and it came to me in a bolt that made the hair on my arms and on the back of my neck stand up, was the reaction of that one child-zombie that had seemed to observe us from a distance.

"Well, Misty seems to only remember what *you* did," Melissa insisted. "And that man keeps breaking into hysterics, saying that you went crazy and just started chopping people up and bashing their heads in."

"Is that right?" Now I was a little annoyed. Not with the child. Actually, her being the way she was had everything to do with how the adults around her had acted. What I wasn't going to do is let some stranger come in here and start painting me as a blood-thirsty lunatic.

I headed out to the lobby area. Luck was with me as everybody—except those on watch—was sitting down to eat. The newbies, or at least the ones that were mobile enough to come out and sit or slump at the table, were present. I did a scan of the faces and realized that, other than Mr. Patton and little Misty, only two others from the group we'd rescued were present. I would worry about names later.

"So…I guess we need to have a group meeting," I announced. Most of my "old" group simply glanced up from their plates. However, it was the reaction from the newcomers that got my irritation meter slamming into the stops. You would have thought, based solely on their faces, that a herd of zombies just walked through the door…led by Satan.

"W-w-we don't want any trouble," the man, Mr. Patton, stammered.

"Well that's really the issue, isn't it?" I snapped. "We plucked your people—the ones still alive—from a bad situation that was only going to get worse."

"You killed—" Patton started, but I cut him off.

"You were eating each other," I snapped. "You had almost nothing left as far as supplies go. We found you and made not one, but two trips to gather you up and bring the ones here that we could try to save. Now obviously many of you were too far gone. And I am really sorry that so many of you died even after we brought you here, but I am not a monster. I put down those of you already dead who had come back as zombies."

"Excuse me," Mr. Patton said meekly. "But am I to believe

that you are saying the members of our group that became ill were...coming back as...zombies? I believe that is the word that you used isn't it? Zombies?"

What rock had these people been hiding under?

"Do you have a better term?" Billy leaned forward at his place in the table so he could look down and see Mr. Patton.

"I imagine there are probably several if we were to have the opinion of an actual doctor," Mr. Patton said with what actually sounded to me like disdain.

"*I* am a real doctor."

Now you've done it, I thought as Dr. Zahn slipped into her normal seat at the table which happened to be right next to Mr. Dean Patton. Perhaps I wouldn't need to say much at all.

"Well then surely you can not expect us to believe that the dead are getting up like some sort of very bad movie and eating people. This has to be some sort of virus or biological weapon," Mr. Patton almost laughed.

"Where exactly have you been all this time?" Dr. Zahn asked as she folded her hands before her and turned her gaze fully on the seemingly ignorant Mr. Patton.

"We have been living in our commune," he said simply.

"What sort of commune?" Melissa spoke up.

"We are simply a group of people who left the material ways behind and sought a more simplistic and basic life," Mr. Patton explained.

"Like a religious cult?" Billy squinted and seemed to be on the verge of laughing. I shot him a stern look and he quickly straightened his expression.

"Some of our members choose to follow certain faiths," Mr. Patton explained. "We had all kinds. Some were atheists, and some kept it to themselves. Religion had nothing to do with our choice."

"So like a hippy commune," Jake Beebe offered.

The look on Mr. Patton's face told me that he was starting to get really annoyed. I guess I could see why. Still, I was not really clear about him or his people, and if he wasn't going to just offer it up, then I guess he would have to keep being asked questions that he didn't like.

"Some of our members are former bankers, corporate CEOs, we were made up of all kinds and classes."

"So then you don't have television or radio in your..." I considered my next word and just decided to say 'The hell with being delicate!' "Compound?"

"We chose to remove ourselves from society after our government had repeatedly failed us and practically wiped out our retirements, our jobs, caused many of us to lose our homes."

Okay, that I could get behind. I understood their logic...at least sort of anyways.

"So you really don't know what has happened?" I pressed.

"Our deliveries of oil for our heating and cooking systems and our gardening supplies did not show up as scheduled. After several days, a few of our people went into La Grande to find out what was wrong.

"When they returned, only two made it back and both were almost beyond understanding as they were delirious with fever. When one of them went into a catatonic state, we were preparing to send for a nearby doctor that comes out and does annual check-ups of our people—we aren't crazy or solely reliant on nature or God to tend our needs," he threw that last line in and glared around the table at all of us. I imagine we'd given him enough reason to feel defensive, so I wouldn't hold it against him.

"Only, just as we were about to do so, Trent came out of his coma. It was his crying that brought us all running. It was the most peculiar cry if you knew Trent. He'd been a welder in the shipyards before and that cry almost sounded like it came from—"

"A baby?" Nickie blurted.

"Yes," Mr. Patton said. He got a far away look for a second, shuddered, and then continued his story.

"When folks went in to check on him, he was up and out of bed...but he was obviously still very sick. His eyes were…wrong. And his tone was certainly off. He attacked people who tried to help him. Even managed to bite a few. When we finally got him restrained, that was when the other fella who had just slipped into his coma an hour earlier woke up. We got him tied down, but a few more ended up being bitten or scratched."

"You didn't start to realize that there was a problem?" I asked. "I'm not doctor, but I have a pretty good handle on what *dead* is. Nobody noticed the lack of a pulse…breathing…some of the basics?"

"We just thought we were missing something," Mr. Patton insisted. "Nobody wants to be the one to say that a dead person is getting up."

Denial. There it was as plain as day.

"But you started figuring out…some of you must have," Jon spoke up. "The first time we came out, you had everybody that was infected either tied down or locked in a shed. So how come you folks didn't start trying to find help?"

"Honestly?" Mr. Patton looked up with red-rimmed eyes.

"That would help," Jon said with a nod.

"By the time a majority of us were willing to accept the possibility…a few of our group had snuck away in the night. They took our only working vehicles and most of our canned food. We always had a pantry with dozens of shelves lined with jars. Our gardens were well-tended and everybody took part to ensure that we were always set just in case of any prolonged stretches of inclement weather."

"It sounds like there is more to this than you are sharing," Jon pressed.

"There was a fight. Only, none of us had guns. Well…none of us were supposed to," Mr. Patton admitted. "The ones leaving had us outmatched. Even worse, they took a few against their will. That was when it got really ugly and a few of us tried to stop them."

"So why not just hike out of that place?" I asked.

"We had everything we needed except for food. We had a little…just not enough to last very long. Plus…" His voice trailed off. After a few deep breaths, he continued. "We were afraid. And we'd already lost so many of our community. Plus, the snow started. Then we were truly trapped. Honestly, we believed that we could hunt. Only, it just seemed like the game had left. Sometimes we would go days without even hearing birds. That was when it started to sink in that there might be problems. And then we realized something that, looking back, is kind of embarrassing."

"What's that?" Jon prompted after another of Mr. Patton's long pauses.

"The sky," he said with a shrug. "Not one single contrail. And none of us could recall when it was that we'd last seen one. And then there was that night when a few of the..." Once again Mr. Patton grew silent. Finally, he spoke, and that first word came out like he was trying to spit a foul taste from his mouth. "*Zombies* came...they attacked a few of us. That was when we decided to build a fence around part of the commune."

"So who decided that it was time to start eating each other?" Jake blurted. He looked around the room at us and seemed embarrassed for a second. "You know that you were thinking it," he finally said to me and Jon.

Mr. Patton sighed again. This one was different, though. He closed his eyes and you could see him wince and flinch. It was almost like he'd developed some sort of facial tick. Tears started to roll down his cheeks, and I honestly did not think that he was going to answer Jake's question.

"We got so hungry." His voice was barely above a whisper and he kept this eyes squeezed shut. "We'd actually buried some of our dead. But then some of the others began to fall. Not from being bitten—we'd secured all of them. The ground became too hard to be able to dig graves. Since it was so cold, we just decided to put them in one of the unused yurts. We would take care of them come the spring.

"But eventually our food was gone. Twice we sent a few volunteers out to try and find something...anything. None of them ever came back."

I tried to imagine what that little bit of Hell must have felt like for those poor people. After all, it was hard enough those first days...weeks. What must it have been like for them to walk out into the world several months into it and discover everything was gone? Couple it with their obvious denial, and they were like zombie room service.

"...when Gail mentioned something about that soccer team that had crashed in the mountains back in the Seventies or something," Mr. Patton said.

I snapped my attention back to him. I was actually curious about how that whole thing had come about. I guess you can't judge somebody unless you have walked a mile in their shoes, but I could not even remotely imagine where things would have to go where I would be able to rationalize eating Melissa...or Thalia. My mind immediately flashed the image of that little girl we'd found frozen to the fence outside their compound. *Great.*

"She tried to laugh it off, but nobody else was laughing. We were all so hungry. And we didn't have anything left for the few children that were still alive. That night, after the little ones were asleep, we went into the yurt and pulled out the first body. After some discussion, we agreed to wrap the heads in burlap so that we didn't have to look at the faces. We removed the clothing and wrapped all of them that night. Then we moved them all around. We went so far as to have each of us go in after the others and move the bodies so that we would hopefully not know who we were choosing...it didn't work."

I looked around the room and saw a lot of expressions. Some were horrified, others simply fascinated. But everybody was paying attention.

"Once we started...it is hard to explain," Mr. Patton finally opened his eyes. "That first day that nobody was hungry...the children weren't crying..."

I'd heard enough. I looked at Mr. Patton and felt something even more profound than pity. It wasn't embarrassment. Whatever it was, I couldn't put a word to it, but this man had seen the bottom.

"I think we've heard enough," I announced. Heads turned my way, some with very visible expressions of relief. "Look, you're welcome to stay. However, you need to understand that things work a little bit differently here than what you might be used to. We have watches, patrols. If you are going to stay, then you will be expected to pull your weight. We have a school program for the children…and also train them how to deal with this new world. That means going outside and learning how to deal with the zombies."

I noticed a few eyebrows raise at that last statement. It was a reality that I could not ignore. Yes, Thalia was better equipped to deal with what was happening than say, Misty. But there was more that she needed to know if she was going to have a chance at a future.

I looked around the room and gave a nod that this was over. It was time to eat and then tend to the daily tasks. One of those tasks would undoubtedly be Emily.

After breakfast, I went in and checked on her. She was drenched in sweat and the smell had actually gotten worse. Sunshine had her heavily sedated. Billy was sitting in a chair a few feet away. Thalia had already taken her spot beside the bed. I was a little surprised to discover the other two children that we'd "inherited" from that group of Muslims that had been here just a short time ago before deciding to just walk out into the woods with several members of their group infected and on the verge of turning.

"Can we sit here, Mister Steve?" Levent asked.

"Of course," I said with a nod. I noticed that Rabia had remained silent and kept her gaze at the floor while waiting for my answer. De-programming wasn't the word, but I hoped that, eventually, she would shed some of that "second-class citizen" mentality that seemed to be imprinted in her head.

"She been awake at all?" I asked Billy as I walked over to stand beside him for a minute and take in the scene. I can't lie, I guess I keep hoping that she would shake this off like a bad case of the flu and be okay.

"She was sorta awake about an hour ago, but she started crying almost immediately and I had Sunshine come in and give her some more stuff for the pain," Billy replied.

I could hear it in his voice. He was possibly even closer to crying than I was at the moment. There was never going to be an easy way to handle this situation no matter who happened to be lying on that bed.

"How long you been in here on watch?" I asked Billy.

"Just a while," he said with a shrug.

"Go ahead and take a break, I'll stay."

He didn't need to be told twice. I imagine nobody wants to be sitting in this room when Emily turns.

I took a seat and watched the kids as they sat beside Emily's bed. There was a lot of whispering, and I would normally have been very curious about what was being said. However, at the moment, I was trying to figure out what I was going to do about taking care of that little girl in the end.

The door opened and Dr. Zahn stepped inside. There was something about her expression that told me I was not going to like what she was about to say.

"Potter and the ones that are conscious are leaving." Her voice was thick with a tone that I almost swore was relief. That was puzzling.

"Leaving where?" I asked. Truthfully, I didn't have a better question.

"Don't know. He just said that he couldn't stay here. Misty refuses to accept that you didn't kill her mother and all the others."

"I guess we can't make them stay."

Now I understood her tone. I was not sure how I really felt about this situation. Sure, we had gone through an ordeal to go get them, but there was just something *off* about them and their whole set up. I couldn't put my finger on it, but these were the type of people like that one guy in *Day of the Dead*, the one who gets bit and has his arm chopped off. This was the type of guy who would open the door and let the zombie horde in if he felt he was on his way out. I couldn't say exactly why I felt that way; it was just a vibe.

"A few people are trying to talk them out of it," Dr. Zahn added.

"What about the members of their group that aren't conscious?" I asked.

"Patton refused to talk about them, but he and the ones that were mobile had a little meeting as soon as you left the room."

"The only thing I don't like about this is the child."

"Misty?"

"Yeah, she doesn't know any better."

The door flew open and Jon stormed in. He glanced at the doctor, and then turned to me. "You okay with this?"

"We can't hold anybody against their will," I said.

"But that child has no business being taken out there by these idiots!"

It seemed that we were all on the same page. I considered the situation for a moment and came to a decision. This could backfire in a hurry. Still, it was time to do something and act like the leader of this group.

"Doc, can you stay in here with Emily for a few minutes?" I asked. She gave me a nod after a brief pause.

I headed out into the entry area to find all of my people standing in little clusters. Everybody was talking quietly, but I saw a lot of the same expressions on people's faces.

I considered for a moment what I was about to do. If things went off with the best case scenario as a result, I might only piss off and alienate a few of my group. And that was when it came down on top of my head. These were *my* people. For some reason that I will never understand, this group of survivors had decided that I was their leader. None of us probably anticipated days like this or decisions along the lines of the one I was about to make. Still, good or bad, I was the one that they were waiting on.

I caught DeAngelo's eye. He had a very grim look about him. Considering how he had stepped in when it came to Levent and Rabia, I was confident that he would support me. Jesus and Jake were on either side of Jon. I could tell that they were agitated. Jesus saw me and I guess read something in my expression. He gave me a curt nod and elbowed the other two.

"Mr. Patton," I called across the room.

He jumped, obviously startled. He had been in the process of stuffing the few things we could spare him and his group into a pack. The two adults and Misty were clustered around looking more lost than anything else.

"What is it, Mr. Hobart?" he said, clutching a hand to his chest like he was about to have a heart attack. If I already had him this spooked, he was in for a world of trouble.

"I will only make this offer one last time." I let my gaze drift across the other two adults that were leaving. "Stay here…at least until things thaw out. It is gonna be tight, and food is a concern, but we have a pretty good set up here. I think we will make it through the winter."

Mr. Patton didn't even wait to see if the others were willing to discuss it. "That is just not possible, Mr. Hobart. You can't possibly understand—"

"You're right," I cut him off. "I think there is something about your little story that you aren't telling. It doesn't seem to connect at all the dots. But I can put that aside and offer you a much better chance at survival than you will get if you leave now. What you are doing does not make any sense."

"Let's just say that our beliefs are not the same and leave it at that. We appreciate all that you have done…you and your people. But I really think this is best," Mr. Patton said. He glanced at the other two adults, a man and woman, who looked as if they would fall over at the first heavy breeze. Still, they nodded!

"And what about the ones that are still unconscious?" I asked. "What do I tell them when they awake?"

"They won't," Mr. Patton said with a sigh.

I was reminded of that television program, *Meerkat Manor*. Several heads around the room popped up at that last statement.

Jesus pushed himself away from the wall and headed into the back.

"Let me save you the trip," Mr. Patton called. "They are dead."

Jesus took off at a run. I was about to lay into this lunatic, but something that Jesus said over his shoulder changed everything.

"One of them was bit!"

Everybody scrambled. Whoever wasn't carrying a weapon moved away from the arch that led to the back rooms. All those who were able, drew whatever they had. It seemed like overkill for just one zombie, but it showed a lot about how ingrained our reactions had become.

None of us needed to assist Jesus. There was a wet chopping sound, and a moment later, Jesus emerged wiping off his blade. He gave me a nod. This most recent turn of events made at least part of what I was about to do feel a little easier.

"Then I guess you are free to go...with one exception," I said.

Sensing where I was headed, Jake and Jon both began to drift towards Mr. Patton and his tiny group. Everybody else just drifted back, creating this huge open space between the four huddled figures and my people.

"The little one stays here," I said. "If you are still alive in the spring, you are welcome to come back. If she wishes to leave with you then, you may take her."

I had no expectation that he was going to accept my offer. And even if he did, I knew that the little girl was going to be a bit of a problem. But that was a problem I was willing to deal with.

"I don't believe that I heard you correctly," Mr. Patton said. He placed his hands on the little girl's shoulders and I knew right then that this was going to end up way past the worst-case scenario.

"I said that you and the other two can leave. The girl stays here with us until the weather changes. You have my word that if you come back, we will let the child decide if she wants to leave with you at that time."

"Mr. Patton?" Misty looked up at the man. She was old enough to get the idea. "You won't make me stay here with that man, will you?"

I was going to have to keep my distance for quite a while with this one when this was over. If she hated me before, then what I was about to do would probably make her fear and lack of trust in me about as entrenched as it could possibly be.

"I won't, Misty," Mr. Patton said.

"I wouldn't make that promise," I warned.

"What are you going to do, Mr. Hobart? Kill me?"

"If it comes to that?" I had to look around the room one more time to gauge my own people. I actually saw a few heads already nodding! "Yes."

16

Geek on the run…again!

"What do you mean?" Kevin asked in a voice barely above a whisper. In his mind a million scenarios unfolded at once. The most likely seemed to be that Willa was actually working for Major Beers and that this had all been a set up.

"We have the president's daughter."

Okay, Kevin thought. That was not in any of the possibilities that he'd been sifting through and trying to brace himself for the impact.

"You mean…" he let it die on his lips.

It was a stupid question. To what other president would she possibly be referring? Shelly Bransen made all the usual news when she selected her university the year after her father's re-election. The nation had been fascinated by this soft-spoken, girl-next-door pretty brunette as she grew up before their eyes.

"She was attending school at Ohio State," Matt said. "I remember the insanity…it was like Hollywood relocated to Columbus that first couple of weeks."

"We went in for her on the same day that her father's airplane crashed," Willa explained. "Even had some Special Forces types with us. When we arrived at the university, it was just more than we were really prepared for. The SpecOps commander tried to play it off, but I could tell he knew they were not going to come out of there.

"The second night after we lost contact with the last of the men who had gone in, Shelly arrived at our camp with a soldier that had been bitten but not turned. That was the first time we realized that the bite was not a guaranteed death sentence. It was actually our call to the CDC that made the news.

"We were supposed to merge with another local unit and do everything possible to get Shelly to NORAD. That was when we started communicating via radio with Major Beers' group. Our CO sent a scout team ahead to try and clear the way. They came across a band of what they thought to be raiders." Willa glanced over Kevin's shoulder at all the other faces staring at her.

"They had already started breaking through barricades and looting civilian strongholds under the guise of appropriating supplies for a "vital" mission. We decided that turning the president's daughter over to them was not the right choice. Technically, we disobeyed our final order."

Everybody was silent for several seconds. A voice on a bullhorn warned Willa that she had two minutes before they started burning everything. The voice that broke the silence caught everybody by surprise.

"Shelly wouldn't want to have anything to do with that nasty major and her people." All heads whipped around to see Erin looking back. The sudden and complete attention surprised the young girl enough to make her take a few steps back. "What?" she finally blurted. "We met during Shari's last tour. My mom *was* a senator, and Shelly liked Shari's music. We went to dinner that night and she was really nice to me."

"I am turning myself in." Willa checked every pouch and pocket, dropping everything on the ground.

"You don't need to do this." Kevin grabbed her arm as she headed for the door.

"Yes," she very gently took his hand off and stepped away, "I do. And you need to get these people out of here. You remember where our group was camped?"

"Yes."

"They will be there for another two weeks. Tell them that Beers is still searching. Scrap the last orders and follow your lead."

"Okay...wait...what?" The door shut in his face and he

heard Willa call out to whoever was outside.

"Maybe they—" Erin started, but was cut off by the distinct sound of a single gunshot.

"Everybody out the back!" Kevin shoved Aleah and Heather.

"But—" Matt started to protest, and Kevin cut him off.

"You want to risk losing a few toes or do you want to die. Now shut up and move!" he hissed.

He grabbed up Willa's things and followed. The group was standing on the back porch. With the exception of Erin they were all already hopping from one foot to the other, the rags that they had tied around them were little help at this point.

Kevin scanned the back yard. The house that was diagonally to the left was one he remembered from several past trips out foraging. That was the first stop. He took off at a jog and simply assumed that the others would follow.

It took longer than he would have liked, but five minutes later, everybody had shoes and socks. They might not fit great, and there would probably be a price to pay later, but right now they just needed to survive the night.

An hour later they were moving through the woods. Everybody had simply shut up and followed—even Erin. More than once he had looked back to ensure they were all still with him. Only once did they encounter any zombies. Three of the things had gotten stuck in a drainage ditch. Apparently they had stayed still long enough for the knee-deep water to freeze. One of them had actually snapped one leg just above where it was frozen in place and was sprawled on the slick surface. Had one of the creatures not been the type to make that baby cry sound, Kevin would have left them untouched.

Just as the first traces of light began to lick at the sky, Kevin brought everybody to a stop. Steam rolled off of them all, but the warmth was being sapped almost as quickly as that steam dissipated.

"Aleah, see that opening in the trees just down at the bottom of the hill?" Kevin pointed.

281

"Yeah," she said with a nod. Already her teeth were starting to chatter.

"I want all of you to make for that. Just on the other side is a housing development that was just getting started. There are a lot of empty lots and a few with the frames in place. There are three houses that are actually finished. They don't have anything in them, but they will make a good spot to hold up. Grab some wood, there should be plenty."

"And what do we use to start a fire?" Heather asked. "None of us has anything except what we are carrying."

Kevin dropped Willa's bag and kicked it to them. "She has everything in here that you will need. I know there is a flint and steel…she might even have a lighter, but just take this and go."

"What about you?" Aleah stepped forward and grabbed his arm as he turned to head back the way they'd come.

"I won't leave Valarie and Shari if I don't have to. I can grab something on the way to deal with the lock," he replied.

"Haven't you done enough?" Heather snapped. "You know as well as anybody that you can't save everybody. We may have to accept this as a loss."

"Not again." Kevin shook his head.

"That isn't your sister!" Heather insisted. "I understand that you have a lot of feelings going on here, but she isn't your sister. And Shari will watch over her. I don't know what has gone on between those two, but she has not let Valarie out of her sight since Beers and her people showed up."

"Look, I understand what you're saying." Kevin hung his head for a moment. "And I promise that I won't do anything stupid—"

"Too late," Aleah sighed.

"But I have to at least see if there is anything that I can do," Kevin continued, ignoring Aleah's quip.

"So what do we do in the meantime?" Matt asked. Truth be told, he didn't really care, he just wanted out of the cold. If Kevin wanted to run off again on some damn fool mission that had next to no chance of being successful, that was his business.

"Wait for me for three days." Kevin pulled away from Aleah and started backpedalling. "If I haven't returned by then, head west following the highway towards Newark and The Basket. You will come to what is basically a wall of cars. That is where Willa's group is set up. Tell them everything. Stay with them. If, for some reason it takes me longer than three days and I am able to come after you, you will be easier to find with them than if you were by yourselves."

Kevin had taken about three steps when something grabbed his arm and spun him around. Before he could react, Aleah's lips were on his. The kiss was long, and Kevin had to try his best to control his body's physical response—he failed. Eventually she let go and he started off again.

This time he heard the footsteps coming up behind him. He spun, prepared to tell Aleah that she was absolutely not coming with him. He was shocked to see Erin bounding through the snow towards him. He glanced past her at the others with a questioning look, but received blank stares and shrugs.

Erin collided with him and threw her arms around his waist. She squeezed tight for a few seconds before looking up with a tear-streaked face. "Please bring my sister back," Erin said through the tears. "She is all I have left and I would be lost without her."

"I can only try my best," Kevin said. He had to fight everything in him to not tell her that he would bring Shari back. He had learned that there was very little that was actually in his control. As it was, he had doubts about his ability to bring himself back alive.

"I know you will," Erin sniffed. She wiped at her face with her sleeves and took a step back, still looking him in the eyes. Her sandy blonde hair was matted to her forehead from being sweaty as well as the lack of washing, but a few strands still managed to float in the wind and get into her eyes. She brushed them away and seemed to stand up just a bit straighter. "You have always done your best, and I am sorry that I have been such a brat. Try to be safe and come back alive. Aleah would be really sad if you didn't."

"Can I let you in on a secret?" Kevin leaned down and whispered in the girl's ear. She nodded. "I would be pretty bummed, too."

He stood up, patted her in the shoulder, and headed back towards Major Beer and uncertainty. He stopped once just before tromping into the woods and turned around to look back. He wasn't surprised to see them all still standing there watching him. He raised one hand and waved, then turned his back, hoping to God that wasn't the last time he would see his friends...Aleah.

***

Kevin moved through the back yard. He could hear all the noise of people yelling back and forth. It was clear that Major Beers and her clan were pulling up stakes and moving on. That, in and of itself, was a good thing. However, it did not bode well for Shari and Valarie.

From what he had seen, this meant that Valarie was as good as dead, and Shari, if she wasn't simply killed, could end up in that brothel tent. He knew that according to what Aleah and Heather said, so far, nobody had been forced into that line of work against their will, but with all that had happened in the past twenty-four hours...all bets were off.

Pressing himself against the fence, he risked a peek between the slats. About a hundred yards off was the entrance to the country club. The carefully erected wall of vehicles had been pushed aside. It looked like an ugly open wound. He was reminded of that first Walmart they had hit back when he was with Cary, Darrin, and Mike. He'd glanced in the rearview mirror and seen the open entry to the store with a few zombies already trickling inside. It wouldn't be long after these goons left that all the undead drawn by the noise would be showing up.

Careful to stay out of sight, he moved along the fence. The next yard had a raised deck and a huge brick fireplace. He was pretty sure he could get up there and be able to see better and remain hidden.

Five minutes later he was proved right. There was only one problem. At first he thought it was his imagination, but he thought he kept hearing a slightly muffled squeak. Sound was tricky in a snowy world. When he happened to glance over his shoulder, he discovered the source.

The reason that he'd not considered that the noise was coming from the filthy sliding glass door that opened in to the house from the deck was because the curtains were drawn. If something would have been there, the curtains would have most likely been torn down a long time ago.

The infant—what remained—had been torn in half. A tiny, splintered ribcage was at least half gone. There was a tiny thing jutting out that took Kevin a moment to realize was part of the spine. The left arm was gone and all that remained of the right was from the elbow on up. It was the remnant of that arm that was sliding back and forth across the dirty glass on the other side of the door. He could barely make out its eyes; they were hardly visible slits on either side of a nose that had been flattened by the indeterminate amount of time that it had spent pressed to the glass.

Since he could just hear it himself, he felt confident that he would not need to go inside and finish it off. In fact, that would more likely alert somebody to his position. His only problem was that the image had burned into his mind with about a dozen other horrifying things that no zombie movie would ever flash on the screen. He remembered when that *Dawn of the Dead* remake had come out, and all the hype over the "baby" scene. That had been nothing.

He started scanning the groups of people—he refused to call them soldiers, it felt like a slap in the face to all the true brave men and women that had served. They were very well organized, no matter what else he felt, he had to credit them with efficiency. They had staggered sentries set up in a picket in several locations. From their positions, they would see anything—

living or undead— coming their way in plenty of time to react.

It took him a few minutes, but he finally located the major. She was walking among her people presumably giving instructions. Then Kevin felt his chest tighten. On a streetlight pole, dangling by her feet was a figure that had to be Willa. The light brown skin had turned gray. The naked figure swiped at anything that went past. Most ignored the naked zombie, but a few people seemed more than a little nervous to have a zombie dangling over their heads as they packed up to leave.

He was no idiot. There was simply nothing that he could do at the moment. He had little doubt as to what his fate would be if he were caught a second time. He continued to watch and wait, all the while, that noise behind him became like an itch between the shoulder blades that he could not scratch.

Around midday, the rattle and distinct growl of a diesel engine echoed across the landscape. A big snowplow eventually came in to view. It exited the country club and turned left! That was the best news Kevin had gotten all day. It was moving away from Newark...away from Willa's outfit...away from Aleah and the others!

Kevin watched the plow head off sending a wall of snow and ice crashing aside like a giant wave. The handful of vehicles fell in behind and headed away, the sounds of tire chains rattling like an army of Dickensian ghosts. He'd waited this long, and his body hurt from the cold. His mind was frazzled from the zombie infant just a few feet away pawing in endless futility at the sliding glass door. Yet now was not the time to be careless.

He had been vigilant. Valarie would be hard to miss. He had seen no sign of either one of his friends during the evac. He should have an answer one way or the other in a very short while. Still, he had to be patient. This could be a trap.

Certainly the major would expect him to return for his people. He was certain that, despite the fact that they had only specified Willa surrender to them, the major had certain designs on *him*. He had gathered that much in their brief meeting.

What seemed like an eternity passed. Having no way to accurately gauge time, Kevin homed in on a single zombie in the distance that struggled along the side of the snow-covered highway. By the time it passed the entrance to the country club, he had to figure that at least an hour had gone by.

During that time, he had felt comfortable enough to move around a bit and stretch. He finally succumbed to the desire to open that sliding glass door and end that infant for good. Afterwards, he rummaged through the house to find a few things he knew he would need later.

No longer able to wait, Kevin crept out and made his way to the entrance of the country club. All the movement from earlier made it pretty easy once he reached the actual highway. He stopped at the light post and looked up at the zombie dangling by its feet. Willa's otherwise perfect flesh had a bullet hole in one thigh, and one bite on the right arm. That was all it had taken. At least that was what he thought until he looked closer. There was a nasty scar on her left shoulder that could only be a healed bite. She'd been immune!

With a single shot from his crossbow, Kevin put an end to Willa. He untied the rope that had been used to hoist and suspend her and eased the body to the ground. It took him a few minutes, but eventually he discovered a small bump with what had to be a needle mark in the center.

"I'll bet the major was pissed when you didn't show any sign of infection from being bitten," Kevin said with a sad laugh.

He wished he had the time to take care of her body with a bit more respect, but time was something he didn't have to spare at the moment. He folded her arms across her chest and shut her eyes. That would have to do.

Jogging up the entry road that led to the where the country club building used to stand, Kevin began to notice a few single stragglers milling about. He hadn't recalled seeing any zombies enter the opening, so that meant that either the wall had been breached…or, and this was a bit more chilling, Major Beers had a few zombies in her arsenal and had chosen to leave them behind for some reason.

He oriented on the general direction of the storage shed that had housed Shari and Valarie. He just hoped that they were still there. As he approached a small ridge, expecting to see the shed not too far away once he reached the top, he heard a peculiar thumping sound. *They're alive!* he thought as he bounded through the snow.

When he finally crested that hill, he skidded to a halt. A dozen or so zombies had the shed surrounded and they were banging on the sides. He counted his bolts: seven. That would not be enough by half. He really only had one option.

Moving as close as he deemed necessary, Kevin cupped his hands to his mouth. "Shari!" he called.

There was a moment where it felt as if the world had come to a halt. That span of three or four heartbeats where he waited and watched every set of undead eyes turn his direction seemed like forever.

"Kevin?" a voice called back.

Several of the zombies that had started to turn his way and come after the newest stimulus seemed to pause, almost as if they had a moment of uncertainty. Then, a few actually continued their turn and headed his way, while the rest returned to their pounding.

"I am going to get you out of there, but I need you to do me a favor."

"Name it! Just hurry and get us out of here."

"I need you two to bang on the walls and try to keep the zombies' attention."

There was a pause, and Kevin hoped that he wasn't going to have to explain this as more of the zombies had abandoned the shed for this new thing that kept getting their attention. Then he heard it, a loud clang of what sounded like something metal being used to beat on the interior of the shed.

Sure enough, the zombies where now all kinds of confused. Or at least that is how they appeared as they would turn one way and then the other. A few continued toward him, and for Kevin, that was perfect.

It took him almost no time to drop the zombies that had chosen to pursue the visible prey. He retrieved each bolt and then circled the shed to find where the zombies were thinnest. One side only had a pair. He moved in slow and took them both down. Systematically, he worked his way around the shed and only twice had to actually stop to deal with a zombie that had been brought by the noise.

Finally he was able to rush to the door of the shed. He pulled the hammer from his belt that he'd scavenged from the icky-baby house. It took a bit more than he had expected, but eventually he managed to bust off one of the door handles that the chain had been run through to keep Shari and Valarie locked inside.

He barely had the door open when two figures from the darkness rushed out and tackled him to the ground. Kevin looked up to see Valarie's ear-to-ear grin just before she planted a wet kiss on his mouth. Shari seemed content to simply bury her head in his chest and squeeze him until he had to physically pry her off.

He climbed to his feet and helped both of them up. That was when the newest problem arose. Both girl's had been stripped of their shoes and socks.

"We are going to have to run through quite a bit of snow," Kevin said. "Your feet are going to hurt, but we will get you shoes as soon as possible."

"What about this?" Shari held up her left hand which also caused Valarie's right hand to join it in the air.

"Cuffs are not that complicated," Kevin said. Although something in his gut told him that this might be worse than the lack of shoes. "As soon as we get across the street to those houses, I will find something and get those off of you."

The girls had already begun the dance from one foot to the other. Standing around and talking any longer was a waste of time.

The trio took off across the snowy ground. Kevin glanced back more than once to make sure they were still behind him because it was so quiet. To both girls' credit, they were plowing ahead. Even Valarie was unusually silent.

As they reached the entry gate, Kevin skidded to a halt. Coming from all directions were singles and small clusters of the undead. They had finally arrived in response to the dinner bell that had been sounded by Major Beers and her people pulling out.

As he scanned the area for the best possible route, he heard a cry from behind him. He turned just as Shari and Valarie tumbled to the ground in a heap. There was a moment where he searched frantically for the hidden zombie that would emerge from the tangle, but to his relief, no such thing occurred.

He reached down to help pull them to their feet. Shari yelped and collapsed, once again pulling Valarie down as well.

"My leg," Shari hissed through clenched teeth.

Kevin looked around to see how much time they had before the leading edge of the zombie wave would hit. He still had a few minutes. Pulling up her pant leg, he couldn't help but wince at what he saw. A few inches below the knee, the leg was bent at an angle that it should most definitely not.

"That bad?" Shari managed through the tears that welled up in her eyes.

"Nothing we can't handle," Kevin insisted.

He looked around at everything for a second and then directed Valarie to move just a bit so he could scoop the former pop star up in his arms.

"Stay right here at my side, Valarie," he instructed. They resumed their trek, eventually reaching the first houses.

Kevin passed several before turning up the driveway of one that had an open garage door that revealed a big open space. Once inside, he set Shari down on a sturdy looking tool bench that was mounted to the wall and then shut the rollup door.

"I am going inside for a few minutes. I will be back, but you two just stay quiet. Hopefully none of them saw us duck in here."

Kevin headed into the house that he already knew from previous excursions to be empty. He bounded up the stairs and went for the closets. It took him a few minutes, but eventually he found several pairs of socks, and some shoes that looked like they might fit, and a couple of coats. He'd even found a pair of boots that were closer to his size. He just hoped that he had time to change into them.

As he reached the landing, he got his answer. The dull slap of a dead hand on the front door sounded louder than any shotgun blast in his ears. It was quickly joined by others.

As he returned to the garage, he found Shari holding Valarie and stroking her hair. "Shh, everything will be okay," she kept repeating.

Kevin had seen some shadows at a few of the windows. Everything was definitely *not* going to be okay. He tossed the shoes and socks to the pair. "Get this stuff on, we can't stay here for long."

He turned back inside and headed to the bathroom. It took longer than he would have liked—several more sets of hands were now banging of various parts of the house—but he eventually found a bobby pin. Rushing back, he was relieved to see that Valarie had her shoes on. Shari, however, did not.

"We don't have time to screw around," Kevin snapped as he strode across the garage.

"I can't do it, Kevin," Shari said in a barely audible whisper.

"Fine, then I will." He bent to grab the socks, but her hand stopped him.

"I can't walk."

"Then I will carry you," he insisted.

"You can't," Shari said with a shake of her head.

"I carried Matt, and you don't weigh anything close to what he does."

"You did it on solid ground. Out there it is all snow and ice. And if you fall and get hurt…" Her voice trailed off at the end as she glanced down at her injured leg. "Valarie is going to need you."

"And your sister is going to need you," Kevin argued.

"She will be okay," Shari waved a hand. "She has all of you...most importantly, as long as she is with you she has a chance to survive."

"We have to at least try!"

"You almost fell twice just getting me here," Shari pointed out. "And those things are gathering outside. That means a fight just to have a shot at escaping."

"But you have to at least try."

"I did...and I can't."

"I refuse—"

"We don't have time for this," Shari snapped, cutting Kevin off. "You need to grab Valarie and run...now!"

Kevin glanced at Valarie. She was watching the entire exchange with a blank expression on her face.

"What do you think?" Kevin asked, not knowing what to expect.

"Shari promised to keep the bad ghosts away," Valarie said with a smile. "She said that if she stays here, she can keep them all trapped in this house forever."

Kevin shot a look Shari's way. She gave the briefest of smiles. "Go, Kevin. And take Valarie away from here."

Kevin sighed. In just the past minute the banging had increased. The garage door was starting to rattle in its frame. It wouldn't last much longer. Almost on cue, the sound of breaking glass could be heard from somewhere within the house. Taking a deep breath, he went to work on the handcuff around Valarie's wrist. With a few deft moves, there was an audible click. Valarie was free.

"I just need one thing," Shari grabbed Kevin's arm. "Don't let me be eaten by those things. I don't want to die that way."

"Valarie, go wait in the kitchen," Kevin said, his eyes never leaving Shari's.

The girl took two steps, but then turned back and grabbed Shari in a hug. The two whispered something in each other's ears, and then Valarie left the garage.

"Try to make it not hurt so much," Shari said as the tears

spilled down her cheeks.

"I…I…" Kevin had no words.

"I'm scared," Shari managed as Kevin moved behind her and brought one arm around her neck.

"Me too," Kevin whispered back.

It took less than twenty seconds for Shari to lose consciousness. Kevin imagined that he could have been quicker if he'd ever actually practiced using a "sleeper" hold. Shari slumped into his arms and began to slide off the workbench. He laid her on the floor and then drew his crossbow. The bolt punched through the forehead and Shari's body spasmed twice and was still.

The idea of retrieving that bolt never crossed his mind as he exited the garage. He took Valarie by the hand and went to the back door. He saw a few shapes milling about, but this was definitely going to be the easiest way back to his friends.

"Come on," Kevin managed around the lump in his throat. Together, they slipped out the door, across the yard, and over the fence.

17

Vignettes XXX

Aaheru entered the dining room and scanned the faces of all those who sat awaiting his arrival. With the exception of that pair of women he had just left in his stateroom and the one man placed on guard at his door, all of his people were assembled. He'd demanded that the ship be stopped and that even the men caring for the engines be present.

His eyes sought one person in particular. When he spotted Ahi, he was momentarily baffled. He had given the man free reign to assign everybody on board with another to prevent anybody from being alone. He thought that Ahi would take that situation and use it to his advantage. While he had not officially made all of his selections as to which of the women would be among his wives, he had felt a bit magnanimous in allowing his trusted advisor with whomever he chose. Ahmes was the only woman off limits and he would have no problem allowing Ahi his first choice. Besides, if she was ever summoned by her pharaoh, then both she and Ahi would certainly see that as an honor. Yet, Ahi had a young man beside him. In fact, it was that one boy who had been banished after being bitten but returned days later without having changed. Perhaps they would talk later and he would clarify the liberties that he had implied to the man.

"My people," Aaheru strode to the center of the open dining area and spoke in what he considered his most authoritative voice. "By now, some of you have heard that we have a saboteur in our midst. Somebody in this room tried to disable our engines. That attempt failed as you can clearly see."

Aaheru watched a few faces in particular. Naturally he had suspicions, and would like to deal with this situation before they reached the islands that dotted the waters of Greece. There were a few that he actually had in mind and had pointed them out to the men that he had tasked with steering the ship.

"Since this coward has not stepped forward, I have decided that nobody shall be allowed outside of their quarters until we reach our destination. Anybody found out by themselves will be tossed over the side. There is to be no exception."

Once more he looked around the room. Still nothing, but like Markata, eventually this subversive would make their presence known. When that happened, he would perhaps demonstrate with his bare hands why it was that the gods had chosen to lead Egypt to her new age.

"You may all return to your rooms now, except for you, Ahi, I need a moment."

The room emptied as everyone did as they were told. Once the room had cleared, Aaheru took a seat and motioned for Ahi and his companion to join him.

"Perhaps you did not realize your position and the opportunity that I afforded you," Aaheru said with a wolfish smile.

"My apologies, my Pharaoh," Ahi said. He immediately went on guard. There was something in the large man's eyes that he did not like.

"No, my friend, perhaps it is I who should apologize for not making myself clear. When I gave you the task of pairing everybody up, I simply anticipated that you would select one of the women."

"I did not wish to make such an assumption, my Pharaoh. I was not aware that you had selected all of your brides." Ahi tried to sound casual, but he felt some of those old fears starting to emerge.

"Well feel free to remedy the situation in the next few hours, and as a consolation, perhaps this strong young man might be given the other half of the pairing that you will break."

Aaheru glanced at the young man and began to realize that

something about this person seemed to bother him. He tried to place it. Ahi saw the peculiar look cross Aaheru's face and spoke out.

"My Pharaoh, this is Nabeh. He is the young man that was bitten but did not fall ill. He fought his way back to us and was granted your permission to remain."

The connection dawned on Aaheru and he clapped them both on the shoulders. "This is even better. Perhaps you will be able to pass on to your offspring this trait that you possess. That will make us even stronger as Egypt begins to rise from the ashes of the old world to claim this new one."

With that, the man turned and left the room. After a brief discussion of what they needed to do once they reached land, Ahi and Nabeh settled on a pair of women. Knowing that Aaheru would likely check up on "how things went" the next day, he instructed Nabeh to bed the woman that night. After all, they had already been together, and would be again as soon as the ship reached land.

Ahi followed his own advice and fulfilled his manly obligation to the woman he'd selected. Of course he also introduced her to the Western Civilization's position known as "doggy style." Through it all, he was able to imagine Nabeh. It was probably just his imagination combined with his borderline revulsion of sexual intercourse with a woman, but Ahi was feeling just a bit ill.

***

Juan steered the small boat into the cove that Frank had pointed out. They had travelled up the river and gotten way too close to the actual city for Juan's liking. What he hated even more was being out in the middle of the river. Anybody and everybody for miles around would be able to see them. That would be even more of a problem on the return trip, but one thing at a time.

"So what makes you think this Donna girl would be here?"

Juan asked as they aimed the boat for the shore and killed the motor. It wasn't like they had been silent up to this point, but he figured that it couldn't hurt.

"Her house is up that hill." Frank pointed to a rather steep slope that was thick with all sorts of brush and growth that could easily conceal zombies.

"Of course," Juan grumbled. "But this seems kind of far from where I first ran into you guys."

"Yeah, but if she is having dreams about her brother, this is the most likely place I can think of to look for her."

Juan did not like this at all. He saw absolutely no good coming from this little trip. It reminded him of that war movie, *Saving Private Ryan*. Last son or not, it made no sense to send a bunch of people after one guy. So you lose eight or ten and get back one? And it was that Matt Damon guy. How fair was it for Vin Diesel to get killed and for that little panty waste to make it to the end?

The boat ran aground and Juan jumped out. Frank was still sitting and had a look on his face that made Juan pause.

"What?" he finally asked when the youngster remained quiet for several seconds.

"Sorta funny how all of this shakes out," Frank said in a soft voice just above a whisper.

"Like what?" Juan didn't have time for a trip down Memory Lane. He would try to find this girl, and if he didn't, he was going back home. Mackenzie needed him right now and he needed to be there.

"I had this huge crush on Donna, but she didn't know that I even existed."

Great, Juan thought, *we are gonna do this now?* He would give the kid a minute or two, but then it was time to move.

"She used to have this big party every single year at the end of school. It became like a tradition. But after fourth grade, it stopped being this big open event. Only the 'In' crowd got invited. I wasn't on that list. I didn't play football, I ran cross country. I wasn't one of the jocks and my folks didn't have much money, so I didn't wear the right clothes or have a car."

Juan leaned against a barren tree and began digging at the grime under his nails with his favorite knife. There was something that Frank was getting to...he hoped.

"I was blown away when she came up to me one day and asked about how to be an Outdoor School counselor. I helped her fill everything out and since I already had an inside track because of being friends with one of the senior counselors, I put in a good word.

"When all of this crap happened, she clung to me like I knew what I was doing. I mean, I'd seen a few zombie movies, but we all know that it never turns out to be like Hollywood, right? The thing is, the night before all of this happened, we kissed after the bonfire. That was the first time I ever kissed a girl that wasn't a relative."

"So now you feel like you have to take care of her?" Juan asked.

"Well...kinda..." Frank stammered.

"Here's the thing, kid," Juan pushed away from the tree and looked up the hill. "You don't owe nobody. You have to take care of yourself now. If you can't handle your own business, then you sure can't be takin' on somebody else's garbage. You follow me?" Frank nodded. "Good, now, we go up, we check, and if she ain't here, we go back. You want to stay on your own, that's your call."

With that, Juan turned and headed up the hill. He was very happy when he reached the top and hadn't had to deal with a single deader. However, at the top was a whole new set of problems. A chain-link fence greeted him and he would have to walk across about ten feet of wide open ground to reach it. The other option was to move down to where the house actually sat. It had a high brick wall sealing off the back yard. Looking either way, the other houses in sight had the same thing going on. But then he would be in the open when he reached the top of that wall. Which led to the other problem. This once affluent neighborhood was a curious beehive of activity. Zombies walked around in singles or small bunches. This was most peculiar considering that most zombies had wandered off on their own little adventures or whatever zombies had going on.

"It's the wall," Frank whispered.

"Huh?" Juan asked as he tried to decide the best way to tell this kid that his friend was screwed nine ways to Sunday if she'd come here.

"This neighborhood had a big brick wall on three sides...and the steep hill and the Cyclone fence is like a fourth wall. You can only get in from one of three main gates."

Juan looked back and down. He hadn't realized it was so steep until now. In fact, he felt pretty damn good that he'd made it to the top and not fallen backwards and broke his neck.

"So you are telling me that this place is totally walled off?" Juan asked. That would make sense why the zombies were still here in such big numbers.

"Yeah, everybody here was doing okay in the money department," Frank said with a dreamy quality in his voice.

"Well a lot of good that did them," Juan scoffed. "Follow me."

With that, Juan took off for the brick wall that acted as the fence to the back yard of the house that Frank had indicated was Donna's. He was up and over so quick that even if a zombie had been waiting on the other side, it would not have had time to react. Fortunately, the yard was empty.

They both had weapons drawn when they scaled the stairs that led up to the raised deck. The sliding glass door was shut. Juan glanced at Frank who shrugged and nodded. Giving a gentle tug, Juan was actually a little surprised to discover it was unlocked. Throwing the curtain aside, Juan stepped in with his arm cocked and ready to take down whatever might be waiting.

He froze in his tracks...arm still in the air. When he was able to shake off the shock, he could only think of one thing to say.

"Tight like a tigah."

***

The village looked like a picture postcard. Chad and Scott both stopped long enough to look over their shoulders. Steam rolled off their bodies and neither seemed to be able to catch his breath.

The screams had died out several minutes ago, but Chad was almost sure that he could still hear Trina calling his name and begging him not to leave her behind.

The three of them had been actually making good time. They stopped at a small gas station and slept in the cashier's booth for a few hours when they could simply not go on any longer. It had been Trina that had woken Chad and Scott. Her eyes were wide with fear and all she could do was point.

Chad had peeked over the lip of the counter and the moment he saw them, he knew they were in serious trouble. A few were already almost on them. If they did not leave right this very minute they were screwed. There had to be hundreds coming up the mountain road. The mob was on their heels.

"Grab the skis," Chad hissed. "We can put them on later, right now we just have to go. This little shack won't stand a chance, and if they trap us, it's over."

There had been no arguments from anybody. The trio had fought their way out the door, having to take on a handful of the leading edge of the zombie herd that had been the reason they'd had to abandon their mission in the first place. Well, everybody except Michael Clark, he had continued on; insisting that he could make the run alone and probably easier without the others to slow him down. Chad had his doubts, but at the moment he didn't care.

They had been able to outdistance the herd with relative ease once they broke clear. Once they got the skis back on, it was even easier. All had been going well until Trina, who was actually leading the way and had to be asked more than once to slow down—a request she didn't seem to hear—rounded a corner and ran smack dab into three zombies.

By the time that Chad and Scott had caught up, there was blood on the snow and Trina was shrieking in pain as another chunk of her arm was torn away by a zombie wearing what looked like a brown uniform of some sort. The other two were obviously soldiers. Chad had thought it odd considering that he hadn't seen a single one since they'd left that FEMA center all those months ago.

Scott had moved forward as if he intended to pull the flailing woman free, but Chad had stopped him. He'd shaken his head and dug his poles into the snow.

"Chad, help!" the woman pleaded.

"She's done," Chad said to Scott without so much as glancing back.

After a few minutes, Scott had finally broken the silence. "You don't think we should have at least put her down?"

"I thought about it," Chad finally tapped the knife at his belt and answered as they continued to push for their destination. "But I just couldn't look somebody in the eyes and kill them. At least with a gun you know it is quick."

That answer seemed to satisfy Scott and they had continued through the day. Finally, they saw the signs and knew they were close. When they reached the outskirts, Chad stopped. At first he admired the idyllic scenery. He knew that it would not be long before hundreds if not thousands of undead converged on this little bastion that had given them all a false sense of security. It was in that moment that he realized that there was no such thing as a safe place.

"So what's the plan?" Scott asked as the two made their way down the main street.

"I'm grabbing Ronni and I am heading up into the mountains," Chad said as they came to a stop in front of the hotel they both called home.

"What about everybody else?"

"They aren't my problem."

"So you are just going to up and leave?"

"Pretty much."

"What about me?"

"You are free to join us...Brett, too. But I'm not staying here and waiting for those things to swarm in and trap everybody inside. And with that many, there is no way that we will be able to keep them out. This place is over."

Scott seemed to consider Chad's words for a moment before he spoke. "We gonna tell anybody?"

"What do you think happens if we do that?" Chad said in an angry whisper. "These people will want to talk about it. By the time they have come to some hair-brained conclusion, that swarm will be here and it is over. Or...there is a run on the food, it turns into mass chaos, and we all kill each other before the zombies get a chance."

Once again Scott was quiet. Chad headed inside, but a few seconds later, Scott was by his side. They reached Chad and Ronni's room and opened the door to find the girl asleep.

"I'll wake her, you go tell Brett. Meet me at the food locker in ten minutes," Chad said to Scott as he opened the closet and began gathering what he deemed to be essential.

Scott nodded and headed out the door at a jog.

Fifteen minutes later, the four of them ducked into the trees and vanished from sight. The people of Yosemite Village went about their business and waited for the food to arrive.

***

The fire had burned down to embers, but the warmth was still so blessedly good. Vix felt the rest of her clothes that she had hanging. Everything was dry. Of course she wouldn't dare sniff them, she knew better. Gemma was curled up in the corner snoring softly and it was peaceful and quiet.

She hadn't been able to believe that one person could talk so much. It seemed like one question had barely left that girl's mouth when three more were already being asked.

She liked the girl well enough, and her decision to bring this girl with her and leave all the others behind was simple. She didn't want any of the blokes because they would try to run things. All of the women except for Gemma had attached themselves to one of the men. Gemma was young, and most likely, she would do as she was told. Vix needed somebody like that if her plan was to work.

By now that group had figured that she wasn't coming back. Most likely they would figure that the two of them ran into some trouble and ended up falling to the zombies. She wouldn't miss any of them. Not to put too fine of a point on it, but they were mostly a bunch of idiots. Had it not been for her husband's hard work, that place wouldn't be as secure as it currently was…for now. Sooner or later, the dead would find them. Gun or not, Nigel and the others wouldn't stand a chance.

Not for the first time, Vix wondered about her friends. Not the neighbors and such, but all the people she had met on Facebook. Many were in America, and she had seen the news reports the first few days. It was simply too crowded over there for anybody to stand much of a chance.

She thought of all those daft conversations they'd had about zombies and vampires. It seemed a million years ago now. They had all agreed on one thing: get away from the big cities. Yet here she was headed for London.

Reaching up and pulling her pack down from where it hung on the doorknob, she opened it and began digging through it for that piece of paper. Her hand felt the plastic baggie and she pulled it out. A glance at Gemma to ensure that the girl was still asleep, Vix pulled that piece of paper out and unfolded it.

The folds had made creases in the paper so indelible that somebody who did not have the writing on the page committed to memory might actually have a hard time reading it. She had no such trouble. As many times as she'd read what was written in fancy script on the page, she didn't so much read the page as recite it.

Her lips moved, and when she was done, they curled up into a smile. Yes, there was a chance that somebody might have the same idea, but a lot of things would need to happen for somebody else to be on the same quest that she was on.

Carefully, she folded the paper back up and put it back in the baggy. Wrapping it in the rag, she stuffed it back into her pack.

It was funny how things worked out. Her friend Reggie had sent this flyer just two days before that first zombie had stumbled into her nurse's station. She hadn't even told Ivor about it yet. She was going to surprise him with a trip.

Thinking of him brought a sharp pain in her chest. Why hadn't she just told him about this weeks ago? Of everybody she'd known, he always believed in her. He would have followed her with no questions asked. Perhaps he would still be alive.

"Stop thinking that way, you silly cow," Vix scolded herself.

Nothing could be served by living with "shouldas, wouldas, and couldas" as her husband was fond of saying. No, she would move forward and do him proud.

Her mind drifted back to one of the conversations that they'd had over dinner. Ivor didn't share her love of zombies, but he always entertained her interests.

"If that ever did happen," he'd said one time in particular, "then I am certain you would be fine…with or without me."

"That's ridiculous," she'd argued.

"No," and suddenly his face grew serious, that sparkle that was always hinting at the smile that always came so easily was replaced by something else. "If something as unlikely as zombies ever happened, you would be one of the few who not only survived, but you would prosper. In fact, a bloke like me might just slow you down."

"Now you're being ridiculous," she'd scolded.

"No, I've never been more serious. You are much stronger than you give credit, my love." He'd taken her hand in his and looked into her eyes with something that was close to sadness. "Given the chance to put all your past behind you, I believe that there is no stronger woman in this world."

Vix wiped at her eyes. *Stupid old lummox of a man*, she thought. He'd always had the right words, which was a feat since he was a man who used very few.

"I'm gonna show them, love," she whispered.

Gemma made a noise in her sleep. Almost at the same time, a cry came from outside. It was one of those cursed crybabies. She hated those more than anything.

Well, tomorrow they would push on. London was two days away at the most. Then it would get tricky, but if everything worked out, then it might be worth it. If it worked…then the world would see what Vix Kirkpatrick was made of…and Ivor would be smiling.

***

"So the two of you were being held just up the road from here?" Danny was doing a pat down of his gear. "Little shack beside the access road, right?"

The girl glanced at Selina who fired off a series of rapid hand signals. After a few seconds, she nodded.

"You think this is such a good idea?" Selina asked Jody while continuing to sign so that Katherine could follow the conversation.

"If we hit them first we have the element of surprise. I seriously doubt if what that girl is saying…err…umm," Jody began to stammer.

The dark haired girl grabbed Selina's hands to stop her. She fired off some signs of her own while looking up at Jody with a smile.

"I am a deaf-mute, but that does not meant I do not have a sense of humor. And since this is how I communicate, yes, that is what I am saying," Selina spoke slowly as she followed the young girl's hands.

"We can worry about this later." Danny grabbed Jody by the arm and began pulling him to the door. "Let's go."

The two men headed out of the room that they had set up as

their camp for the next day or two. The idea was that they could use this location in the basement of what was apparently the local high school as a base and run into the town to search for supplies before continuing on.

As they reached the door that opened to the outside, a hand grabbed Jody's arm. He turned to see the young girl looking up at him with a smile. She wrapped her arms around his waist and squeezed. The she went to Danny and did the same thing. Afterwards she made a gesture of touching her fingertips to her mouth. Jody looked up at Selina who was standing a few feet behind.

"That means thank you," Selina said.

"How do you say you're welcome?" Jody asked.

"Hold your hand in front of you and move it across like you are inviting her in," Selina said, demonstrating the gesture.

Jody mimicked it, and then touched the girl on the top of her head. "Now stay here with Selina and we will be back in a few minutes."

The girl glanced at Selina, who quickly fired off a series of gestures. Danny opened the door and peeked outside before grabbing Jody and pulling him along.

A cold rain was falling. It was coating everything with a sheet of ice. Already there was a shimmer to the power lines that still hung limply overhead, and several of the branches on nearby trees were sagging with the burden.

"Freezing rain," Danny observed. "Might be able to use that to our advantage when we go into town."

"How so?" Jody asked.

"The zombies are gonna have a hell of a time walking on it."

"So will we."

"Yeah. But we are much more able to focus on our balance. Zombies just walk wherever without thinking. There will be some busted legs when this is done. They will have a much worse time of it than us."

Jody shrugged. As they started across the parking lot, he

almost landed on his ass twice. Eventually they reached the grass that ran alongside the access road. It was much easier going from that point.

The road stretched on and made a gentle turn. It was just around that corner where they were supposed to find the people who had held Katherine and her friend prisoner. From the sounds of it, these guys were scavengers and had a pretty decent stash of goods. Since there were no plans of leaving these animals alive, Jody was actually fairly confident that they would make a good score when this was done.

He and Danny separated and went to their own version of sign language as they closed in on their target. They would strike hard and fast. Jody actually felt his heart begin to race. This was no zombie hunt. They were actually going to take out living, breathing men. He'd almost forgotten what that felt like.

They rounded the corner and Danny was the first to throw up the 'Halt' sign. Jody froze. His eyes tracked to where the other man was pointing. Three bodies littered the road. Their target just happened to be three men at this location. Jody did not believe in coincidence.

He flashed a signal for Danny to go wide and come around from the other side. It would take him a few minutes to get into position. Jody waited until Danny vanished behind a building before he moved forward cautiously.

When he got close, he began to notice a few details that heightened his already alerted senses. The blood was relatively fresh. The pools around two of the bodies were still a deep red. However, it was the third body that had his attention.

Jody moved closer. His eyes darting around as he sought even the slightest movement. Finally he was kneeling beside the large man. He felt around the neck and confirmed his suspicion. This man had been killed by somebody up close and personal. His neck had been snapped. That was quite a feat considering the man's size. This was one big boy, easily tipping the scales at over two hundred and fifty pounds.

He reached down to his belt and was just about to draw his

Ka-Bar when a familiar voice whispered in his ear close enough that he felt the warmth of the owner's breath.

"If you pull that out, son, I will have no choice but to kill you."

***

"Just keep your hands out so I can see them," Chuck Monterro warned. "I ain't here to cause you any trouble."

"That knife point in my back seems to say something else," the young sergeant replied.

"Listen, Jody, if I would have wanted to kill you, we wouldn't be having this conversation."

Chuck moved back a step and then edged his way around in front of the young man. He glanced down at the dead body now in between them.

"This your work?" Jody asked.

"Yep." He saw no reason to lie. Besides, if he gauged this kid right, he would imagine that he would probably have done the same thing given the opportunity. "They had some kids held prisoner. The kids escaped and they were just about to go hunt them down when I showed up."

The young man just nodded. Perhaps he wasn't buying the story. *Well*, Chuck thought, *can't do much about that right now.*

"The thing is," Chuck continued once it was obvious Jody wasn't going to say anything, "them kids are still somewhere close by. Saw them myself as I was coming down the road."

"And what exactly were you doing way out here?" Jody scoffed. "How come you aren't back with the captain and the folks of Bald Knob?"

"Same reason you ain't," Chuck said with a smile. "We both know that place is gone. Too many of them things and no solid plan or defense against a group that big. Hell, we were barely equipped to deal with a few hundred. That mob had to be—"

"Thousands," Jody breathed.

The two stood in silence for a few seconds. Chuck shrugged

309

and sheathed his knife.

"Probably shouldn't leave this just sitting around," a voice called from the porch of the shack.

Both heads turned to see Danny standing there with a crossbow cocked and aimed at Chuck Monterro. Jody let a breath out that he hadn't realized that he'd been holding.

"Nicely done, private," Chuck made a few casual claps of his hands. He put his arms out to his sides. "Now, you gonna use that thing or keep running your mouth?"

"Danny," Jody called, "he could have killed me. He didn't."

"This time," Danny said through clenched teeth. "You know what kind of person he is. He hung two of our guys just the other day. Had us rounding up people like cattle. Who knows what else."

"If you are gonna use that thing, son—"

Chuck "Slider" Monterro's sentence was cut off abruptly when the shaft from the crossbow caught him in the center of the chest, piercing his heart. He was more than a little surprised, but mostly, Chuck Monterro was relieved. He would have had to kill both of those boys sooner or later. Now...now he could finally rest.

18

A Trip to the Woods

It had only been a few hours since Patton and his little flock had left. In the end it had been more Jesus and Jake standing there fingering the hilts of their swords than anything that I said or did. Dr. Zahn had pumped something into Misty that put the little girl down. We could deal with her later.

I was standing on the porch when Billy and Fiona came stomping out of the woods. I waited for them patiently, just hoping that they had news that would not involve us having to kill living, breathing people. I'd done it, but it still haunted me, and I doubted that it would ever go away.

"They headed east when they got to the road," Billy reported. "I don't give them a week."

So maybe I wasn't killing them directly, but it was sort of a moral gray area, wasn't it? If you see somebody drowning and don't bother to throw them a life preserver...

"They brought this on themselves," Fiona said, obviously reading my expression. "You didn't actually kick them out. They were leaving anyway. In fact, you did just the opposite in demanding they leave the girl."

I tried to let that sink in, but I still felt responsible. My actions had led to their eventual decision to risk it out in the wild instead of stay here where there was food and shelter.

The two of them both went in and left me to my thoughts. There had been so much in the past several hours. I had to wonder if life would ever settle into anything like a routine. Maybe just a few days where absolutely nothing happened.

"Steve."

I knew that tone. Hell, it didn't seem like there was any other. I turned to find Sunshine standing in the door with Cheryl Coates. Both were in tears.

They didn't need to tell me. I may not be the brightest bulb on the tree, but I'm no idiot. I just nodded and moved past them. I felt their hands brush me, like they could take away some of the pain or something. Or maybe they just wanted to let me know that I wasn't alone. But that was a lie. When it came to what was about to happen, I could not be any more alone. None of them would have to do what was required of me. None of them could 'share' in the experience. This one would be all mine…and so would the everlasting pain that came with it.

The entry area was a sea of faces. I noticed Dr. Zahn, Melissa, Jon, and Thalia missing. Everybody else was standing on one side of the room as far away from the door that opened to where Emily waited like that distance would somehow help.

I walked to the door and took a deep breath. I knew for a fact that once I walked through it, nothing would ever be the same again. This wasn't like a hot bath or jumping into a pool where you just plunge in and get past the initial shock. This was a shock that would last until the day I died.

As my hand clutched the doorknob, I suddenly realized just how full of crap all manner of fiction used to be. Whether it was movies or television, there just seemed to be this magic surge of inner-strength that consumed the hero of a story when confronted with something terrible. Maybe that was what I was waiting for as I stood here. I think the real truth was that I was scared.

When I turned the doorknob and opened the door, my brain did its best to shield me. The room swam and I didn't really see anybody or hear anything except Emily. Her tiny frame was on the bed, the white sheet that was pulled up to her chin had obviously just been changed and seemed to bathe her in an ethereal glow.

"She is sleeping now, Steve, but I don't expect her to last the night," Dr. Zahn whispered in my ear.

A Trip to the Woods

I glanced at her and wondered for whose benefit she chose to whisper. Everybody in this room—Thalia included—knew what was happening and had experienced it so many times. This was not some sort of secret.

"Are you sure about doing this yourself?" Jon asked.

I had a million things that I could say to what seemed like such a simple question. Instead, I just looked at him. His expression indicated that he got the gist of my thoughts.

I moved beside the bed and looked down at her. I did my best to block out the stench. I just wanted a moment with Emily that I could keep safe in my heart for when the sun came up tomorrow. Unfortunately, whatever it was that did this was bent on ruining that possibility. Her face was a waxy shade of sickly yellow. There was a single black vein that snaked its way up from her neck and bloomed into a varicose web that marred her left cheek.

"Steve," Melissa was at my elbow, she had Thalia by the hand, "we'll be right outside."

I nodded. One by one, each of them said something to Emily, and then left. I only heard Thalia.

"Bye, sissy. I promise to teach Buster to shake like you wanted."

How could something that simple be able to break me in half? I held it until I heard the door shut, and then the tears came in a torrent. I prayed to God or whatever is in charge that I would eventually be able to stop.

I have no idea how much time passed, but eventually I was able to breathe again. I wiped the sheen of sweat off of her face with a nearby towel. When I was done, I considered that towel briefly. I was supposed to just place it over her face when she stopped breathing and then there was a spike and a mallet sitting just to my right on the table.

Could it really be that easy? I wondered.

My eyes drifted to the window. I could see the coming clouds that signaled yet another storm. More snow would mean that it would be even harder for the zombies to reach us. It also meant that we would have a rougher go of it if we needed to leave for another food run. And with each passing day, we came closer and closer to being wrapped in a sort of arctic cocoon with no assurances of what we might become by the time we were able to escape it.

"I'm sorry, daddy," Emily whispered in a voice so faint that I was almost certain that I had imagined it.

I looked down to see her tracer-laced eyes looking up at me. Tears were trickling from them, but instead of looking shiny and bright, they just looked rheumy and sick. I wanted to say something, but the words all died in my throat.

"I'm scared," Emily whispered, and then her eyes closed again.

I was certain that this was it. I still held the towel in my hand that I was supposed to use to cover her face. I watched her chest, and it continued to rise and fall, but in shorter, more agonizingly small bursts.

I looked at the window once more. A few snowflakes were already starting to fall.

I unfastened the restraints and scooped Emily up in my arms after unlatching the window. A few short minutes later I was wading through the snow and out into the woods. I kept Emily pressed close to me and could still feel her breathing.

She weighed almost nothing in my arms as I pushed myself to move faster. I needed to be as far out into the woods as I could before she stopped breathing. It was like a deadly game of 'Hot Potato' at this point.

My only real fear as I pushed on was that I would not realize when she stopped breathing. She would die and come back and tear into me before I knew what had happened. Nothing could have been farther from the truth.

I felt her body shudder once and then go still. My brain was trying to tell me that she would turn instantly. It always took time; maybe a few minutes, maybe hours. But it was never instant. Still, I was embarrassed when I stumbled to a halt and dropped her unceremoniously to the ground.

I drew my blade, knelt down, and pulled the sheet back. I kept repeating to myself over and over that as soon as her eyes opened and I saw what she had become, that I would end it. I kept trying to tell myself that it was an end to her suffering, but how did I know? How do any of us know?

All we know for certain was that once you died, you came back as one of those things. But they did not seem happy or sad any more than the ants in an anthill. We saw them as evil or monstrous because they were a threat to our lives. Yet not one of those things had actively sought me in some way that would lead me to believe it was after me alone. We'd already seen them go after a noise and continue on when whatever had cause that sound had long since moved in another direction. They didn't hunt us so much as stumble upon our location.

A low moan broke the stillness. I looked down just as Emily's eyes opened. In them, I tried my hardest to see anything of the little girl that I had come to know and love.

I moved away and watched as she struggled free of the sheet that she had been wrapped in. The snow offered her little help as she broke through the crust and sank in it, momentarily disappearing from view.

Slowly, she rose to her feet. Her head moved in that jerky bird-like fashion and her limbs were like a wind-up toy that was in its last fits before becoming still until wound once more.

"Oh, Emily," I breathed.

Her head snapped my direction and she seemed to freeze in place. She tilted one way and then the other as if considering me. This was very similar to the behavior of that other child-zombie from outside that compound. Any other zombie would already be stumbling towards me, wanting nothing more than to take a bite out of me. Yet, this zombie that had once been my Emily simply stood and seemed to study me as much as I studied her.

I was careful to keep my hands away from any of the hilts sticking up from my belt. I don't know what I hoped for. Did I think that she would mouth the words, "Good bye" or something? Yet there I stood, unwilling to draw a weapon and kill the child that I had taken as my own all those months ago.

I remembered all those times of reading to her and Thalia. I remembered that day beside the trench when we discovered the zombie of her dad, Randall Smith. I can still hear every single word she said to him that day as she said farewell to him before we torched the whole bunch.

Yes, I was very aware that this was still a zombie standing just a few feet away. But, so far, she had made no move to attack.

I don't know how long we stood there, but eventually, she turned her back on me and walked away. I stood there until she had vanished through some trees. Then I stood there some more. I kept waiting for Emily to come back.

It was almost dark by the time I returned home. When I walked through the door, questions came from every side. I ignored them and went to bed. The dreams began almost as soon as my eyes closed.

I dreamt of Emily. Not the zombie, but the little girl. In the dream, she laughed.

CUSTOMERS ALSO PURCHASED:

JOHN O'BRIEN
NEW WORLD
SERIES

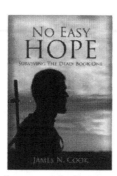

JAMES N. COOK
SURVIVING THE DEAD
SERIES

MARK TUFO
ZOMBIE FALLOUT
SERIES

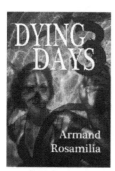

**ARMAND
ROSAMILLIA**
DYING DAYS
SERIES

HEATH STALLCUP
THE MONSTER
SQUAD

SHAWN CHESSER
SURVIVING THE
ZOMBIE APOCALYPSE
SERIES

The Dead Return
May 30, 2013:

Confrontation
Book 6 of the DEAD series